M000282239

To Carry the Horn

Karen Myers

To Carry the Horn

The Hounds of Annwn: 1

Karen Myers

Perkunas Press • Hume, Virginia

To Carry the Horn

The Hounds of Annwn: 1

Perkunas Press
12142 Crest Hill Road
Hume, Virginia 22639
USA

PerkunasPress.com

Author contact: KarenMyers@PerkunasPress.com
Cover illustration: Ann Mei

Published 2012. First Edition.

Trade Paperback
ISBN-13: 978-0-9635384-0-6
ISBN-10: 0-9635384-0-3

Library of Congress Cataloging-in-Publication Data

Myers, Karen, 1953-
To carry the horn : the hounds of Annwn : 1 / Karen Myers. -- 1st ed.
p. cm.
ISBN 978-0-9635384-0-6
1. Fox hunting--Fiction. 2. Fantasy fiction. I. Title.
PS3613.Y4726T6 2012
813'.6--dc23

2012040017

CONTENTS

CHAPTER 1

I did it! He's finally gone, dead, finished. A few snicks and snecks, and there he was on the ground, wasn't he, throat twitching. And they just stood around, didn't they, deluded like fools by the spell, that wonderful spell he gave me, he was right about it, all those hounds and nothing they could do.

The mighty prince. Ha. One less for you. I remember how he helped you hold him down before you cut him open…

Hush, hush, no, don't think about that.

He won't be holding anyone down anymore, will he, no, not him. Not with those hands. I've got them now. I have my own plans for you, don't I.

Time to run all the way home now. They'll never catch me, I'm too clever, I'm too slick.

Such a long time to wait but we're all ready now.

~

Misplacing a pack of hounds was not on George's "to do" list this morning.

"Come on, Mosby, get moving," he said. "I don't know how they got way over there either, but you can hear 'em. Let's roll."

He leaned forward, using his legs to urge the horse into a canter on the narrow trail. The damp grass muffled the rhythmic pounding and filled the air with a tangy mid-autumn scent. Most of the leaves were still clinging to the trees, and the wild grape vines, draped wherever the sunlight penetrated, obscured his view, but he could clearly hear hounds giving tongue off in the distance. Sounded like the whole pack was on. One voice would lift, then several in chorus, then single voices again. As always, the hairs on the back of his neck rose. They were somewhere on the far side of the woods, and the trail looked like it was headed in that direction.

He turned his head at a flash of white and the sound of twigs breaking to watch a big whitetail bound across the path before him.

He sailed over a fallen branch, then spun around to stare at him boldly.

A magnificent buck—what a rack, twelve points at least, George thought, turning to admire him as he rode by. Why's he just standing there looking at me, with his great brown eyes and his flared nostrils? What's he waiting for?

As he cantered past he swung his attention back to the front, startled to find two small trees lying fallen together across the trail just a couple of strides away. He hastily settled himself for the jump, his gaze fixed on the topmost part that his horse would need to clear, and beyond. Not until Mosby rose to spring easily over the barrier did it occur to him that he might better have spared a glance upward, as a high branch materialized from the side and swept him out of the saddle.

The fall knocked the wind out of him when he hit the ground, with a thump to his head. He paused before trying to move, taking stock. Nothing felt broken. He rolled to the side and pushed himself up, his snug knee-high boots making it awkward to bend his legs fully as the calf muscles swelled. This wasn't the first time he'd come off a horse and he felt it in the usual places. The woods had pulled back into a little opening after the fallen trees, and the glare from the sunlight made him blink. Odd. He'd had the impression that the trees were still enclosing the trail after the jump when he looked ahead as Mosby rose.

He tried to clear his head and focused on the sound of a horse grazing. Good, at least Mosby had stayed with him instead of running off in a panic after losing his rider. The reins trailed on the ground and he heard the bit clattering as the horse munched around it.

He limped stiffly over, picked up the reins, and led Mosby forward a few steps, looking for injuries or any evidence of impeded movement, but the horse seemed sound. Well, that's a blessing. Better me sore than him.

He couldn't hear the hounds anymore, nor John's horn. Couldn't hear the foxhunt at all. Maybe catching up wasn't going to be so simple. He could already imagine the lecture he'd be getting from the huntsman for letting this happen.

John needed to know about his delay. He pulled his cellphone out of his hunt coat's inner pocket. No signal, as usual.

Off came the leather riding gloves, and he used his thumbs to type a brief text message describing what had happened and where he was headed. The cellphone would look for a signal every few minutes and would forward the text if it found one. Out of habit he pulled out the pocket watch chained through his vest's buttonhole to check its time against the cellphone. He stood a moment, running his thumb across the engraving of St. George and the dragon on the back of the watch before returning it to his vest. As he shuffled the cellphone to his left hand to put it away, it dropped from his fingers—his old injury kicking in again. He bent stiffly to pick it up.

Standing there with the leather reins in his hand, he put his gloves back on, turning around to see where he'd fallen. He wasn't going to take that jump again, but maybe there was a way past it that rejoined the trail.

The tangle of tall pokeberry bushes on the edge of this little clearing were thick and unbroken. No trail was visible, much less any downed trees.

That can't be right.

He continued turning in a full circle and scanned the woods all around, methodically. There were two openings for paths, but both were on the far side from him and no fallen trees were visible from here. Still holding the reins and bringing Mosby with him, he walked all along the margin, peering past the thickets whose leaves were just starting to turn color.

When he stood at the openings of the two paths, he found he could see some distance along them. They were true rides, larger and better defined than deer trails, but without droppings or hoof prints to show that any horses had traveled them recently.

A shiver went through him and his stomach tightened. There was no way into this spot, other than the rides he hadn't used.

Well, George, pick a path and worry about it later. You have to get to the hounds.

He'd been headed west when he last had a clear sense of direction. His hand reached back into his other inner pocket for his GPS tracker. Power, no signal. That's strange, he thought, as he put it back. All it has to do is line-of-sight up to a satellite, not find some cell tower on the ground. It's usually reliable.

Good thing I brought backup, he thought. He hauled out a small, well-worn brass compass from his left vest pocket, attached where a fob would have been on his watch chain.

Using his compass he confirmed that the right-hand path started in a westerly direction, toward where he'd last heard the hounds. Alright, he thought, the sensible plan is to just try and get out of the woods directly so that I can orient myself and make contact with the hunt as quickly as possible.

He led his horse back away from the margin a few feet into the clearing. He checked the saddle girth, then tossed the reins over his head. At six foot four George was used to looking over a horse's back from the ground but gray Mosby, a Percheron/Thoroughbred cross, stood 17.2 hands high at the withers, or just two inches short of six feet.

You'd think someone my size would have less trouble mounting but I had to fall for a horse too tall for me, just like everyone else, he thought. He'd been unable to resist the dark smoky dappled gray gelding with his silvery mane. As Mosby aged he would gradually lighten until he became white. Always going to be a problem keeping a white horse clean, but he's worth it. "Aren't you, boy?" The horse cocked his near ear back at the sound of his voice.

George lifted his left foot into the stirrup, careful to keep the toe of his boot away from Mosby's ribs. With his hands on the front and back of the saddle, he bounced on his right toes twice for momentum and hoisted himself up, swinging his right leg over and settling into the saddle with a comforting creak of leather.

He adjusted the fit of his hard hunt cap. Time to get back to where I belong.

George roughly remembered the layout of this property from his years of adolescent trespass, but it was a big place, several thousand acres, and many of the details had dimmed over time. This wooded covert was new to him, but no private woodland in this part of Virginia was very large. Can't cost me but a few hundred yards to get clear of all this, he thought.

His current trail was clearly intended for horseback, with no tight spots. Even so, he held Mosby to a walk, trotting where he could, since the path was unfamiliar. Too late cautious, but I'm not going to be surprised a second time. He watched for the thinning of the trees ahead, eager to get out and see the Blue Ridge to the west.

The woods seemed to extend into dimness indefinitely in this direction, and the mid-October day was turning cooler.

He checked his compass again. Still going west, not in a circle, so how's it possible I'm not out by now? These woods weren't here twenty years ago, but these trees are older than that. He thought about retracing his steps and trying the other path from the clearing, but he knew it went in the wrong direction, or at least started that way.

Alright, then, when in doubt, double down. Let's pick up the pace. He sent Mosby forward at a stronger trot, using his horse's momentum to rise in the saddle on every other stride to smooth the movement as he been doing all his life.

The ground began to fall away to the south, the trees finally opened up a bit, and the path entered another small clearing which was not, he noted with some relief, the one he'd started from.

As he brought Mosby to a halt to recheck his bearings, a nearby rustle on the right caught his attention. George saw two hounds just inside the woods, all by themselves. They ran silently into the clearing, looking for scent.

His years as a whipper-in took hold and he lifted his hand with the furled whip in a warding-off gesture, saying, "Get back to 'im," in an authoritative tone, to send them back to the pack and its huntsman. The hounds glanced up at him in acknowledgment and turned back in the direction they came from, but he hardly noticed, stunned.

Those aren't our hounds, not white hounds with red ears. I thought those were mythical. He chuckled uncertainly, remembering the Welsh tales his father had told him when he was a child. He looked around at the trees, the sunlight flickering on the autumn leaves as the breeze caught them. It all seemed very ordinary. Well, I suppose it can hardly be the Wild Hunt, in broad daylight. Maybe someone's lost dogs? They looked like working hounds, though.

He glanced down at the hounds on the buttons of his coat. Maybe they're Talbot hounds, he grinned. If I'm wandering dreaming in an endless woods, might as well have the legendary beasts of grandfather's ancient family to keep me company.

Wouldn't he be pleased at my invoking the old lineage, back to the Norman Conquest. He smiled wryly. Better never tell him I think a man should do his own deeds, not lean on those of his ancestors.

Still, he sat up straight like a Talbot of old, and headed after the errant hounds, seeking enlightenment.

The couple of hounds led George to the edge of the trees at last. He picked his way after them with care and paused to take in the view, a welcome relief after the enclosed woods.

He gazed southwest down a gradual slope of upland meadow. Glancing right automatically, he was relieved to see the smoky wall of the Blue Ridge, running north-south like a compass line laid out on the earth. From this angle the ridge line seemed quite high and completely wooded. The air was crisp and clean, with a chill rising despite the cloudless sky.

His eyes followed the two hounds, obediently loping down the slope ahead of him. Before him was a familiar scene of hounds and riders, but this wasn't the Rowanton Hunt. Several hunters were dismounted, gathered around someone on the ground while others held their horses.

He examined the riders more carefully. What's with the clothing, he wondered. They look like reenacters for a Revolutionary War event—tricorns, long coats, and bright colors.

A small group of mounted men near the hounds wore something that seemed to be hunt livery, green frock coats, longer than any he had ever seen in use, with prominent turned-back cuffs, and brown boots that rose over the knee.

The nearest hunt servant glanced up as the two hounds rejoined the pack and looked along their back trail, spotting George sitting his horse at the edge of the woods above him. He called out to one of the men standing over the fallen figure and pointed. The standing man followed his gesture and then dispatched two of the riders next to him up the slope.

George quelled his momentary panic at the strangeness of the scene and stood his ground. That must be the master of this hunt, he thought, by the way he gives orders. Who are these people, and what are they doing on Bellemore land?

As the riders cantered up the slope, he got a closer view of their gear. Swords and long hunting knives? That's eccentric even for a private pack. These clothes look genuine, worn and comfortable, not stiff and unused like costumes.

The hair rose on the back of his neck and for a moment he had to resist the urge to turn and flee. His pride stiffened him, that, and the knowledge that Mosby wasn't built for speed. Whatever this is, it's real, he told himself. Deal with it.

He decided to take them at face value, kicked his rational disbelief firmly into the back of his mind to await a better moment, and rode forward slowly to meet them.

He stopped just before the first rider reached him and looked him over as he approached. The man was tall and dark, wearing a blue frock coat with a long buff inner vest. Must be what they call a weskit, George thought. He nodded to him, and they waited a moment for the second horseman, a brown-haired man on a bay gelding. They eyed his own gear in some puzzlement, though they said nothing about it.

The first rider bowed his head before speaking. "I'm Idris Powell, and this Ifor Moel. My lord Gwyn would speak with you, sir, if you please."

My lord Gwyn? Conscious of the revolver holstered at the small of his back under his coat, George briefly considered resisting, but what would be the point? Instead, he let his well-schooled Virginia manners take charge.

"My name's George Talbot Traherne, whipper-in for the Rowanton Hunt, and I seem to have gotten lost on Bellemore land."

"What's happened here?" he said, pointing with his chin at the fallen man. "I'd be glad to help, if I can."

The three of them cantered down to the group of standing men and the man in charge came forward to meet them. George dismounted to speak with him, not wanting to loom over him on horseback.

He saw a tall man accustomed to authority, lean and fit, with gray eyes in a dark weathered face and black hair starting to silver. He was dressed with dignity and quiet richness, his thigh-length coat of green wool cut away in front, partially covering a long matching waistcoat. The color matched the livery of the hunt staff, but the details were more elaborate and the cloth of higher quality. His cream breeches were cut full for ease of movement. White sleeve ruffles extended beyond the coat sleeves with their broad turned up cuffs. He wore no stock around his neck, but his shirt collar was closed by a green silk scarf. His high boots were brown and well worn.

He held himself rigid in some strong emotion as George approached, and said stiffly, "I'm Gwyn Annan, and this is my land. What's your business here? What do you know of this?" He pointed behind him.

George was startled to recognize the name but it was impossible to make sense of it—perhaps this was a cousin? He opened his mouth to tell him about the hunt meet today at this fixture, but before he could speak his eyes followed the gesture and he looked down at the fallen rider on the ground.

One motionless outstretched arm ended in an oozing stump. A reek of blood rose in the clear autumn air, more blood than he could see through the tangle of men standing around the body. Why, that fellow's been killed, he thought, shocked. This isn't from a fall.

Where are his hands?

George was speechless for a moment. Into the silence Idris Powell announced from horseback, "My lord, this is George Talbot Traherne. He declares himself a huntsman."

At the name, Gwyn's face froze, and he turned back to George.

"Who is your mother?" he asked, staring at him intensely.

George's tore his attention from the dead man to the man before him, puzzled by the question and the focus of his attention. "Léonie Annan Talbot." He stressed the "Annan."

"And hers?"

"Georgia Rice Annan. I was named for them both."

Gwyn Annan closed his eyes briefly, and bowed. "Welcome, kinsman."

CHAPTER 2

Kinsman?

George had no trouble recognizing the name. There was a Gwyn Annan who was the father of his grandmother Georgia, but he had gone to France with his son in the 1950s, soon after her marriage, and vanished. George didn't know much about her family. This must be a descendant from that line.

Bellemore had been vacant since then, kept in good repair by a farm manager, and supervised by a lawyer from Culpeper for annual repairs and cleaning from an apparently inexhaustible budget. It had been part of the Rowanton Hunt territory long ago but closed as a fixture for decades. Rumors of the current heir returning had been confirmed when the senior Master of Foxhounds, his grandfather Gilbert Talbot, received an invitation to hunt there today, mailed from the lawyer's office under instruction. Could this be the heir? He called it "his land."

That made some sense of who he was, but couldn't explain the clothing, or the dead man lying bloody on the ground.

Gwyn recalled himself first. "We'll discuss this later. I must see to this outrage now."

He looked up at Idris. "Take everyone who will go back to the manor and see that they're well provisioned, with apologies for the abrupt ending of their sport today. Make sure you listen to their complaints. I want to hear their speculations about this affair afterward."

Idris nodded, turned his horse, and headed over to the main body of riders to begin organizing a general withdrawal.

Turning to one of the men beside him, Gwyn said, "Thomas, take some of these standing here to clean poor Iolo's body as best you can. We'll tie him onto his horse for the trip back."

The appointed man, weatherbeaten and competent, gathered two to help him and they began a quiet discussion about what to do.

Gwyn turned back to George. "Idris named you huntsman. Is it so?"

"Not quite. I've been whipper-in for many years, both to my grandfather and then to his successors, but it's not how I make my living. I've hunted hounds, on occasion, filling in for our huntsman."

"Did you send those two hounds down to the pack?"

What was he getting at, George wondered.

"Yes. I'm sorry if I've interfered but it seemed clear that they weren't on a trail and not with the pack where they belonged. I'm afraid I just reacted as I would for my own hunt."

"And they obeyed?"

"Well, of course." The question surprised him. The hounds always obeyed him—they knew him well after all, he thought. Maybe these hounds didn't know him, he reconsidered, but it was a common enough command he gave them.

"Then I put you in charge of the pack for now to bring them home, if you would. As you can see, someone has killed Iolo ap Huw, my huntsman and foster-son." He couldn't keep the affection and grief from his voice.

Taken aback, George thought, what have I walked into? And then he mulled it over, just how would I take a strange pack home, I wonder?

He looked over at the hounds, both bitch and dog hounds milling about silently, a mixed gender pack. They were white with small reddish-orange markings, especially on the ears, and most were broken-haired rather than smooth.

Obviously someone needed to bring this pack back, and this Master, grieving and facing an emergency, asked me for the respect due his office. Hunting etiquette required George to make himself useful and he resolved to put all other speculation aside until the hounds were back safely. "Alright, then, I'll give it a try. Who's the senior man among the hunt staff?"

Gwyn pointed to the one who had first seen George at the edge of the woods. "That would be Owen the Leash." Owen had been watching their conversation since he arrived, sitting his white horse at some distance from the pack.

George remounted and rode over to Owen, introducing himself and explaining his assignment. "How are you organized?"

Owen pointed out the other three mounted staff. George could see that they surrounded the pack but not closely, keeping them together like cowboys driving cattle. Only one, rather younger than the others, got close to the hounds. "Iolo it is who leads them and throws them into covert after their quarry. We three follow behind to keep them from turning." His gesture excluded the younger man, and his expression made it clear he thought of the hounds as threats, not partners.

That was odd, George thought. Whippers-in usually operated from the side, to keep hounds together and stop them hunting separate trails on their own, or from the front, to turn them away from hazards like roads. They didn't drive them forward or prevent them from turning back altogether—hounds were only too eager to hunt.

"And what about that one?" he said, indicating the younger man.

"Oh, that's Rhys Vachan. Of the blood he is."

An odd expression. What did that mean?

"Where are the kennels, and how far?"

Owen said, "We've come about five miles, hunting across the high ground. It would be three miles back, without detour." He pointed west toward the mountains.

"What happened to the huntsman?"

"We stopped to water horses and hounds, and Iolo brought them up to the woods here. A whirling cloud, twice the size of a man it was, sped over the ground from the west and aimed directly at him. With a howl, and blood, the cloud passed over the slope. There's outraged some of the hounds were, and a few trailed it and gave tongue, but they lost it and returned."

The tale was fantastic, but he seemed to be sincere enough. "Have you ever seen anything like that before?"

"No, never. It's cursed Gwyn is."

George let that pass. He didn't like the way Owen described the hounds, as if they were enemy troops to fend off. Maybe the other fellow would be more in tune with the pack. He raised an arm to the young Rhys and waved him over. Rhys was fair-haired and beardless, looking to be in his early twenties.

"My lord?"

"I've been tasked with bringing the hounds home. What do you suggest?"

Rhys replied straightforwardly enough, but George could hear the doubt in his voice. "If you're not afraid, then walk among them for a few minutes and let them smell you." George could see Owen's eyes widen at the idea. "Then if you mount and ride forward, they should follow when you call them."

"Sounds like a plan. I don't know the way, so please stay close to the pack when we head off and let me know if I go astray."

"As you wish." Rhys rode off to what would be the point of departure at the head of the pack.

George looked down at the pack and saw about fourteen couple of hounds, assuming they counted their hounds in pairs for speed like everyone else. "How many should there be?" he asked Owen.

"We left with thirteen and a half couple." That would be 27 hounds. George half-smiled at the old hunting joke that you should always have an odd number of hounds out, since it was the odd hound that found the fox.

"Are they all here?"

"Yes, my lord."

George walked Mosby past Owen and around to the far side of the pack. Before dismounting he glanced back and saw the bulk of the field moving off west at a slow canter. Three men were tending to the body on the ground, but the remaining dozen or so, and all the hunt staff, were watching him attentively. No doubt they expect to see a stranger's discomfiture, he thought. Alright, then. Let's disappoint them. He stood in the stirrups, swung his right leg over behind him, and dropped down. He drew the reins over Mosby's head and looped them over his left arm, giving him a solid pat on the shoulder. Then he walked into the pack.

The first of the hounds came to him, and he could feel the undivided attention of the remaining men and dead silence outside the rustle of the pack. Ignore them. Concentrate on these hounds. The dog hound sniffed his boots daintily, then raised himself on his hind legs prepared to brace his front paws on George's chest to inspect his face. He was enormous, and shaggy, more like an otter hound than a foxhound. George took a step back and let the hound drop lightly down to all four legs where he stood almost at waist level. George put a hand on his head and crooned to him, "Hey, puppy. Good old puppy."

The dog hound stepped away and was succeeded by two dancing white bitches, whose interest was kept at ground level with a knee and some adroit dodging. One by one he made the acquaintance of each hound as he walked through the pack. He marked a few boisterous youngsters as likely young entry, hounds getting their first experiences of hunting with the pack, but otherwise they came to him in an orderly fashion, calm and courteous.

These are lovely hounds, he thought. I'll bet they'll come along just fine, especially if they've already had a run.

Then Owen edged a bit closer to watch his progress. Immediately, the hounds nearest to him raised their hackles and set up a low, almost subliminal, growl. They turned to face him with a sinister sort of focused alertness. The deep noise increased in intensity and threat, like the wavering hum of a hornet's nest. The bystanders, who had begun moving normally, once again froze to watch, and Owen backed hastily away, the hounds quieting when he did. George had never seen this behavior in hounds before. Maybe they're right to be cautious of this pack, but it doesn't make any sense.

He resumed his progress through the interested hounds. As he led his horse forward, George saw that the hounds sniffed him casually but kept out from underfoot, while Mosby placed his feet carefully and came along behind him without any fuss. George made his way through the pack trying to make sure that he touched and was smelled by every individual hound. He was overwhelmed with first impressions, but there were a few hounds that he particularly liked the look of.

He called over to Rhys, as he approached the front of the pack. "Who are the leaders?" Rhys pointed out several hounds, including one dog hound named Dando, the first hound that had come to greet him.

"They'll follow Dando anywhere," Rhys said.

"Let's put that to the test," George said, as he mounted up.

He sat easily on Mosby and looked over to the rest of the hunt. The departing field was no longer in sight. The dead man's body had been wrapped in someone's cloak and tied across his horse's saddle. George caught Gwyn's eye and raised his eyebrow as a question. Gwyn nodded, and George stepped out.

He put himself at the head of the procession since the hounds usually led the field with their huntsman. He turned in the saddle and summoned Dando with a "Come along, Dando, puppy," and the white hound cooperated as if they had hunted together for years. The pack paced tranquilly behind him, then Owen's men, and then Gwyn and a man leading Iolo's horse with the grim few who had stayed to help. Rhys rode nearby but behind and off to the left, calling out general directions. They headed west, toward the Blue Ridge.

~

Gwyn took his place at the head of the remnant of the field, behind Owen the Leash. Glancing back at the dismal procession behind him, his stomach tightened and he could feel his shock and horror begin to give way to a boiling rage.

Iolo, his foster-son and companion of hundreds of years, slain in his prime like an animal, in the midst of his work. Reluctantly he admitted his own sense of guilt in the matter; Iolo wasn't murdered because of any crime he'd committed. Killing him two weeks before the great hunt was a master stroke aimed at Iolo's lord instead.

For twenty years Gwyn had felt his enemies picking at his control of the hunt, but he never thought they would move so directly against the huntsman. He knew one of them had to be his sister Creiddylad, but he wasn't sure what part she played. He felt the old familiar heartache at the thought, but Owen the Leash was hers, and he could no longer think of her as innocently involved. There were certainly others, though. He detected the hand of at least one other and thought he could name him: Gwythyr. Surely his sister wasn't working together with her ex-husband—that he wouldn't believe.

He'd have to invite his brother Edern, he thought, without delay. No more standing in isolation pretending he was strong enough to fend off any attack on his sovereignty.

What would he do for a huntsman? He didn't think Rhys could do it, and he couldn't imagine what would happen to him if he tried it and failed.

What about this unexpected apparition, Georgia's grandson, pulling the hounds somewhat raggedly along in front? Too convenient, just dropping in like that. Was he planted there?

Should I believe the implied lineage? The man was in his early thirties. Standing on the ground, our eyes were level, so he's about my height, but so much broader. That's those Norman Talbots, I wouldn't be surprised. He didn't recall Georgia's mother very well, she had died so young, but he had stayed twenty-one years to raise his daughter and see her wed, and it was to her he looked for comparison. The hair looks like mine, but he has her mouth and her green eyes. I suppose it must be true. To think that little Léonie had such a son. When I saw her last, she was trying to push that horrid pony over a jump of her own devising, and winning.

It must be almost sixty years since I last wore clothing like his, the red coat with the collar in Talbot colors of dark gold and red piping, those uncomfortably tight breeches, and the knee-high black boots. I'm surprised so little has changed.

What's this fellow like? He reached out to him with his mind and recoiled. He tastes rather… odd. Human and fae, clearly, but there's something else, something dark and alive. Is it part of his blood? Georgia's Gilbert Talbot was normal enough, but who was this man's father?

Gwyn watched his performance with the pack as they followed the side of the slope westward along open ground at a walk. The hounds were staying together, for the most part, and Rhys helped keep them from breaking left.

Maybe he'll do, Gwyn thought, better than risking Rhys for the purpose. Let's keep him around for a couple of days and look him over. Perhaps I can persuade him to stay for the great hunt.

George kept the pace to a walk to accommodate the dead man on the led horse. Ahead the open ground widened as it began to descend to the west as well as the south, and he saw from above a village surrounded by fields in an enclosed upland dell that extended to his left down the slope. A stream of some size descended from the north end and ran through the village, and he spotted an arched stone bridge and the first roads he had seen here, dirt trails wide enough for vehicles.

Lifting his eyes, he made out a large stone building with a wall around its grounds about two miles away across the vale and north on the far side, partway up the slope, backed against the woods that continued uninterrupted up to the ridge line. The building was well-sited, with good views in three directions, and pennants in green and gold blew from each of the square fort-like front corners.

He looked a question back over his shoulder at Rhys who nodded. "We follow that road across and up to the manor," pointing at a minor road between fields that began a short distance below them.

Just one problem: the hounds weren't ready to stop for the day.

By ones and twos they were slipping away to check out nearby coverts as they passed. Rhys intercepted the ones on his side, but George couldn't stop the others effectively, and Owen and his men were useless, trailing behind them and avoiding his gaze. It was like trying to control a handful of water with a mind of its own, and getting worse by the minute.

He could feel the eyes of the silent riders behind him and his stomach clenched in embarrassment. You'd think I'd never done this before, he thought, but then he'd never tried with strange hounds.

Finally, in exasperation, he called loudly, "Pack up," and echoed it with some swallowed curses. To his astonishment, the hounds on the edges lifted their heads and moved closer together, like so many lambs.

Really? The next hound that started to drift away got a "Pack up, get back here" with some backbone, and it worked. A shiver went through him. They shouldn't obey a stranger so easily. Something unnatural about this, he thought.

People in the fields stood and watched. He saw that the bridge met a larger road that paralleled the stream on the eastern side, and that his current path led directly to the crossing. The stream was large and a bit rough—would the hounds cross at the bridge or through the water? It would be easier to control them if they stayed together.

He called over to Rhys, "Will they cross at the bridge or try to swim?"

"Over the bridge."

George nodded.

Houses and other buildings stood along the main road, but he saw few people as he approached with the pack. Most of the buildings were made of stone, with a few wooden dwellings. He looked for the typical old Virginia houses, in wood, or stucco, or even logs, but these were very different, though porches were common enough. The bridge was stone with timber flooring and rose smoothly to a high point in the middle.

As he passed the first building on his right before the crossroad, he could see well into its interior main room from his elevation on horseback. Two faces pressed against a window, a man and a woman. Glancing at the other buildings, he saw more faces at the windows. Almost all the people he could see were indoors. There was little noise other than the moving hounds and horses, and he cleared his throat uneasily.

He paused deliberately at the bridge, expecting that the hounds would break to drink anyway. They loped to the edge of the stream and lapped eagerly, but made no attempt to cross. After a few moments, conscious of the waiting procession behind him, he called the dripping Dando back to him and headed across the bridge, Mosby's feet clopping hollowly on the wood. To his relief, the hounds fell in behind him, or more likely behind Dando, and the whole pack crossed up and over.

He turned right, up another, smaller, road that kept pace with the stream on this side, clearly just for local use. He noted one woman who looked about his age, dressed in gray, standing on a porch in front of a baker's shop. She alone remained outside to watch the hunt go by. Nice that someone else trusts me with these hounds, he thought. Good thing she doesn't know how little control I actually have.

He touched his cap to her.

~

As George approached the manor he'd seen from across the river, he discovered that what he had taken for a wall was really a sort of impenetrable living palisade enclosing the grounds. The opened gates were solid wood set in a stone wall that extended for ten feet on either side before joining the palisade. The passage between the walls smelt of damp stone as he rode through, passing under a manned stone archway.

He came out into a sunlit park and gardens that surrounded the manor house, though the grounds behind the house were hidden by interior walls extending from the sides of the house out to the palisade.

George picked up the pace to clear the path behind him for the main procession. At Rhys's direction, he circled along a path to the left that avoided the front grounds and brought the pack in behind him with their sterns waving, in good order. Owen the Leash and his companions maintained a discreet and constant distance and followed him. Behind him the procession moved across the grounds at a solemn pace to his right, along a wide path bordered with low bushes, now in autumn foliage.

As George came alongside the main building with the pack the full extent of it became clearer. Standing three stories high, its extended square corner towers in front gave it the impression of a fortification. The tower corners were connected by the three levels of a stone portico across the front of the building. The first level had a recessed grand entrance. The building was rough-hewn stone, and overall the manor seemed like a cross between a small castle and an English country house of the more rustic variety, both defensible and comfortable.

The back lacked the fortified corners of the front. About halfway down the manor house's side a two-story stone wall extended in a curve out sideways and back to the palisade, matched by another wall on the other side. It was large enough to stand on, crenelated for defense, and protected by a pair of large solid wooden gates, now standing open.

As he crossed through the gateway in this curtain wall he discovered many extensive outbuildings arranged neatly with straight lanes between them, like a Roman outpost. Far more space was enclosed behind the curtain walls than in front of the manor. From his position he could see several stables and a variety of workshops which must include a blacksmith, since he could hear an anvil ring. There seemed to be small dwellings, mixed in with the rest. It reminded him of the interior of a castle yard, but much larger and laid out more elaborately. The builders had left a space open between the back of the manor house and the first of the outbuildings that flowed up the slope, and more space was left open along the palisade that surrounded it.

It was also noisy—an establishment this size required many people—and the sudden silence that spread as he came into view with the pack was striking. Rhys cantered ahead of him toward an isolated area not far from the palisade on the left that was clearly the kennels, and he followed at a walk with the hounds.

Rhys bent over his horse to issue orders to a couple of boys in red. They turned and opened the kennel gates, disappearing inside. He straightened up and beckoned him in.

George brought the hounds into the kennel yard, followed by Rhys, and the gates closed behind them. Owen and the other hunt servants remained outside and turned away.

The kennels were large and elaborate, with the resident hounds raising a racket as their packmates returned. Working with Rhys who knew the hounds, and helped by the kennel-boys who held the gates and pointed out where the hounds belonged, George directed first the dog hounds, and then the more biddable bitches into their respective pens. The younger hounds had their own quarters separate from the older ones. Finally the yard was empty and each hound was where he belonged.

The boys in red came up for more orders, and George realized with a start that they weren't boys at all, but small folk, one bearded, dressed in red jackets and wearing leather breeches with low boots. All were comfortable with the hounds and clearly functioned as kennel-men. He tried not to stare rudely at them. Time for some answers, George thought.

George turned to Rhys. "What now?"

"The lutins will see to the hounds. Come with me and we'll find a place for your horse." George swung Mosby toward the gate and followed him, wondering what on earth a lutin was.

One of the small men opened the yard gate for them and shut it behind as they left, with a clang. The noise of the busy establishment had resumed.

George pulled up beyond the closed gate. "I should be headed home," he said. "I'll be missed." He didn't bother asking for a phone—he doubted he'd find one here, wherever "here" was.

Rhys apologized with his eyes. "Gwyn will want to speak with you, please. We might as well make your horse comfortable in the meantime."

No arguing with that, even if it was a delaying tactic, as it seemed. Surely he wasn't suspected of being involved in that death. There were now two gates, a village, and several miles between him and the woods where he met the buck. He felt more like a guest than a prisoner, but if he was wrong he might as well let Mosby rest up while he tried to get answers from Gwyn. No point in putting Rhys on the spot if he's just obeying orders. Besides, he suspected he would need their willing assistance to get home.

Rhys and George ambled to the nearest stable where two more of the small men in red came out to greet them and take their horses. George dismounted and followed the one who was leading Mosby inside, wanting to be sure of his horse's comfort.

As Mosby was led into a loose box, George asked, "What shall I do with my gear?" Rhys pointed to a room at the end of the stable aisle, clearly a tack room. "You'll be assigned a chest during your stay. Come see."

The lutin silently handed him a basket that had been hanging on the stall door. George unclipped his sandwich box and wire cutters from the saddle and added them to the basket. Then he unbuckled the girth and removed the bridle. Mosby bent his head to some fresh hay and oats in a manger and a welcome wooden bucket of cool water, while one of the grooms began rubbing him down, standing on a stool to reach high enough.

George used the advantage of his height to pull off the saddle and pad, and another groom took them from him, along with the bridle. With the basket in his hand, George gave Mosby a pat on his hindquarters and followed Rhys to the tack room to claim an unoccupied chest. Several were stacked up in the sunlight streaming through the window, and more in the dimmer corners.

Wouldn't hurt to have a bit more light in here, he thought. He stood in the doorway looking for a light switch. No power? He looked up to confirm his suspicions—no lights. But what's that next to the window? He walked over and stared at an ordinary oil lamp hanging from a hook on the wall, like a sconce. It seemed so normal, in this place, but where did it come from? It was the first thing he'd seen that didn't look like it was manufactured here. A shiver went up his spine at the incongruity.

I'm not the only thing in the wrong place.

Meanwhile Rhys and one of the lutins had pulled out an empty chest and opened it.

"How shall they mark the chest and stall for your stay, my lord?" Rhys asked.

George looked around and saw no names or even letters or numbers on the chests, only a variety of what seemed to be symbols drawn in charcoal on small wooden shingles hung on hooks. They were largely simple geometric shapes or drawings of an animal, reminiscent of heraldic signs. He recalled seeing similar charcoal drawings on some of the stall doors.

He thought of the old Talbot arms that hung in his grandfather's dining room, gold on red. "A lion rampant," he said whimsically, without thinking, but Rhys nodded and it was clear he understood the heraldic term's meaning: "standing to strike."

"Very well. I would judge that your task is done. Allow me to return you to my lord Gwyn."

Rhys preceded him to the front of the dim stable. As George paused on the threshold behind him, he heard light running footsteps and a bright form leaped at Rhys, causing him to stagger lightly. George's eyes adjusted and he saw a young teenage girl dancing about his guide. Her blond braid bounced along her back over her simple rose-colored dress.

"Did you see it? What did it look like? Is he really dead? They won't let me in there. What about the stranger? Did he do it?"

Rhys grabbed her shoulders, smiling, and forcibly held her in place to slow her down. "What courtesies are these to our guest?" he said.

George emerged from the dimness of the stable entrance and she stopped, abashed, staring at him.

Rhys said to him. "Please excuse this ill-mannered display." He looked at her sternly, if fondly. "Allow me to present Rhian, my sister. Rhian, this gentleman is George Talbot Traherne. He's brought the pack safely home for us."

She brushed the loose wisps of hair off her face and dropped into a courtesy, glancing up at her brother to see if this was acceptable. George smiled down at her. "No, I didn't do it." Her cheeks reddened.

She rose and said forthrightly, "Thank you, sir, for your deed and please excuse my unbridled words."

She took her brother's arm and accompanied them to the house.

CHAPTER 3

How could she have said anything so embarrassing, Rhian thought. Would she never learn to hold her tongue?

As they walked to the manor house, she pulled back on Rhys so that they were walking more abreast of each other. That way she could get a better look at their guest. My, he was big, taller than Rhys, a bit, and broader. Are all humans this large? There was something about him that reminded her of her foster-father, but it was hard to say what, since his face was so expressive, constantly changing, while Gwyn's was always so careful.

She glimpsed him smiling, not broadly, but quietly, to himself, as if he found everything amusing. Including her clumsy manners, probably.

She sighed silently. Well, at least he looked too kind to hold it against her. She decided he couldn't have been part of Iolo's murder. The news had traveled very quickly with the first hunters back from the disaster, some of whom saw it happen and were pleased to tell anyone all about it. The one day she has to miss hunting and look what happens. She was determined to get a look at the body herself, but so far they'd turned her away. Never mind, I know how to get in there after hours when everyone's asleep.

Who would be huntsman, now? It seemed like it must be Rhys, but she worried about that. He didn't want it, might not be any good at it. It was so unfair. She was the one who wanted it, not him. She could do it, she knew she could. She'd been practicing, in the kennels, with Isolda's help. She'd almost had Iolo persuaded to take her with him. Almost. Would it have made any difference? Or would she be dead, too? She shivered.

She looked over at George again as they approached the nearest of the three rear entrances. How had he managed it? Could Gwyn hire him, maybe?

As they entered the hunting room, she sneezed at the smoke from the fire that took some of the chill off the stone walls. She checked to see if anyone else was there, in the comfortable chairs by the fireplace or at the small tables that marched along the right side, but the room was empty. She glanced at the pegs on the outer wall and saw the usual mix of gear, both military and hunting. with several bows, a few swords, and a couple of lances with cross bars. Many of the pegs were empty.

So, nothing out of the ordinary was going on, just everyone busy with something else.

Rhys turned to her and unbuckled his belt with sword and hunting knife attached. He put the two blades together, and wrapped the belt around them to make a neat package. "Would you do me the favor of returning this to my room and bringing me my normal belt while I attend to our guest?"

She looked at him, surprised. He didn't often ask for casual favors like this, the way he would a friend, much less appeal to her duties to help him as host.

Pleased not to be treated as a child, she nodded at him with appropriate dignity. "Certainly, brother."

She took the weighty bundle in both arms and ran off through the doorway on the left.

George and Rhys followed her more sedately, entering a large hall with open double doors to the outside on the left wall. It was flagstone paved and the walls were rough stone, like the exterior walls. An archway at each end pierced the long wall opposite the outer doors, and George could see an immense great hall within. Along the outer wall on the far side of the outer doors a staircase led both up and down into cellars. He could smell something roasting through a door at the far side of the hall across from him.

Nearest to him on the left was an enclosed area with doors, like a large set of cloakrooms. Rhys nodded at it. "For your convenience." George opened a door and discovered tidy if basic indoor plumbing.

After the emptiness of the first room, this hall was busy. Servants and attendants bustled through the open doors and archways, and from the kitchen opposite came a boisterous and continuous noise. Rhys snagged an older man with an air of management about him. "Do you know where my foster-father is?"

"In council, I believe."

Rhys strode off with George, calling back over his shoulder, "Send us some refreshment there." Without waiting for a reply, he led George into the great hall in the interior of the manor house.

The very image of a medieval banqueting hall, this cavernous space rose three stories. George noted a raised stone platform with steps all around against the left wall, bearing one row of long tables and chairs. The main floor was flagstoned, wide and empty. Against the right wall, beneath a minstrels' gallery, stood an orderly pile of long trestle table platforms and supports, with low benches in stacks beside them.

The hall was well-lit and George turned his head to see why. Behind him was a great central hearth along the wall shared with the back hall he'd just left. The chimney rose up internally along the center of that long wall and, at the level of the third floor, was surrounded on both sides by a series of tall windows. The afternoon sunlight poured through and illuminated the space. No windows were cut through any other wall. Tapestries and banners clung to the stone surfaces of the upper walls, their colors faded and hard to discern. The ceiling receded into dimness with a hint of carved beams.

On the wall opposite the hearth was a large archway. George glimpsed the entrance hall at the front of the manor house through it, but Rhys didn't head that way. Instead, he drew George after him to a closed door in the left wall on the other side of the raised dais.

The sound of steps from behind halted them, and they turned to find Rhian running up with Rhys's belt and a simple hanging knife. "Can't I come in with you?" she pleaded.

"You know he won't allow it. I'll come find you after and tell you everything. Well, almost. Will that satisfy you?"

She hung on his arm anyway, and when he tapped on the door and then opened it, she came through with them, lingering in the doorway.

George saw a large comfortable room, plastered along the inner walls. The one outer wall across from the open door was wood-paneled and filled with bookcases and papers. In the half of the room near the entrance stood a great table, half-occupied now with several people. Gwyn was seated at the narrow end furthest from the door, listening to an earnest discussion. Behind him, in the back half of the room, were desks and tables, and more stacks of papers. A fire had been laid in the hearth behind the desks, but it hadn't been lit.

Paintings, mostly portraits, hung on the plastered walls, along with several oil lamps. A number of small tables and chairs were scattered beyond the council table. On the right, another closed door led to the front of the building.

Gwyn looked up as they entered. He caught Rhian's eye and raised an eyebrow. She sighed melodramatically and turned away, shutting the door behind her.

George remained standing near the door while Rhys walked the length of the table and approached Gwyn. Gwyn raised a hand to halt the conversation around the table.

Rhys came to a halt. "My lord, the hounds are safely back in kennels and all's well. Our guest's horse has been seen to, and I've brought him back to you."

"My thanks, foster-son. Please be seated while we finish our business."

Raising his eyes to George, he continued, "Please wait a few minutes, kinsman. I would speak with you privately."

Answers at last, I hope, George thought. Who are these people? Will they let me leave wherever this is?

Rhys and George removed themselves to some comfortable chairs beyond the great table. A quiet tap on the door they had used was followed by a servant bringing in a tray with food and drink. Rhys waved him over and he set up on a small table between them. A fresh round crusty loaf, butter, ham, cheese, and several apples, with flagons of cider and water, tempted their appetite. George's pocket knife was short for the purpose, so Rhys used his belt knife to cut for them both. He poured out some cider into glasses where it bubbled quietly along the sides.

George's stomach overruled his growing concern about how he was going to get back home. They ate in pleasant silence for a few minutes, concentrating on the food. The cider was sparkling and mildly alcoholic.

Rhys raised an eyebrow at him. "My foster-father called you kinsman?" he asked.

"I don't understand it myself. I know of someone with that name, but this can't be him, he'd be dead," George said.

A quiet scratch on a nearby closed door leading to the front rooms of the manor house caused Rhys to shake his head and rise, opening the door to let in two small white terriers, long haired and wiry-coated. The noise in the front rooms beyond them vanished again once he closed the door.

The terriers promptly parked themselves in front of the food and waited, quivering. "Nothing wrong with those noses," George said quietly, trying not to disturb the discussion around the table.

"They are scamps and rogues, and my lord is excessively fond of them." Rhys smiled. "Allow me to introduce Taffy and Myfanwy." He patted the seat of the chair he occupied and Taffy hopped up into place, rewarded with a tidbit of ham. Myfanwy looked up imploringly at George, so he obliged her with the same invitation and welcomed the bit of warmth along one leg, kept contented by small but frequently solicited bribes.

The conversation at the other end of the great table was intense but quiet, and George couldn't make out much of it.

Gwyn rose. "Let me know what you find immediately. We'll continue this in the morning. If you'll excuse me…"

They pushed their chairs back, nodded, and left through the door to the great hall.

Gwyn came over to Rhys and George in the corner. "Any left for me?"

He pulled another comfortable chair over and sat down. Rhys handed him his own glass and refilled it with cider, cutting him some bread and ham. Gwyn looked over at Taffy in Rhys's lap. "Well?" The terrier jumped down and hopped up to Gwyn's seat. Myfanwy studiously ignored him to keep George's nice warm leg. Gwyn chuckled. "Traitor," he told her.

Silence persisted while Gwyn took a few bites. Then he sighed, put his glass down, and looked directly at George. "We have much to discuss."

George cleared his throat. He could finally ask the most important question.

"Where am I?"

"There's no simple answer to that. This is still Virginia, after a fashion, and yet really more a reflection of Virginia in another place."

George nodded to himself. Well, you knew it was something like that already, didn't you, he thought. He took a deep breath.

"If you're about to say that I've been carried off by the Fair Folk to Elf-land, I'm not sure I can well dispute you. There's too much concrete reality in all of this." He could hardly believe that he'd actually said this, but he truly had no good rational explanation to hand.

Gwyn smiled. "We would call it the otherworld."

Maybe this will make more sense from another direction, George thought.

"You've called me 'kinsman.' What are we to each other?"

Gwyn approached the topic indirectly. "My kind are very long-lived and we've been in this new world for centuries. From time to time, some of us are accustomed to visit your human world, and sometimes we stay for a while, as a change."

Suddenly George rethought the brief introduction in the field. Not a cousin in the Bellemore family, perhaps. "You're the father of my grandmother Georgia Annan, aren't you?"

Gwyn nodded. "And thus your great-grandfather."

Rhys had been silent so far but at this he grinned. "That would make me some sort of cousin, wouldn't it?" He sounded pleased.

George recalled the Bellemore estate history. It was often empty for a generation or two, and then re-occupied by an heir in the male line. Gwyn returning periodically under a new guise each time?

"Does my grandfather Talbot know?"

"I'm not sure what he believes. I departed soon after their marriage. It was time; I'd remained long enough that my unchanging appearance was beginning to cause remark. I claimed a son in Europe from a first wife to create an appropriate heir, as I've done before, and left my daughter an inheritance of all but the actual estate and its furnishings."

"How could you leave your family?"

"It must always be so. Her mother was gone, and I'd seen her into adulthood with a husband. I've looked in from time to time. Does she live still?"

George was horrified. Doesn't he keep track of his own daughter? With an effort he held his face expressionless.

"She's becoming frail. Does she know what you are? She inherits none of your… traits?"

"I never told her—it wouldn't be kind. We have few children and, when we have children outside the blood, they mostly gain little of us except our affection."

If that, George thought.

"Did you ever meet your granddaughter Léonie, my mother, before she died?"

"I didn't know she'd died." He was silent for a moment. "I often saw her in the woods of Bellemore, on her pony. We had many pleasant, if anonymous, chats."

Rhys laughed. "You named your estate 'Bellemore?' Did you tell your grandfather?"

George gave him a bewildered look and Rhys turned to him with a flourish. "Cousin," chuckling at the salutation, "you see before you the great Prince of Annwn, Gwyn ap Nudd. His father is the great lord Nudd of the Silver Hand, called these days Lludd Llaw Eraint, ruler in Britain, and his father is the mighty Beli Mawr, our highest present power. Hence 'Bellemore.'"

Gwyn said smoothly, with an unruffled expression, "Word play's not uncommon in Virginia estate names. I didn't ask him for permission, nor yet you, pup."

"Wait a minute," George said. "It may be taking me a while to catch up, but I remember some of the old Welsh stories from my father. If you, sir," nodding to Gwyn, "are the Prince of Annwn, then those hounds would be the Cŵn Annwn, the Hounds of Hell."

Gwyn nodded.

George was taken aback at his calm agreement, then laughed uncertainly into the silence—no wonder everyone was afraid of them. "How did I survive that?"

Gwyn looked at him. "Sometimes our blood does come out, after all. Those of my blood are in sympathy with our beasts, and so, it would seem, are you."

George wondered. It was true that hounds and horses were biddable for him but he had never tried teaching them anything out of the ordinary. He looked at Myfanwy in his lap. "Would you sit up for me, my lady?" She glanced up at him and rose to waggle two paws in the air, eyes agleam. "Thank you," he said faintly, popping another bit of ham in her mouth.

Before he could explore the dozens of questions that came to him, he pulled his mind back to the basics.

"Can I return? Or have I already lost years, as the stories say?"

"Yes, you can return. The stories are wrong; time passes the same in all worlds. Do you wish to return? Can you not stay the night, at least?"

George thought about it. He wanted to find out more about this place and his new relatives, but he felt the tug of his home and his responsibilities. "I will be missed and I don't want to cause distress, nor should they send searchers on a fool's errand."

He remembered the text message he'd sent a few hours ago. He pulled out his cellphone and saw that the message was still unsent; there had never been a usable signal since the disastrous jump in the woods. No GPS signal either. A chill went up his spine at this confirmation that he was in a place without cell towers or satellites, or even, presumably, electricity.

As he fumbled with his gadgets, Gwyn said, "We have agents in your world. We could get a message to one that would be delivered this evening to, say, your grandfather."

George was tempted. He wanted to explore this unexpected heritage, at least briefly. "If I return, can I come back?"

"Perhaps, but I don't know for certain if you can do it on your own."

Ah, there's the subtle prod to reinforce the offer. I'm being played, George thought. He's got something in mind, and he's being very smooth about it.

Alright, George decided. "If I can get a note delivered to my grandfather, I'd like to stay a little while. Thank you."

Gwyn smiled at him. "Excellent. You'll find paper and pen on my desk. Rhys, please arrange a room for our kinsman." Rhys departed on the errand.

With apologies, George lifted Myfanwy off his lap and walked to the desk on the far side of the room where he found an ink well with a dip pen and smooth rag paper. What could he possibly write? He settled for truthful and obscure.

Grandfather,

I can't explain right now, but something completely unexpected has come up and I may be away for a few days. Mosby and I are fine, and I'm very sorry to have caused any worry. Could you please ask Bud to look after the place and the animals for me? Please tell Sam Littleton at my office that it's a family emergency; Bud has the number.

Fondly,

George

His farm manager, Bud, could look after things for a few days. He'd have to defer a proper explanation until he understood more about what was happening. Perhaps his Talbot grandfather comprehended more about his wife's family than he let on.

He gave the sheet to Gwyn who folded and sealed it. He stepped into the great hall and stopped a passing servant. "Send Idris Powell to me."

After a few moments, Idris entered. Gwyn handed him the sealed sheet. "Get this to Mrs. Catlett as soon as possible, this afternoon, for immediate delivery to Gilbert Talbot. She knows who he is." Idris nodded and left.

George was startled. He knew Mariah Catlett slightly, a middle-aged woman who rode quietly but competently in the first field of the hunt.

Rhys re-entered the room. "Good. Rhys, take charge of your kinsman until dinner, if you would." He turned to George, "I'll speak with you again later this evening."

Dismissed, George and Rhys returned to the great hall. Rhian was sitting on the steps of the dais, waiting for them.

Rhys informed his sister, "Rhian, allow me to introduce your kinsman. He's Gwyn's great-grandson."

Rhian brightened at the news. She sprang up and then courtesied formally.

He continued, "He'll be spending the night so at least some of your questions will be answered."

Rhian looked George over critically. "What will he wear tonight? Everyone's staying, too curious to leave." George frowned; he hadn't considered the matter of evening dress here. Rhian was right—it would be poor manners to be improperly attired at what promised to be a formal event.

"What's it matter?" Rhys said.

With a great look of scorn, Rhian ignored him, "We had better sort that out now; there won't be time later after kennels. Let's see what's in his room."

Looking tolerantly over her head at George, Rhys shrugged and the three of them passed through the great archway to the front hall and the main stairs.

Gwyn moved to his desk and straightened up after George, wiping the pen and capping the inkwell. He took advantage of the rare solitude to consider his options.

This was the first time a human descendant had ever come to him. On those few occasions when he thought it appropriate, he had brought one with him, usually permanently. They had adapted well and lived out their lives, as humans do.

This one, however, seemed to have been thrust upon him. It wasn't surprising that he'd been unaware of his existence; there was little point in tracking his ever more diluted blood in the human world indefinitely, especially with their short lifetimes. But how did George get here? And why was it so timely? He discarded the notion of coincidence with barely a moment's consideration.

Who was interfering in his affairs? Was it the work of a secret ally or an enemy? Enemy seemed more likely—why would an ally be hidden?

The prudent thing would be to have nothing to do with him and to refuse the bait. Unless, he reconsidered, it would be better to keep him close and forestall any damage by controlling him, letting whomever was behind him think him deceived.

And yet, all that he could see of George so far persuaded him that he was not only who he said he was, but that he was also an independent player, unaware of Gwyn or the otherworld. What to believe?

Surely if he intended to deceive he would feign great family affection and desire to stay. Instead, he's taking it slowly and a bit reservedly, as if he distrusts me and would truly return to his home in a day or two.

If he's genuine, then he's taking it well, better than some of his predecessors.

Well, what choices do I have? I must have a huntsman or risk losing everything. Remember how Arawn was weakened until finally he failed the great hunt. That was cleverly done, too, using Pwyll as a distraction and a test. I helped bring him down, and I remember the methods. He glanced at Angharad's painting of his investiture as Prince of Annwn at the hands of his father.

I had help then, in the moment of crisis when it counted. It shouldn't surprise me, I suppose, to find help again. And if I'm wrong, at least I'll have a chance to control it.

Alright, I'll take George at face value for now and try him as huntsman. If he can do the job, and if I can persuade him to stay long enough, then I may survive this for now. If not, I must fall back on Rhys, and that's not likely to succeed. Better to gamble on the possible unknown over the known impossible.

Let's see how he performs in company this evening.

As they entered the front hall, George discovered grand stone stairs ascending on either side of him to a common mid-story landing above the archway from the great hall, then rising in a single course to the next floor. The pattern repeated itself again as he peered upward. The wide double doors in front, a match to those in the back hall, were closed, but windows on each side showed a view through a square-columned porch and down the extensive front grounds.

On either side were smaller archways and formal rooms, crowded with people and movement. A few were still in riding costume, but most had changed clothes. George took them for the members of the field that had been sent home early. Servants passed through with refreshments and had been doing so for some time, to judge by the noise level.

Rhian ignored them and bounded up the stairs, Rhys and George following at a more dignified pace. She waited for them at the top of the stairs. "Where did you put him, Rhys?" she called down.

"In grandfather's room. It has a view of the kennels." Turning to George as they climbed the stairs, he said, "The second floor's for guests and the third for family, but many of our family are only occasional visitors, so they have permanent rooms on the second floor which we use also as guest rooms when they're not present. On crowded occasions, we have additional quarters in the yard." He pointed in the direction of the grounds behind the house.

The top of the stairs opened up into a formal sitting area, with a double-door that led to the second story of the porch. They turned right along a corridor that George realized surrounded the interior shell of the great hall downstairs. There wasn't time to examine the paintings and colorful objects hung everywhere, but he got a good look at some of the weaponry from many periods and various cultures. As he passed one battle ax scarred from use, he thought, these may be decorative, but I notice they're not bolted to the wall. Handy for an impromptu brawl.

After passing two doors on the left, Rhys opened a third and led the way into a good-sized chamber. "This is the room that my grandfather Edern ap Nudd uses when he's here. He hasn't visited for several years."

George saw a high canopied bed, a wardrobe and chest, and some chairs and low tables in front of the unlit fire in the hearth on the right hand wall. Colorful rugs lightened the floor. He walked over to the narrow, tall windows on the opposite wall, stepping around the desk below them.

To the left, his view was blocked by the fortified corner tower and the curtain wall that he'd ridden through, but to the right he had a good view of the left interior of the yard, with the nearest stables and, through a gap in the buildings, the kennel pens beyond. They covered much more ground than he'd realized; he'd only seen a small part of them before.

Rhian meanwhile had opened the wardrobe and was looking through clothing which he assumed belonged to her grandfather. It held several coats of antique cut and breeches. "Oh, Rhys," she cried, in tones of despair, "This won't do—Grandfather's too thin for him."

Rhys looked over at George by the windows. "I'm afraid you're rather broader about the shoulders than she expected." To Rhian, he said, "I have an idea. What about Rhodri's robes?"

"Oh. Yes, that might work." George widened his eyes in alarm—he was conservative in matters of dress and "robes" had alarming connotations of gaudiness and vulgarity.

This was going to be a problem, he realized. *Staying in a family bedroom, wearing someone else's exotic clothes, dropping in on a dinner where they all know each other, except for me. Am I the only human around?*

Rhys caught some of his expression and reassured him. "Don't worry. Rhodri wasn't the first to travel to the east. Many of us follow those fashions. You'll fit in fine." He headed for the doorway. "Come with us."

~

They left the chamber door open behind them and continued down the corridor, turning right after passing another door. Rhys ticked off the left-hand rooms along the back wall as they passed them. "Baths, and the rooms for servants brought by our guests."

After turning right again and passing another door, Rhys opened the next door on the left. George realized this was the matching room to his own on the opposite side of the manor house.

What a difference, he thought, as he stood on the threshold. Where George's room was quietly comfortable, this was a riot of colors and textures. He paused in the doorway and tried to make sense of it. The ceiling was draped with yellow flowered silks giving the impression that the entire room was inside a Persian tent. Overlapping layers of colorful eastern carpets covered the floor, leaving little bare wood visible. Instead of sturdy chairs, large cushions were scattered before the hearth, and the bed crouched low to the ground. As George walked over the deep carpets to the windows, he saw chests along the wall and a low desk, to be used while sitting on the ground.

The view from here gave him his first look at the extensive kitchen gardens. Orchards, gardens, and animal pens ran most of the way to the palisade, inside another curtain wall.

Beside him, Rhian was busily opening chests and poking through the bright fabrics within. "What sort of colors do you like, cousin?"

"Dark and sober ones," he said, repressively.

Nothing daunted, she pulled out a long-sleeved kaftan. It was a midnight-blue satin, almost black, with a damasked dark gray allover figure of tree leaves. Quiet lines of embroidery in burnt orange, pewter gray, and gold in a similar tree-leaf pattern ornamented the cuffs, collar, and divided front. To match it she found loose breeches and a long-sleeved tunic top of the same color. A little more probing unearthed a very long dark orange and gold sash for the tunic, clearly intended to wrap around more than once. The breeches were designed to blouse over at the knee and tuck into boots. "This will go well with your boots and save us one difficulty, at least," she said.

She laid these clothes out on the bed. "Jewelry?" she asked.

"No," he replied, absently, looking at these garments. If he were attending a costume party, he might actually wear such things. Despite the richness of the materials they seemed neither flimsy nor feminine to him. The tunic and breeches had a good weight and the kaftan was thicker than it looked. He held it up against himself and it seemed large enough.

Alright, he'd have to take their word that this sort of clothing was acceptable, and try not to look out of place. He'd show them a human could handle anything, even uncomfortable social situations. He smiled crookedly.

Rhys had his back to him, on his knees going through another trunk. "You'll need a belt knife, at least." He pulled out a knife with a sheath that curved at the tip. The blade was about five inches long. "You stick that in the sash," handing it backward to George without looking.

And that would help, George thought whimsically, as he took it, pulled out the blade, and flourished it in the air. Anyone messes with the human, I'll teach him better manners at knife point. Too bad I can't do that back home.

Home. What would his grandfather think of all this? What does he know?

Rhys stood up. Opening the door, he snagged a passing servant. "Please take these things to Edern's room and have someone prepare them for our guest for dinner."

Turning to George he said, "We have more than an hour before we must appear. This is when I usually do my kennel duties. Would you care to accompany me?" Addressing his eager sister behind him, "And you can come, too, properly dressed." Rhian dashed up the back stairs to change.

CHAPTER 4

Rhian came running up behind them and they paused to let her catch up. She had changed to breeches, boots, and a long jerkin over an old shirt. The leather jerkin was too big for her and George suspected it was her brother's, outgrown. It had clearly visited kennels before, judging by the paw prints left behind. She'd bound her braid up in a kerchief to keep it clean and donned worn leather gloves.

George looked over at Rhys as they stood before the kennel gates. "What are your duties here?"

"I've been learning mastery of horse and hound. I must understand everything about the hounds, their training, and the management of kennels. I can't set people to their tasks if I don't know those tasks myself. We two," looking fondly at his sister, "have the blood for it, as well as the inclination, though Rhian can handle hounds better than I can."

"What will you do now that the huntsman has died? What will happen?"

Rhys and Rhian exchanged serious looks.

"Iolo's death is a disaster. He was my lord Gwyn's foster-son, and has been the huntsman for the pack since Gwyn's rule began. I don't know how, or if, we can continue."

"If you don't have anyone suitable, wouldn't you get a huntsman from somewhere else and then go on after some interval?" He could see from their faces as he spoke that it was much more serious than that.

Rhys shook his head. "The hunt must go out on Nos Galan Gaeaf, the night of the first day of winter, the change of the year, to hunt in the old way. Our lord Gwyn must provide justice and be seen to do it. Not to do so would break the ancient compacts and I don't know what would happen. I think he might lose the hunt and perhaps, with it, all of Annwn, this realm."

Rhian stared at him. "Could that really happen?"

Rhys nodded soberly.

George said, "So maybe it's a political enemy, then. The killing might've been targeted for this purpose, aimed more at Gwyn than Iolo. Does Gwyn know who his enemy is?"

"He has, we have, many enemies, but they're not usually secretive, especially about their victories. Perhaps we'll hear a boast in the next few days."

"When's this deadline, the night of the first day of winter?"

"I don't know your name. Our neighbors in the old country called it Samhain."

All Hallows' Eve, thought George. "Can't anyone else hunt the hounds? What about Gwyn? Or you?"

"Gwyn rules here, he doesn't lead the hunt himself. It's been two years since I was released from my weapons-master to learn about the hounds, but it wasn't to be huntsman. I don't know that I'm capable of it, nor is it my ambition. We don't have that much time for me to learn, either—just two weeks."

Sounds like they've got a real situation on their hands, George thought. Too bad. Glad it's not my problem.

Rhian ran ahead to the gate of the kennel yard and opened it. All three walked in, Rhian closing the gate behind them, and George paused to get a better look now that he no longer had a pack of hounds surrounding him.

The kennels had an enclosing wall of stone raised to well over a man's height, whitewashed and bare of encroaching vegetation. The yard itself was flagstone paved, slanted slightly toward drains along one edge. Two large unroofed pens stood on either side with solid walls halfway up, separated by a third pen. Through a doorway in the solid wall at the back of each pen, George could see a roofed area with long benches built along the walls. A solid door, now open, allowed the inner portion to be closed off from the weather, and windows alongside the door admitted light.

The hounds erupted off their benches when they heard the gate open and stood in the front of their pens to watch them, barking and standing up against the metal bars to inspect their visitors. The middle pens were empty.

The dog hounds were housed together first on the left, followed by the empty pen and then the bitch pack. On the right, he saw the same gender division for the younger hounds in their first season, not yet full-fledged members of the pack. Past the two pens of youngsters was one more small enclosure, apparently empty. "For whelping?" he asked Rhys, who nodded.

Just beyond the pens in this yard were entrances to the kennel buildings on either side. They followed steam and a smell of meat into the left entryway. In a room just off the entry two younger lutins were stirring large cauldrons suspended by chains over a fire, one with boiling meat, and one with something that resembled porridge. A third one, older, was bent over, mending a leash at a table.

"Any injuries today?" Rhys asked the lutin at the table as they entered.

"No, all are well."

"And Holda's rash?

"Healing. She'll be able to go out again soon."

"Master Ives, this gentleman's George Talbot Traherne. He's our guest for a while, and a kinsman." All three lutins nodded. "George, this is Ives, the kennel-master."

"I'm pleased to meet you," George said. "The yards are splendid and beautifully maintained, and the hounds are magnificent." Ives straightened with pride and nodded his thanks.

"These are Tanguy," indicating a small lutin with a beard, "and Huon." The youngster, beardless, smiled at them.

"Rhian," cried a voice from the entry. "I didn't think we'd see you today."

A young lutine dressed in red under a long dirty coat ran up to embrace Rhian. She was much smaller though clearly a few years older than Rhian. Ives beamed at her indulgently.

"My daughter, Isolda," he said to George. "I can't keep them apart." He paused, "Would you care to see the hounds?"

"Indeed I would, if you can spare the time." The girls brightened.

"Excellent," Rhys said. "I'll turn to some of my other duties here, and Ives can return you to me when you're done."

Ives picked up a dirty garment to throw over his clothes as a kennel coat and led them further in to a corridor that ran along the back of the building. "We'll do the dog hounds first. They always expect it, conceited beasts."

Their boot heels rang on the flagged floor. On the right they passed rooms for gear and equipment. On the left, the solid doors at the backs of the pens were matched with windows on each side so that one could look in on the hounds on their wide benches. An outer door stood at the end on the right, and George could see through the window alongside that it led to two turnout yards along the inner wall of the kennels, each of an acre or more, surrounded by high fencing.

Having reached the farthest pen on the left, the first pen George had passed on his way in, Ives paused with his hand on the latch. "I was told you brought the pack back today. Did they give you any trouble?"

George described how he had walked through them and treated Dando as the leader. "Most of the people here seem afraid of them. Isn't it the same for your folk?"

Ives smiled in his beard. "It's not us they hunt. We send our souls elsewhere and punish our own. They hunt the tall folk, human or fae."

"Who were they hunting this afternoon, then?"

"Oh, well, we haven't so many villains that we hunt them every day," Ives chuckled. "Mostly they hunt deer, for the pleasure of the company."

He opened the door. All the hounds had risen off the benches along the sides at the sound of their voices. They stood quietly, their tails waving slightly.

Rhian pushed past George to single out one hound, white with red ears and little other red on him. "This is our Dando." George walked over and renewed his acquaintance.

Ives pointed out individuals and described their breeding and characters. "Iolo and I plan, er, planned, all the activities."

"I'm sorry for your loss," George said. There was silence for a moment.

The group returned to the corridor and this time Isolda walked ahead with Rhian to enter the bitches' pen. As Ives and George followed, they found Rhian sitting on one of the wide benches with a hound next to her.

"Look, Master Ives. Anwen's sore needs tending," Rhian said. George peered over Ives's bent head. The hound's licking was keeping the sore from closing.

"Thank you, my lady. I'll take care of this." He pulled a lead from his belt, looped it over the hound's collarless neck, and brought her with him out to the corridor.

Back in the cook room Ives brought down a small closed jar from a shelf and put it on his low worktable. He sat down which, at his height, brought his head close to the standing hound's shoulder.

"Would you hold her for me, Rhian?" Rhian stepped forward to oblige.

He opened the jar and dipped a finger in the salve within. George smelled a bit of rotten egg and recognized sulfur. He couldn't identify the other herbal scents.

Ives gently smoothed the ointment over the sore, then took the bitch's head between his hands and murmured, "Do you leave that alone now, my girl."

He held the lead out to his daughter. "Isolda, return her, please."

As Isolda walked back down the corridor with the hound, accompanied by Rhian, Ives rose and led George outside and across the yard to the matching entry on the other side.

Standing in the doorway, George could see a door on the right and a corridor beyond. Ives opened the door to a large room on his right. It contained a desk, worktable, chairs, and many shelves, as well as a small fireplace on the far wall separating this chamber from the whelping pen. A shuttered window opening was on the same wall, not far from the desk. Papers and gear were scattered on the desk, and the shelves held books and boxes.

"The huntsman's office," Ives said.

The room seemed to George as if it expected its owner to return at any moment. "It's a good arrangement." He pointed at the shutter. "He can see into the whelping pen from there?"

"Yes, and the heat warms the wall as well. When necessary he can bring the bitch and pups right in."

George admired the intelligent setup. "And those empty pens separating the hounds are for feeding or for gathering the chosen ones for a hunt?"

"Both, and also for occasional use as an infirmary, if the whelping kennel's occupied."

Footsteps sounded outside and Rhys appeared in the doorway, with Rhian. "I fear I must interrupt and return you to the hall. We'll be wanted for dinner soon."

George turned to Ives. "Thank you, master, for your time. I hope we'll have the pleasure of meeting again."

They went back out through the first yard and shut the kennel gate behind them. The bars of the gate cast long shadows on the ground as the sun started to disappear behind the Blue Ridge.

George felt the pull of that huntsman's office. What would it be like to hunt these hounds, to shape their breeding and make them his own? He envied the next man who would slip into that post.

They entered the manor through the back hall and ascended the stairs together. Partway up, they almost collided with a manservant hastening down who came to a halt and moved to the side to let them pass. George glimpsed a face, distorted as if arguing violently with himself, that smoothed as he bowed his head. He made note of his appearance: brown hair with broad streaks of white along the temples and a rigid, locked demeanor. The man's apparent internal conflict caught George's attention, but he didn't know what to make of it.

They climbed past him and heard his steps descend. George looked at Rhys who shrugged. "He's in the service of Creiddylad, my lord Gwyn's sister. I don't know his name."

Rhian unexpectedly burst out, "I hate him."

They both looked at her in surprise. "He stares at me like he wants something."

Rhys cocked an eyebrow at her, and she blushed. "I don't mean like that. When he does it, it's slimy, nasty." She shivered.

He spoke to her, seriously. "If he ever bothers you, says or does anything, you come tell me." He looked her in the eyes. "I mean it."

She nodded.

On the second floor landing, Rhys and George parted from Rhian who continued up to the third floor. Rhys came as far as George's room to confirm that the clothing for the evening had been freshened and returned. "Would you care to bathe? There's enough time for it."

At George's eager assent, Rhys said, "There should be a robe and foot gear in the wardrobe, and everything else you need in the bath room."

"I must ask, Rhys. Of all the mundane things to find in this world, I didn't expect indoor plumbing."

With a grin he replied, "His peers may consider my foster-father a decadent, fallen fellow for consorting rather too freely with humans and adopting some of their innovations, but even they admit he's a very *clean* decadent."

It would be beyond good to take off these clothes that had been well exposed to horses and hounds and get clean, George thought, even if he had to put the damn boots back on again afterward.

He turned to the wardrobe and found both a flannel robe and loose backless slippers, as promised. He pulled off his boots with relief and stripped off the rest of his clothes. At a loss for what to do with them, he draped them over one of the chairs. He took the gun which had been holstered at the small of his back, unloaded it, and put both the cartridges and the weapon into a drawer. He added the GPS device, and pulled the cellphone out, too, but dropped it with his left hand and had to stoop to pick it up again and dump it in the drawer. The rest of the contents of his pockets he emptied onto the dresser.

Standing there for a moment, he flexed his left hand and rubbed it with his right. Hasn't been getting any better, has it? The doctor said the numbness would improve, but I think this one's going to be a lifetime companion, like an old football injury. Well, you come off enough horses, these things are bound to happen. Awkward to keep dropping things this way, though.

He donned the robe and cracked open the door to peek into the hallway. No one there. He left the door open a crack and headed for the baths, just two doors down the corridor.

A small anteroom led to four main chambers, their doors ajar. The near two were clearly toilet areas, with pull-chains that emptied cisterns for flushing and shelves with basins for washing. The one on the right was for men, to judge by the stand-up options.

The next two rooms held the baths. He assumed the one on the right was also for men but was cautious about sticking his head in. More basins stretched along the wall leaving most of the room for a large steaming pool with square sides, like a Roman or Japanese soaking bath. A man was already in residence, only his head visible. His gray hair and long drooping mustaches were soaked but he popped his eyes open and grinned at George.

"First time in one of these? You'll get used to it, my boy, I promise you. Wash your hair and rinse off over there, then come on in."

George found soap and a straight razor. Careful, he told himself, try not to cut your throat. He bent over a basin, washed his hair in tepid water, and managed a quick shave, not without a few nicks, while peering into a small mirror. He looked around for a way to empty the basin, and the fellow from the pool called out, "Just toss it down that drain over there," pointing to the corner. George did so and refilled it. This time he took a wet cloth, dabbed it in soap, and used it to wipe off as much of his body as he could reach. Emptying the basin again, he filled it one more time so that he could rinse off the soap.

At last, he walked to the edge of the bathing pool and stepped in. It took him a moment to get used to the steaming hot water but once he sat down on the built-in bench along the side, it felt wonderful. The soreness from his fall at the jump began to ease.

"Not bad, eh? Gwyn thinks I come here for the hunting, but it's really the baths. I'm Eurig ap Gruffudd, from up the valley. Are you that fellow who brought back the pack?"

"Yes. I'm George Talbot Traherne."

"I can't understand it. Human, aren't you?"

"So I thought, but apparently Gwyn has a… connection to my family."

"Ah, took on one of the locals, did he? That boy has always been fond of the ladies. Ever since we arrived he's been improving the native stock, so to speak."

George was startled to hear Gwyn referred to as "that boy" but then Eurig did look significantly older.

"Can you tell me about this place? What's its name?"

"You mean the manor here, Gwyn's court?"

"Yes, and the village."

Eurig stroked his mustaches. "Why, this is Greenway Court or, in the old tongue, Llys y Lon Las."

"But that's the name of a local spot in my world, Thomas, Lord Fairfax's wilderness hunting lodge."

"Is it now? I remember Thomas Fairfax well. Gwyn brought him here once for a visit, oh, must be a couple of hundred years ago now or maybe a bit more. I suppose he liked the name. He stayed a few weeks, hunting every chance he got. He was very pleased with the great hunt, as I recall. Shook Gwyn's hand stoutly afterward, he did."

He pursed his lips in reflection. "There was this one lass, what was her name? Dilys, that's it. She caught his eye, and no wonder, with her black hair, and dark eyes. She's gone now, but not before giving him a son. You may have met him, Thomas Kethin?"

George shrugged. He couldn't keep track of the names yet.

"The village is Pantglas, or Greenhollow."

Appropriate enough, George thought. Maybe he could find out more.

He said, "I never thought of, well, the otherworld as part of America. Can you tell me how your kind got here?"

Eurig settled a bit deeper in the water, like a walrus, clearly pleased to be asked.

"Certainly I can. Let's see, where to start… Our own histories go back to the advancing and the passing of the ice, several times; before that we know little. We had the lands mostly to ourselves, for a long time, we and the various small folk, and the old humans, the hunters, and then the new humans moved in alongside our world, following the herds and then planting their crops. The small folk were fascinated and, I'll admit, so were we, for a while."

George was mesmerized. The end of the last ice age, from a fae's point of view.

"There are some who hold that the old humans, the ones suited to winter, never truly died out, that they took our blood from the children we gave them and became the new men of today. Others find that a shameful notion and give it no countenance, but I've noticed there are sports among the humans that seem like throwbacks to one of my kind.

"We settled down into territories on the newly freed land as the waters rose and the rivers shifted, and we carved out domains. My folk stayed mostly in the west. Not many are still alive from those foundation times, and most of our kind were born much later, but I myself have met Beli Mawr, Beli the Great, and he saw it all.

"The more we came to know of humans, the more we withdrew beyond their notice and avoided visiting their world. Gwyn always believed there was something to be learned from them, and he's visited often. Many think him eccentric, but I, for one, am happy with plumbing, oil lamps, and all the rest. I remember what it was like before, well enough. Besides, we can't really escape the connection between our worlds entirely. Most of the pleasant little novelties in our fashions come from you, and even our names take on the coloring of the human languages surrounding us as time passes. There are just so many more of you, and you're so very, very busy all the time," he said with a snort.

"We came here, to your new world, not long after Gwyn's father created him Prince of Annwn. We knew there were lands in the far west but no way-finder had ventured the journey and made it possible before. It was restful here, for a time, like a return to our distant past. Different tribes of your kind were here already, in the human world, and we kept out of each other's way."

He smiled in reminiscence, then pulled himself a bit more upright in the bath.

"But it didn't last. Our original local humans had their inevitable little wars, and then your colonists arrived with theirs, and it all became very lively as they sorted it out. We kept mostly to ourselves in our world, peaceably enough."

"This killing of Iolo changes everything," he concluded, subsiding into a brooding silence.

"What will happen?" George asked.

"The vultures will descend to see if Gwyn will lose his kingdom. We have many enemies. None of us likes the idea of change."

The two of them sat in companionable silence for a few minutes, George pondering the deep history of these people and how shallow his life seemed in comparison.

"Well, my boy, we'll not solve this tonight. I must be dressing." Eurig stepped out of the bath. "I'll see you again soon."

George was shocked by the many scars he carried, like a battered veteran warrior. After Eurig left, he toweled off vigorously, donned his robe, and followed.

Back to his room, George discovered that it had been invaded in his absence through the open door. Myfanwy had managed to jump to the bed and was lying proudly on the blanket at the foot of it, wagging her stump of a tail. "You little devil. Well, I'm pleased to see you and glad of your company."

He closed the door behind him and surveyed his fine borrowed clothing on the wardrobe hangers. He poked through a chest of drawers and found stockings, shirts, neckerchiefs, and gloves. The breeches had a drawstring at the waist, making the fit easy. The stockings came above his knee, and he tied his breeches below the knee, to act as garters. He saw with some surprise as he pulled them on that his boots had been brushed while he was out of the room, restoring much of their gleam. The breeches bloused out over the top of the boots in a most piratical manner.

He stood up and took down the tunic, slipping it on over the breeches. It fit well enough, coming to mid thigh, with slits up either side almost to the waist for ease of movement. The heavy satin felt smooth over his chest. The tunic had no pockets, but the breeches did, and the slits in the tunic made it easy to reach them.

He looked around for the sash and saw it on the bed. He reached for it, but Myfanwy, intent on his movements, anticipated him and pounced first. "None of that, my dear," he admonished, but was enticed into playing tug-of-war with her for a few moments anyway. Then he took the sash and thought about how to arrange it—wrapped all the way around without ends showing, or ends dropping down? He ended up wrapping it around his waist twice, with both ends dangling down for a foot on his right leg.

Now for the kaftan itself. He lifted the robe off the hanger and slipped it around him, settling it across his shoulders. Everything fit well, with the bottom of the kaftan coming to mid-calf. He strode about the chamber experimentally to see how it moved and discovered that it flowed back properly as he walked rather than just hanging on him. It was wide enough to meet across his chest though there was no way to fasten it.

He glanced around the room for a mirror and spotted a small one mounted on a swiveling frame sitting on the chest of drawers, with a comb and a clothes brush next to it. Thank heavens, he thought, and combed his hair which was nearly dry. Then he took the brush to the end of the sash that Myfanwy had beaten him to and removed as much of the evidence as possible. He took a look in the mirror and thought, it's not half bad. He tilted the mirror in its frame down to catch a glimpse of the rest of him. It'll do, he thought, always assuming everyone else isn't in black tie or its equivalent.

He took his pocket watch from the drawer and ran his thumb across the dragon engraving, then unhooked the compass from the other end of the chain. In lieu of an actual watch pocket or vest buttonhole, he fastened the chain around the drawstring of the breeches and slipped it into his right pocket. The knife Rhys had found him was on top of the chest. He slipped it into his sash on the left, under the top wrap and over the bottom one so that the end of the sheath was visible.

He thought about his conversation of a few minutes ago. That Eurig fellow seems to be a vassal of Gwyn, part of the local aristocracy. Most of the others I'll meet tonight will probably be the same, and they're not all likely to be friendly. I imagine there'll be both political and social rivalries here tonight, and I'm not going to have a clue about the factions.

It'll be like an Edwardian country house party where I'm the only stranger, the only one who doesn't know the history and the alliances, and that's going to be damned awkward. Well, it may only go back to the Norman Conquest instead of the last ice age, but my Talbot blood can make itself useful and stiffen my spine for me, if nothing else.

It's only for one evening. I can uphold the honor of mere humans for that long.

CHAPTER 5

Myfanwy's yip announced the presence of visitors. George opened his door to a quiet knock and let in both Rhys and Rhian. Rhian wore a simple green gown with a modest bodice and low shoes. She had twisted up her blond hair and teased out a couple of curls. Rhys was dignified by a very dark green frock coat with an ivory waistcoat and loose white breeches. Instead of boots he wore white silk stockings and shoes suitable for dancing.

Rhian exclaimed over George's attire and had him walk back and forth to check the effect. "It really needs a turban, don't you think, Rhys?"

"Not happening," George told her. "I don't see any horsehair wig on Rhys."

Rhys shuddered. "That's one style we didn't pick up from your examples."

He bent over Myfanwy. "I see you've adopted our guest." Looking up at George, "This is very high approval, you know."

"I am conscious of the honor she does me," George said, smiling. "Come along, pup, you don't want to be trapped here all evening."

George bade her out the door and waited for the others, then followed and shut the door behind him. This time Rhys turned right and led him to the front stairs. George sighed: so it was to be a grand entrance.

He heard the buzz of conversation long before they reached the staircase. They descended and found small groups in the front hall catching up on gossip and politics. George was relieved to see several other men in robes, and noted with satisfaction that his attire was rather more somber than the peacock displays of some of the others. Some of the women were also in oriental-style dress, where the wrapped robes emphasized willowy forms.

As soon as the crowd caught sight of George the noise diminished, then recovered almost immediately with a polite resumption of conversation. A stately middle-aged woman with dark hair in a yellow silk gown came up to them. Rhian curtsied lightly, and Rhys bowed. "You're looking well, my lady. Allow me to present to you our kinsman, George Talbot Traherne. George, this is Creiddylad, my foster-father's sister."

George remembered the name from the back stairs conversation earlier. He bowed.

She greeted him with a token smile on an unreadable face. "Welcome. We've been discussing today's events, as you might imagine, and many are anxious to meet you." To look me over, you mean, thought George, keeping his face smooth. This was his aunt, three generations ago. It was difficult to balance a terminology that implied distant ancestor with a living, breathing person not much older in appearance than himself.

As he looked over the crowd it struck him that all of his first impressions of people were going to be unreliable. He was no doubt younger than almost everyone in the room except his two young friends, younger by centuries in most cases, surely. They can probably see right through me. It'll be hard to keep secrets here.

As Rhys began to introduce him around, George muttered, "You realize I won't be able to remember them all."

"They won't expect you to."

Gwyn swept up from the left, conversing with Idris Powell as he strode along. He nodded as he passed by and entered the great hall. The crowd turned and began to follow in small groups.

As George came through the archway in turn he saw that trestle tables and benches had been set up along the two long sides leaving a wide empty space in the middle. Many tables were still stacked unused along the left hand wall beneath the minstrel gallery; clearly this space could accommodate a much larger crowd than tonight's guests.

To his right, people began to take their seats at the long table on the raised dais at right angles to the two rows of tables on the hall floor. Rhys and Rhian walked up the steps, bringing George with them.

All the seats were on one side, with their backs to the wall. Looking out into the room he saw that the seats on the main tables were also on the outer sides. As servants began to bear in platters of food and pitchers of drink, he understood why—they left the inner side free for delivering the food. Serving tables along the outer walls held additional pitchers and trays. Gaps between the long table rows gave them passage space. He leaned toward Rhys quietly and asked, "What happens when there's a big crowd? Do they occupy both sides of the tables and fill the floors?"

"Yes, and very awkward it is. Noisier, too."

George estimated the dinner party at about 50 guests and noticed that the hum of conversation was indeed relatively quiet and decorous. Centuries of practicing their manners, he thought. I wonder if they have loud party drunks? Perhaps those are weeded out young. People who live together for hundred of years must have cultivated the art of good manners for friend and foe, else feuds would surely become too deadly. If you can't get away from your enemies altogether over the years, better to cleverly insult them than to come to blows on every occasion.

The sound of soft music made him lift his eyes to the minstrel gallery all the way across the hall. It was hard to make out the instruments from here, especially since he could only see the upper bodies of the musicians over the parapet, but he thought he heard viols and soft winds—oboes, perhaps?

By now, most of the guests had found a seat. George's eye was caught by Eurig with his drooping mustaches at the head of one of the tables on the main floor. Eurig smiled at him encouragingly. Next to him was a matronly figure who must be his wife. George smiled back.

About a dozen people sat along the table on the dais. Gwyn held the middle with his sister Creiddylad seated on his left, another woman and man beyond her, and an older woman on the far end. Idris Powell was at his right hand. He's more important than I realized, George thought, maybe an adviser, or a second-in-command. Gwyn has no wife? Perhaps she's just absent, or maybe there isn't one at the moment.

Rhys was seated next to Idris, then George and Rhian. He turned to his right where Rhian sat silently and smiled at her. "Have I taken your seat?"

"Oh, no, you're our guest."

"But I'm sorry to be your only dinner companion this evening."

"That's alright. I like to watch."

He leaned toward her conspiratorially. "Then do you mind if I ask you all sorts of questions? I want to know more about this place."

"I'd be pleased to help."

"To start with, who are all these people? Do they live here or are they guests?"

"Most of the year we're about a dozen in residence and dine informally with our senior staff. Of course there are often visitors, and when we hunt many of the local families join us. Since most of them live at a little distance, it's not unusual for them to spend a few days here. Some have small permanent guest lodges on the grounds, and others stay here in the manor. As the harvest is completed, more and more join us for the end of the year."

"The year starts in two weeks, yes?"

"That's right, on the night of the first day of winter. Some of these here tonight from far away have come for that. In a few days, we'll be full up to the rafters and some will have overflowed into the village."

"Do they come for a new year celebration or for the hunt?"

"Both, of course. No one misses the hunt, unless they can't ride at all. I don't know what will happen now that Iolo's gone."

George glanced down the table. "Does Creiddylad make her home here, like you do?"

Rhys overheard him and leaned in with alarm on his face, murmuring, "Hssht! That's a topic for another place and time."

My first screwup, George thought.

Servants appeared and laid out plates and silverware before them. George picked his up to examine it more closely. It looked like ceramic and the material was thin rather than heavy, but it felt like no plate he had ever seen before, and rang almost like metal when he tapped it with a fingernail. The surface was subtly textured, decorated with a horned stag inside a green-leafed border. The only marking on the back was an imprint of an oak leaf.

It came to him suddenly that his behavior was ill-mannered and he hastily put the plate down, but Gwyn caught his eye and seemed pleased with his obvious admiration. Rhys's plate was decorated with two crossed swords inside the same border, and Rhian's had a group of daffodils, but they were clearly all part of the same set. "These are the work of one of our own," Rhys told him, proudly. "Maybe you'll have a chance to meet her."

"Are they all different, like these?"

"Each is unique. They're stronger than they look and rarely break, so by now she just makes a few of these every so often to keep up with our need."

The silverware was also artisan-made. Only forks and spoons were supplied; each diner brought his own knife. There were even simple linen napkins. Not quite as medieval as I expected, George thought.

The servants brought in platters for each table and set them down. Like a conventional Thanksgiving feast they bore a distinct preponderance of new world foods: potatoes, sweet potatoes, corn, acorn squash, and some sort of broad beans he didn't recognize. The meats were venison and roast pork with apples, and there were loaves of crusty bread and plates of cornbread, dripping with butter.

Rhys said, "Some lords, I understand, revel in the fine goods and exotic foods that they bring from afar. My foster-father's one who would rather boast of his local goods and produce. Not only does he prefer them, but in these weeks before the new year, with his far-traveled guests to impress, he's quite insistent about the display. Even our way-tokens take up the theme, with their turkeys and corn stalks."

"Way-tokens?"

"Our domains are guarded. Each lord's tokens provide passage through the ways and ease what would otherwise be long tedious journeys. We don't cross oceans lightly, and avoid them when we use the ways to visit each other."

Why should I be surprised, George thought. Something like that must've taken me from Bellemore to here.

"Rhodri, who's loaned you his clothing unwittingly, is one of our great way-finders. If he returns for the great hunt this year while you're with us, you can ask him more about it," Rhys said.

No one had yet touched the food. Gwyn pushed back his chair and rose to address the gathering.

"Let us tonight honor our huntsman, Iolo ap Huw. To Iolo!"

The crowd echoed back, "Iolo!"

The servants wore a green livery, similar to the hunt staff in the field. Looking down the tables, he saw other servants, dressed in various liveries. Pointing them out to Rhian, he asked, "Are those some of the servants your guests bring?"

"That's right. They make themselves useful at dinner, otherwise we'd be overwhelmed as we fill up with guests."

George noticed the servant he had met on the stairs on his way up to change, with the white streaks at his temple. He was dressed now in a dark ochre livery, serving tables at the end of the hall. Rhian followed his gaze and commented, "Creiddylad didn't bring him on earlier visits. He walks around staring at things. He doesn't just stare at me, he stares at Rhys, too."

"Do you know his name?"

"No, but I'm going to find out. He's only been here a few days."

Rhys on his other side was attending to Gwyn and Idris, so George focused on Rhian.

"What are your interests? Do you hunt?"

Rhian glanced sharply at him to judge if he really wanted to know. She looked down at her plate and said, with fierce intensity, "I intend to be the huntsman someday." George hid his surprise. "I can do it, too. I know the names of all the hounds and the horses and the hawks and most of the other beasts. They listen to me. I'm better at it than Rhys, even Iolo said so.

"My foster-father says I must learn to run a great estate, as Rhys learns fighting and hunting and governance. So I must be in attendance on my elders for part of my education. That's why I missed the hunt today—I was in the yard with the crafts-master in the morning and with our housekeeper for the afternoon. Gwyn doesn't know that I attend on Ives and Iolo when I can." Catching Gwyn's glance, George suspected that perhaps Gwyn did know.

She continued earnestly. "He won't let me sit in council yet. He says I'm too young. But I know as much about the family's hounds as anyone, and I understand the great hunt."

George looked at her, puzzled.

"There must be a villain for the hunt each year who *deserves* it, who requires justice. It's the tribute we pay to justice and law. To choose someone unworthy is an insult. To choose an innocent would be far worse."

George asked carefully, "He's killed by the hunt?"

"Yes, of course. The hounds bring him down. They know their duty. Once a year the hunt is not for sport or game for the table. And then we all of us live under the law for another year."

George was shaken to hear such matter-of-fact words from her. This wasn't just a comfortable medieval dinner at a rich man's hall. This was also a place where life or death came at the hands of one… man? Godling? He could understand killing someone in hot blood, but who could launch a pack of hounds at someone, however much he deserved death? Who could put him to such terror?

Gwyn thought, his face impassive, if I have to listen to one more vulgar joke from Mederei Badellfawr, I may kill her myself and get my sister another bodyguard, one that won't make her the butt of bed preference jokes.

He watched the unseemly amusement to his left and brooded behind a bland face.

Idris's report about the public gossip was no surprise, but not informative. Some dwelt on the details of Iolo's death with an exquisite feigned horror, but he was looking for active plot sympathizers, not character flaws in his usual guests.

Under the table where none could see, he clenched his fist in frustration. He could smell the beginning of an endgame designed to stop the great hunt. He'd been waiting for something like this since the death of Islwyn eighteen years ago, he'd never believed that accidental. First Iolo's young kinsman, and now Iolo himself.

He noted Ceridwen's attempts at the end of the table to draw out political opinions from Madog. Good luck to her. He'd tried to penetrate that mask for decades, ever since Creiddylad began bringing him with her as part of her entourage. Where did she find him? What does he want?

Are they lovers?

Why should that matter to me still? He tried to distance himself and look at his sister with objective eyes. She's looking tired, he thought, and worried. What's she worried about? Iolo was never a great favorite of hers, too much on my side during the fights with Gwythyr. But she did provide Owen the Leash and his men when we needed assistance. Maybe I'm wrong.

He looked out into the hall at his retinue and guests. A few noticed him and nodded, Eurig for one, good fellow, but his black mood was not lifted. I've ruled here too long, he thought. They want to see me fall, just for a change. Fools. Any new dynasty strong enough to defeat me would sweep them away and install its own sycophants and hangers-on, dispensing their properties without a second thought.

A movement caught his eye, and he saw George picking up his plate in obvious admiration. Well might he admire it, he thought. Angharad's works were things of beauty, from the mundane table service to her fine paintings. That's one good thing to have come from his reign, providing a home for her.

He listened in on Rhian's intent conversation with George. What servant of Creiddylad's were they talking about? He looked out into the hall but couldn't tell whom they meant.

Rhian was maturing quickly. She still had the awkwardness of quick-growing youth, but listen to her, she wants to be huntsman. Gwyn had heard something of this before and started to dismiss it again but now he paused and reconsidered. Iolo had mentioned the possibility to him not long since.

She's not a child any more. She's of an age where one makes these choices seriously. She has the background for it, and the fierceness of character. Only youth and its uncertainties stood in her way. The oddity of her gender was more than made up for by the advantages her blood would give her.

She wants to help, which is better than I can say about many of these here tonight. Why not let her? She's too young to hunt the hounds but, assuming we all survive the next two weeks, she should begin formal training under someone. She needs to start learning more about politics, too. Time for her to join her brother.

He looked up as a servant entered from the back hall and came up to Idris with a folded paper.

Idris leaned over to him. "It's a note from your son-in-law to his grandson." Gwyn gestured for him to deliver it.

Idris leaned over behind Rhys to George, handing him a note. "Your grandfather has sent you a reply."

This was unexpected. George unfolded it.

George,

I think I know what may have happened to you. If I am correct, then you have my best wishes and certainly my envy. Come tell me about it sometime, if you can.

Don't be concerned about your mundane affairs. This is only Saturday; if you are still away by mid-week, I will contact your office again and tell them you need a leave of absence. Bud and I can look after your home for a while.

Your grandmother wishes you to pass along her greetings, if you should find that appropriate.

Love,
Gilbert

Gwyn was looking at him with polite curiosity. "Your daughter sends her greetings," George told him. Gwyn smiled warmly.

Rhian asked him, "What's it like, where you come from? I've been there, but only briefly, and never spoke to anyone."

"You'll have to visit me sometime," he replied. "I have a small farm where I raise hay and a few horses."

"What about your kennels?"

"The kennels belong to the Rowanton Hunt, not to me, and are located on its property, down the road. It works like a small business where hunt members contribute funds, pay for the expenses, hire any necessary staff, and appoint one or more masters of foxhounds to direct the hunt and cover unexpected costs. Our huntsman's a professional, someone who earns his living this way. Most of our whippers-in are honorary, hunt members who aren't paid, like me." He could see her filing this information away.

"I've seen part of my foster-father's lands. Is all the hunting done there?"

"Oh, no. Each foxhunt has an assigned territory, so that we don't conflict with each other. Within those broad regions we must find landowners who allow us to ride over their land. Of course, some of our hunt members are also landowners, but many landowners aren't hunters, just friends of the hunt. The goal is to find landowners whose properties connect with each other to give us enough contiguous land to hunt. So when we hunt, we must start the hounds and riders within bounds and then keep them there to pursue any fox or coyote they put up."

He continued, "Of course, that's not a problem at a fixture as large as your foster-father's Bellemore. The only challenge there is to keep hounds away from any roads along the edge."

"What's a fixture?"

"We hunt regularly, but each time we meet at a different assigned location to start. That landowner's property is a fixture. Hunt members get a fixture card at the start of each season so that they can plan appropriately."

"I don't understand—we always start from here."

"Our hunting territory's about 30 by 40 miles, with landowners scattered throughout. We could never leave from kennels on foot with the hounds, except for the very closest fixtures."

"Oh. Then you must travel the day before," she said, working it out.

George stopped. "Um, do you know about cars and trucks?"

Rhian looked uncertain. "Those are like wagons, yes? But no horses. I've seen them, from the woods."

"They can cover 60 miles in an hour, or 25 on bad roads. No need to travel the day before."

She was too polite to express her disbelief, but George could see that she was skeptical. "Truly," he assured her. "We have amazing machines."

Rhys, who had been listening to their conversation, asked, "So you must do things very differently, then, in your country. For hunting, I mean."

"Not in the ways that matter. Hounds are still hounds. We may transport them to a meet instead of walking them there, but after they arrive, I imagine it's very much the same. We just have some additional tools. Things have changed enough that we hunt with a pack for sport, not for food, and our choice of quarry features animals that are usually able to escape successfully. Many people hunt just for the pleasure of riding cross-country and talking, since horses are no longer part of our everyday lives."

"Many of our guests are the same," Rhys said, laughing. "Doesn't matter what we're doing out front. They're too busy plotting and gossiping to notice."

By now the serving platters had been removed and dishes of fruits and nuts were scattered along the tables. The guests clustered in relaxed groups chatting quietly. George saw that the staff in guest livery were also seated at the far end, catching up on the meal, while Gwyn's staff served them.

He asked Rhian, "So how does that work? Do your staff eat elsewhere so they can serve the meal now?"

"Most of the household staff eat before dinner, below the kitchen, but those involved in meal service eat afterward. We serve the guest staff at the end of the meals in the main hall, since there wouldn't be room for them all in the staff dining rooms below-stairs."

They were looking at the guest staff during this discussion, and George noticed the odd fellow with the streaked temples again. He was speaking to no one, and his eyes were fixed on the archway to the back hall at George's right.

George turned his head to see what he was staring at. Two men were standing just outside the hall, ill at ease, looking toward the dais. Idris saw them, too, and beckoned them over. One shook his head, and they didn't move. Idris pushed back his chair and descended the steps, going to meet them in the archway. They showed him something wrapped in a cloth and his back stiffened. George glanced back at the end of the hall; that servant was smiling quietly at the events in the archway. George thought, he likes this. No, he's been waiting for it. What's going on? What does he have to do with it?

Gwyn watched with foreboding as Idris left his seat. When he turned in the archway to look at him, Gwyn summoned him with a gesture, and the whole group came in and up the steps of the dais to stand across the table before him.

"What have we here, Idris, that so disturbs you?"

"My lord, these men have come in from their guard duty to show me what they found hung on the gates of the southern wall. It's not suitable for this company to view."

"Show me." Gwyn pushed back his chair and stood, feeling a hollow forming within him. He trusted Idris's prudent caution but he was done with circumspection. Everyone should bear the consequences of this struggle, as Iolo already had. Only two weeks were left.

The two men cleared a space on the table. Standing with their backs to the hall, they placed a bundle on the wooden surface and unwrapped a linen cloth. Idris reached in and held up, by the twine connecting them, two fresh severed hands.

Distantly, Gwyn felt those seated on either side of him push back and stand in shock. His attention was narrowly fixed on the dangling bloody horrors. The crowd in the hall couldn't see clearly with Idris blocking their view but understood that something significant had happened.

The musicians in the gallery above had a better view, and the music faltered and stopped.

He heard himself say, "Anything else? Were they hanging or in this cloth?"

One of the men volunteered, "My lord, before my patrol, I was eating my dinner. This cloth held my food. I didn't want to carry them...," he broke off, but everyone understood him. "Hanging from the higher latch of the gate, they were."

Idris said, "This note was with them," handing him a square of parchment.

Gwyn read it silently. He bade Idris turn to the assembly and display the ugly trophy, while he read aloud, with an even, cold voice, "I have taken your hands. Soon it will be your heart, and then your head, as it always should have been."

After the initial shock, the dead silence was slow to recede.

Gwyn straightened and felt a chill descend. He called his majesty about him, and summoned them to council before striding off the dais.

~

George looked away from the horrible objects and down the hall. As he half-expected, one face watched without surprise, with ill-hidden pleasure.

Gwyn stood rigidly, drawing the light, as the hall darkened around him. He seemed to grow, though his stature was unchanged. George could feel moving powers and a growing chill in the air, and the hair on the back of his neck rose. I could believe in fairies and gods now, he thought. May he never be angry at me.

"We'll meet in council, now," Gwyn said. "If you know ought of this, make it known."

He glanced to his right. "Join us, kinsman, and you also, foster-daughter." George suspected he had overheard their conversation at dinner. Rhian nodded solemnly.

His own visceral reaction surprised him. This was a deliberate taunt of some kind, and it was to someone in his family, however remote. He was indignant on Gwyn's behalf, as if Gwyn needed his help.

Gwyn strode from the dais and into his council chamber, shutting the door behind him. Idris re-wrapped the bundle and returned it to his men, with orders to place it with Iolo's body. George caught his arm to suggest that they keep everything, including the twine and cloth. Idris nodded and passed that along as well.

Conversation returned slowly to the hall, and people began to approach Idris to see if what they knew or saw might be of interest to the council session. He drew a couple of them to his side, and the rest he dismissed, with thanks.

Other people had already tapped on the closed door and let themselves in. Idris took his small group, including Rhys, Rhian, and George, and they passed in as well, the last of the assembly.

CHAPTER 6

Gwyn sat motionless at the head of the long table. He kept a tight rein on his fury, but it was a struggle and he noted the uneasy glances sent his way by the twenty or more people finding seats. The last ones in brought up chairs from the end of the room to make a seating area within hearing distance. He saw George and Rhian off to the side together, the table being full with his senior family and staff. Madog and Creiddylad's bodyguard had the good sense not to intrude.

Gwyn waited for everyone to settle. "Many of you met with me earlier today in preliminary discussion, but now I ask you to begin again, in an orderly fashion, so that we may all dwell upon events and perhaps discover the truth of what has happened. Only then can we make sound plans for action."

Into the awkward silence Idris said, "Did anyone see anything unusual before Iolo's murder?"

Gwyn nodded. "Yes, not all of you witnessed that. Who first saw the whirlwind?"

Rhys spoke up. "When the hounds stopped moving forward, I turned back to see why. Iolo was looking at the Thirty Acre Wood, and I saw this black shape swirling out toward him."

"How did Iolo see it first? Did anyone here see it sooner?"

A woman on the outskirts declared, "It seemed to me that Iolo heard it, because I saw his head lift before he turned. Something caught his attention."

A man spoke up. "There was a snap, like a breaking stick, just inside the woods. I was close to it and heard it plainly. I looked to see what it was, expecting a rider or perhaps a deer, but saw no one, only the sudden whirlwind."

"Thank you, Thomas. Did anyone else see the start of things?" No reply.

Gwyn continued. "I'll supply the next portion. I saw the whirlwind come straight to Iolo. It was black and higher than a man on a horse. The hounds set up a baying and growling, but Iolo didn't move or speak."

He paused. This is when George would have arrived, he realized. "The whirlwind enveloped Iolo and pulled him from his horse. The horse bolted, and I couldn't see what happened on the ground. Can anyone tell us?"

Idris spoke up. "Something flashed within the whirlwind, as if from steel, and there was blood. It rose and continued east over the fold of land where we lost sight of it, and Iolo's body was left behind."

Rhys added, "Most of the pack were excited but being leaderless they stayed in place. Three couple, however went off in pursuit, giving tongue. Two couple turned before reaching the eastern covert, and the other couple entered the woods…"

"Where I found them running mute and headed them back to the pack," George said.

Another woman spoke from the outer ring. "I rode after Iolo's horse, who was frantic, and brought her back."

"Was the horse injured?" Ceridwen asked.

"There were scrapes on the saddle, but I saw no blood. I don't think the whirlwind injured the horse, at least not directly."

Gwyn paused a moment to consider. "So, this was the death. What can we learn from this?"

George asked, "What was the stick that broke? Has anyone looked into the woods there to see if any trace of the whirlwind or maybe some less formless enemy can be found?"

Idris replied. "Nothing's yet been done in that regard. It would be good to look further in the morning."

George said, "If you happen to have bloodhounds, perhaps they'd be helpful. Scent can linger for a day or two."

Gwyn said to the assembly, "He means a lymer or other trailing hound." He looked over at Rhys, questioningly.

"Yes, we have three we can use. The lutins keep them."

Gwyn concluded, "Then we have a clear action. Idris, Thomas Kethin, Rhys, and George will make a band at first light, with tracking hounds, to look over the edge of Thirty Acre Woods where the whirlwind was first seen. Rhian, please join them." She nodded silently, eyes wide and back straight with pride at being included.

Gwyn was pleased. This sort of decision would be appropriate while not revealing any of his suspicions prematurely. Still, it would seem unnatural not to discuss enemies in this open group. He must be careful not to let the conversation stray.

"Next," he continued, "Who is our foe? I thought it might be an enemy of Iolo's, but this note," waving the square of parchment, "declares otherwise."

George leaned over Idris and asked to see the note, and Idris passed it back to him.

He looked it over and said, "I can't speak to motive, but we have several physical clues that might help. This parchment appears to have older writing underneath scraped away which could provide a clue about where it originated. The marks on the saddle, the wounds on the huntsman, and the way the hands were tied and hung, all might be helpful if looked at closely."

Useful boy, Gwyn thought. Keep them focused on physical clues, not motives.

Ceridwen said, "There's also a question of access. Who was at the hunt and in plain sight, who was here and not therefore at the hunt, and who isn't on either list? Who could hang something on the gates and not be noticed, and when were the gates last seen empty? Who can't account for their whereabouts at various times of interest, once you identify what those times are?"

Creiddylad spoke for the first time. "The motive seems clear enough. Someone wants to stop the hunt."

Gwyn regarded her expressionlessly. Odd. Surely someone also wanted him dead. Which was more important to her?

"Yes, my dear," he said, "but that's rather unspecific."

Ceridwen said, "As your kinsman suggested, looking at this logically will narrow the alternatives. Taking the note as it stands, Iolo doesn't represent your 'hands' in all of your duties, but only in one: the hunt. Now that we are but two weeks from Nos Galan Gaeaf, I think the simplest and likeliest motive visible here is to undermine your chief responsibility, the foundation of your rule, killing you as well if possible."

Creiddylad looked away, tight-lipped, as if in disagreement.

Time to put a stop to this speculation, Gwyn thought.

"I agree with this reasoning. The meaning of taking my head is obvious, but the reference to my heart is clearly symbolic, like my hands. I would like to know who's meant, with some urgency."

"Just as importantly for all of us," Ceridwen said, "how will you hunt the hounds?"

"I have some thoughts on that subject which I will share with all of you later." No one looked pleased at his evasion, except Creiddylad who seemed blandly unconcerned. He narrowed his eyes at that.

"Ceridwen, I'd like George to go with you tonight, to look carefully at the injuries before tomorrow's ceremony."

"As you wish," she replied, regarding at George with an appraising gaze.

Gwyn stood and addressed the assembled guests. "We'll honor Iolo ap Huw at dusk tomorrow. For now, let's get what rest we can. Thank you all."

The meeting broke up as people rose from their seats and either departed or clustered together in small groups for further discussion.

~

As they left the council room, George turned to Ceridwen who stood, waiting for him. At her gesture, Rhian joined them. He was glad to have her name, since she'd been too far from him at dinner to have been introduced. "Ma'am, I'm sorry my words made work for you. How can I help?"

She replied serenely. "My lord Gwyn no doubt sought to combine these activities into a suitable bundle, since I serve him both as scholar and healer. Thus I can bring you to see Iolo's body, and take notes as well. My student here," smiling down at Rhian, "...can make herself useful, I'm sure."

The three of them went first to inspect Iolo's horse and saddle. Rhian led the way to the same stable George had already seen. They each picked up a lamp from a table near the entrance and lit it.

As they walked down the main aisle, George looked for Mosby's stall. His eye was caught about halfway down by a piece of wood with a charcoal sketch of a rampant lion hung on a stall door, and he walked over to peer in. Mosby stood quietly, dozing. George continued on without rousing him.

A groom, disturbed by their lights, came to meet them, and Ceridwen explained quietly what she wanted. He brought them first to look at Iolo's horse, a chestnut mare with a wide blaze. The groom led her into the aisle where there was less danger of fire than in the stall, and they hung their lamps on high hooks, placed for that purpose.

All three visitors checked her over but she seemed none the worse for her ordeal, and the groom returned her to her stall.

Next he brought them to the tack room with Iolo's gear, a different room from the one George's chest occupied. Iolo had two chests, each marked with a straight hunting horn. The groom opened the one on top, and brought out the saddle and bridle for them, then left.

"See, they've been cleaned already," Rhian said. The bridle bore no marks, but the offside saddle skirt did show scratches, as the woman at council had declared. It was hard to say what they were.

"Did Iolo wear spurs?" George asked Rhian.

"Yes, dull ones."

To Ceridwen he said, "See, some of this may be his spur as he's dragged from the horse, but what about the rest? There's one track here like three parallel claws."

Ceridwen bent over the saddle and looked carefully. She reached through slits on the side of her blue gown and petticoat, and pulled out a small notebook from the pocket tied to her waist underneath. Sheets of paper were strapped across the middle, and the cover held a fountain pen and some loose wipes in a packet. She sketched a copy of the saddle's marks, with some notes.

The groom returned, bringing another lutin with him. "He cleaned the saddle and horse. I thought you'd want to speak with him."

Ceridwen thanked him, then questioned the second groom. "Are these marks on the saddle skirt new?"

"They weren't there when I cleaned it yesterday."

"Was there any dirt or blood today, anything besides these marks?"

"No, my lady."

"What about the horse?"

"She was dirty from carrying the body, but that was all."

Ceridwen put the notebook away and let the grooms escort them out of the stable, taking their lamps from them as they departed.

It was mid-evening and dark, but enough light came through the windows of the buildings in the yard that they had no difficulty following the paths between them.

Ceridwen led them up the same lane as the stable but on the other side of the kennels. On the other side, well away from the manor, a few buildings were grouped together, isolated on either side from their neighbors. She explained as they walked. "Here's our infirmary, where we treat the sick or wounded, and naturally here is also where we prepare the dead."

Lights were visible in one of the buildings, and they entered.

Ceridwen looked over at Rhian. "I think this is the first time you've been here?" Rhian nodded and visibly swallowed.

George felt the damp chill in the room they entered, a stone platform like a bench running at worktable height all along one wall and a prominent drain in the middle of the floor. A body lay under a coverlet on the platform. One attendant in a brown gown with a large striped apron sat at a desk writing in a ledger. She stood up at their entrance.

"Hefina, we've come to look over the body. Did they also bring you the hands?"

"Yes, my lady. Let me show you."

She led them to the body and pulled back the coverlet, folding it down to the feet. The body was washed and freshly clothed. The hands were in their proper place, with the sleeves of the shirt covering the joins. Cloth bound the neck, and there were no visible wounds.

George saw a strong, fit, bearded man with brown hair gone half-gray and a darkly weathered face.

"I see he's prepared for the ceremony tomorrow. I must ask you to disarrange that to show us the wounds."

"Yes, my lady. He was covered with blood and dirt when they brought him to us, but the only wounds we found when we cleaned him were the missing hands, and the cuts across his throat which bled strongly. There were also some lesser scratches along the leg."

She pulled up the sleeves on either side to show clean cuts above each wrist. George remarked to Ceridwen, "One stroke each, no mis-strikes. After death, maybe?" She nodded.

Hefina rearranged the sleeves, then unwrapped the cloth around the neck. Three deep parallel gashes crossed the throat, now neatly stitched shut. "This is what killed him," she said.

Ceridwen said, "These are the same spacing as the saddle cuts." She added more illustrations and comments to her pocket notebook. "You mentioned cuts on the leg?"

Hefina tied the neck cloth back together before continuing. "Yes, my lady." She unfastened the breeches and pushed the material down in front to expose the top of the right thigh. The long shirt preserved Iolo's modesty. They could see there an interrupted trace of the same three cuts on the outside of his leg, superficial in depth.

Ceridwen asked, "Did you preserve his clothing, and the other items that accompanied the hands?"

"One moment, my lady." Hefina refastened Iolo's clothes and raised the coverlet back up carefully to re-cover the body. "Idris Powell warned me, so I've kept everything over here." She led them further down the stone bench. Iolo's clothing was spread out, garment by garment, blood-stained and torn.

A quick look showed that most of the clothes had bloodstains, primarily from the cut throat, and the ends of the sleeves were both stained and ragged. The breeches showed slashes that corresponded with the cuts on the leg, and they saw more such scratches on the upper garments where multiple layers had prevented penetration to the skin.

Ceridwen posed a question to Rhian. "What can you tell us about these sets of triple cuts?"

"They're not the work of animals."

"And why do you say so?"

"An animal that extends a forearm to slash narrows its claws as it draws in, and when hind legs are used to disembowel, its claws are widened as it pulls down. There might be a brief stretch of parallel lines, but not for any extended distance, and with several marks like these, on the clothing and the body and the saddle, they wouldn't all be alike."

"Well reasoned," Ceridwen said, "and I quite agree."

George had moved to the boots, standing upright and uncleaned. "What about these marks? They look like heel scuffs." After years of cleaning his own gear he knew well the marks of something standing on a boot, whether a horse's hoof or someone else's foot.

Rhian looked. "The mark of the heel on the left toe can't be Iolo's—it faces inward. And it can't have happened before he mounted, for he would have seen it and wiped it away."

Ceridwen said, "So. We have a person's foot, and unnatural claws. This isn't just murder but deception and illusion, meant to terrify."

They passed along to the twine used to tie the hands. It had been cut to free them, leaving the knots intact.

George asked, "Is there anything remarkable about the material or the knots?"

Ceridwen picked it up and felt it carefully. "Our twine here in Annwn is made of cotton, and we buy it from your world like our other cotton goods. This isn't cotton, but hemp, what we use in other regions where we grow it ourselves. I don't know why one of our own should have hempen twine."

She handed it to Rhian. "Feel it, smell it, taste the difference."

She turned back to George. "The knots are ordinary, but I would assume this came from the pocket of a visitor, who knew nothing of the details of our local fiber industry and had no reason to think it different from what he was used to."

She continued. "This inspection of physical evidence has been very useful, in unexpected ways. It's often fruitful to incorporate an outsider's point of view." This last was directed at Rhian, instructively.

As they left the building, George suddenly realized: this all happened a few hours ago—it's still the same day. I feel like it's been a week since I mounted up this morning. He stopped dead in the lane for a moment, overwhelmed by the strangeness of the buildings all around him in this not-quite-Virginia, and the not-quite-humans who were claiming kinship.

Ceridwen looked at him sympathetically. "You'll feel much better for a night's sleep, and morning will come early for you." She parted from them before the house and strode off back up the lane between the buildings, leaving Rhian and George to re-enter the manor through the double-doors.

"She's right, we'll need our sleep. I'll see you to your room," Rhian said.

She took a lamp from the hall table, lit it, and handed it to George, and lit another for herself. She brought them up the back stairs again, and left George at his door.

He entered and closed the door behind him, suddenly glad of a refuge where he could take private stock of the events of the day. His hunt coat had been brushed and hung in the wardrobe, and he saw that the rest of his garments had somehow been cleaned during dinner. That eased his mind about clothing for tomorrow, but next time he visited, he'd have to pack a little better. I'm getting giddy, he thought, this isn't a vacation spot. Who knows if I can ever get back home, or come back here again if I do?

He stripped for bed, hanging his borrowed robes in the wardrobe for someone to return after he was gone. He could get used to the feel of satin and silk.

There was a faint scratching noise against the door. Not again, he thought, but then reconsidered. I'd like the company, and at least I can count on her not to claim to be a relative. He opened the door and, as he expected, Myfanwy trotted in and hopped up to the bed via a bedside chair, making herself comfortable on the folded blanket at the foot.

George closed the door behind her and turned the lamp down low. The bed felt wonderful. He settled in, determined to review his options, but sleep claimed him before he got past "I'll just give it one more day." When Myfanwy walked up the covers beside him and poked his arm expertly with her cold nose, he raised them for her without waking, and she burrowed alongside him in the warm nest.

CHAPTER 7

The knock wakened him. He blinked at Rhys who opened the door and stuck his head in. "Breakfast in fifteen minutes."

The room was dark and George turned his lamp up before leaving the warm bed. He put on the hunting clothes he had laid out the night before, and added his usual pocket contents, including the gun at the small of his back. After liberating Myfanwy, who was waiting patiently at the door, he headed quietly down the dark hall.

Lights were hung and lit in the back hall, so he returned his lamp to the night table there and sought out the voices he could hear in the hunting room.

A crackling fire gave a warm glow to the handful of people clustered around the small tables. He joined Idris and Rhys at one table, and saw others dressed and ready to go about their business in other small groups.

Servants brought in trays of cold food: bread and sweet rolls, ham slices, hard-boiled eggs, cheeses, and fruit. Besides water, there were steaming pots of tea. George asked Rhys, "Any hope of coffee?"

"I've never had it. What's it like?"

"Dark, bitter, and eye-opening."

Idris smiled. "I've had your coffee before. This tea's harsh enough for me." They fell to in silence.

Rhian joined them, in breeches and a long-sleeved jerkin, and then a dark, weatherbeaten man came in through the outside door. Idris introduced him to George as Thomas Kethin. He remembered him speaking in Gwyn's chamber last night, and then realized where he'd heard the name before. This was the the fellow Eurig named as the son of Thomas, Lord Fairfax. He looked competent and hard. Wasn't he the fellow who took charge of Iolo's body on the ground, George thought.

As each finished their hasty meal, they took a cloth from the tray and wrapped some food into a packet to take with them.

George followed their example, making something small enough to put in his sandwich case. They rose as a group and walked out to the nearby stable.

Grooms stood standing there with their horses, tacked and ready. George looked Mosby over, checked the fit of the bridle and the set of the saddle, and tightened the girth. All of the small gear from his chest in the tack room had been reattached, in the right places.

Rhys rode over to the kennels while the rest of them assembled at the gate in the southern curtain wall. In a few minutes Rhys rejoined them, accompanied by a two-wheeled pony cart driven by a middle-aged and taciturn lutin. Two white hounds looked out from their crates in the cart. "This is Orry. He'll help handle the hounds," he told George.

The sky was beginning to lighten as they headed out the gates of the curtain wall and down alongside the great front lawn. There was a pause at the palisade while the main gates were opened, and then they were on the road just as the sun rose.

Idris led the party at a brisk trot down to the bridge and across. George spotted a few lights in the village as most people were just rising, but they found no one outside yet as they passed though. Once they reached the eastern fields, Idris slowed to a walk to give the horses a breather. They went slowly up the slope, keeping to smooth ground for the sake of the pony cart.

Once up on the plateau, it didn't take long to reach the scene of yesterday's chaos. Rhian rode over to the blood-stained spot, her eyes searching the ground. She dismounted and picked up two bits of dirty cloth. Holding them out to George, she said, "See, I thought we might find these. The cuts that took the hands also clipped the ends of the sleeves." She tucked them into a pocket of her jerkin and remounted.

They couldn't see anything else of interest at the spot where so many feet had already walked. Idris turned to Thomas Kethin, "Where was it you heard the sound and saw the whirlwind first?"

Thomas led them to the woods on the right, about 100 yards away. As they left the trampled part of the field where the riders had milled around the day before and came to smooth tall grass, they found a clear trail, leading from the woods, made of broken grass stems and small crushed plants. The slant of the early morning light picked it out plainly. The party rode to one side so as not to damage it.

Thomas halted them at the edge of the woods. He dismounted, handing his reins to Idris, and entered the woods on foot, careful not to disturb the traces that remained. He didn't go far. Just a few yards in he stopped and bent over.

George called out, "Don't touch whatever it is. We want the hounds to get a clean scent."

Thomas returned. "There's a broken spell-stick in plain sight, and footprints behind it, though none in front."

"What's a spell-stick?" George asked Idris.

"It holds a spell, which is released when it breaks. The user doesn't need any powers of his own." Idris turned to Thomas. "Did you recognize the style?"

"I need to pick it up," he said.

George had seen bloodhounds at work before and had some idea about how to proceed. "The hounds also need to smell it. We can do both. Orry," he called, "do you have some sort of clean cloth we can use to hold something?"

Orry climbed down from the seat of the pony cart and reached behind it into a leather bag. He brought a clean rag over to the riders. "We use these for bandages. It should be clean." He went back to the cart and began to prepare the hounds for work.

George shook the rag in the air with his gloved hand to dislodge as much as possible of whatever scent clung to it, then gave it to Thomas, with instructions to pick up the spell-stick carefully.

When Thomas returned, they all bent over the pieces as he turned them around, held by the rag. It was a natural stick cut cleanly at each end and about a foot long in its intact form. The bark had been removed, and it was now broken into two pieces. Red characters had been painted on it, but not in any alphabet George was familiar with. "Can anyone read this?"

Rhian said, "I've seen this before but I can't read it. Ceridwen should look at it."

Idris asked Thomas, "How's the trail?"

"Clear prints and traces. I can work it backward while the hounds try to work it forward."

"We'll do that then. Wait until we're sure the hounds can find a scent trail, then track it back as far as possible."

Orry brought the two hounds forward, on leashes. They were white all over with pendulous ears and wrinkled faces, heavily built, a bit longer than tall. Except for the color they looked like bloodhounds to George. Why, these are Talbot hounds. His delighted grin brought an inquisitive look from Idris.

George leaned forward and pointed out the emblem on his hunt coat buttons. "We call these Talbot hounds, the old English Southern hound, said to descend from the hounds of St. Hubert. No one knows what relationship the name has to the name of my family, but the name's very old. I never thought to see one."

They planned the course of action. The hounds needed to be handled from the ground, on leashes. Idris and George remained mounted. Thomas declared he would lead his horse behind him as he tracked through the woods. "Not the first time we've done this," he said.

Rhian joined Orry on the ground and took one of the hounds. Rhys tied his own horse and Rhian's to the back of the cart, and mounted the seat to drive along behind them.

Both the hounds sat quietly by Rhian. She introduced them to George. "This is Arthur, and that one Roland. Give me the spell-stick."

Thomas handed it to her, holding it in its rag. She held the rag in her open hands and bent over the hounds, urging them to smell the broken stick it held. They obediently buried their muzzles and inhaled deeply. She stood, wrapped the rag around the pieces, and thrust them into a deep pocket on her jerkin.

Orry and Rhian walked the hounds to the visible trail in the grass and gave them a long line. Heads down, they immediately struck out at a trot, away from the covert. Thomas turned in the opposite direction, leading his horse, and re-entered the woods.

The hounds pulled strongly toward the trampled grass with its stains and paused at the spot. George watched how they concentrated several yards to the east and commented to Idris, "Watching bloodhounds, you can see how scent moves, flowing with the ground or moving in a breeze. Looks like there was just a little air movement from the west since the attack. We're lucky we had calm weather last night."

At Rhian's quiet urging, the hounds moved on, to the east and south. Idris confirmed this was the direction the whirlwind had taken after the kill. Together, the party followed the hounds over the fold in the ground that had hidden the whirlwind's escape. The grass was both shorter and sparser here, as the soil changed character, and the physical trail was harder to see, though still visible in the slanted morning light. The hounds followed a scent trail that was parallel to the visible one, but off to its left by a few yards. As they approached another covert, the visible trail and the hounds tracking scent converged.

Rhys and the pony cart couldn't enter the woods here, and went around to the far side to wait for them. Orry took a few steps, then called out, "Footprints, here."

Idris looked down. "Man-sized, with a heel like a boot. There might be a cut on the inner right heel, though it's hard to be sure."

George took a look. There hadn't been much left of the scuff mark on Iolo's boot, but at least this was consistent with it. He ventured, "So, however the whirlwind was created, this was a man before and after, yes?"

"Looks that way," Idris said.

The hounds took them through the woods, following a strong trail that had been sheltered from the wind. They met Rhys on the other side waiting with the cart. From here, they could see across and north to the manor, though most of the village was tucked into the river fold between and largely hidden.

Eagerly pulling at their long leashes, the hounds brought them by a footpath down to the river, striking it south of the village at a ford. Orry and Rhian let them drink, then led them through where they struck the line again, crossing the road and the western fields toward a wood.

Idris called a temporary halt. "This trail has been turning in a curve, and now it's headed back to the manor. Rhys, take the cart up the road and look for us at the main gate. If that turns out not to be right, we'll send someone to tell you."

Rhys turned back to the road and the tracking party followed the hounds into the woods on a clear path that began climbing the slope toward the manor. It didn't take long to follow that back and come out, as Idris had predicted, at the back of the palisade.

George got his first clear look at the structure. Trees of several types and all ages stood packed so tightly together that even a hound couldn't get through. For as far as he could see, there was bare grass in front of it, but no foliage ventured into the open space, down to the height of a man. Above that, there was something… wrong about the branches. He wouldn't have wanted to climb into these trees.

"They feel dangerous," he said to Idris.

"They're part of our defenses. Enemies don't pass through them."

"How thick are they?"

"Ten yards in most places."

The hounds had led them upslope along the bare space and stopped. The densely packed trees of the palisade were disrupted here. Two trees had decayed, and the undergrowth around them had been penetrated by a low tunnel. It contrasted sharply with the vigorous growth on either side.

"This isn't natural," Idris said, "nor has it been here long. We patrol this regularly."

"It's not easy to see if you're not looking for it. It could've been here a while," George said.

The hounds indicated clearly that the scent led them here, but they whined and wouldn't cross the open space to the palisade.

George sympathized. He didn't want to get any closer himself, and Mosby was also restive. He noticed that the others were also staying as far away as the open perimeter would permit, Orry and Rhian comforting the hounds.

The sound of a rider coming up from the right drew their attention. Thomas Kethin appeared and joined them. "I came out of the woods on the back trail but close to one of the footpaths, and I lost the track there. I could see you headed down to the ford below me, so I crossed over at the bridge to join you and met Rhys coming up the road. I've left him down by the gate."

"Where are we, do you think?" Idris asked him.

"By the shape of the slope, I'd say we're roughly behind the balineum. The west branch can't be far from here, where it enters under the ground."

They could faintly hear the busy yard on the other side of the palisade.

Idris decided. "We'll go around and find the exit point. You stay here, in case it isn't obvious and we need the sound of your voice as a guide." Thomas nodded.

"George, ride down and send Rhys up here. The way's smooth enough for the cart, and we can move the hounds with least disruption that way. You can wait for us below."

George turned downslope and trotted down to find Rhys at the gate. He told him of their discovery so far and sent him up to Idris.

While he waited, he thought about the hole in the palisade. Not just a murderer, but apparently within the grounds, one of their own. That should get everyone's attention.

~

The whole party rejoined George at the gates, with Orry driving and the hounds in their crates. Idris led them up the grounds and back through the curtain wall where they'd started. He continued back to the palisade, passing the kennel buildings and yards on the left.

When they reached the palisade, George saw that it was smooth and dense on this side, too, and a space of about twenty feet was kept clear in front of it. Idris took them at a walk along the inner edge of the gap, upslope away from the kennels.

George got his first good overview of the entire yard, which he estimated at about 200 acres. As they moved along, he saw straight lanes leading down to the manor, with buildings on either side and many people occupied with their mid-morning tasks. How would they find one person in this huge establishment?

The kennels were clustered behind him, with the stables and other buildings laid out in ranks on his right on one side of the lane as they walked up the slope, facing them. Nearer to the palisade wall were workshops, warehouses, and a blacksmith.

The next lane brought more workshops on either side. George recognized the low infirmary building and its morgue from the night before on the north side of the lane, near the manor, and some small dwellings on the south side.

Idris called a halt as the infirmary line of buildings came into view. George saw a cluster of buildings at the edge of their path up at the top of the next lane. Since the land cleared for the yard was on the slope of the hill, the west palisade marked the local highest point, and these buildings were sited on the highest ground within the palisade.

Large windowless stone buildings stood upslope in the group, and then what were clearly laundry and public bath buildings were placed downslope, with steam rising in the crisp air.

Rhys turned to George as they stopped. "We're famous for our balineum, the baths. It's truly miraculous what Ceridwen was able to accomplish. We'll never want for water, between the west branch and the underground streams, and buried pipes carry water to all the buildings."

Rhian joined in. "Ceridwen's always telling me how much we learned from the Romans."

George looked over at the manor below them. The third floor roof was just even with the highest of these buildings, so pressure and gravity must be adequate to convey water to that height.

Idris said, "I was here when Creiddylad set this rear palisade. The lower one for the front grounds came much later. All in one spring we planted it, from seeds and seedlings rescued as the land was cleared. We worked from the end of one rising curtain wall to the other, while others raised the first buildings. Then, in a single night of the full moon, she sent us all indoors and walked the length of it. Come morning, it was a deep line of well-grown saplings thickly sprung."

"How do you maintain it?" George asked.

"It maintains itself. Don't ask me how. The trees don't seem to age past maturity."

He turned his face to the palisade and shouted, "Thomas!"

A voice responded from the other side, just a bit in front of them.

"I thought this was about the right place."

They dismounted and led their horses, trying to look carefully at the palisade without getting too close. Mosby was skittish, eying the trees nervously.

Idris said, "This won't do. Rhian, will you hold them for us?"

Rhian retreated a few steps and the others handed her their reins.

"From here we can't see the postern gate and, more importantly, its guards can't see us. The balineum shelters this spot from view in most other directions. Ah—here it is."

He called back over, "Thomas, come in at the postern gate."

He pointed to a slight unevenness where one trunk stood a little further into the path. On the other side of that tree, George saw a low decayed area, free of vegetation. His skin crawled this close to the palisade, as if it broadcast a subsonic hum. No wonder the animals kept away from it.

Idris called over to Orry who waited at the cart. "Hitch those horses and bring the hounds back, with Rhian."

He leaned his full body a little toward the wall, as if bracing himself against a strong wind. He smiled at George's expression. "I like to test myself against it, see how close I can get. I don't know anyone who can touch it."

George wondered about its defensive properties. "Can it be burnt? Could you blast a hole through with cannon?"

"It doesn't burn. I've traveled with Gwyn and I know what your cannons can do, but gunpowder isn't the same here. The first time I encountered it, I brought some back. It would hardly burn, much less explode. When I asked Ceridwen about it, she told me it wouldn't work."

George thought ruefully of the revolver he was carrying under his coat. Good thing I didn't rely on that.

Orry and Rhian brought the hounds to the inner edge of the path. Rhian unwrapped the bundle from her pocket and let them smell the broken stick again as a reminder. After a bit of casting about they settled on a trail leading directly to the balineum and ended at a back entrance to one of them.

Rhys sighed. "That's it, then. End of the trail."

He turned to George. "It's the back of the bathing rooms. We could look inside, and see if maybe something was dropped, or stashed. Sometimes you get lucky."

Rhian said, "We should at least bring the hounds to the front of the building; he had to have left it later."

"She's right," Idris said. "I'll go with them. You two look into the baths."

Rhys opened the door and they walked into a small bare anteroom. Before them were entrances to two main rooms. "Let's try the men's side first," Rhys said, pulling open the right hand door.

George felt as though he'd entered a Roman movie set. Steam rose from several small rectangular pools with seating ledges. Decorative mosaics featuring hunting scenes and vegetation covered the walls, floors, and depths of the baths themselves. The echoes that George associated with indoor pools were muted by fiber mats and wooden furnishings. He glimpsed other rooms off to the side with shelves for clothing and towels. No one was currently using the baths.

Rhys and George split up and covered all the rooms in the building, including the women's baths. With no current occupants, the search went quickly, and they discovered nothing.

George smiled at Rhys's obvious disappointment. "It was always a long shot. Let's join the others."

They found that the trackers had had no success of their own. The hounds couldn't pick up the scent again, though they walked around the entire building.

"Rhys, I believe Orry's work here is done. Please thank Master Ives for me and rejoin us at the manor," Idris said.

Rhys nodded. They all returned to the cart to unhitch and remount their horses, then Idris led Rhian and George a bit further along the palisade to the postern gate.

George discovered how a gate in this palisade was possible, despite the repulsion effect of the trees. A square stone tunnel, large enough for two mounted men or a small cart was built all the way through the palisade. The stonework on either side and above it extended about fifteen feet, and it was barred at each end by a gate. He realized the stonework on the main gates was for the same purpose, to insulate users from the palisade's effects, but the main gate was so much wider that he hadn't felt any of the repulsion using it.

Idris told George, "It takes strong men to stand guard here and to use the tunnel. The one part of completing their basic military training that all the men dread most is the assignment to stand watch here. Not all of them can do it. Some of the horses can't manage it either, but we have a few that've become accustomed to it."

Thomas emerged through the gates and joined them.

Idris said, "I think we've done everything we can for now. I don't believe I could get permission from Gwyn to parade everyone in the compound, guests and locals alike, before those hounds, even though it's the most efficient way to identify the killer; too many political problems with that."

"Very frustrating," George said. He felt his shoulder blades twitch with the knowledge that a murderer was in here with them.

Idris looked at him. "Thanks for your help. Thomas and I need to report back to Gwyn, and he'll want to see you for the midday meal, but I don't have other instructions for you in the meantime."

Rhian spoke up. "I'll take charge of my kinsman and deliver him to Gwyn when he's needed."

"Alright, my lady, that should do."

Rhian waited until the two men had started down the slope and turned to George with a conspiratorial air. "I've a favor to ask. Isolda and I have errands to run in the village and we were told yesterday that we must have an escort while this villain's still at large. Wouldn't you like to see the village?"

"Well schemed," he said with a smile. "Just one problem—what good would I be as an escort with nothing but my bare hands?"

"Oh, we can get something for you from the armory."

"I hate to disappoint you, but my people aren't all trained in edged weapons. We play at it, sometimes, but it's been many years since I last held a foil or a saber." It was surprisingly humiliating to admit this. He was so comfortable with firearms that it had always seemed enough for self-defense. Now he found himself in a place where that wouldn't do him any good at all.

Her look of surprise was comic. "I hadn't thought of that. Come with me anyway, there must be something you're familiar with. We can always get you a club, you're so much bigger than me it might do." George looked at her sharply with that last line, but she kept a straight face.

They headed over to the barracks area behind the stable and hitched their horses in front of one of the stone buildings. "We have more weapons in the manor's armory towers, but this is closer," Rhian told him as they went in.

Several men were engaged in practice sessions and others were cleaning weapons and armor. The walls were hung with dozens of swords, axes, and other medieval-looking items. George thought he could identify halberds among the pole weapons, but lacked the technical vocabulary for some of them. He pointed at one of the spiked clubs. "Think a morning star would be appropriate for the drive into town?"

Rhian didn't deign to respond to the tease. "Hadyn, can we borrow something for our guest?"

A broad-shouldered man looked up from a nearby bench and put down the sword he had been sharpening. "George, this is our weapons-master. Hadyn, my kinsman came here unexpectedly and thus not well-armed."

Turning to George, she said, "I'll put our horses away. Isolda will want to drive in. Meet you at the curtain gate?" George nodded and turned his attention back to the weapons-master.

Hadyn looked him over. "What sort of weapon will I get for you, now?"

George wasn't eager to explain the differences between the life he led and this more active one. At least he had done some fencing in college. "Where I come from few are warriors, and it hasn't been my training either. As a student I've handled small-sword and saber, but only as a sport, not mounted or in combat." He flushed with embarrassment at this confession of incompetence before this group of trained men.

Hadyn kept his face expressionless. "You'll be on horseback, is it?" George nodded. "Then a saber's a good choice. You can use it mounted, and large enough you are to fight with it on foot."

"Your hand is big, I see." He took one down and felt its weight, then handed it to George to try.

George drew it from its scabbard, having first made sure the grip and guard accommodated his large hands. Hadyn had chosen well. Then he backed away and fell into a fencing stance, swinging it experimentally to test the weight and reach.

Hadyn took a similar saber from the wall and turned to face him. George pulled himself up. Though it shamed him, he felt he must explain. "Master Hadyn, I'm very out of practice even for sport, and not competent to prevent harm in a friendly bout. Could we do this with practice swords, or protective clothing?"

The weapons-master smiled slowly. "Don't you worry about it none. You'll not be harming me, nor I you."

George nodded. Alright, then. He must know what he's doing.

He executed a salute and returned to an opening position, his hand grasping the hilt lightly enough to maneuver quickly, and firmly enough not to lose the sword from a *prise en fer*. He circled warily, waiting for Hadyn to make the first moves. The weapons-master probed along each of the lines George recognized, and let him execute basic parries to block the attacks. George then returned the favor by attempting to press an attack from various directions, none of which came close to succeeding.

Hadyn took back the initiative and, in a series of attacks which went by in a blur, effortlessly touched George with point and blade in several places. He pulled up and nodded to George. "Well, there is some training you've had, but you fear too much to do harm. You must lose that. For today, if you meet anyone with a sword, it's running away I think you should be doing, or maybe throwing something." He turned and rehung the saber he had used.

George swallowed his pride and held his tongue. An accurate enough assessment, after all.

"We hold training for the beginners from mid to late afternoon. Welcome you are to join us, while you're here."

George thanked him. He looked at the sword belt and hanging straps and decided not to humiliate himself further by asking how to fasten it, taking the whole tangle with him.

CHAPTER 8

George made his way to the curtain wall holding the saber in his hand with the belt wrapped around it. Rhian was standing next to a simple wagon drawn by two small horses, and Isolda was up on the wagon seat grasping the long reins in her gloved hands.

Rhian grinned to see George unwrapping the belt from the saber with obvious confusion about how to put it on. "Let me show you. I learned on Rhys."

She took the belt out of his hands and tied it around the outside of his coat, passing the excess length around the strap into a loose overhand loop that left the end hanging tidily flat against his coat. She fastened the two hanging straps suspended from the belt on his left hip to the two rings of the saber scabbard and adjusted it for length so that the sword was at a comfortable length to be drawn. She showed him how to wear it long, with the sword hanging diagonally, when on horseback without a scabbard mounted to the saddle, or how to re-hook the base of the shorter strap to the spare hook on the belt to make it hang straight and out of the way while walking.

Suitably armed, George handed Rhian up to the wagon seat next to Isolda, then walked around to the other side, looking into the wagon bed as he went by. There were several items tied down, most notably an excited terrier puppy in a small crate wagging furiously on a scrap of blanket. "A puppy?" he asked Rhian.

"That's for Angharad. Her dog died and she wanted a new puppy. Her name's Ermengarde."

The wagon also held a saddle with its girth, and several different packages wrapped in cloth and twine.

"That's all?" he asked as he swung into the seat next to Isolda.

"Plus the orders in our pockets, so there'll be plenty of stops," Rhian said.

Isolda was dressed for work in a long leather jerkin and red skirt, with leather gloves. She seemed little larger than a child, and George wondered if she had enough strength to handle the two sturdy little horses. There were only two reins, one from the outer side of each cob. Their bits on the inner sides were connected to each other with a short strap.

She looked up at him. "I don't often have the opportunity to indulge my pleasures this way, since our errands tend to be bundled together and others get to do the driving. Thanks for making this possible."

Rhian said, "Isolda wants to work with the horses, but not as a groom. They tell her she's not big enough to ride them, but no one has forbidden her to drive."

"Big folk like to talk about their size and strength, but even the biggest is smaller and weaker than a pony. You don't master a horse, you train it."

Sensible words, thought George, and they made her seem older again. "May I ask your age?"

"I'm eighteen to Rhian's fourteen. We've been each other's companions from our youngest years."

"You get her out of trouble, I expect?" he asked.

"I'm only one of a long list in that regard," she said, not losing a beat.

"I get myself out of more scrapes than any of you ever find out about," Rhian said, defending herself.

They trotted on in this way down the road and into the village. The houses on each side gave way to combinations of houses and shops as they approached the bridge. Their first stop displayed a hanging sign with loaves of bread and a bee painted on it. They hitched the horses and all went in.

George inhaled the wonderful bakery scent and felt his stomach rumble in response. About a third of the small shop was given over to a counter, where Rhian headed immediately to chat with a tall man wearing a flour-sprinkled apron.

George wondered about his age. It was odd to think of these people in ordinary occupations. Did they hold them throughout a long life, or did they try them on for a while and move on to something else?

The rest of the store was devoted to shelves with jars of honey and preserves, and sacks of dried fruits, nuts, flour, salt, and sugar.

He said to Isolda, "I would've thought every household baked its own bread."

"And so they do, most of them, but the bakery ovens are available for all, and it's easier to buy additional supplies from one place like this. And sometimes it's just simpler to buy specialty items here. The manor's too large not to do its own baking, but we're filling special orders from some people who have particular favorites they can't get there."

"I saw sugar. Do you grow it here?"

"No, that's part of what we import from your world. Honey's more common for us, but sugar expands the possibilities."

As they left the store, the baker brought out several packages that he loaded onto the wagon, and Rhian handed raisin-studded rolls to her companions as a treat. George wolfed half of one down before he slowed and tried to analyze the contents. He could taste honey and cinnamon, and the fruits seemed to be not just raisins but other small dried bits of apricot and apple. "That's the best sweet roll I've ever tasted," he declared in sincere praise. The baker beamed with satisfaction.

The next two stops were homes where Rhian hopped down and delivered packages to those who answered the door. Isolda explained. "Some of the manor staff and guards have family here. There's always a call for deliveries in both directions."

The next shop had a pipe and oil lamp on its sign. They all went in, and George was amazed to find something like a rural country sundries store. A woman strode out of the dwelling space at the back as they came in and Rhian walked over to her, pulling a list out of her pocket. George, with Isolda, wandered about inspecting the goods with fascination.

He located several varieties of oil lamps and lanterns, and pottery jugs of lamp oil. He picked up a lamp and saw "Aladdin" marked on the bottom. "Another import?"

"Along with the lamp oil. I've heard it was very exciting when these replaced the vegetable oil lamps. Candles are still popular, though, for some of those who..." She broke off, embarrassed.

"Who don't like human influences?" George suggested. Hardly surprising, after all.

"I'm afraid so," she said, with an apologetic glance.

She continued. "We like matches, too." She pointed at boxes of common matchbooks, wrapped in paper. "But lighters are even better." And indeed there were baskets of cheap disposable lighters in garish colors.

There were also items of local manufacture on the shelves, decorative and functional carved wood pieces and simple pottery. George saw dishes, but nothing like the plates from last night's dinner. He called over to Rhian, "Someone told me the plates last night were made locally. Who was the potter?"

"That's Angharad. You'll meet her when we deliver the puppy."

"What about hardware?" he asked Isolda. "Nails, tools, and so forth?"

"There are some items here, but most of that will be at the smithy."

As they walked over to rejoin Rhian, George's eye was caught by a basket of pipes. "Of course, that was on the sign. Do you import tobacco?"

"I'm not sure whether tobacco or cotton is the greatest treasure here. We had cotton before your kind were growing it here, from the east, but tobacco was unknown to us before we established Annwn and discovered it from the tribes. Even those who don't approve of trading with humans find it hard to resist tobacco, though there are still a few who find it distasteful."

George missed his own pipe. "I'm fond of it occasionally myself."

The shopkeeper overheard and turned to him and asked, "What sort of mix is it you like, then?"

"I use a blend of dark Virginia and perique."

"Ah. Try this, then." She walked over and plucked a jar of tobacco from among several others, and removed the lid for him to sniff.

He inhaled a lovely dark moist aroma with just a hint of sweetness. "Smells wonderful," he said, with a smile.

"Shall I get you some, now?"

"No, thank you. I won't be here long enough, and in any case I didn't bring a pipe with me."

At this, Rhian turned to him eagerly. "Please let me get you a pipe and fixings, as a kinship gift. It's a matter of small cost but would give you something to remember us by."

"I can't have you spending your money on me," George said.

She looked at him with dignity. "I'm young but I'm hardly poor. You must let this be my decision."

George assented with a good grace. Rhian and the shopkeeper laid out suggested pipes for him. He picked up one, in a free-form bent style, and admired the straight grain of the sides and the bird's-eye of the bottom. It had a horn stem and bit. "Do you import the brier, too?" he asked the shopkeeper.

"No, long ago we brought some from overseas, when we introduced our kin to tobacco. Specialists grow it here now. Our pipe-maker's at the other end of the village, and I blend the tobaccos myself."

She got him a deerskin roll-up pouch for the tobacco, a small tool to use to keep the airways open, and a disposable lighter. She handed the pipe, in a loose leather sleeve, to Rhian, who presented the whole bundle to George, with a little bow. "Please accept this as a welcome gift, cousin."

He took it from her solemnly with both hands and bowed in turn. "I am honored, kinswoman." He tucked the pipe and tobacco pouch into separate chest pockets inside his coat.

The affection indicated by the simple gift touched him. He would miss this little sister he'd never had.

They covered the rest of their home deliveries on this side of the bridge, and then trotted over to the far side, where the houses and shops along the main road were larger and more people were about. Starting at the south end, their first stop was a mill where Rhian ran in to pass along an order for flour of various kinds for the manor, for later delivery. They stopped twice more to hand over personal packages, and worked their way back up to the bridge.

At the main crossroads on the north side by the river stood an inn. Its signboard displayed the top half of a man with the antlers of a stag. "That's the Horned Man, where all the traders stay," Rhian said, as they drew up there. Isolda stayed with the wagon while George hauled out the saddle and girth at Rhian's direction and followed her into the inn, carrying them for her.

A lutin wearing an apron was cleaning up the room. Rhian asked him, "Where's the guest who requested a saddle repair?"

"Seeing to his horse."

Rhian thanked him and they went out a side door to a courtyard with an open roofed area for sheltering vehicles and a stable on the far side.

As they crossed the courtyard they saw another lutin inside the stable through the doorway, with a taller figure looming over him menacingly. George slowed down as he felt suddenly light-headed, his senses expanding, and his ears moving back on his scalp. Something screamed *Alert!* though he couldn't identify what was so alarming.

He touched Rhian's arm from behind, discretely. "Danger," he whispered. "Come away."

She hesitated in her stride for just a moment as she listened but didn't look back. As he watched, her face aged and altered. Everything about her appearance subtly changed, until she was an older plain servant in worn clothes. George felt gooseflesh rise, but he held his face still to mask his surprise and lowered his eyes as she led them directly into the stable and up to the groom.

"Here's the gear you sent for repair. They told me to bring it straight over. This is the gentleman, is it?" Her voice was coarsened and unremarkable.

The lutin looked relieved at the interruption. "See, my lord, your saddle's been repaired, as you required. The best harness makers are up at the manor, as I told you."

A thin dark-haired man with an air of command straightened up at their entry. He was dressed in traveling clothes, leather breeches and sturdy coat, and looked ordinary, but George's hair was still up on the back of his neck and he knew this man was not what he seemed. His appearance was at odds with the sense of menace he radiated, and he carried a small-sword at his side in a well-worn scabbard.

George slung the saddle onto a bench and laid the girth on top. He backed casually away from any furniture that might inhibit his ability to draw his sword, keeping his head down and doing his best imitation of a country bumpkin.

The traveler looked them over and dismissed them, telling the groom, "Pay them. I'll settle with the innkeeper later." He strode out of the stable toward the inn.

Rhian dropped her glamour and turned to the lutin. "It's me, Maonirn. Who was that?"

"My lady, he arrived three days ago, by himself. He says he's waiting for traveling companions and I hope they turn up soon because no one wants to serve him. I offered to repair his saddle for him when he asked, but he insisted it go up to the manor instead. He calls himself Scilti."

"What does he do all day?"

"Stays in his room, mostly, coming out to glower at us from time to time." He paused. "We were sorry to hear about Iolo, my lady."

"Thank you. We'll honor him this evening at dusk. Please spread the word."

She resumed her glamour before leaving the stable and held it all the way back to the wagon. Isolda looked at her with alarm. "What's happened?"

"A stranger at the inn's not what he appears to be. What alerted you to him, kinsman?"

"I don't really know. I felt like a deer who suddenly hears a branch break. Everything came alive for me, and I knew he was wrong in some way. Deadly."

"He could be looking out of a window. I will keep the glamour until we are well out of sight, and resume it again when we come back."

As they continued up the road, George asked her, "How do you change your appearance that way?"

"Almost everyone can do it, but I don't know how to show you. You *think* yourself different. If you do it a lot, you get more expert at certain choices."

"It changes your sight and sound. Does it change for real, or only in the mind of a beholder? If someone's looking that you don't know is there, is it changed for him, too?"

"I don't know. A mirror reflects the glamoured form to the wearer."

"Can you change your scent, too? Does this work on animals?"

"I've never thought of that. I don't know anyone who's tried it."

"And if you can change your scent, does it change your scent trail for real, or only in the mind of an animal that's present? And if it changes your scent trail, what happens when you drop the glamour? Does the scent trail change back? Surely not; it's a physical trace of separate particles, after all."

Isolda looked at him. "All good questions. Ceridwen should know the answers."

George continued to chew at the problem in silence. I wonder if a camera or microphone captures the glamoured form or the original. If he was in a world with different possibilities, he wanted to understand their limits. The stranger had made him feel vulnerable, and he didn't enjoy the sensation.

~

The last stop was some distance north of the inn, on the right side of the road. A good-sized cottage with autumn flowers around it in abundance and a large porch stood bordered by an access lane on its far side. Isolda turned the wagon down the lane and into a cleared space between several buildings.

A woman emerged from one of the buildings dressed in working clothes and cleaning her hands on a cloth. "Well timed," she said, "I was just proposing to stop for a while."

George recognized her as the woman he'd seen the day before as he brought the pack back, the one who hadn't been inside. She seemed about his age, tall and calm, with dark auburn hair gathered into a single braid down her back and gray eyes. I wonder how old she really is, he thought.

Everyone climbed down from the wagon, and Isolda led the horses over to a trough for a drink before hitching them to a post.

Rhian did the introductions. "Angharad, this is our guest George Talbot Traherne who arrived yesterday. He's a great-grandson of Gwyn. George, Angharad's the maker of those plates you asked about last night, among her many other talents."

George said, "I noticed you when the pack came through the village, outside the bakery. You weren't indoors, unlike almost everyone else."

"I have no fear of the hounds. Speaking of which, did you bring her?" she asked Isolda.

Isolda bent over the crate in the back of the wagon and lifted out a sleepy terrier puppy. "My lady, allow me to present Ermengarde." The puppy yawned in her face, then licked it, wriggling.

Smiling, Angharad carried her toward the back door of the cottage. "Come in and have some tea."

"We can't stay that long," Rhian said. "We must be back before the mid-day meal. I wanted to show George some of your work, though, since he so admired our dishes."

They entered a large kitchen and were greeted by another terrier, eager to inspect Angharad's armful of puppy. She put the puppy in a wicker basket near the wood stove and supervised the first encounters. "Cabal's been lonely since Bran died. Look at him now." Cabal was wagging his stump of a tail furiously as he lay down on the floor on his belly watching the puppy as she bumbled out of the basket and began exploring.

Angharad left them to it and led her guests into a large front room, filled with light and color. Brightly decorated plates and plaques hung in every small space, leaving room for paintings in watercolor and oils on the larger surfaces. Ceramic statues gleamed from the fireplace mantel. Woven textiles covered the cushions and furniture.

The first cat that George had seen since his arrival stretched on a cushion near the window and hopped down to inspect the visitors.

George paused to admire the room as a whole, then walked slowly around the edges examining the items on the walls. "All of this is your work?" he asked Angharad.

"Not the woodwork; I don't build furniture these days."

"They're extraordinary," he said, stunned by the quality of what he saw. This was a serious artist, he realized, in a wide variety of forms. The watercolors were landscapes, mostly scenes of the Blue Ridge in various weathers. The oils were a mix of landscapes and penetrating portraits. The pride of place was given to an antique oil portrait over the fireplace, the distilled essence of an older man with an intense and commanding gaze.

"Who's that?"

"My second husband, Cai. I painted it many years later," she said.

Here in this room of bright colors, something about her seemed even brighter and filled his gaze. Tough act to follow, that husband, George thought, mesmerized. But I'd like to try.

"He was exhausting," she continued, "But then he was rarely home. It was a very long time ago." She smiled quietly and refocused on her guests.

"I took up ceramics here in Annwn, and textiles are a new interest for me." She gestured at the fresh fabrics. "Gwyn lets me work in peace."

Isolda spoke up. "It's getting late and we're expected back. I'll get the wagon."

Rhian and George said their good-byes, leaving Angharad in the kitchen admiring the puppy, now lying fast asleep against the delighted older dog.

Before they left Angharad's lane, George reminded Rhian to resume her changed appearance, in case anyone was watching from the inn. She held it until they reached the bridge and crossed over.

As they drove back up the west road to the manor, George asked Rhian, "Is Angharad another relative? Is she married?"

"Oh, no. I'm not sure who her last husband was, but she's been alone for many years. I think she likes it that way. She came to Annwn in the early days, but not at the very beginning. You'll have to ask my foster-father for more."

Quite the older woman, George thought. *She must look at the three of us as puppies, the lot of us.* Her solemn face and gray eyes had a hold on his imagination. *Too bad I can't stay. I'd like to see that smile again.*

CHAPTER 9

Rhian and George dropped off as Isolda pulled up in the manor yard. They offered to help her unload, but she waved them off as others came from the stable to meet her.

Rhian checked the position of the sun nervously. "We must hurry. Rhys and Idris are expecting us."

They walked quickly into the back hall and into Gwyn's council room where they found Idris, Rhys, and Ceridwen already present. Food was laid on a sideboard, cold meats from last night's meal. George and Rhian filled plates and joined the others at the council table.

Gwyn greeted them. "Just in time. Ceridwen told us of the wounds on Iolo's body and the marks on the saddle. Idris, please report your findings."

Idris spoke of their early morning tracking expedition. At the appropriate time, Rhian pulled out the broken spell-stick and placed it on the table for all to see.

Ceridwen bent over it without touching it directly. "This is made by one of my kind. The writing's clear enough: 'Be thou masked in wind and fury.'" She touched it carefully with one finger. "It wasn't made here in Annwn."

She looked up. "This was given to someone who couldn't work his own disguise."

Idris continued with the tale and described the recent tunnel through the palisade.

"But this isn't possible," Ceridwen said, rising. "I must see this.' She made as if to leave immediately and Gwyn gestured her back down.

"You and Creiddylad shall inspect it when we're done here." To Idris, he said, "Did you post a guard?"

"No. We were fairly discreet when we found it and it's possible the enemy doesn't know what we discovered. I left Thomas Kethin there to loiter about plausibly and try to spot any unusual interest." He looked at Ceridwen. "I don't think we should make our knowledge plain with an inspection, my lord. Better an escape route we know about, than plugging this one and not finding its replacement."

Gwyn nodded, but Ceridwen was still troubled.

"I must see it somehow, though. I don't know how this damage could be done as you describe, and therefore I don't know if we're vulnerable in some more serious way along the entire palisade."

Gwyn acknowledged her concern. "You and Creiddylad will go out riding this afternoon, with Thomas in attendance. No one should see you inspect the damage from the outside if you're cautious. We'll avoid drawing attention to the inside portion until we have some better sense of our enemy's plans."

Idris finished up with the fruitless search at the baths.

Ceridwen then took up the tale. "I've asked among the guards about traffic and that won't be finished until tomorrow morning as they come off shift. But I can tell you already that it's unlikely to be helpful. On the one hand, there's been quite a bit of gate traffic, both from our guests and their entourage and from our own people. On the other hand, with this tunnel, why would our enemy need to use the gates?"

Idris said, "It was in my mind that he may have used the gates on the way out, when he was in a hurry and use of the tunnel entrance might have been seen. Clearly he returned in secret, as you suggest."

George felt obliged to speak up. "There's one guest servant I saw at dinner who caught my attention with his eager watching of the entrance of the guardsmen. He seemed pleased while everyone was shocked at the package. I don't want to make too much of it, but he bothered me."

Rhian said, "You know the man, the one with the white streaks."

Gwyn nodded. "Part of Creiddylad's staff. I haven't noticed him much."

"That's because he stays out of your way," she said. "I've seen him duck into other rooms when he sees you coming."

"Oh?" Gwyn said, with sudden interest.

George was alarmed for Rhian's safety. "Does he know you've seen him do that?"

"I don't care. He'll not scare me in my own house."

Idris said, "Unwise. An enemy discovered and desperate is never to be despised."

Rhian persisted. "He follows me around, and sometimes Rhys. I think I'll pay him back and watch him, instead."

Gwyn looked at her sternly. "You'll do no such thing. Even if your suspicions have merit, better not to alarm a spy than to scare him into deeper hiding or, worse, force him to hand off the task to an unknown confederate. We have other ways of keeping an eye on him." He looked at Ceridwen, who nodded thoughtfully.

Rhian spoke up again. "We ran errands in the village today, it's why we were late. Do you know who's at the inn?"

She recounted their encounter. "If our kinsman hadn't warned me, I would have blundered in unprepared. I think he took us for servants. There's something wrong about him. I don't see any reason for him to be hanging around."

It was Rhys's turn to look alarmed. "Are you sure he didn't recognize you? No one greeted you by name?"

"George made me keep the glamour up till we were out of sight of the inn, and had me resume it on our way back down the street later."

Rhys nodded at George approvingly. "A wise precaution. How did you know he was glamoured?"

"I couldn't exactly tell you. Can't work very well if you can see through it," he said.

"But normally you can't detect a glamour," Ceridwen said. "Did you know it was there, Rhian?"

Rhian shook her head.

Ceridwen summarized their results so far. "So, it seems clear that the attack on Iolo was made by a man disguised by magic, probably someone else's magic, implying he has none of his own. He may have used artificial claws as weapons, presumably to suggest a creature not a man. He may have written the note and hung the hands, or that might have been done by a confederate. He knows of a breach in our defenses, made with unknown means, and perhaps may have created it himself. He's likely here now, under our noses, and he may know of our discoveries. He's made threats of additional violence, referring to a past history of some kind. He's most likely one of the guests or part of their entourage, given the foreign nature of the twine."

"In addition," she continued, "we have two unusual characters who may or may not deserve our suspicions and who may or may not have had anything to do with the murder, or each other."

George said, "It's not too late to bring back the bloodhounds and have them match the spell-stick to a person, if they went through the entire population, though with each passing hour that becomes more difficult. You could also do a search, looking for the weapon or anything else that matches the evidence, like the twine."

"Neither of these are attractive alternatives," Gwyn said. "They might not work, and at best will implicate just one person, assuming the murderer and the note-writer are the same. Much worse, they will certainly alert the enemy, who's likely to be more than one man acting alone. Even if we catch one, what about the possible others?"

"No," he said decisively. "We'll continue in more subtle ways. Ceridwen will finish her interviews so that we can be seen to be looking into it. The inspection of the palisade damage will be done as covertly as possible. We'll look into these two people but without alerting them. Whatever we find, we must assume there are other enemies we haven't yet identified."

He stood. "Iolo was killed for a larger purpose. Bad enough that he was the victim, but worse that it wasn't even personal. We don't know the full purpose yet, but it must revolve around Iolo as huntsman, and therefore around the great hunt in two weeks.

"The hunt will happen. It must happen, both for its own sake and our realm's benefit, but also because I won't be moved in this way like a pawn by powers that wish me and mine no good." This last was spoken with quiet ferocity.

The others rose from the table and moved to the door, but Gwyn asked George to stay, closing the door behind them and returning to the council table.

"I haven't had the time to speak with you at length and would like to know you better. Can you tell me more about your arrival yesterday morning?"

George was eager to discover why, and how, he'd gotten here. Maybe this time he could get someone to agree on a plan to send him back.

He described how he'd followed the sound of hounds along a strange path and been distracted by the deer, before coming off at the unexpected jump.

"So, you heard the pack baying, and that's what sent you to them. Was it your pack you heard, or mine?"

"I thought it was mine at the time, of course, but now I think not, that it must have been yours."

Gwyn said, "They bayed at the murder. So, at the moment of Iolo's death, the way was opened to you." He paused. "You were brought here, I think."

"By you?"

"No, not by me. What was the deer like, that you saw?"

"A big buck with a magnificent rack. The noise drew my eye and I had a clear view. He was quite pale, with dark eyes, and he just stood there and watched."

"I detect other hands at work in this," Gwyn concluded.

"Does that mean you can't send me back?" George's heart sank.

"It means I should understand why you're here, first," Gwyn said.

Gwyn continued, "Tell me more about your encounter with the stranger at the inn. What made you think he was a threat?"

"I've thought about that, and I can't say. It's almost as if he smelt wrong, though that's not it. I knew his appearance was a lie."

"Oh? Could you tell that Rhian was glamoured?"

"Well, I saw her altered form, of course, and I knew what she looked like normally, but, yes, I think I also knew it was false independently of that."

Gwyn stood and his appearance abruptly changed to that of an older man with a stooped back. "What do you see?" he asked with a quavering voice.

"I see and hear the change, but I know in some fundamental way that it's not true. I can't see your real form directly, but I know it's there. It's hard to explain."

Gwyn dropped the glamour and sat back down, thoughtfully. "This isn't typical for one of us. A glamour works unless some counter magic prevents it. There's no sensing of the true form otherwise. A skilled man can hold a glamour for a year and not be detected, as Pwyll did."

Who was Pwyll, George wondered.

"Tell me of your father," Gwyn said.

With some reluctance, George opened up the sunny memories of his childhood, blighted by the ending.

"Conrad Traherne. There's not much to tell, since I was a child when they died. My mother, your granddaughter Léonie, met him in Wales when she was about 22. There was some family story, never very clear to me, of getting lost in a woods and rescued at dusk. He worked as a gamekeeper and was away for days at a time while my mother wrote at her desk. I don't know where the money came from, but we had a snug little cottage off against the woods by itself, with our neighbors at a distance. I had my pony and freedom to explore, and life was very good."

George looked off into the past. "He was a lovely man when he was home. He would tell me stories and take me into the woods for adventures. He had this amazing knack for spotting animals and not disturbing them, and I would try to imitate him on my own when he wasn't there, to make him proud of me."

He glanced back at Gwyn, who was listening attentively. "I don't really know what happened. One evening they went out together for a walk, and they didn't return. I was nine years old, and sick with worry by morning. We had no phone. I was just about to take my pony to the next farm to find someone when a policeman knocked on the door to tell me there'd been an accident.

"He wouldn't say much. I sneaked a look at his notebook when he was washing up, and saw something about wild animals. That's also where I saw my father's right name for the first time: Corniad Traherne. I showed them my mother's address book and they contacted my grandfather. I met him the next day, and he took me back to Virginia."

And how strange it is, he marveled, *that I so rarely think of them. I never went through their things when I got older. I know grandfather has them. No longer. As soon as I get back I'm going to start asking questions.*

George went to the sideboard to refill his glass and sat down again. His mind was in turmoil. *How's it possible that I never asked? It's as if a veil's been torn away and now I can see how odd that is.*

Aloud, he said, "I never heard of any other family on my father's side, but I don't actually know."

"What about your own family?" Gwyn asked. "Your wife and children? Who's waiting for you?"

Who, indeed, George thought. Aloud, he said, "I've never married, and there's no one special at the moment." He looked down at that. He wanted children and was unhappy he hadn't found the right woman yet.

"Still, I have a good career. I run a small software firm," he smiled at Gwyn's blank look, "but I'm at a point where I'm, well, bored by it." There, he'd said it, admitted it out loud. "I live on a small farm, and visit my grandparents regularly. I go foxhunting. It's a very quiet, dutiful life."

"And you find it constraining and unsatisfying, I think," Gwyn said.

George shifted uncomfortably in his seat. "Yes," he said shortly. "But it's what a man does, making his way in the world. No one said it had to be fulfilling."

Gwyn rested one elbow on his chair and gestured with his hand while he summarized.

"You're certainly my descendant, but you have skills I don't recognize in glamoury. Your father is, at the least, unusual. Someone has brought you here, when we have a need for friends and a suspicion of enemies. I think I may know now who the player is on that side, an old but tricky ally."

George hoped for more details but Gwyn went off in an unexpected direction instead and George held his tongue.

"Let me tell you a bit about us and our current situation."

"I am old, and older than old. I remember the coming of the new humans before the ice, watched it push them south in the old world, and watched them return when it retreated. My sire and his are older still. We die, in time, but the longer we live, the more powerful we become. Unless we die by violence."

George was prepared for something like this after last night's history lesson from Eurig, but it still took his breath away.

"We form families, of course, but many of our marriages are alliances of power and don't last more than a few decades at best. We have children, but not many and not often, and they make their own way in the world. Eventually, even that stops. I expect no more siblings, but now and then I'm still tempted myself."

George smiled privately at Eurig's judgment last night about Gwyn being "fond of the ladies."

Gwyn continued, "The great houses mind their realms with smaller lords in their retinue, and they strive with each other over old grudges, new ambitions, or just out of boredom. Not all of us take the path of direct power; there are craftsmen, warriors, solitary dwellers, travelers, scholars, and all the flavors of any people that you might expect. We live long enough that many try their hand at a variety of activities and become expert in several.

"Some of us, like me, have children outside our own kind. Most of those lead short lives by our reckoning, in the outerworld, and come to nothing in particular, but sometimes they come back to us with true skills and some powers. A few are living here now, though none of mine."

"It would be interesting to meet them," George said. "Do you yourself have children in the current generation? What of Rhys and Rhian?"

"I have no young children at the moment. You must realize that, with our long lives, we rarely know our much older or younger siblings well, so our greatest bonds are with our parents and our own children. To connect us across the lineages, we typically foster each other's children. It broadens their education, and a foster-parent can be more objective about discipline and training than a natural parent.

"When my brother Edern's son Rhys died, I offered to foster his young children. The Rhys you've met is Rhys Vachan, Rhys the younger. He and his sister have lived here for nine years. He's now 22, and she 14. It's quite unusual for full siblings to be so close in age, and they wouldn't be parted from each other, so they came together when she was old enough. They're dear to me and I hope they'll stay all their lives, but in any case I'm responsible for their rearing and, most importantly, their safety."

Gwyn paused. "I wasn't always the Prince of Annwn. It was a great honor to receive the realm, but many of my enemies date from that time. I was quick to remove it to the new world and to keep the ways obscure until I was better prepared, but for many centuries now we've fallen into a regular practice at the time of the great hunt of opening our ways to all who would come, as if we were all at peace. You understand, better to appear to be so strong that you needn't show concern, yes?"

George nodded. This was all very interesting but it wasn't getting him home.

"Now we're paid for that with treachery and murder. And in truth I have even older enemies, in particular Gwythyr ap

Greidawl. He was at one time betrothed to my youngest sister Creiddylad until I rescued her, at her request. It was a bitter fight, and many died at my hand whose families still wish me ill. For this old grudge I must meet Gwythyr every Nos Galan Mai at the spring equinox and strive again. Sometimes I win, sometimes not, and Creiddylad leads her own life at our father's in the meantime, or on the lands that I gave her, accordingly.

"The great hunt is the heart and purpose of Annwn. All the mighty families come to see the world's justice meted out. There are lesser hunts throughout the year but the one on Nos Galan Gaeaf is the one where all the ways are thrown open and no one can predict who will be pursued and where they will lead. For the great hunt to fail, or not to happen, would be disastrous.

"This murder of Iolo is a blow aimed at the great hunt, at the balance of the world, and at my realm. I can't allow it to succeed. You understand?"

George nodded again.

"Good. That's why I want you to serve as huntsman on that night."

CHAPTER 10

Huntsman!

I didn't see that one coming, George thought. I just want to get home. He sighed inwardly.

Alright, let's think about this like a job interview. I'm offered a new position, but to be fair I've done it before when someone needed to cover for John at the Rowanton Hunt. This involves a new pack, a new breed of hounds, and a strange territory, but there are people who can guide me with that. Two weeks is an absurdly short time, but perhaps it's possible.

But this is the Wild Hunt we're talking about. Someone will die at the end, however well deserving, brutally and in pain. And, in some sense, the whole world will be watching.

On the other hand, what a challenge. George felt the pull of that thought.

"What would happen if I turn this down?" he asked.

"I don't know. Rhian may someday grow into this, she wants to, but she can't do it yet and under these circumstances. Rhys might be able to, but this isn't the way he's inclined and a lack of enthusiasm might well be fatal. I could do it, but it's not permitted. Beyond that, there's no one. Iolo shouldn't have died, and so we're not prepared."

He continued, "Besides, I think you were brought here for this. At the moment of Iolo's death, a new huntsman appears. It can't be coincidence. I think your father's kin may have something to do with it. It's the right answer. Even if it fails, it's better than not to try."

George protested. "I have a life of my own in another world. It's one thing to visit, but I hadn't thought of uprooting it altogether."

"Let's make this just for the duration of the great hunt. After that, if we're all still here, we can decide together if it should continue."

"May I give you my answer in the morning? I need to think about this."

"That would be acceptable." Gwyn looked at him directly. "I must warn you, many will be hoping for this to fail—my enemies who want to see me fall, traditionalists who won't tolerate a mixed blood in the role, and those who just dislike humans altogether. Some of them might take steps to ensure you won't succeed."

George translated soberly: if this fails I may not survive to worry about it.

"If you accept, you'll need to study with Ceridwen. She can help you explore your talents."

And I'll also need to spend some time with the weapons-master, Hadyn, and become competent with physical defense, George thought.

Aloud, he said, "I assume I can have whatever resources are necessary to get the job done? I'd want Rhys and Rhian involved."

"You'll get all the assistance you need." Gwyn rose. "I'll await your answer tomorrow."

George stood at the dismissal, nodded, and exited the room thoughtfully.

He walked out into the yard and stopped someone passing. "Where can I find Ceridwen?"

The man pointed out her dwelling—two stories high, of stone, and just beyond the infirmary. He knocked on the green door. The servant who answered asked him to wait and returned with Ceridwen.

"I'm sorry to interrupt you," George said, "but I wanted to take a few minutes of your time today. Should I come back later?"

"No, this is fine. I thought I might see you. Was your discussion with Gwyn… interesting?"

"Indeed," he said dryly. "He offered me a job."

She nodded. "And you have reservations." Clearly she knew this might happen. She must've already discussed it with Gwyn.

"More than that. He implied strange things about my father and speculated on inherited abilities. I need information, badly, if I'm to make any sort of rational decision, and I was hoping you might be able to help."

She smiled and led the way back into a large study, more of a library, with comfortable chairs, a desk, and great piles of books both on and off the shelves. A low fire crackled cozily, and they settled into two armchairs before it.

She gestured for him to continue.

"I don't understand what I might inherit from Gwyn, three generations back." He recounted the conversation about detecting glamours, and the earlier one about sensitivity to animals.

Then he told her about his father, and Gwyn's remarks about being brought deliberately, and his father's kin. "I don't understand any of that."

The servant brought tea, and she served them both. "As to what you may inherit, that's never predictable. Most commonly, the child of mixed blood has little or nothing, but not always. You've made your life, or part of it, with animals, and so I think that talent may be true, if unexplored. You'll have to experiment to see what you're capable of there. For the glamour, yes, that's unusual. I can detect one, sometimes, and perhaps Gwyn can, but we don't discuss it since it's more useful as a hidden advantage."

She looked at him. "There are other things to test. Can you cast a glamour yourself?"

"I wouldn't know how to try."

"As you sit there, think of yourself as an old man and try to convince me of it, silently."

George let himself feel shrunken and tired, conscious of small aches and a certain tremor in his hands. It was acting a part, but persuading himself instead of an audience. He looked over at Ceridwen, keeping to character, then released it.

"I think you may have it in you. I could see the glamour, dimly. You'll need to work at it, but it's a skill like any other."

She looked at him speculatively. "How old are you?"

"Thirty-three."

"Remind me, I don't see many humans. Do you seem young for that age?"

"It's hard to know what normal feels like, of course. My hair hasn't started to gray yet, nor receded, but that's not all that unusual. I feel well, but then I keep fit for foxhunting. I'm good for my age, but young? How would I know?"

"It's possible you have some of the longevity, too. We mature at the same rate as humans, until middle age, and there we linger for a very long time."

She took a sip of her tea.

"What Gwyn suspects about your father is much more of a surprise. Let me see if I have this right."

She summarized. "You hear the pack at Iolo's death, then see a pale stag, then, a bit precipitously, find yourself in the otherworld. Is that correct?"

"Yes, that's about it."

"Your father had no kin of which you are aware. He had a special affinity for animals. He worked in the woods. He vanished, with your mother, in the woods."

"Yes."

"Do you know what 'Traherne' means?"

"I just know it's Welsh."

"It means 'iron-hard,' more or less. And 'Corniad' is 'the horned-one,' like a bull or a stag."

She paused, exasperated like any professor facing a dullard at George's apparent lack of comprehension, and spelled it out for him. "Gwyn thinks your father was a manifestation of Cernunnos, the lord of beasts, the great hunter, and that he brought you here for a purpose."

He felt the blood drain from his face. Another stunner, he thought. He had seen archaeological portrayals of Cernunnos, a seated man with the antlers of a deer, but this implied a living god of some kind.

He shook his head in denial. "There's a limit to my suspension of disbelief in the last couple of days, as I find myself here in the otherworld talking to near-immortal relatives, and we may have just hit it."

Ceridwen smiled sympathetically. "We do have gods, they just don't concern themselves with us very often, and the distinctions between our highest lords and our gods aren't that great. Even our gods can die or vanish. Cernunnos is one of our old ones and, perhaps, still enjoys taking a hand in our affairs. He's the ultimate sponsor of the great hunt."

George said, "Never mind, I just can't associate this with my father. If you're both right, I'll just have to think of it as another unusual set of traits, like wiggling my ears." He muttered, "I'm beginning to feel like a specially bred hound."

Ceridwen said, "I've never seen Cernunnos myself, nor met one in whom he took an interest, either indirectly or directly. This should be most intriguing."

She paused. "A personal question, if you will. Why were you named George? Who named you?"

"I asked my parents that, since I was teased as a boy for such an English name in Wales. My mother said it was after her mother, Georgia. But my father always joked about it being a fine name for a dragon slayer."

"Let's hope that's not prophetic."

The fire crackled in silence for a moment as bits dropped off the logs on the andirons into the embers below.

George stirred from staring into the fire to glance at the andirons and chuckled. "I've been meaning to ask. Whatever happened to the 'fearing the touch of cold iron' tradition of the otherworld? Everywhere I look I see perfectly ordinary iron objects, not to mention the weaponry."

Ceridwen laughed. "We don't know where that legendary guidance came from, but we sometimes play along with it, for the gullible in your world. It's useful to pretend to a false weakness and be underestimated."

"I don't suppose garlic or crosses matter, either?" he asked.

"We're not vampires." At his surprised look, she said, "Yes, I've read some of your books. Besides, consider your premises. We're not part of Christianity, so those religious symbols are as irrelevant to us as signs to scare off the 'evil eye' are to you, and garlic's used symbolically to ward off the evil and the unclean; we're neither."

"But King Arthur's court is traditionally Christian."

"We do take on the trappings of the human world over time, in fashions and language, and in names, so you'll find occasional Christian names among us, if few actual Christians. And Arthur's part of our history. But the stories you know have been very much modified in your traditions to conform with the needs and uses of the times. Sometime, when we have more leisure, I'd be glad to correct your understanding of that period."

She continued, "There's one more trait I've thought of from Gwyn's line that may be relevant. Perhaps you found your own way here, having received the call. Has anyone described to you what a way-finder is?"

"Rhys mentioned something. Is Rhodri one, the fellow I borrowed the robes from? He also said something about tokens, but I didn't quite understand."

"Our realms in the otherworld lie in different areas, but all are connected to each other, and sometimes to the human world, in particular places. You could ride out that gate below and eventually come to the realms of Gwyn's father and uncle, but it would take months and you would pass through much wilderness and danger along the way. You would even cross oceans. The ways are direct routes, shortcuts, either open to all or warded.

"A few of the high lords, and some of their descendants, can find new ways not yet in use, and claim them for ownership. Gwyn allied himself with Trefor Mawr, one of our greatest way-finders, when he found the first ways to the new world. He built settlements around the important locations. After he moved Annwn here, Gwyn let them be known and used, primarily for traders. They require tokens for their use. It's not hard to obtain such a token, but the number of travelers a token can accommodate is limited. We don't want armies to appear on our doorstep, after all.

"Gwyn also maintains at least one private way for family and friends, and those tokens are few. For the great hunt in the fall and the striving with Gwythyr in the spring, which are public events, he issues tokens for the guests, good for one use only. Not all guests are… friends.

"Rhodri has great talent as a way-finder in this current generation. Like any young man—I suppose he's about your age—he's swept up by the novelty of seeing other lands, but I expect he'll settle down eventually. What I wonder is if you yourself have inherited any such talent and found a new way to the otherworld, as Gwyn did when he first visited your world from here."

George couldn't help thinking, I look for answers and get nothing but more questions. Aloud, he asked, "How can we test that?"

"Quickly, without thinking about it, close your eyes and point to the spot where you entered this world."

He closed his eyes and held out an arm, as though he were a compass. He felt a bright pull to the southeast and pointed in that direction. "There."

"That's right," Ceridwen said.

"But I don't understand. I looked for it when I woke up and couldn't find it."

"You looked with your eyes, not your mind. Didn't you?"

"True." He nodded.

"They can be hard to see until claimed, even to their finder."

He closed his eyes, and this time thought of himself as a sonar detector, sweeping around in a full circle.

"You're right. Now that I'm looking, I can see five more."

Ceridwen started. She rose abruptly. "There should only be three."

She walked swiftly to her desk and pulled out a scroll from a shelf behind it. She unrolled it on top of the desk, shoving stacks of paper to the side carelessly, and weighted it down. "Come here. Show me."

He walked over and looked down at a map of the area that seemed to cover about ten miles across, with the manor and its palisade in the center. The Blue Ridge and the local stream were clear, and Greenhollow with its bridge, but this was the first overview he had seen. There were cleared farms but no other visible settlements, and no roads over the mountain.

"Let me find north," he said. George had an excellent sense of direction, and he confirmed it with his compass. Ceridwen looked at the device with interest. He moved the scroll to conform.

I wonder how you can tell distance, he thought, if it's like stars where "small and close" looks the same as "big and far away." He closed his eyes again and pointed to his entry spot in real space. He opened them, leaned over the map, and placed an inkwell on it as a marker. "I know the distance of this one, close enough. I'll use that as a gauge of distance for the others."

Reclosing his eyes, he identified the most obvious one, south of the village near the road. Ceridwen confirmed that as the Travelers' Way. It was further than he would've thought, so it seemed that the sense of 'big' was easily confused with 'close.'

The next was a small one in the direction of the gate, which Ceridwen marked in the clearing before the main gates. "That's the way for guests," she said.

George stayed close in and identified another small one, very nearby and due south. "That's the Family Way. It comes out in the kennels."

"No other defense needed?" George said.

"The family doesn't fear the hounds, and we wanted the endpoint to be something easy to guard, if it was going to be within the palisade."

George swept around west of the manor. "There's one here, in this direction. Judging by these others, I would say it's very small and fairly close." He put a smooth stone from the desk on the scroll where woods were indicated, west of the palisade, not far away.

He pinpointed the last one. "Here, north of the manor. Medium-sized?" Looking at the map, he dropped a small paperweight in a cleared field halfway up the ridge. "Somewhere along this line, depending on its real size."

Ceridwen looked shaken. "We know nothing of these last two. I must tell Gwyn and Idris immediately."

~

George stood on Ceridwen's doorstep, watching her hasten off to the manor. He saw the armory across the lane and was reminded of the afternoon training sessions. Never too soon to start. How bad can it be, someone my age with a bunch of youngsters, he thought, wincing in anticipation. He walked over and caught sight of the weapons-master within.

"Master Hadyn, thank you for the use of this sword. There was no opportunity for me to embarrass myself with it, but that's all to the good."

Hadyn's mouth quirked.

George continued, "You mentioned training for the beginners in the afternoon. Do you think I could join the session today?" Might as well find out how long it's going to take me to become competent enough to hold up my head.

Hadyn nodded. "We start in an hour. Keep the sword while you're here, you'll need it for training."

George thanked him and returned outside.

Now for the hounds.

~

"Quiet down, now," George told the hounds at the kennels as they crowded up against the bars of the pens and began to bark in excitement. And they did, not violently as if turned off at the switch, but cooperatively, as if they understood him. It was the same command he gave to his dogs at home when they got noisy, and while he'd noticed that it usually worked, he assumed it was nothing more than their familiarity with the words and the tone of his voice. These hounds didn't know him, but it worked on them, too. It can't be this easy, he thought uneasily.

He looked over the yard with his new attention to the travel ways and spotted the small presence in the center. He couldn't see anything as he circled around it. It can't just suck people in, here in the middle of a public space, he thought, and he nerved himself to walk right through the spot. It tingled slightly, but nothing happened. Perhaps you need a destination in mind, or one of those tokens.

He entered at the doorway on the left at the end of the yard and found Ives in the same place as yesterday, plaiting a thong for a riding whip at the table while other lutins stirred the cauldrons.

Ives looked up and smiled. "Thank you for letting Isolda practice her driving skills on you this morning. They don't all take her seriously around here."

"That was Rhian's doing, but it was a pleasure. She's quite competent. What does she hope to do with this line of work?"

"Our families work with the animals, here and on the farms, but we tend them rather than using them for our work. I know of a few who've taken up riding on ponies or small horses, but we think them rather odd. Driving's more unusual yet, and Isolda's the only girl I know who's ever taken an interest.

"Most of the wagoners are big folk, strong enough to move heavy freight around and control the big horses. She's fine with the horses, but I think she'll need to stick to carriages for people, where the freight can move itself. There's enough of a call for that for her to do well, if she wishes."

He put down the leather work in his hands. "Was there something I can do for you?"

George considered how much to reveal. "I've been asked to see what I could do with the hounds, based on skills they think I have."

"Do you know who will be huntsman, then?" Ives said, rising from the table.

"They're weighing their options. Do you have any opinions they should know about?"

"The great hunt must happen. If she were older I'd recommend Rhian, but I think it's too soon."

"Not Rhys?"

"He's not dedicated to it, and the hounds would know. He's fine as a whipper-in, but it's just one step in his training for him, not a life. The same for Rhodri, who also came through here in his time, as a whipper-in."

Ives looked at George speculatively. He has some idea about my situation, George thought, but is too politic to mention it first.

"Let's take some of the bitches out into the paddock and see if they'll listen to you," Ives suggested.

They went down the corridor to the bitch pen, where all the hounds jumped down from the benches at their approach. Ives picked out three couple of hounds and released them into the corridor. He looked at George and said, "They need to go down to the end and out that door into their yard."

George understood the implied challenge. "Are the yard's outer gates closed?" Ives nodded.

George addressed the hounds. "Alright, ladies, pack up." They looked at him and settled down in the corridor. He pushed his way through, making sure to focus on each one and give her a touch as he went by.

He led them to the outer door at the end of the corridor and went through it, blocking the hounds with his body as he checked to see the yard was empty and its gates were closed. The fence enclosed about an acre and a half. Then he opened the door fully and released the hounds to run in the grass for a few moments and let off some steam.

Ives named the hounds to him. "They're a mix. I gave you four biddable hounds, one good but stubborn leader, and one shy but good trailer that the others pick on. If this group will listen to you, you've a good chance with all of them. That Rhymi there is the head bitch."

George watched them run about, sniffing the markings from the other hounds and anything else they could find. Rhymi was a powerful hound, with a few scars to show she didn't lead a peaceful life in kennels.

He walked out to the middle of the yard, leaving Ives leaning against the fence. "Rhymi," he called, "Come."

The hound's head went up and she trotted over to see what he wanted. "Pack up," he called to the rest of them. With their leader already in place, they weren't hesitant to join in.

The shy one got too close to the others and was snarled at. "Ah, ah, ah," George said sternly to the offender, who looked surprised at the reprimand.

Ives spoke from over by the fence, carefully expressionless. "Never heard that one before."

George flushed. "I think all domestic animals speak 'cat' as a second language, since they all seem to know 'scuss' and 'ah, ah, ah.' Works for me, anyway."

He turned and called out, "Pack up," without looking back. The three couple followed him in tolerable order as he walked around the yard. He kept watch from the corner of his eye, and as one paused to investigate a leftover bone in the grass, he told her, "Leave it," and she returned to the pack.

It was exhilarating to work with the hounds this way. He knew this level of communication wasn't normal, and that's why it had never occurred to him to try it before. On those occasions when he had been working as temporary Rowanton huntsman, he assumed the smoothness of the pack was just the good training by the real huntsman of which he was able to take advantage. This time, he was looking for the difference, and he could feel it. If he put enough serious intent into his voice, the hounds took him seriously in turn. It wasn't orders and obedience, but more like a musical dialogue where he led and they agreed to follow, mostly. This was like the golden thread that huntsmen speak of connecting them to their hounds, but with much more specificity.

He tried an experiment. He pointed at Ives, now standing watching a few steps away from the fence. "To Ives," he told the pack. They looked at his gesture and headed in that direction. He wasn't sure if they understood the directionality only or the destination, but they stopped at Ives rather than continuing on to the fence, and then he knew: they understood the name. A shiver went up his spine and his ears pulled back on his head.

"Pack up," he called, and they returned. "Alright, ladies, enjoy yourselves," he dismissed them. They bounded off to continue exploring in the yard while George walked over to Ives.

"That was very interesting," George said. Maybe this would be possible. But a little group like this inside an enclosure didn't prove much. Could he do this dance of command and persuasion for a pack five times this size? Much more doubtful.

As if he could hear his thoughts, Ives warned him. "They won't all be so cooperative, Cythraul particularly. Still, you clearly have what you need to hunt them."

"I'd need to know the standard commands Iolo used, his horn calls, all the things they're used to."

"Of course."

No point dodging the obvious, thought George. "So, do you think I can do this, just to cover until the great hunt? Do you think I should?"

"I think you can, and I don't know who else could, if you don't."

I can see where this is headed, George thought, as he walked back to the armory. Now, what about my real life? Can I just drop everything at work for a two-week sabbatical? Do I really want to? Well, why not? Sam's been itching for an opportunity to run the whole company. This can be his chance, and I can do a serious evaluation when I get back. Two weeks of no electricity or other mod cons will be plenty for me, though no doubt I'll want to come back for visits, if that's possible.

All of this assuming I can actually do the job. A job that ends up with someone dead.

As he entered the armory, he stopped one of the young men inside and asked about the training class. Together, they joined a group at one end of the building where Hadyn was waiting for them.

George reminded himself, this isn't about sport and exercise. Someone killed a man yesterday with a claw-blade, and everyone was shocked by the murder, but not by the violence of it. What would I do in a world without guns if someone came at me with a knife? Or a sword? Better learn quickly.

He hadn't anticipated his first assignment from Hadyn.

"Partner up with young Brynach there," he told George.

George glanced over at a boy in his teens, slender and not quite full grown, who looked startled at the match-up. Well, I told him I didn't know much and I guess he's taken me at my word, he thought. I must be half again his weight. Hope I can keep from hurting him.

He walked over and introduced himself. "Where I come from we do very little combat training in earnest, so assume I know nothing." Brynach looked dubious but held his tongue.

Hadyn began with unarmed defense exercises. George knew just enough to bend his knees and keep a lower center of gravity, but he was completely inexperienced in this area and let his partner take the offense.

Brynach danced around him looking for an opening. When he incautiously circled in too closely, George stepped toward him, turning away at an angle, then put his hands to the floor to support his weight, and swung his back leg around low behind him to sweep Brynach's legs out from under him. They were both surprised, Brynach, because he hadn't expected it, and George, who had never thought it would work. He leaned over to give Brynach a hand getting back up.

"I never tried that before," he said, apologetically.

"How's it done?" Brynach asked.

George showed him the direction and weight shift he'd used. He looked around and saw that the other pairs were mostly using grab and leverage moves, rather than blows.

There were only three hand blows the untrained George could think of that would be useful in real combat: a punch to the solar plexus, a chop to crush the windpipe, or a palm thrust to the nose for bone splinters to the brain. He could see that the common leather jerkin and other torso clothing worn here might make a chest blow less effective, and that the closed shirts, stocks, and other throat defenses might be adequate as well. He had no experience in facial blows and thought the risk of an amateur breaking his hand in the process was fairly high. Most of all, he didn't know how to practice any of these without running the risk of serious damage to his partner.

This left wrestling, about which George knew less than nothing, and his inexpert recollections of oriental martial arts maneuvers staged by the movies. With his weight advantage he was willing to close and grapple, but again he had no idea how to achieve any effective result without hurting his partner.

He decided to set a trap. As they circled, Brynach staying in front to avoid another leg sweep, George dangled his left arm out in front temptingly, and Brynach went to grab it. Instead, George caught his arm in a strong grip, brought his right hand down to join it, and dropped backwards into a roll using his weight and Brynach's momentum to pull him off balance up and over his shoulder onto the floor with a thud.

That caught the attention of some of his neighbors, who paused to watch as he demonstrated what he'd done to Brynach. "This is part of an organized system of martial arts which I have seen but never studied. I can't teach it, I just know of a few gimmicks," he said.

He returned to the sparring. No fight was ever won by defense, so he determined to wade in and take his licks. He didn't want to hurt his partner, so he decided to aim for pinning him flat. Brynach was game and stung him as he dodged, but couldn't move him. George got a hip behind him as they grappled and was able to toss him to the floor.

Hadyn came by to offer criticism. "Brynach, what is it you've learned, now?"

"Big doesn't necessarily mean slow. How do you counter size and strength?"

Hadyn turned to George. "What shall you tell him?"

"Keep a lower center of gravity and make the most of the strength you have, and remember, your center of gravity will keep changing as you finish growing. Counter my weakest positions with your strongest and avoid the rest, or use them against me if you can."

He considered for a moment. "Also, I think you underestimate my reach. You dodge the hand where it is, not where it could be. It's not how long my arm is, it's how long the whole lunge is. As in sword fighting, a pivot of the hips or a lunge changes all the angles and closes the distance more quickly than you're prepared for."

"And what have you learned, then?" Hadyn asked George.

"How very little I know about unarmed combat. I especially have no idea how to inflict serious damage in a real fight. I haven't had a fist fight in earnest since I was a boy. That means I also don't know how to spar without injuring my partner." That last was said with a significant dark look at Hadyn for the uneven match-up.

Hadyn smiled. "Worried you'll break him if you get lucky, is it? You hold your body well, and you have some sensible moves, but you need to build this from the ground up. Brynach, spend the rest of this time with him, on the basics."

George was mollified to realize Hadyn had set the match unevenly not to humiliate him but to give another student an opportunity to practice outside of his weight class with a better chance of success. This isn't a roomful of people waiting to watch you fail, he thought. You're just another student here.

For the next half hour, Brynach showed him some standard positions, moves, and counter moves, and gave him a few kata-like sequences to practice on his own. George thought this might be the first time Brynach got to teach someone who knew less than he did, and he knew from experience how that solidifies one's own understanding. His respect for Hadyn's expertise as an instructor grew.

After a break of a few minutes for water, the group switched to weapons work, shrugging on some chest protection. This time Hadyn matched George with an older man who handed him a blunt saber and bowed.

"I'm Helyan." He was calm and confident.

George introduced himself and warned, "I had some training many years ago, but not in earnest, for real combat."

They sparred for a while. Helyan got in several strikes as George learned in painful detail just how rusty he was, but gradually he fell back into the old groove and began to push the attacks, getting through Helyan's defense for an occasional strike.

They paused for a moment to catch their breath. Helyan said, "You need to press more. I can feel that you're held back by something."

"You're right. I learned this as a sport, not as a fighting skill. There were rules about acceptable moves and, of course, you weren't supposed to try and really hurt your partner."

"Well, there are no rules in battle. Avoid head blows while sparring, for now, but otherwise have at it."

This time, when they resumed, George went on the attack immediately. He pressed Helyan back as they sparred, even though Helyan was able to deflect most of the strikes. George could feel himself getting into the rhythm of it, shutting out distractions and focusing on predicting the next moves of his opponent. Eventually he backed Helyan up to a wall and they stopped.

Helyan conceded. "Much better. What are your thoughts?"

"I can see some of the limits of what I've learned. Many of your successful strikes would've been illegal by my rules, and so I had no planned defenses for them, leaving me completely open. For real combat, I'd like a *main-gauche* of some kind, a weapon for the left hand, or at least something wrapped around my arm."

"You're stronger on offense than defense, it's true. Are you familiar with small sword?"

"I've trained with something similar."

Helyan gave George a light rapier with a blunted point. "Let's see."

George went on the attack, beating the *foible* of Helyan's blade, the front part, with the *forte* of his own, the strong back part, repeatedly. He got in a lucky *prise en fer* that popped the blade out of Helyan's grip, but was unable to duplicate the maneuver. Helyan got in most of the touches.

Hadyn observed the last few engagements. "What do you think, Helyan?"

"He can move to the intermediate group, with some coaching."

Hadyn raised an eyebrow at George expectantly for his commentary.

"I need to get past the sport restraints into real combat usefulness. I've lots of holes in the basics."

"You also need to learn knife fighting, one and two-handed, just for the fundamentals."

George agreed. He eyed the wall of medieval weapons. "I take it that's for the advanced classes?"

Hadyn laughed. "No one's expert in all of those. You'll pick your favorites and learn a bit about defense against many of the others."

"What about weapons at a distance? Bows?"

"Aren't bows part of your hunting training already?"

George considered how to explain. "Our weapons from a distance are completely different, and I'm told they won't work here."

Hadyn said, "I'll set you at shooting practice next time, if you're still here."

The training session was winding down. The participants removed their protective gear and started to don the clothing they had discarded. George shook Helyan's hand and thanked him, making a point of seeking out young Brynach and doing the same.

Everything hurt. His muscles were sore from the unaccustomed exercise, and there would be plenty of bruises soon.

He checked his watch. There should be time to bathe before the gathering for Iolo.

~

As George entered the baths, he discovered Eurig once again relaxing in solitary possession of the soaking pool. He joined him quickly, sighing appreciatively as the hot water began to do its work.

Eurig looked over his latest collection of rising bruises. "Did you badly irritate someone, or do I recognize souvenirs from Hadyn? I remember the look from when I used to train."

"It's always sobering to confirm how little you actually know. I'm useless as a warrior here, though I suppose that can be fixed. It's just that our ways are so different."

"You're thinking of guns, aren't you?" At George's surprised look, he continued. "Yes, we do know about them, and there've been some enterprising trials, but they don't work here. Ceridwen supervised most of the experiments—you might want to speak to her about her conclusions."

George shook his head. "It's not just that guns have replaced many of your weapons, it's that we don't have much of a warrior culture anymore. Except for our professional soldiers," he said. "I know how to shoot, though many of us don't, but I don't know much about knife fighting or unarmed combat, and that's still as basic a need as ever."

He chuckled ruefully. "There's an old Persian saying about training a man to ride, shoot, and speak the truth. I figured I was done with that, but here it turns out I must go to school again, to reclaim the honor." After a pause, he said, "But I must say it feels good, feels real. We've buried so much of that in our world, pretending we've somehow grown beyond it."

Eurig nodded. "It's good to do the work you feel born for. Many of my kind try on one thing after another, and are never satisfied. We live long, but some can waste the whole time never settling and growing deep roots.

"My Teg and I have been together all our lives, and I wouldn't have it any other way. It's not that we don't grow and change, it's that we do it together and grow into each other at the same time. It's hard to explain the worth of that to these youngsters."

Envying that lifelong partnership, George changed the subject. "Can you tell me what will happen this evening for Iolo? Where and when?"

"They'll take him down to the manor gates and the procession will go north from there to Daear Llosg, the Burnt Ground, where all roads meet. It's not far, but most will ride, and there will be some carriages. We'll assemble at the south curtain wall gate. Would you care to ride with us?"

"Thanks, that's most kind of you."

"I'll knock on your door when we're ready to come down, in a few minutes."

Back in his room as George dressed, he debated adding the borrowed saber to his robes. If I put it on and no one else is wearing a sword, I can always take it off and hang it on a hook in that first room with the weapons on the walls and reclaim it later.

When he opened his door to Eurig's knock, he was introduced to Tegwen in the corridor. She was a comfortable sort, with gray hair and plump cheeks, and she looked as if no crisis could ever disturb her. Her brown brocaded skirt was split for riding. George bowed over her hand, and she smiled at him approvingly.

"Such manners," she said to Eurig, "and so young." George sighed to himself.

Eurig was resplendent in a quiet way in brown and gold, and was wearing a heavy saber. He looked over George's clothing and nodded, "You'll do fine."

CHAPTER 11

As they mounted up at the stables, George saw Isolda waiting atop a large open carriage quickly filling with her father and several of the kennel staff he recognized. Others were piling in as he watched. They were uniformly attired in more formal clothing than he had seen before, with dark red coats and weskits and buckskin breeches. Some had families with them, the wives and daughters in dark red skirts. These lutins had probably known Iolo all their lives, George realized, and now he was gone.

A few lutins were mounted, but there were more than could fit in one carriage, and he saw that the other drivers were not lutins. Isolda showed no discomfort among her peers, and George nodded encouragingly at her across the distance, bringing a smile to her face.

He walked Mosby over to Eurig and Tegwen, and they led him to a place in the procession that was forming. At the head were Gwyn and Creiddylad, Rhys and Rhian, with Idris and others following. A group of guards rode close behind.

Next came Ceridwen and a low open wagon carrying Iolo's body encased in a decorated wooden coffin. Eurig's group formed up behind them. As they moved slowly down to the main gates, George looked back and saw the long tail of the procession behind them, a mix of riders and carriages.

At the gates, there was another, smaller, group waiting to join them. Eurig leaned over to him, "People from town, come to pay their respects." George spotted Angharad among them, on a coal-black horse with a compact well-muscled frame. She was dressed in gray, and her auburn hair was the only bit of color about her. She nodded at him as their eyes met.

The two groups merged and turned left up the road to the north. After clearing the palisade of the manor, the road passed through ever denser woods on both sides, and continued to ascend the slope of the Blue Ridge obliquely as it went.

As they rode, at a walk, George realized they were headed in the general direction of the way he had pointed out earlier in the day, and he tried to locate it again. He was startled to realize that the road seemed to be headed precisely there. He could see that Idris was on the alert; perhaps Ceridwen had told him.

Less than a mile from the end of the palisade the road widened out into an open meadow of several acres with a few patches of bare rock exposed. The main road continued north, but there was a footpath leading down from a gap in the ridge above them, running alongside a small stream. Tegwen, on his right, said, "Crossroads, water, fire, stone, woods. It's a suitable sacred place." The words caught his attention and he looked down at her, startled to see a saber of her own fixed to her saddle on the left.

There was a bier waiting in front of a prepared pyre of criss-crossed logs, and Iolo's body was brought there for final farewells. The procession pulled off to the side to allow enough room for everyone to assemble.

George excused himself and rode over to Idris. "Did Ceridwen tell you? I think that way is right over there," facing upslope and pointing to the right.

"Yes, that's why we have so many guards. She thought it might be focused in this spot. Is it open?"

"How would I know? It seems like all the others at the moment."

"Tell me immediately if it changes. Only you and Gwyn can see it well, and he's occupied with other responsibilities."

He let a look of frustration cross his face. "I don't believe this is coincidence. What if someone killed Iolo, knowing we'd bring him here, where we're all gathered together, outside our defenses? I don't like this at all and advised Gwyn not to come."

He shook his head. "He wouldn't take the prudent course."

He turned and positioned several of the guards between the bier and the place George identified, and more of them near Gwyn, but he was hampered by the need to stay clear of the ceremony itself.

George put himself mentally on guard, trying to maintain a sense of the way at all times, like listening for a particular background noise. He positioned himself at the back of the crowd around the bier, his back to the dormant way, and a good downslope view in front of him.

The individual visits to the bier gradually lessened, and Gwyn nudged his horse forward to stand beside it.

"Today we make our farewells to Iolo ap Huw, foully slain. I knew him all his life and his father before him. None was ever so worthy as he to hunt the Cŵn Annwn. He will be sorely missed, and I vow to find his killer and bring him to justice." He gestured, and several of the guard bent to lift the coffin to the pyre while Gwyn drew his horse aside.

In that moment when all eyes were on Gwyn, George felt a change of atmosphere, as though a window had been opened. He whirled Mosby about and saw a mounted archer appearing out of thin air just behind him, already drawing on Gwyn. He shouted. Idris, who had been keeping an eye on him, had began to yell at the guards, but it was all taking much too much time.

George threw his right rein to his left hand and closed his right hand on the lower edge of his flowing robes. He flung up his arm with the heavy satin widespread, thinking to block the archer's view. The arrow went right through the material, but he hoped there'd been enough resistance to change its course.

He didn't turn to see what happened but dropped the robe and drew his saber awkwardly, launching Mosby up the hill against the lighter horse and rider. Mosby took his intent and, after a brief gray passage, the upslope meadow vanished around them and they barreled into the other horse, knocking him over.

Around them three riders stood in an open field on a river bottom. They were startled at the crash of the archer's horse and George's unexpected appearance, but drew their swords and made for him.

I am in so much trouble, George thought distantly, but his blood was up and he was already looking for a target. He discounted the archer crushed to the ground and pushed Mosby after the nearest approaching rider. I'll have a better chance if I can take them one by one, he thought.

Time slowed as the two of them neared each other. George reflected on his own advantages of weight and height versus his opponent's probable experience. The only way this is going to work is if I go berserk on him and give him no time to realize my own lack of skill.

He yelled like a banshee and brought his saber forward like every charge of the heavy cavalry scene he'd ever seen. He bore down on his opponent bearing to the right and parried his blow, then struck him from behind as he passed. The man wove in his saddle, clearly injured, and George spun Mosby around in a loose circle at a canter to focus on the other two.

They had taken the opportunity to bunch together and began an approach at a slow trot. Oh, well, George thought, it was too much to hope that I could do that again. He brought Mosby back to a gallop and aimed for the same angle of attack, from his own right, since he would only be more awkward from the other side.

The outer rider split away as he got closer, to get him from behind, but George put it out of his mind and focused on the one in front of him. An explosion of sound behind him made him break off, and as he swerved, he saw that Gwyn had appeared and was taking on the second rider.

George curved Mosby around and returned to his initial target, only to see that he had turned and was galloping swiftly away down the field.

Gwyn's opponent did the same. George knew Mosby couldn't catch them, but looked at Gwyn hopefully.

"No, we can't stay. They're the ones holding this way open, and eventually they'll remember that. We must leave or be trapped here."

George wasn't ready to stop. "Who are they? Can't we learn anything from these?" gesturing at the archer still trying to free himself and the one he had wounded, now sitting dazed on the ground having fallen from his horse.

"I've seen all I need to. Come with me now."

George subdued himself to Gwyn's urgency. With Gwyn beside him, he passed through the way again.

Things had changed back in the mountain meadow. The guards were drawn up in formation surrounding the way and prepared for some sort of breakthrough, and the armed guests had drawn swords and moved in front of the non-combatants.

Idris cantered up to Gwyn in a fury. "You should've waited for us to join you."

George had cooled off enough to realize what Gwyn had risked coming after him that way. Perhaps no one else could have seen the way to follow them.

He bowed to him in the saddle. "Thank you for saving my life," he said.

"And I thank you, for deflecting that arrow and pursuing the enemy. You did well, for a man in his first sword fight."

"I was lucky," he said. And besides, it was exhilarating, he thought. The reaction might hit later, but it would be worth it.

His blood pumping, he smiled fiercely at Gwyn. "I'll take that job."

Gwyn returned the smile, and they trotted down the slope together.

With the guards firmly in place before the way exit, and the way dormant to George's senses, the remainder of the ceremony went smoothly. Iolo's body on its pyre was consigned to the flames, and the procession returned to the manor gate. George rejoined Eurig and Tegwen on the ride back and told them what had happened in detail, buoyed by his success.

Friends from village and manor stood about in parting conversations, those who weren't coming up to the manor for dinner. While George waited for the crowd to clear, he looked for and located the guest's way that Ceridwen had described. A path split off from the main road to a cul-de-sac, and the way was clearly there.

He turned to Eurig and asked, "What happens when someone using a way is confronted by someone going in the opposite direction?"

"It's not a problem. Ceridwen once explained to me that a way's like a tunnel that allows smaller tunnels to pass through. There are size limits to each way, so if one tunnel in use is as large as possible, perhaps a second tunnel can't come into existence, but I don't know anyone who's done the experiment. Ask…"

"Ask Ceridwen. Yes, I get it."

Eurig smiled. "Well, that's her job, isn't it?"

The remnants of the procession entered the yard and began to disperse. George walked over to the carriage that held Ives and his kennel lads. "Could I speak with you a moment, Master Ives?"

He dismounted and Ives walked off to the side with him. "You've decided to do it," he said, looking at George's face, still flushed with excitement.

"Yes, and I'll need all your guidance not to be an unnecessarily disruptive force. I may make changes, but they must be done deliberately, not from ignorance. Can I count on your help?"

"Of course. Iolo would've wanted that."

"I've committed myself for the great hunt, not beyond, and one of the first things I must keep in mind is any transition afterward. I don't yet know what Gwyn may want, but I'd like to start to place others as junior huntsmen and whippers-in, to ride with me and to grow into the positions, at least eventually if not right away. I haven't seen her yet with hounds, but I believe Rhian may be one such candidate and I plan to find out. Do you see any problem with that?"

"She works with the hounds all the time. If Gwyn will permit it, that would be a good idea, for when she's older."

"I'll ask Gwyn's permission, and speak to Rhian."

He continued, "What time tomorrow would you like to see me at kennels, to begin my instruction about Iolo's routines?"

"The kennel lads start at dawn, and Iolo would come before breakfast to ensure all was well, then return to start his work after breakfast. He was usually free in the afternoons."

"I'll need to do something about clothing, and I have plans for weapons training in the afternoon, but otherwise that should work well. I'll see you after breakfast in the morning."

~

George walked to the council room door off the great hall. Dinner was being set up, but not yet ready.

He stuck his head in the open doorway, saw Gwyn alone, and knocked on the door. "May I speak with you for a moment, sir?"

Gwyn nodded him in.

"Some procedural matters… How do I acquire things like work and hunt clothes or other small items that I need?"

"Ifor Moel, whom you met at Iolo's death, is our steward. I'll ask him to meet with you to find out your immediate requirements."

"Once I get pen and paper, I'll need to send another note to my grandfather, without urgency this time. Is that something I should ask Idris about?"

"Yes, he'll arrange connections with the human world for you."

George paused while he considered how to ask without seeming rude, and just spit it out. "Please forgive me, but why isn't there any huntsman in waiting for Iolo, no backup?"

Gwyn looked pained. "We simply didn't envision the need. It sounds foolish now, but Iolo had been hunting the hounds for so long, we couldn't imagine training someone for a role they'd never get to play."

"I'd like to start changing that. I'd like to begin training novice huntsmen and perhaps other staff, for when I leave."

Gwyn nodded.

George said, "I think Rhian's interested. If so, may I begin with her?"

"Certainly," Gwyn said. "But you hesitate. What is it?"

"It seems to me that Iolo was killed to injure you, to prevent the great hunt. If so, then by taking the job I've painted a target on my own back. If they think I can do the great hunt, then they'll also want to eliminate me."

He continued. "I'm alright with that. In fact, if I can get them to aim at me, we may be able to expose them better. I think I can hold their attention on me, but there's a chance that any trainees may also be at risk, as potential threats."

Gwyn said, deliberately, "Rhian's very dear to me, but she's almost a woman and must make her own choices. If she wishes to do this, after your warning, then please coordinate with Ceridwen and Ifor Moel who between them govern much of her education."

"One last question for now, sir. How long do I have to train, that is, when do we next hunt?"

"Say, for deer, a week hence on Tuesday, and thereafter following the usual schedule."

"Alright, then," George said. One week to find out how to hunt this pack, in front of guests who didn't all wish them well. What have I taken on?

~

Gwyn returned to his speculations about the way at Daear Llosg after George left. The way had no sense about it of distance, as many of them did, and he couldn't tell just from that where it had led to. The sun's position was unchanged while he was there—by habit, that was the first thing he checked. So it must be here, in this new world. He recognized the trees and other vegetation, so it mustn't be too far away, south or north, but there was little else he could use to pin down the location. Certainly he didn't recognize it, and he had traveled everywhere in his own domain.

He considered returning there tomorrow through the way, if it was still there and still open to him, but that would be horribly imprudent. If the way closed and no other one was found, he might find himself hundreds of miles from home just two weeks before the great hunt, and that couldn't be risked.

Who was this enemy who used the ways as a fundamental tool for his attack? Way-finders were always more common in his bloodline than in others, and he knew them all. Maybe not, he thought.

George was a new player. How did George sense this way? When Ceridwen had rushed in to tell him about his discoveries earlier, he was disinclined to believe her. After all, he couldn't sense it, from here, and George's blood could only be a diluted reflection of his own. But he knew now that couldn't really be so—the way was there, and George had located it.

Oh, he didn't doubt George was his descendant, but what was his father? This tale of Corniad Traherne sounded like the kind of game Cernunnos might design, but he didn't think George was a conscious agent, more like a piece Cernunnos had created and put into play to do what he could. That he blended both his own and Cernunnos's blood was just the sort of twist he would enjoy.

Could he be huntsman for the great hunt? If he can handle the hounds, he'll still have to handle the great hunt itself, with its ways and its quarry, and he's never even seen it before. Iolo wasn't a way-finder, and Cernunnos didn't move through him. So why has Cernunnos presented me with this new player, so very different, and why now?

He hasn't taken an active hand since the downfall of Arawn and the resettlement of Annwn here in this new world, away from the political strife of the old. Arawn lost his place because he proved himself unworthy, and Cernunnos himself brought him down. At least, that's how I see it, Gwyn thought. My father would disagree.

My own conscience is hardly clean, he thought, shying away from exploring the great void where his wrath and frustration caused him to so betray himself when he held his enemies in captivity. He thought he was bearing his own righteous punishment, with the struggles on Nos Galan Mai, but maybe Cernunnos felt differently, maybe he had proven himself unworthy, too, and it was just taking a while for the hammer to fall.

Was George here as a help in his time of trouble, or as a replacement?

CHAPTER 12

George emerged from the council room to discover the pre-dinner crowd beginning to assemble in the front rooms. He headed directly across the great hall to a large library and music room which was the counterpart of the council room on the other side of the house. On the right, the doorway led to the hunting room with its weapons at the back of the manor, but here it was all wooden shelves, hanging instruments, and carpets on the floor. The shared wall with the great hall was lined with simple upright chairs for musicians, and the rest of the room sported comfortable armchairs and tables for talking or listening.

Not many people were in the room yet. He spotted Rhian with Rhys and walked over to them.

Rhian gripped his arm, "Everyone says you're going to stay for the great hunt. Did you really save my foster-father and then charge through the way and kill several soldiers?"

Startled, he said. "Not exactly. I just got carried away and had a brief encounter, after which Gwyn arrived and rescued me. Where did you hear all this?"

Rhys said, "Eurig's been telling your tale, and it grows with each retelling."

"Oh, no." He shook his head ruefully. "Well, nothing I can do about it now. Rhian, could I speak with you for a moment?"

"Shall I leave?" Rhys asked.

"Maybe you should hear this, too. I've spoken with Gwyn, and he's given me permission to begin training novice huntsmen for when I have to leave again. I'll put the question to you first, Rhys. I understand you've been whipping-in for Iolo. Are you interested in learning to be huntsman?"

"I will if I must, but I'd rather learn to govern, like my foster-father. My heart wouldn't be in it."

"I thought that might be so. Rhian," he said, smiling down at her eager face, "last night you mentioned a wish. Is that still true?"

"Oh, yes!"

"It would mean long hours and hard work, and will take some time away from your other studies."

"I can do that."

"Pay attention. Those who killed Iolo may try for me, and for any trainees. There's real danger here. Gwyn said you could make your own choice, though I have misgivings about it."

Rhys looked down at his little sister. "Rhian, I fear for your safety. It's your choice, but if you do this I insist you learn more serious fighting skills."

"Yes, I will," she said earnestly. "And yes, I want to do this, very much."

"Alright, then. I'll see you at kennels, mounted, immediately after breakfast."

"There you are." A voice hailed them from across the room as a tall man with light brown hair strode briskly over. He looked to be about George's age. "I know those robes, don't I?" he said, with a smile.

"George, this is our cousin Rhodri who was gracious enough to lend you clothing last night. Without his knowledge." Rhys turned to Rhodri. "Sorry, cousin, there was nothing else to fit him. This is our newly found kinsman, George Talbot Traherne."

George extended the right half of the robe as he had in the meadow to show the arrow hole. "And just see what a mess I've made. Very sorry."

"Well, you'll just have to keep them, then. I never did like such a somber color anyway." And indeed he was dressed in vivid robes himself, purple with swirls of gold and scarlet.

Rhodri continued, "I heard about the excitement at the burning ground. Welcome, kinsman. You seem to have arrived just in time to be useful. Always the best way. And speaking of ways, I understand you've learned some interesting things. There's to be a meeting after dinner this evening to explore the topic, Gwyn tells me."

As they stood around chatting, waiting for dinner, George was taken with the easy family ways of his companions. It struck him that he was part of the same family, that they really were kinsmen. With Rhodri, someone his own age, he felt less like a visiting uncle and more like a brother. As an only child raised by grandparents, it was a very odd sensation to be adopted like this. Mustn't get too used to it, he thought. They have their own lives to lead, and so will I, when I return.

~

Rhian could scarcely focus on Rhodri's banter with her brother and George for all the excitement buzzing in her head. It was finally going to happen. Her cousin had persuaded Gwyn to let her understudy as huntsman. And Gwyn let her join the council, too. He could hardly resume throwing her out again now.

Don't get too carried away, she told herself sternly. They may be treating you like a grown-up, but you're a very junior one. Now you can find yourself in a whole different kind of trouble, maybe get yourself killed. You'll be responsible for hounds, and they can be hurt or killed, too.

This sobered her.

The huntsman has the welfare of the pack, the staff, and the field following as his responsibility, she thought. People do get killed, hunting. You're asking to take that on, too. It's not just about fun with the hounds.

She looked up at George. What sort of leader will he be? I wish I'd seen him bringing the hounds back, and him not knowing how to speak to them. You know, I'm glad I'll have a mentor to show me what to do. It seems so easy and wonderful when you dream about it, but that's a child's dream. She stood straighter. I'm not a child any more.

What'll happen after the great hunt? Will I be expected to carry on as huntsman after George? There was a thought to made her stomach clench. Better do my best to learn while I can.

What will self-defense training be like? I'll have to talk to Hadyn.

Wait till Isolda hears about this.

~

Tonight, more people were at dinner, and Rhodri joined the family group on the dais, seating himself between George and Rhian. He kept up a running commentary on the notables in the hall.

"Have you met my lady's guests?" he asked, *sotto voce*, nodding his head at Creiddylad in reply to her nod of recognition. "That bodyguard of hers, the famous Mederei, is a stunner, but rumor has it that they are mutually otherwise engaged." Rhys, on George's other side, choked on his wine and Rhian's eyes widened.

"I've never liked the look of that Madog fellow," he continued. "Some permanent guest of hers. He doesn't say much but he's always around, watching. I've heard he lives over here somewhere, but not as part of Gwyn's court. Why is that, do you suppose? Where does he go when she leaves? Ceridwen sits down there probing him but I don't think she learns much."

"If Gwyn thinks he's a threat, why does he invite him?"

"He's Creiddylad's guest, and Gwyn forbids her little. Besides, if he's an enemy, better to keep him close."

George encouraged him. "What else can you tell me? Who are the other players and what are the factions?"

"Oh, except for Creiddylad it's pretty friendly right now. Those are almost all locals, out there, and they're mostly a good sort, more worried about marriage schemes and farming than treason. Wait until the big players arrive in the next few days."

"What will that be like? I have to, well, debut in a week as huntsman."

"They won't approve, for starters. They don't like change, and they don't much care for humans, however willingly Gwyn may acknowledge your descent. Most think it wrong to dilute the blood; they think it's a weakness on his part that they can exploit.

"It'll be interesting to see whether their concern for the continuation of the hunt outweighs their distaste for the proposed huntsman. After all, what choice will they have? Many would like to see Gwyn embarrassed, as a setback to the growth of his power, but that doesn't mean they want to see this realm lost to him and all their holdings put at risk. They're not prepared for that."

"Somebody is," George said, "or Iolo would still be alive."

"Very true. Don't forget you have active enemies already in place. They couldn't have anticipated your presence disrupting their plans. If you can hunt the hounds, then you must be eliminated, too, or Iolo's murder will have been pointless."

He looked directly at George. "They may wait to see if you'll fail, first, before moving against you. I would. Or they may just take the simple route and dispose of you anyway, to return to the original plan. And, incidentally, to demonstrate that Gwyn can't protect his own people."

"If there's an emergency, who can I rely on?"

"Of these here, Idris and Ceridwen. Don't trust Creiddylad—guard your tongue and your person from her and hers. If you're caught outside the grounds," he looked over the guests, "Eurig, there, is a good choice. His lands are the first large settlement to the north beyond Daear Llosg. Everyone discounts him as past his prime and out of circulation, but he likes it that way, encourages it. He's unquestionably loyal, cunning as a badger, and well prepared. He also clearly approves of you, which will count in your favor with many of the others."

Idris leaned over Rhys and passed the word: there would be a meeting after dinner.

The same group was gathered around the council table as the night before, with the addition of Rhodri.

Gwyn started by saying, "If anyone doesn't already know, let me say that my great-grandson George has agreed to hunt the hounds for us on Nos Galan Gaeaf. The first public hunt will be in one week's time."

He asked George to recount the events on Daear Llosg, and followed up with his own actions. "These were unmarked warriors. They carried no colors, and I didn't recognize them. The arrows were fletched in the old style." He reached behind his seat and tossed an arrow onto the table for all to look at, the one that had missed him. George noted the bright yellow fletching. "The other end of the way must be based locally—it was the same time of day and weather."

Ceridwen asked, "What's been done to shut this way?"

"Idris has posted guards around it for tonight," Gwyn said. "I want George, Rhodri, and you with me there at mid-morning tomorrow."

George leaned toward Rhodri and muttered, "I'll be in kennels. Can you fetch me for this?" Rhodri nodded.

Creiddylad spoke up. "Shall I attend, brother?"

"I don't know why this should interest you, sister, but you must do as you please."

"I wonder why you are taking your kinsman away from his kennel duties, brother. He'll need all his time to prepare."

Because I can see the ways, thought George, but something cautioned him against saying anything about it. He noted that she considered him her brother's kinsman, not her own.

Gwyn replied smoothly, "Because I wish it, sister."

Ceridwen reported the results of interviews with the guards, now that they had all checked in. Unsurprisingly, there was simply too much gate traffic to provide any useful information.

"And the spell-stick?" asked Gwyn.

"Frustratingly anonymous, my lord. Some clues in the writing make me think it isn't local. We tend to keep older words longer here, as colonies do, and where we'd use one word, a more modern one's been substituted. Anything to add, my lady?" she asked Creiddylad.

"No, I could do nothing with it."

After a few more questions, Gwyn dismissed them, and the meeting started to break up.

After Creiddylad left the room, George turned to Rhodri at the table. "I clearly need more information about this whole 'way' business, and everyone tells me you're the expert. Can we spend some time on this, and soon?"

"Let's do it tomorrow, with whatever Gwyn has planned. It's good you said nothing about it in front of Creiddylad. Keep it a secret as long as possible."

As he re-entered the great hall, George felt a touch at his elbow and turned to discover Ifor Moel standing behind him with a handful of papers.

"My lord Gwyn has asked me to provide for your needs while you're here. May we go to my office to discuss it?"

He led the way outside to a stone building next to Ceridwen's. A central area with seating was surrounded by several rooms set up as offices. Ifor said, "Many of the people who administer Gwyn's lands take a room here, for offices, except for those like Iolo or Ceridwen who need their own elsewhere. The important records are kept in Gwyn's council room, but all the day-to-day material's here."

He opened the door of the first room on the right. Shelves lined the walls and chests were piled high at the far end. At Ifor's gesture, George took a seat in front of a heavy wooden desk. "The second floor's used for storage, but I fear we're filling the place up."

Ifor hauled a ledger down and opened it at the desk. Dipping a pen in ink, he started to make notes on a piece of paper.

"Iolo's customary expenses included the maintenance of his horses. Your own horse will of course be supported, but you'll need at least two more."

"So," he continued, "you should take over Iolo's three horses for now. Look them over and see if they suit you."

He paused to make a few notes.

"Then there's the matter of livery and other clothing. Iolo's coats won't fit you but perhaps the shirts can be adapted for work. Certainly you'll need appropriate clothing for hunting immediately, and you'll need work clothing for the kennels, evening clothing, and ordinary wear. Boots and shoes, too. And all of this as quickly as possible, since you must be properly clad when the public hunting resumes in a week."

He rubbed his chin. "I'll ask Olwen to send someone to measure you and go through Iolo's clothing to rescue anything suitable. She can oversee most of the work you need, but for the footwear and outer garments you'd best see Mostyn in the village, as soon as possible. You'll find him a few shops up from the inn. Just tell him it's Gwyn's request and let him guide you."

"I don't quite understand. Don't Iolo's horses and goods go to his family?"

"Iolo has no recent family and left no instructions. In such cases we would let his friends choose keepsakes and disperse or store the rest, but Gwyn has asked that we leave his house alone until after the great hunt. I suppose he envisions installing Iolo's permanent replacement there.

"Now, for the kennels themselves. Ives will go over kennel budgets with you and do most of that. You can take what you need from the armory, but I don't think our armor will fit you and you won't be here long enough for that to become an issue. Ask Hadyn—you've met him?—what he suggests as a temporary measure for protection."

"One more thing," Ifor continued. "Normally we'd fee a huntsman quarterly, but Gwyn has asked me to give you this now, as a courtesy to a kinsman." He unlocked a drawer and took out a small leather pouch which he handed to George. "I recommend you carry a bit of this around and secure the remainder."

George took the pouch without opening it and slid it into a pocket.

"Thanks for all your help," he said.

"I suggested to Gwyn that you could also use the services of Iolo's man, Alun, while you were here, and Gwyn agreed. I'll have him seek you out in the morning."

"How are people like Ives and Alun paid?"

"My office sees to the fees of the kennel staff. Private servants are paid by their employers, but Alun's been taken care of until after the great hunt. Iolo's replacement may bring a man of his own, of course."

"What would happen to Alun then?"

"I imagine we can find him another position somewhere." Too bad for him, George thought. I wonder how long he's held that job? Has he always been a servant?

Well, no point making waves until I understand how all this works.

It's good to get some pocket money, but what exactly am I to Gwyn, retainer or kin? How much difference is there?

CHAPTER 13

The chime on George's pocket watch woke him well before breakfast, and he headed down for a quick bite. He set out for the kennels early to see if he could begin looking through Iolo's office before the appointed time with Ives.

As he reached the kennel gates, a man approached him. "You're the new huntsman, then?" he asked. At George's nod, he continued. "I'm Alun. Ifor Moel sent me to make myself useful to you."

"I'm glad to meet you, Alun, and grateful for all the help you can give me. Let me first offer my condolences on the death of Iolo."

Alun nodded soberly. "How can I help you?"

"Well, what were your usual duties for Iolo?"

"Breakfasts and simple meals. Keeping the house in order—he wouldn't let me tidy his office there." He nodded with his head in the direction of the huntsman's office. "Errands of all kinds."

"Do you live at Iolo's house, then?"

"Indeed, and have these last thirty-five years, since I was a lad."

"I don't know what'll happen after the great hunt, but let's keep everything the way it was until then, anyway. I'll look to you to let me know if I'm doing something wrong or asking for something unusual, yes?"

"As you say."

"Please come with me to the huntsman's office. I'll want to write a note to my grandfather, and you'll need to give that to Idris for delivery. You can help coordinate the rest of my schedule while we're at it."

They entered at the kennel gate. George noted that Alun kept to the middle as they crossed between the pens, but was more prudent than scared of the hounds. He looked in at Ives's usual place and found him busy with the kennel-men.

"No hurry, Master Ives. Alun and I will be in the huntsman's office whenever you're ready."

They walked over to the office.

George said to Alun, "I seem to have taken on multiple responsibilities for the next two weeks, and they're bound to conflict with each other, especially since one of them, the huntsman's job, is already a full-time activity. I'll wait till Ives arrives so we can both hear about my huntsman tasks. Did you and Ives coordinate this way for Iolo?"

"No, just helping with his domestic needs, it was."

"Do you mind my broadening your tasks, in areas other than hunting?"

"That would be interesting." Alun was unwaveringly polite and George couldn't yet tell when he was being sincere. He decided to assume he meant what he said.

"Alright, then. First, where I come from we don't use swords. I must become decent at it as soon as possible, and I want to train with Hadyn's men in the mid-afternoon session whenever I can. My most important job may be the great hunt, but I need to stay alive to do it.

"Second, I need clothes. I've been put in Edern's room in the manor but I came with almost nothing but what you see, and it doesn't seem like I'm going to be able to borrow clothes easily. Ifor Moel was to have someone go through Iolo's looser garments to see if there's anything I can use, but otherwise I'll need ordinary clothing, hunt clothing, and enough fancy clothing not to embarrass myself while I'm here. I gather some of the clothing's made here, at the manor, and for some I must visit the village, someone named Mostyn."

He plucked at his hunt coat. "I can't keep wearing the clothes I came in for long, so I'll need your help to sort that out as quickly as possible, and to tell me what's appropriate attire. Right now, my borrowed robes have an arrow hole in them. How do I get that repaired? And I'm very tired of wearing these boots all day.

"Third, Gwyn and Idris have me doing some other tasks for them. I'll be interrupted this morning for one of them which will take me away for a couple of hours. I expect that could happen again unpredictably. I may need you to relay messages for me when I have disruptions like that. If people can't find me, it would help if they could come to you for my schedule.

"Last, I want to set up some study time with Ceridwen. I don't know yet if that will be scheduled or irregular, but I'll keep you posted. Will all this work for you?"

"Easy enough it is."

"Great, that will be a big help. Give me a moment while I put together the note to my grandfather."

George found paper and pen on the desk.

Grandfather,

Your father-in-law conveys his respects to you and grandmother. He has requested my assistance in a family matter, and I have accepted. My services are expected to end sometime in the first week of November.

This is, of course, unplanned but it's not untimely. Sam Littleton, my COO, is perfectly capable of running things. Please offer my apologies and tell him that a family emergency has called me out of the country for two to three weeks, and I'll let him know as soon as possible when I'll be returning. Ask him to run the place as if it were his own in my absence; I promise not to second-guess him when I return. To explain why he can't reach me by email, tell him it seemed the best way to give him truly free rein.

Can you help Bud get whatever he needs, and perhaps take in my dogs if necessary?

Love,

George

He folded it and wrote his grandfather's name on the outside. He gave it to Alun and said, "Please get this to Idris and ask him to see that my grandfather receives it. No special speed's required."

Alun tucked it away in a pocket.

George looked at the desk with an eye to bringing pen and paper to the desk in his room. "Alun, I've seen some people use fountain pens, the ones with an internal ink reservoir. Are they common here? How can I get one, ink, too, to use both here and in my room? I'll need paper, too."

"I'll find you what you need."

"A small notebook for a pocket would be very useful, too. How does this work? Do I give you money for these things, or does Ifor Moel?"

"You have, Iolo had, a small amount for food and other items. I keep a list, and he refilled it at need, paying whatever part was personal himself. The rest, with the list, goes to Ifor Moel. I'll let you know if we're running low."

"I'll make time for the trip to Mostyn in the village today, if I can, after lunch. Can you come with me? Um, do you have a horse?"

"Indeed I do. I'll look for you then."

With a knock on the open door a middle-aged woman came in with a bundle of clothing.

"I'm Olwen and I thought I better see to this task myself." He stood up to greet her and she looked him over. "My, there's broad you are."

"Thanks for making the time for this, Mistress Olwen."

"Happy to help. Alun," she said, "I brought these things of Iolo's to try, from the pile of possibles you put together."

She dumped the clothes on a chair and held a shirt against George's back to check for likely fit.

"Good. Some of these will do. Let me take your measurements properly and Alun and I can sort this out for you."

As he stood there in his shirtsleeves with arms outstretched, Olwen measuring, and Alun writing down whatever she said, in walked Ives, with Rhian on his heels.

Ives laughed. "It's good to see you getting something done, then."

George explained the upcoming morning's interruption and his hopes for fitting in some time in his daily schedule for training.

"I'd like you and Alun to coordinate. Hunting has the highest priority, and he'll help with everything else. Can you start by telling me what Iolo's daily work was like?"

"Iolo would come before breakfast to check on the hounds as they were released into their yards, then back home for breakfast. After that, we either walked hounds or prepared the pack for hunting, during the season."

"What's the hunting schedule?"

"Tuesday, Thursday, Saturday, with adjustments for the special events."

"Gwyn told me to take the pack out in public a week from tomorrow, for deer. We should keep to a hunting schedule for this week, but only for staff. Do you normally take out just the one pack, or do you have multiple packs, as some hunts alternate a bitch or dog pack?"

"We keep a single pack going and hold back just the unfit or young ones. Our busiest period runs to the great hunt, when we're filled with guests who must be entertained. After that it slacks off a bit until we end the season in the spring, to let the deer raise their young in peace, or until deep snow shuts it down."

"I don't understand how there can possibly be enough game to support all this hunting in territory close enough to reach in an hour," George said.

"We try not to hunt more than three miles away from kennels. That means it's an hour to get there, two to four hours hunting, and an hour to return. For special events, we can put the hounds in wagons and make a day of it. We have four directions and multiple terrains to choose from, so as long as we don't run the same spot more than once a week it works. After all, we're not hunting primarily for the table, and there's no shortage of deer."

"So that's a four mile travel radius, pushed out by maybe five more miles in a hunting loop, so perhaps a nine mile radius. An oval, yes? Or do you cross the mountain?"

"No. It's a lopsided circle, with the ridge line as the western edge."

"Is there a map of the territories? Something with names I can study?"

Ives walked over to a large map hanging on the wall. "Here's where we're scheduled to hunt for the next few days." He pointed out four spots, and George wrote down the names.

"Where will the great hunt be held?"

"It'll start from the bridge at the center of the village, but the path can't be predicted. The quarry's unidentified, at least initially, and the ways are open."

"What?" George said.

"On that night, the hounds can follow wherever they wish. Sometimes the quarry attempts to escape using a way, but that's no barrier. Sometimes he's already distant and a way must be used to reach him. We don't know how it will go, but the hounds know."

George made a note to himself to find out more later, in detail.

Changing the subject, he said, "I've asked Rhian to join us for hound walking and hunting as a junior huntsman. I want her to ride in my pocket, as we say, and learn everything she can." Turning to her, "I'll want to hear a quiet running commentary from you naming the hounds to me and telling me whatever else you think is useful. I'll explain what I'm doing, and why. We don't have time to do this the traditional way, with silent observation and long apprenticeship."

She nodded.

"Do you have enough horses to use them every day for this? And that reminds me, Ives. Ifor Moel told me to use Iolo's horses, three of them. Could someone show them to me?"

"I'll have Isolda do that. The gray won't be up to your weight. Rhian, you could use that one."

She said, "That would give me enough."

"Alright, I'll use Mosby today and tomorrow. Please ask Isolda to show me the horses as soon as she can."

He continued, "Now for this morning's tasks. Where do you walk the hounds? Who comes along?"

"We typically walk them out, on horseback, about three miles each way. We stay to the roads as much as possible and then find a field where we can take them for a drink or otherwise exercise them as a pack, before returning. We should start soon—shall I have Owen the Leash get his men together?"

"Ah. Please explain to me what their role is. What Owen said led me to think that he's there to protect the followers, not keep the pack together. Is that right?"

"Yes."

"What exactly is everyone afraid of with this pack? Do they actually threaten the followers?"

"They only hunt man at the great hunt but, you know, they're not friendly to everyone and no one wants to take a chance. There are stories…"

"If we had more staff like Rhian and Rhys, would we be able to handle them like any other pack of hounds?"

"I think so."

"Then why don't we try to do that? Do you know anyone else who could start learning to whip-in?"

"Would he have to be part of Gwyn's family?"

"I don't care who they are, if they can handle hounds without fearing them."

Another knock on the open door, and Rhys stepped in.

"Alright then, looks like everyone's here," George said. "Shall we get started? Wait—what will I do for a horn?"

Ives told him, "Iolo's horn went with him, but there's another on the mantle." George stuffed the small straight silver horn between the buttons of his vest until just the slightly flared bell protruded. "And there's the horn for the great hunt," pointing to a locked cupboard.

"We'll look at that later. Let's go."

They went out to the yard, leaving Alun and Olwen sorting through clothing, and found that Mosby as well as the horses for Rhys and Rhian were already tacked up and waiting for them. George checked his girth and mounted up.

Ives called to him, "Do you want the whole pack?"

"What the hell, bring 'em all. May as well find out the worst right at the start."

The hounds were collected into the holding pens on either side before release into the kennel yard. George told them to pack up and Rhys helped hold them in a concentrated group along one side away from the main gate. All this took a few minutes.

Owen's men were visible waiting beyond the gate. Ives opened it just enough to let in a lutin mounted on a small roan horse. The two of them walked over to meet George.

"This is Benitoe," Ives said. "Isolda suggested him, and I sent him a message to join us. I'd like to give him this opportunity to whip-in with the hounds, if you agree."

"I'll be glad to give it a try. See if you can find anyone else for me, so we can have some spares."

Benitoe looked to be in his late twenties. He gave a serious nod to George, then moved into place to be ready to control the pack on the side opposite Rhys.

"All set, everyone?" He looked around. "Alright then, open the gates."

They walked slowly into the main yard of the manor, and Owen's men took up position behind them. George put himself at the head of the pack with Rhian directly behind him, and Rhys and Benitoe covered the left and right flanks toward the rear. The younger hounds looked around curiously, but the hunt staff held them all together in a pack.

They went through the gates in the curtain wall in tight order, with George muttering, "Pack up," insistently, conscious of the many eyes upon them. So far, so good. His attention lagged for an instant, and suddenly the younger members of the pack broke free into the front grounds within the palisade to go exploring.

"Hold up!" he roared at the hounds that remained, while the two whippers-in tore off after the miscreants. He stayed with the obedient hounds thinking dark thoughts, Rhian quiet behind him. Knowing the sinners couldn't hear him, he tried reaching for them anyway, with his will. He found he could feel them faintly, and he called to them silently, "Pack up." Astonished, he saw heads raise and look back at him. He did it again, and this time added the horn call. They turned and loped back, with Rhys and Benitoe behind encouraging them all the way.

George brought his half of the pack along to meet them, and held the reunited hounds to let everyone settle back into place.

"Let's try this again, shall we?"

George led them down to the main gate without further incident and Rhys directed them down the road to the right, and then up a small lane to a farm with an open field surrounded by woods, fenced for cattle. Rhys cantered ahead and opened the gate, closing it behind after everyone had passed through.

George moved a ways into the field, gesturing to Owen to take his men off in one group along the fence. Holding the pack together, he praised them in a calm, low voice, "That's my good hounds." As he pointed to individuals, Rhian named them to him and he used their names as he talked to them. He tried to touch them with his mind at the same time, as he had done in the manor yard, starting to get a sense of them as individuals.

Dando, the lead hound, was like a captain: dignified, responsible, sensible. One active larger hound, with red-tipped ears and no other markings, caught his eye. He was constantly on the move, pushing the limits. He asked Rhian to name him. "That's Cythraul."

Rhys grimaced. "Watch out for Cythraul. He's well-named 'demon.' Great strike hound, but not easy to work with."

He recognized the head bitch Rhymi, from his experiment in the kennel yard the day before. To his newly sensitive mental touch she seemed like a determined, no nonsense leader. Other personalities were starting to solidify for him as he watched the hounds interact and Rhian supplied names for him.

"Alright, we managed to get here without losing any, which I consider an excellent first step. Let's find out how biddable they're going to be."

He told them to pack up, then led them partway down the field. He tried to keep an awareness of them behind him so that he could feel if any strayed, and that seemed to work. He felt one hound drifting before Benitoe moved his horse in to remind him to return to the pack.

"Alright, hold up." George came to a halt, and the pack stopped with him.

"Pack up." This time he moved out at a trot, and the hounds kept up. He brought them in a tight curve then stopped again, giving them more warning. They stayed together without urging from the whippers-in.

"This is delightful," he said to Rhian. "I could get used to this."

"They're cooperating now, but it'll be harder when they're hunting and excited," she said.

"Can you sense them as individuals without looking?"

"Yes, but then I already know them all."

George called out to Rhys and Benitoe, and pointed at a small spring-fed stream running down the field. "I'm going to take them for a drink."

This time he started at a canter, and the hounds stayed together behind him. He held them a few yards from the stream, before releasing them to drink.

He waved Rhys and Benitoe in. "Any difficulties?"

"Not after that first break," Rhys said.

George looked at Benitoe directly. "How is it for you?"

"They treat me as a regular whipper-in, as I hoped they would."

"Rhys, I gather that they're used for buck but also sometimes doe, yes? The hounds I've hunted have only one target, or one group of accepted targets, such as fox and coyote. All else is forbidden. I wouldn't be able to tell them 'fox today, coyote tomorrow' except by bringing them someplace where there's only fox or only coyote. How do these hounds know which game is wanted?"

"That's part of the huntsman's job. I'm not sure how it's done."

Rhian spoke up. "Iolo would show them what he wanted, here," tapping her head. "I've felt him do it. It's not the sight of a stag that he showed them, nor even the scent, but the feel of it.

They remember buck differently from doe: different scent, different location, different excitement."

"And the great hunt's quarry is more different yet?"

"I imagine so, though I was never close enough to feel him do that."

"I don't know how a deer hunt feels. How will I show the hounds what I want?"

"I suppose you'll have to learn like the young hounds, from example and experience." She grinned.

"We hunt deer tomorrow. Think you can show the hounds what's wanted?"

"I think so."

"Have you held the pack before?"

"No, not yet."

"Then now's a good time to start. Try packing them up and taking them partway down the field like I did."

Rhian turned serious. "Pack up," she called. The hound who were still drinking lifted their dripping heads, and joined the others on the bank headed back to her. Rhys and Benitoe drifted back into their proper places to support her.

She looked about to make sure she had them all. "Move out," she told them and started at a walk, the pack following behind her.

Next to her, George tried to sense what she was telling the pack and found he could pick up most of it. Her style was different from his own beginning fumbles, more assured and more detailed.

When Cythraul started to follow a scent, Rhian spoke, "Cythraul, pack up." George felt the reinforcement of a mental rebuke as well as the verbal one, directed at just the one hound and marked by his own signature, distinct from all the others.

"Hold up," she cried, and they stopped.

"Alright, then," George said. "You know, I think we may actually be able to hunt them tomorrow, as long as we're doing it in private like this. Benitoe, I assume you don't know the names of these hounds?"

"Not yet."

"Then you and I both need some quick lessons. Let's start tonight after dinner and work through one pen per evening with Ives or one of these two," gesturing at Rhys and Rhian. "I want us to be reasonably accurate by the end of the week. The rest of you, don't hesitate to correct us if we get it wrong."

He set a test for the staff. “Rhian, take the pack to the gate and hold them there while Benitoe rides ahead to open it. I’ll take over and bring them back. Rhys, you and I will ride behind.”

Rhian was startled. Hold the pack herself, already, and move it out?

She nodded at the request and assumed an air of confidence. Ignoring the butterflies in her stomach, she walked her horse to the head of the pack. It would be just like a few minutes ago, and that had worked out alright.

“Pack up,” she said, bringing them with her and away from the huntsman. When they looked back at George, she bespoke them and drew their attention back to her.

Back and forth she led them, and then to the gate which Benitoe held for her.

She wanted to shout—I can handle the hounds by myself. Something in the back of her mind added, well, in perfect conditions anyway.

I don’t care, she insisted to herself. It’s a start.

CHAPTER 14

After the hounds returned to kennels from their walk, George joined Rhodri at the curtain wall.

"Have they been gone long?"

"They just left a few minutes ago. How'd it go with the hounds? I heard you provided some entertainment here, as you departed," he said, gesturing to the grounds in front of the manor house.

"Well, we're learning. Other than that, it actually went much better than I expected," George said.

As they reached the road and turned left, they cantered to make up some of the ground, dropping back to a walk as the slope began to rise.

"Time for my lesson," George said. "Everyone says you're the expert—tell me more about these ways. Who can see them?"

Rhodri turned serious for a moment. "There are old ways that everyone knows about that many have enough skill to use. Those who can't hire guides. Those are like public roads."

George nodded.

"To use a way you must be able to 'see' one end, or be guided there, and you must be able to enter. Public ways, or unclaimed ones, can be entered by anyone. Private ways require permission, and that's usually in the form of a way-token of some kind."

"Who makes the tokens? What can they do?"

"A token's made by someone who has power over the way, the lord of a place or his way-finders, if he isn't one himself. It's a spell tied to a small piece of wood, specific to a particular way, and it can be limited to a person, or limited to a number of uses, or limited to a period of time, or limited to just one direction, or any number of restrictions."

"So that's why walking through the spot occupied by the way in the kennels didn't cause it to open for me," George said. "How was it I could chase that archer through the way he used? I didn't have a token."

"He would have functioned as a guide, perhaps. But really I think from what Ceridwen says that you're a way-finder yourself, like me, and it's much harder to keep us out if we set our mind to it. It let in Gwyn, too. Maybe it recognizes more than one owner, since you penetrated it without a token. Normally a private way would be closed, and even a way-finder would need a token to penetrate an actively barred way, though he could probably detect it."

Rhodri raised a hand to contradict himself. "On the other hand, the way Gwyn opens for the start of the great hunt is always in the same place, but I can't detect it the rest of the year. There's something like that for the way Iolo uses at Nos Galan Mai for new whelps. Those ways seem to be stable but hidden somehow, and many way-finders who don't have our experience insist, from their books, that hidden ways can't exist."

"How do you close a way?"

"Its owner ties it to himself or to a few others and issues no other tokens."

"Can you shut a way held by someone else? Can you keep it from being reopened?"

"That's the interesting question Gwyn's going to try to answer, I think."

Dozens of questions flooded into George's mind, and he tried to sort out the most important ones.

"Can you make a way or only find them? Is it 'way-finder' or 'way-creator,' or are they the same thing?"

"There's a lot of debate on this topic, complicated, as Ceridwen will tell you, by the fact that few of the adepts have been inclined to write about it in detail. There are people who claim to have created ways, but that's hard to prove afterward and no one's been able to demonstrate it at will before witnesses. I've never made one, myself, as far as I can tell, but only found existing ones that weren't known or detected closed ones."

Rhodri continued, "Now, the great hunt often uses ways that weren't known, the hounds acting as guides, but were they there already or did something else, make them? And in front of the hounds is their quarry, once he's been identified. Can he also use ways without tokens and, if so, how does he make or find them? It's unlikely that he just happens to stumble across them, they're not common."

George's head spun with the possibilities. "How does the great hunt get home, if they cross one or more ways? Presumably no one would have tokens."

"The hounds bring us all back to kennels and we must follow them. Stories are told of those left behind making their way home the long way, if at all. I've looked for the hounds' ways, afterward, and not found them. I don't know if they cease to exist, or if they're just hidden. My personal belief is that they're destroyed."

"If they're hidden or destroyed, who are they hidden or destroyed by? Who owns them?"

"Good question," Rhodri said.

Was this religious mystery or superior science? George itched to do some experiments.

He asked, "Why was I able to detect two ways no one else knew about?"

Deadpan, Rhodri said, "I hadn't arrived yet."

George smiled. "So you can detect them, yes?"

Rhodri closed his eyes for a moment. "I feel the one we're approaching at Daear Llosg, but no other I didn't already know. Show me where the other one is."

George repeated his mental sweep of yesterday. The small one in the woods west of the manor was still there. He pointed an arm in that direction. "There."

Rhodri looked again, inwardly. "I can't feel it. How very disconcerting. Perhaps it's another hidden way."

"How would the one from yesterday be different?"

"Perhaps its use by you and Gwyn opened its ownership, in some way?"

George stopped on the road.

"I want to do an experiment. Come, stand with your horse along this line." He lined up Rhodri to face the small west way. "Don't move."

George walked several dozen yards up the slope along the road. He oriented Mosby on the same way.

"The intersection of the two lines our horses are on should tell us where the way is. Can you picture that?"

"We're not far enough apart for much accuracy, but let's try this again at Daear Llosg. It's a good idea."

They entered the meadow to find Gwyn and Ceridwen standing near the way and Idris with several guards nearby. George had no trouble seeing it, but Ceridwen seemed to be looking at a slightly different place. He dismounted, handing his horse to a guard to hold.

"Can you see it?" he asked her.

"Not well at all. It's just an ill-focused blur for me, not like most ways."

"Then why don't we mark the spot?"

He picked up some loose stones and sticks on the ground and walked over, outlining the space the way seemed to occupy. It was large enough for several horses. When looking through the spot casually, the way was not visible at all, but when George concentrated directly at it, he could barely make out a landscape on the other side, like a very faint window at some distance.

He walked around behind and discovered it had little depth from the sides. He could sense it from the rear, but it was like looking at the back of a television set, nothing to see.

"Can you see into it?" he asked Gwyn. "Do you know where it goes?"

"I can see the river meadow. I don't understand why it's still open like this. It should've been shut by its owner."

Rhodri joined them and presented his theory about compromised ownership after Gwyn and George had forced their way in.

"Then we should be able to continue to use it," George said. "Let's go find out whose land that is."

"That would be unwise," Gwyn said. "They've had all night to prepare an ambush just out of our sight behind the opening. It's not likely to be close enough to someone's dwelling to allow us to gather a quick identification, and I'm not prepared to mount an expedition with just a few guards. I'd prefer to shut it down, if possible, or at least lock it thoroughly from our end."

"And just how will we do that, if you're not the owner?" Rhodri asked.

"I was rather hoping you'd have some suggestions, now that you're home."

"If we have some ownership in it now, can't we tie it down in some way, as with a token?" George asked.

"And how would you go about doing that?"

George hesitated. He thought it could be done, but he had no idea just what to do.

"Go on," Gwyn said. "Try whatever you think might work."

George stood straight in front of the way and concentrated. He visualized it: a clear oval shape with a flattened bottom, wider than tall, with its destination faintly visible. He intended to build a mental door across it, but instead he found himself lacing it shut, drawing a broad dark green strap like a ribbon diagonally across it, catching it somehow in the edges and stitching back and forth in one direction, then turning 90 degrees to weave back across it. The way didn't pucker closed, but the wide interwoven lines filled all the space between and held, like a taut trampoline. Finished, it glistened like a wet leaf and vibrated faintly.

George could still feel the way, but there was no longer any sense of locational presence behind it. "I think I've done something," he said. "Will it hold?"

Gwyn and Rhodri looked, then Gwyn tried to walk forward into the way, and nothing happened.

Gwyn said, "I've never seen a technique like that. What made you think of it?"

"I don't know. It wasn't quite what I intended. I had more of a door in mind than something woven, but it just happened."

"Can you undo it at need?"

George looked closely at the woven closure and tried to perceive it as a whole. "There seems to be one bit that says 'pull here.' I don't know what would happen."

"What do you think, Rhodri?"

"I think he's closed it, alright, and I'll bet he can open it again. I've never heard of such a thing. It's still there, but inaccessible, and you know it's hard to keep me out."

Gwyn recalled how hard it had been to keep Rhodri out of places he didn't belong. "Well I remember," he said. "That's why they sent you to me for your growing up."

He saw that Rhodri was puzzled by George's feat, but he understood far better just how impossible it really was. This was a technique for handling the ways that was unfamiliar to those of his line. Another touch of Cernunnos?

Could George open my own secured private ways, for the family? Could he find ways of his own, or even make them as

Cernunnos seemed to do, and keep them secret? He didn't seem to understand the significance of what he'd just done, but Gwyn was more sure than ever that he was a wild card played by outside forces. Were they benign or was George a threat?

None of this showed on his face, of course.

"I think we can dismiss these guards," he told Idris.

He continued, blandly, "Now, what about that other way?"

Rhodri and George demonstrated George's triangulation technique, this time using the entire width of the meadow as a baseline. Gwyn admired this simple method of locating a way at a physical location to avoid an uncertain estimate of distance. Both Ceridwen and Idris were in agreement about the location of the two intersecting lines.

"My lord," she said, "that's beyond the palisade to the west and a little south, but not very far. It should be right in the middle of the woods."

George spoke up. "Your enemy knows we know about this way here, since we've both used it. There's nothing to be gained by stealth. But they don't know we've identified another one. We should try to keep them in the dark about it."

That was an unexpected show of tactics for a stranger to this world.

"It would mean leaving it open," Ceridwen said.

"More," George continued. "It would mean taking only a very small party to locate it physically, and trying to devise some way of spying on it. Can that be done?"

Is this some plan for an ambush, to reduce this party to a small size? Better to go along with it, forewarned, and appear to be unsuspicious.

"We'll go there now," Gwyn said. "My kinsman's correct to suggest we do this circumspectly, so we'll approach it by a wide circle, then return here so that we can come back to the main gate from the expected direction, as though we'd simply lingered here. We don't know who are the traitors and their spies, but there's no sense in making this easy for them."

He pointed his horse west to take the trail. *Let's see how this plays out.*

As they rode upslope to sweep left around the back of the manor, Gwyn dropped back to walk next to George, leaving Ceridwen with Rhodri and Idris.

"How was the hound walking this morning?"

"It went surprisingly well, except for a brief break as we left, out where the most people could see it, naturally."

Gwyn smiled slightly. "That may be just as well, since the more competent you appear, the more dangerous it may be for you, if they decide the death of Iolo wasn't enough."

"True, I suppose."

They walked on for a moment.

Gwyn looked at George sideways, as if he wanted to ask something George might object to. He said, carefully, "I've heard that you've made some interesting staff choices."

George bristled. "Did the words 'girl' and 'lutin' figure in the telling?"

"Maybe so," Gwyn said mildly.

"Do we have a problem?"

"Not with me." Gwyn kept a straight face.

"Well, alright then."

George took a deep breath and continued. "Rhian has what she needs to be huntsman, if she wants to. She's very young and has much to learn, but she could do it today and have a good chance of pulling it off."

Gwyn nodded and listened attentively.

"I want to build up a staff of potential whippers-in and maybe start to develop additional huntsmen. I've asked Ives to identify candidates. While I don't want to make many changes in a temporary position, I think there hasn't been enough thought given to succession plans, and I want to get that going, including juniors as necessary. It may be that lutins don't have the necessary powers to be huntsman for the great hunt, but I don't see why they can't be part of a pool of whipper-in talent."

"I concur," Gwyn said.

George decided to take advantage of how much interest Gwyn was taking in these details and his opinions.

"Then there's the matter of Owen the Leash and his men. How old is that tradition? How necessary is it?"

"It's not an old tradition. In fact, now that I think on it in the light of recent events, there's been a very interesting sequence of circumstances over the last twenty years or so. First we lost some whippers-in to death and other duties so that we were understaffed. Since Iolo refused to use anyone besides family, we were down to Rhys. Then Creiddylad expressed concern that there was insufficient control for the pack and urged me to take steps."

"Where did Owen come from?"

"From Creiddylad, him and his two companions."

"What do they do when they're not being a fence behind the pack?"

Gwyn looked nonplussed. "I don't really know." He called forward, "Idris?"

Idris dropped back to join him. "Yes, my lord?"

"What do Owen and his men do all day?"

"Cause trouble, my lord. They laze about and gossip. None of our decent folk will talk to them, but there are always those who like to complain."

"Why haven't I been told?" Idris was taken aback by the stern look that belied the mild voice.

"Well, no one was sure if we should look to you or your sister for their discipline, and I was reluctant to bother you with so slight a matter."

George asked Gwyn, "What would happen if you decided you didn't need them to protect people from the pack? Would they get other positions? Would Creiddylad take them back?"

Gwyn spoke slowly, "I think she'd send them home. But she continues to drop the occasional word about danger from the pack and how glad she is that they're there."

Idris said, "I don't like it, my lord. If the huntsman doesn't need them, we shouldn't have such people around."

"Why did Iolo tolerate them?" George asked.

"Habit, custom, indifference I suppose," Gwyn said. "He ignored them and concentrated on the hunting. It wouldn't have occurred to him to augment the whippers-in with lutins or non-family, and so he may just have been waiting for things to return to normal as more family inevitably became available." He glanced at George, consideringly. "We tend to take the long view on such things."

Gwyn pursed his lips, coming to a decision. "Do you need them?" he asked George directly.

"I don't think so. I think we can control the pack without them, and even in my short time here I've overheard them undermining your authority."

"We've been complacent about these gradual changes. No more. They shall return to Creiddylad."

"If I may," George said, "we shouldn't show your hand in this. If we're not reacting to shadows, then this is some sort of long-term and subtle plan only now coming to a head and we shouldn't arouse any suspicions that you've perceived it. How about we make me the cause instead? I can pick a fight with them and make a very public scene insisting on their departure, under threat of my huntsman duties. You would seem to have no choice but to indulge me, and your enemies would be confused about your degree of knowledge."

"This is well thought of, my lord," Idris said.

Gwyn nodded briskly. "Yes. Do it soon. If we're correct in our suspicions, they'll need to take some action to replace those particular agents or spies, and we may be able to detect that. The more we can force them to react instead of just waiting for their next move, the easier it'll be to spot them."

George said, "I'll set it up for this week. Thursday, maybe, the second staff hunt. I promise to create quite a stir."

As they approached their destination along the woodland paths behind and past the manor's palisade, George paired up with Rhodri.

"Still can't see this one?" he asked, pointing.

"No, and it bothers me. How many others are hidden from me?"

They came to a wide spot in the path, otherwise undistinguished. George dismounted. "It's right here." He drew his boot heel in the dirt to show orientation and extent. "Seems about right for a single rider, maybe two."

Gwyn looked at Rhodri. "Anything?"

Rhodri shook his head.

"We can't detect this," Gwyn said. He sounded disturbed. "What do you see through it?"

George concentrated. "A gray passage ending in more woods, though not these right here. Looks like the same weather and time of day, so I imagine it's relatively local."

"Can you seal it?"

George tried to look at it in that special way. "I think so, but if I do, the owner will know about it. I don't think we should."

Gwyn remarked to Rhodri, "I wonder if we could've seen the other one, before it was activated or before we'd gone through it? I saw it when we brought Iolo's body, alerted by Ceridwen's warning, but it may already have been prepared for the attack."

To George, he said, "I do believe you, kinsman, but we've never encountered ways that could be hidden from us, only rumors that such exist."

While Rhodri described for Gwyn his attempts at finding the ways used by the great hunt that also seemed to be hidden, George wondered how his barely sensed skills could be so different from his ancestor's. Weaker, that would make sense. But how could they be more powerful?

"It seems that hidden ways are a real thing, then." Gwyn turned to Ceridwen. "Is there anything you can set up to identify a user of this way or to let us know when it's used?"

"I can't include the way itself, but that isn't really necessary. I can easily enough set traps in this spot to detect any traffic, however it arrives or departs. I'd know when this spot has been used, but not the identity of the user."

George had been listening. This had possibilities. "If you set up traps on the edges as well as traps in the middle, would you be able to tell by the sequence what direction the person was going in? For example, if he trips the northern perimeter, then the center where the way is, and then no other perimeter, he has presumably entered the way. Can your traps provide that much specificity?"

"Yes, and that's a good way to detect something hidden. Like looking for the shadow of the thing cast by its actions rather than the thing itself."

Ceridwen picked up twigs and bits of wood to hold the trip spells, and distributed them around the edges and near the way. When she was done, George scuffed out the mark of his boot heel in the dirt and remounted.

As they turned back along the path, Ceridwen glanced behind them and a breeze stirred, resettling the leaves and removing any signs of their presence.

CHAPTER 15

After grabbing a quick meal, George strolled out to find Alun waiting for him, as planned, mounted on a dark bay cob and chatting with Isolda. George walked alongside them to the main stable.

He greeted Isolda. "I'm glad to see you. I want to give Mosby a rest, so I thought I'd try out one of Iolo's hunt horses. I was hoping I'd find you so that you could tell me about them."

"And I was looking for you to hear about the hound walking this morning. Did Benitoe do a good job for you?"

"He was fine." He smiled. "Do I detect some special interest in his regard?"

She colored faintly. "We are good friends and I'm interested in his advancement," she said demurely.

Alun waited outside as they entered the stable.

"Iolo's horses are in a group, here," she said, leading them over to some stalls on the right about halfway down the aisle.

George saw the big chestnut mare with the wide blaze that he had examined by lamp light two days ago.

"This is Llamrei. She's good, solid, and dependable."

The next stall held a large black gelding without a speck of white. His eyes blazed with personality and a bit of temper.

"That's Afanc, and a monster well-named. If you can master him, he'll bear you well, but he's a handful."

Last in line was a medium-sized gray gelding, neat and trim. George saw why Ives thought he wouldn't be up to his weight.

"This is Llwyd," Isolda said. "I understand that Rhian will be using him as a third horse." George nodded.

"Let's do the hard things first. I'll try Afanc for this afternoon's ride."

One of the grooms brushed him and tacked him up in the aisle, transferring George's saber to a saddle scabbard.

George patted him all over and stood by his head, crooning. "Well, my lad, shall we go for a ride?" Afanc's ears twitched at this.

George reached out as he had with the hounds, and suddenly the whole stable receded to background noise as he focused on Afanc. The gelding's personality was strong, and George felt curiosity warring with general cussedness.

He gathered the reins and mounted quickly, giving Afanc little time to protest. He sensed him contemplating a rhetorical buck and told him, "None of that, now." He felt Afanc's surprise, and then acceptance.

Isolda said, "That went well."

"He seems like a fine fellow. I'll enjoy him." Through their bond, Afanc sensed the meaning and arched his neck in pride.

After they crossed the bridge in Greenhollow and turned left at the Horned Man inn, George asked Alun, "Do you know the folks who work here? There's a guest I want to find out more about, without raising any notice."

"It's easy to stop for a drink either now or returning. If we listen carefully, we can learn without asking questions."

"I think the man I'm interested in may be dangerous, but I also don't want to scare him somewhere else where I may not be able to find him again. I'm also too easy to recognize, especially in this red coat."

Alun thought for a moment. "It would make sense for us to put up our horses here for the errand at Mostyn's. We could linger in the stables coming and going, and the grooms have a lot to say. And we could still be having that drink."

"Good idea."

They turned in at the stable entrance and dismounted in the yard, handing the horses to the groom that George recognized from the day before.

"Hello again," he said. "I'm sorry, but I've forgotten your name."

"It's Maonirn," the lutin said, as he took their horses. They followed him into the stable.

"We'll be an hour or two at Mostyn's," Alun told him. George meanwhile looked about to be sure no one else was in the stable. He had no sense of anyone nearby.

"Maonirn, is that Scilti fellow still around? He gave me a scare yesterday."

The groom warmed to a sympathetic audience. "Aye, and as troublesome as ever."

"I thought he was waiting for someone. What does he do all day?"

"Keeps to his room when he isn't out on his horse for hours."

"Where would he go? We haven't seen him at the manor."

"I don't know. But he's not been in a good mood when he returns, I can tell you that."

~

The tailor's shop turned out to be a small house fronting the road on the same side as the inn. At the knock on the door a middle-aged man let them in and directed them to a back room where a large table dominated the center and the only spaces not occupied by shelves and drawers were two large windows and the doorways.

Alun introduced them. "Mostyn, this is Gwyn's kinsman, George Talbot Traherne. He's come to us directly from the human world on an unexpected visit and will be staying for some time. He's taking over Iolo's job while he's here. Gwyn has told Ifor Moel to make sure he's outfitted for the hunting by next week."

George said, "I won't be here that long. That's a lot of fuss for a week's worth of clothing."

Alun looked at him sternly. "You must be properly attired for the honor of the family and the great hunt."

Mostyn glanced over his Rowanton Hunt clothing. "Is this hunting attire you're wearing?"

"The breeches and boots are conventional for riding of many sorts, and the shirt, vest and coat are particular to my hunt and the general style of foxhunters."

"Are you wanting more of that, then?"

"No. I guess I would need appropriate hunt clothing for here, and work clothes, and something to wear in the evenings that's suitable. Olwen," he looked to check that Mostyn knew who that was, "is handling some of the basic items. Alun has a list."

Mostyn and Alun looked over the list for a few minutes.

"You'll need two hunt coats, one simpler for everyday, and one better for actual hunting. Also one coat for kennel work, in drab. Two weskits to match, four hunt shirts, Olwen to take care of more shirts and the under garments. Three sets of breeches, one for dirty work by Olwen. Stockings, from Olwen, and footwear.

Shoes for everyday, high boots for hunting. What style is it you prefer?"

"I want hunt clothing to be both proper and quiet, the simpler the better, in whatever colors are customary. Lots of pockets inside and out. Plenty of ease of movement. Allow room for undergarments for warmth, top and bottom, in case it gets cold."

He thought for a moment. "Let's see… what else? Oh, I need to carry a saber."

"And a hunting sword," Alun reminded him.

"Alright, and a hunting sword. I have gloves for riding, but if it's cold enough I may need a warmer pair, and I need work gloves—maybe there are some already at the kennels I can use?" he asked, looking at Alun.

"For boots, I need enough room at the foot and ankle for a second pair of short wool socks, for warmth."

"Low-heeled, the shoes?"

"Flat-heeled, the shoes," George said. "I mean normal height, not elevated. Boots, too."

Mostyn walked over to the shelves and began pulling out bolts of cloth. Strong dark green wools in various weights were prominent.

"The typical color of our lord Gwyn's livery, this, and the color that Iolo favored."

He draped a medium weight over George's chest to see the effect and nodded approvingly. "Take off your coat, then, and I will measure you."

Dictating numbers to Alun to write down, he began the same process on George that Olwen had, earlier in the day. George resigned himself to stand there patiently.

Mostyn commented on the pistol holster at George's back. "Shall I leave room for this as well?"

"Forgot I had that on. Habit. Yes, you might as well allow a bit of room for that, and enough clearance to access it. Maybe I'll swap it for a knife."

"And then there will be evening wear," Mostyn said while he was working. "What's your fancy, then?"

"Something simple and quiet. I'm used to black but if that's not customary, then a dark navy or some other sober, dignified color."

"Not much used outside of livery, black is. Iolo used a darker green, to indicate his role and support Gwyn."

"So he embodied 'huntsman' in the formal affairs?"

"So it was."

If I do that, George thought, they won't think of me as anything else. Always good to be underestimated.

"Alright, then. I'll do the same."

Alun warned him, "Not all of Gwyn's kinsmen wear livery, even as hunt staff. Rhodri was a true peacock, he was, though he maintained one coat in livery."

George waved a hand. "It's fine by me. I don't want to be noticed so much as a kinsman. Besides, I'm too large to be decorative."

Mostyn said, "Someone else must come in for the shoes and boots. Wait a few minutes while I see if he's busy."

Ah, a perfect opportunity, George thought. He said, "I have an errand to run up the street for a moment. Can you and Alun work together till I return?"

George found himself up the street at Angharad's lane before he could raise enough objections to stop himself. This is idiotic, he raged silently. You're not going to be here long, and you'll seem like a child to her, given the difference in your ages. Don't be bothering her.

He'd stayed awake a while last night thinking about it. Finally, he'd concluded that he wanted to see more of her regardless and was determined not to be shy about it. Nothing ventured, nothing gained.

As he entered the work yard, he saw an open door at the further workshop building and knocked on the door frame. She emerged into the light, dusty from her work and wearing a smock covered with paint stains. A few tendrils of hair had escaped their braid and floated around her face.

"It's good to see you again," she said, looking for his horse.

"I'm sorry to interrupt your work with no notice like this," he said, "but I've come to town to be fitted for clothing and wanted to stop by for just a moment. As you may have heard, I agreed to serve as huntsman for Gwyn until after the great hunt."

"Yes, it's a subject of great interest to us all," she said politely.

He flushed at the neutral remark. Was she teasing him? He hadn't meant to sound like he was boasting. Doggedly persisting, he said, "Since I'm not leaving immediately, as I thought I would be, I want to take the opportunity to become better acquainted with people. There wasn't enough time yesterday, but I'd like to see your work in some detail, if you'd care to show me."

He quickly added, "Not right now, of course, with no warning."

She considered for a moment, her face unreadable. "Would you like to come tomorrow for the mid-day meal? I'd be pleased to show you around."

He could breathe again. "That would be very kind, thanks. I'll be doing my first hunt, tomorrow morning, privately, with just the staff. Assuming I don't lose all the hounds or end up dead in a ditch, I'll come as promptly as I can."

One side of her mouth quirked at the dire predictions. "Perhaps I could attend this private hunt myself? That way you needn't worry about being late."

Really? She'd do that? "I can't guarantee any sport," he warned. "This will be my first attempt at deer instead of fox."

"That doesn't matter. I'd be interested to see it anyway, and from the start, at kennels."

"I'd be pleased to have you, and it'll put me on my mettle to have an audience," he said, wryly. "I'll see you, then, in the morning."

He turned to go, then turned back, dismayed. "Wait, do you know when they usually start? I haven't asked yet." He laughed at himself.

She smiled at him. "Right after breakfast. You'll need to eat early."

He smiled back. "Alright, then. I'll see you at kennels."

Walking away, he thought, that went well. He was surprised she wanted to watch the trial hunt, and concerned it wouldn't go well, but that was a worry he could handle. Better to embarrass himself in front of someone who was interested, than not to spark any interest at all. He didn't know what could happen in just a couple of weeks, or where it might lead, but he was old enough not to want to waste any time in finding out.

Angharad watched him walk down the lane and out of sight. He didn't look back, but his head was tilted as if he were talking to himself. Probably replaying the conversation to see what he could've said better, if she knew men. She grinned.

It never really got old, she thought, this dance between men and women. This descendant of Gwyn was so young and yet so bold, judging from yesterday's fight at the funeral. The unconsidering courage of youth, perhaps? But someone had taught him manners, and it gave him a poise beyond his years. And after all, he'd had the nerve to ask her, which few did. Why not get to know him better?

He's certainly not a child, she thought, remembering how she'd had to look up at him as they stood together. He was like a wall, standing in front of her. No wonder his gray horse was so large. She felt a warmth that had been absent for a while as she drew his body in her mind's eye

It would be interesting to watch him wrestle with this job he's taken on, hunting the hounds, not to mention the challenge he'll face with the great hunt.

She turned and walked into the building, absently making her way as she considered how best to compose his form for the painting she had in mind.

George found a cobbler waiting for him in Mostyn's shop. They discussed shoes and boots, took more measurements, and set delivery for later in the week.

Mostyn told him, "I'll need to see you soon for fittings. When can that be?"

"I'll be here tomorrow afternoon. Is that too soon?"

"I'll have something by then. Come by when you can."

As he walked back to the inn with Alun, a thought occurred to him. "What about Benitoe and Rhian? Won't they need hunt coats like staff, too?"

"As family, Rhian could dress differently, if she wants, but Benitoe should be properly clothed."

"Another item for Ifor Moel, then. I guess we'll find out what the spending limits are, at this rate."

"It's unlikely that Gwyn would place any barriers in your way, for the honor of the hunt."

They stopped in the main room of the inn for a beer before returning, and the innkeeper brought it to them himself.

"So this is our new huntsman?" he asked Alun. He nodded at George. "Huw Bongam, I am, at your service."

"Pleased to meet you. I've just been visiting Mostyn." Better to feed the gossip than make them dig for it, George thought.

"He'll take good care of you. They say you come from the human world. True it is I've never seen a coat fashioned like that."

"That's so. This is my first visit."

"And what do you think about it, then?" He rocked back on his heels, waiting expectantly for an answer.

George considered, what do I think about it, indeed? The last three days had been startling, exhilarating, and somehow compelling. "I feel at the same time like I'm having an adventure and like I've come home," he was surprised to hear himself say.

The innkeeper smiled broadly. "So it's like that, is it? There's a place for everyone, I say. Maybe this is yours." They raised their glasses to the wish.

George asked him to sit down, since the common room was otherwise unoccupied in the middle of the afternoon.

"I met a guest of the inn yesterday and I'd like to know more about him. Quietly."

"You mean that Scilti fellow, no doubt. There's not much I can tell you. He says little and smiles less. No visitors, out all day, and the only time I hear from him is when he has something to complain about."

"How long will he be staying?"

"He's been here a week, he has, and no sign of leaving."

"Unlike us, I fear. We need to get back."

They finished their drinks and picked up their horses from the stable.

CHAPTER 16

Weapons-master Hadyn greeted George at the afternoon session. "I hear it's well you did with a saber yesterday."

George snorted. Was it only yesterday? "My blood was up, so I didn't stop and think how lucky I was until afterward."

More seriously, he said, "Since it looks like I'll be here a couple of weeks, I'd like to come whenever I can to improve, with your permission. I'll try for every afternoon, though I'm sure that won't always work."

"That's what we're here for, isn't it?" He outlined a set of activities and partners to take George through an abbreviated education in saber, mounted and afoot, small-sword, knife-fighting, and defense against the more common weapons.

"My size should be an advantage in unarmed combat, but I don't know how to use it. Could we include that as well?"

"Yes, and you'll need archery, at least the basics. Might as well pull a bow with those muscles."

They walked over to the other end where the trainees were already practicing. George was startled to see Rhian among them, but glad to see she was taking it seriously. Hadyn interrupted the training session for a moment to make general introductions while George stripped down for sparring.

"It's stale you'll get fighting each other. This one," hooking a thumb at George, "will be a challenge, being neither a cadet nor a professional. He hasn't trained with you yet, so you don't know what he'll do." He paused. "Neither does he." This generated some suppressed laughter. He looked up at the tall, broad man standing ready and taking this joshing in good humor. "Try not to hurt the wee man, now, or there'll be no hunting for any of us." That raised smiles all around.

After dinner, George hastened off to the huntsman's office to look over the hunting territory for the next day. Rhian came with him, and they found Benitoe already waiting, with Ives.

"Thank you all for coming," George said. "Let's start with a hound lesson, and then let them get their sleep. I want to begin with the dog hounds, all of them, and those bitches we'll be using tomorrow. I'd like your advice on which hounds to take out." This last was directed at Ives.

"Iolo would draw up a list, and I'd tell him of any problems."

"And I'll do the same but I don't know the hounds well enough yet, so let's make that a gradual process. Let's leave out any young entry for tomorrow, but otherwise which ones do you suggest?"

"Deer at Two Pines," he considered. "Well, it's not a big fixture, nor very far. There are deer in those woods who raid the cornfields, and the crops are high. I'll show you who I think should go, and you can make the list as we go along." They headed over to the hound pens, Rhian and Benitoe walking beside them.

"Will we have an audience tomorrow?" Rhian asked.

"Not officially, though I met Angharad this afternoon in the village and she asked if she could join us and watch. So we'll have an extra reason to try and look professional."

They pulled some chairs into the corridor outside the dog pen, and Rhian fetched hounds one at a time on a lead at Ives's bidding, starting with Dando.

George and Benitoe looked him over carefully, trying to get his markings and bearing fixed in their mind. George held his head and opened his awareness to see the hound's personality: there it was, calm, responsible, the captain of his team. "Can you sense their presence?" he asked Benitoe.

"I don't think it's the same way you do in the family, with each individual. But we lutins feel their pleasure and distress. That's why we tend the hounds and horses. It makes hunting difficult for us, where we must take sides with the hounds and against the quarry, whom we can also feel. That's why so few of us help with that directly."

"Does this make a problem for you, with other lutins?"

"They don't all approve, certainly. But horses are for work, not just grooming, hounds are for hunting, and death's the fate of all."

Ives added, "Benitoe's not the only one. I've spread the word around, and you may have a few more recruits after they see how he does."

"Well, I was pleased with his work today, you can tell them." Benitoe colored faintly.

The next hound was Cythraul. Even here in kennels, George could feel his restless, probing nature. One by one they brought out about twenty dog hounds.

When the last one was returned to the pen, Ives invited them all to follow him in. There by lamplight he challenged them to name each individual hound as he pointed it out, and then gave them names and told them to find the owner. George found that matching the feel of the hound to its name and appearance helped cement its identity for him.

They moved the chairs to the door of the bitch pen and brought out those hounds that Ives recommended for the hunt tomorrow. George used the pocket notebook that Alun had found him and a fountain pen to record the names as they went along. He thought it might be too messy to use on horseback, but he'd yet to see any equivalent of a pencil here and made a note to bring along a bit of cloth or soft suede as a pen wiper.

After Ives had given them the same test with the bitch hounds, they returned to the huntsman's office.

"Did Iolo keep a hunt journal? Where are his records?"

Ives indicated a leather-bound volume on the desk. "That's current, and there are the older ones." He pointed to a wall of similar notebooks.

"I'll take a look at those later, then."

He copied out the list from his notebook onto a clean sheet of paper and gave it to Ives. "This is what you recommended, yes?"

Ives checked it and nodded. "I'll post this on the wall over my table across the way. The lads in the morning will use it to assemble the pack."

"Let's discuss staff, then. Any other volunteers yet?"

"There are some interested who want to wait a few days, till after the great hunt." Ives paused. "I've heard there's been some comment about this morning's staff."

George spoke carefully. "Gwyn mentioned as much. I asked him directly if there was a problem and his exact words were 'not with me.' I intend to do as I see fit about hunt staff and I believe I have his backing. I can't make this less uncomfortable for any volunteers, but I can promise them support for as long as I'm here. Rhian? Benitoe?"

Rhian grinned. "I don't care what anyone thinks. This is what I want to do and Gwyn said I could."

Benitoe said, more seriously, "I do want to do this. I knew it might create a problem but that's what it's like for the first ones to make a change, isn't it? I have friends who are watching to see what happens and I won't be the first to back down."

"Alright, then. Please let me know about anything you can't handle, or anything that looks like it might cause a problem down the line. The hunt staff's a family—we must trust and support each other."

He continued, "Now, about mounts. I've spoken to Ifor Moel. Rhian, Iolo's gray gelding Llwyd is now officially one of your mounts for hunting. Does that give you enough mounts?"

"Oh yes, I have two of my own. That's perfect."

Looking at Benitoe, "What about you? Tell me about your situation."

"Few of us have horses of our own, but then few of us wish to ride. There are about a dozen like me here, and we have a group of three large ponies and four small horses among us, too few to even ride out on together, all at once. The roan I rode today is one of them."

"For you to hunt and hound walk regularly, you'll need at least two suitable mounts, and three would be better. Ifor Moel has given me the means to supply you, but how's it done? Where do you get more?"

Benitoe turned a puzzled look to Ives. "I don't know. Most of ours are cast off mounts for the children that we pick up one at a time."

Ives rubbed his chin. "I can get word to Brittou, down valley. His mistress Iona raises ponies and small horses for the younglings."

George said, "Let's get three, then. If we get more volunteers among the lutins, that'll give us some leeway to accommodate them quickly. How long will this take?"

"It would be fastest if you and Benitoe went together, you to meet Iona and him to try mounts with Brittou. You'll want to found a good relationship with her, for next time."

I'll be gone by then, George thought, but let it pass. Meeting her would do no harm.

"Alright, we'll make room for that this week. Not tomorrow, but maybe Wednesday, after the hound walk. How far is it?"

"Naught but an hour south of of the bridge."

To Benitoe he said, "Will you have enough to last you until then?"

"Yes, I'll swap out among my friends."

"Good. Next, I'd like to see all the staff in livery for their official duties, for hunting of course but also for hound walking. It shows respect for the office, it shows professionalism to outsiders, and it will help suppress any criticism if we present a united appearance. Rhys, of course, is already suited. I went today to Mostyn to arrange clothing for me. Rhian? I'm told that family can choose to dress differently."

She protested. "I should be in livery like everyone else. I'm not playing at this."

"Benitoe, what about you? It seems to me that all the lutins go around in red, even if it's not quite a uniform." George let the question about why they all wore red dangle unasked.

"Red's our traditional color, but I'd be very pleased to be in livery with the rest of the hunt staff."

George nodded decisively. "Then you must both go to Mostyn for suitable clothes. I'll be going to the village after the hunt tomorrow. Please come with me, and I'll tell Mostyn that you must be suited as soon as possible and in any case before the first official hunt next Tuesday."

That was another item ticked off his agenda. Now he could concentrate on the upcoming hunt.

"Now let's cover the plan for tomorrow. My only understanding of hunting deer *par force du chien*, with a pack, is what I've read in medieval hunting books, where gamekeepers look for specific stags the day before or morning of the hunt. Lots of discussion about whose *fewmets* are larger, and so forth. All very colorful, but is that what you do here?"

"I've heard about that from Iolo," Ives said. "Too elaborate for us simple country folk."

"So how does it work, then?" Benitoe and Ives were silent, and he looked over at Rhian, and she laid it out for him.

"You find the stag of the territory, here," Rhian said, tapping her forehead. "You look for the lord in his domain. He'll feel different from the lesser males, 'cause he's the boss."

"Explain to me again how the hounds are directed to a particular quarry."

"You show them what you want. Not the scent, you can't do that, but what it was like for them the last time they found that scent. They'll understand, from that."

"So I picture for them the excitement of following the particular quarry, or type of quarry, in this case the arrogant stag of the herd."

"That's right," she said.

"And I can't do that without having felt how they reacted last time. Therefore," he said to the rest of the group, "since I wasn't here last time, we're going to rely on Rhian for this tomorrow, so I can learn. If she can put them to a buck that she and I find, then I'll know what to do next time. We'll have to feel our way with this, in these three private hunts we've been allotted."

George asked Rhian, "Do you know how this territory's hunted? Which coverts are drawn first?"

"It depends on the wind. If it's from the west, Iolo took this sequence." She demonstrated on the map. "But sometimes he reversed it, and I don't know why."

"Alright, we'll hunt to that plan, if it seems to make sense when we see the spot. Of course, as soon as we find, the plan will go out the window, but we need to start somewhere."

He looked around the room.

"Let's try to meet like this the evening before each hunt for a while. I'll pass the word along to Rhys. I'll probably be spending my evenings in here anyway, going through Iolo's materials."

Turning to Ives, "What time do we start, on a hunting morning?"

"Hounds are released to their yards at dawn, and we assemble the pack in their pens shortly after. Everyone breakfasts early, and staff's in the yard a half hour before departure, ready to go. Iolo was usually there an hour early."

"And the departure time?"

"Right after the main breakfast. Most of the field eats early as well."

"I'll see you in the yard tomorrow, then, an hour beforehand," George told Ives, "and the rest of you shortly thereafter."

Thus dismissed, they rose and departed, leaving George alone in the office.

After they left, George thought about the carrying capacity of this territory for whitetail deer. If this hunt took a buck every time, hunting three times per week for a six month season, that would be about eighty deer. But roughly 20 square miles of mixed agriculture and woods, well watered and sheltered, could probably carry 300 deer or more, from which such a harvest could easily be sustained. In fact, to keep the population in check they must allow some doe hunting, too, perhaps in other forms, unless of course there were deer predators about. I wonder if they still have wolves here. Has the coyote come east for them to take its place, if not? Mountain lions? How close is the congruence between the worlds?

The hunting logs should tell me quite a bit. He sat at the desk and drew Iolo's current hunt journal in front of him, opening it up at the last non-blank page which was about half-filled. He admired the heavy rag paper, made to stand up to the ink without bleed-through.

The last entry read:

Friday, 16 Hydref

Hound walked to Daear Llosg. Young ones are sticking to their elders without couples. Keep an eye on Aeronwy, her packmates listen to her.

Owen the Leash continues to make trouble. Openly disputes me in public. Must speak about him again to Gwyn. Also, push for more staff of the right sort.

Well, now he knew how to spell that place where Iolo's cremation took place.

The dates seemed to match up, which come to think of it was odd. Did they have their own Gregorian calendar reform, or did they just calibrate it to the human world, which probably cared more about it? He had a momentary vision of a brightly colored auto parts calendar hanging over Ives's desk, and shook it off.

George sighed. He was seizing on distractions and putting this off. It was his duty to maintain a hunt log like this, but he didn't relish his first entry. He thought for a moment, then added:

Saturday, 17 Hydref

On this day Iolo ap Huw hunted hounds at Thirty Acre Wood. There he was slain by person or persons unknown in the form of a whirlwind.

He paused, then decided he had better sign it to mark the transition and carried on.

George Talbot Traherne

Sunday, 18 Hydref

On this day Iolo ap Huw was sent to rest before his friends at the setting of the sun.

Monday, 19 Hydref

Hound walked with all hounds to (George stood up to look at the map and see if he could properly name it) Beaver Brook. Lost half the pack briefly in the front yard but all recovered and behaved properly for the remainder of the walk. Junior huntsman Rhian and first-time whipper-in Benitoe are shaping up well.

Holda's rash and Anwyn's sore are healing.

He laid his pen down and turned to the front of the journal. It used the English notation for weekdays and years, but kept what seemed like Welsh names for months. It wasn't hard to translate them. "Hydref" was clearly October, and he saw from earlier years that the next month would be "Tachwedd." The year was recorded ornamentally with a great flourish on Tachwedd (November) 1 each year, and there was a multi-page entry about the great hunt to accompany it.

He supposed he'd be writing that entry himself, this year, if nothing went wrong.

This volume had about 400 pages, numbered by the writer as he went along. Most pages had three or four days recorded on them, so a full volume might hold a daily hunt log for three or four years. The spine was stamped with the opening year, with space left for the closing year, and a volume number. This was volume #498.

George put the journal down and walked over to the shelved books which held the matching volumes. The most recent were at head height, receding in time as they went down. Similar volumes with periodic minor variations in shape went back to 1410-1412

(#291), and then the size and shape changed drastically. He drew out volume #290 and discovered its pages were made of a thin parchment instead of paper. It contained many fewer pages, but they were much larger, so each volume held about the same information. The handwriting was recognizably the same as Iolo's most recent records, though the shape of the letters were a bit different.

The earliest volume on the shelves in this series was marked 475-477 (#1). But there was an older series with a different shape shelved just beyond them which picked up at year 471-475 (#313). He picked up the #313 volume, the latest in its series and compared it to #1 in the newer series. #1 seemed to still be Iolo, but the last of the older series was clearly written by somebody else. Iolo's predecessor?

The ink on the parchment was dark and the writing perfectly legible, but not the language.

The dates were clear, though the weekday names were different, and he could make out some names. He suspected this was an old form of Welsh.

He put them both back. Where he would have expected 312 more volumes in the older series, he only found about twenty bound in codex form, like books. Then the cases of scrolls began and continued to the bottom, closed up against the damp and rodents.

He straightened up and backed away from the shelves as his hair rose on the back of his neck. He could feel his ears moving back on his scalp with the frisson of the uncanny. Had one man been writing hunt logs for 1500 years?

What a resource this was. Even if it was restricted only to hunting matters it would still mention in passing their arrival in the New World, their interactions with visitors, and who knew what else.

He moved to the next set of shelves. Here were the breeding records. He brought the most recent volume to the desk.

There were hound names he recognized from the current pack. He flipped through it quickly, trying to find evidence for outbreeding, any introduction of new bloodlines, but nothing obvious stood out. If these hounds have been inbred for centuries, they'd have all sorts of defects, he thought, and that's not the case.

They'd also be very similar, and that's not entirely true, either. Look how different Cythraul's personality is from Dando's.

This gave him an idea. He went back from the present looking for Cythraul's bloodline, and didn't find it. That's odd, he thought, here's Dando, for example. Cythraul seemed to him to be about four years old, like Dando. Dando's litter was whelped in Ebrill (April), so he looked at the corresponding period in Iolo's journal (in the volume before the current one) and located the entry.

Thursday, Mawrth 28

This evening Holda whelped 3 dogs and 2 bitches without difficulty. This was her 2nd litter.

A few days later, Iolo recorded the names and descriptions of each puppy, including Dando.

That didn't answer the question of Cythraul's origin, however. George idly turned the pages as he thought about it, and his eye was caught by another entry.

Sunday, Ebrill 30

On Nos Galan Mai, from the usual spot, I returned with two hound whelps, the dog to be named Cythraul, and the bitch Rhymi. I have put them to Holda to nurse, and she accepted them.

This raises more questions than it answers, thought George. There seems to be outcrossing coming into the bloodlines, but from where? And what is "the usual spot?"

Following a hunch, he went back to April 30 from the previous year.

Friday, Ebrill 30

This Nos Galan Mai I brought back from the usual spot the dog whelp Goronwy and the bitch whelp Elain. I put them to Briallen to nurse.

These hounds would now be five years old and may well have been bred. He went back to the recent breeding records, and there he found both Goronwy and Elain used as stud and dam with others in the pack. The record for their progeny showed the breeding for their partners back four generations, but on the side for Goronwy or Elain, it was bare where their ancestors would be listed.

So, thought George, it seems like the source that created the Cŵn Annwn is still contributing to the bloodline. Let's hope Iolo told someone else where these whelps come from, or this pack will be in trouble in a few generations.

Yawning, he checked his watch and decided the rest would have to wait for another evening. Tomorrow was a hunting day.

CHAPTER 17

George rose at dawn and made a brief meal, brushing off any last crumbs as he entered the kennels. He'd left word at the stable to saddle Mosby. He wanted a familiar horse under him while trying to hunt a strange pack for the first time.

Spotting Rhys as he walked in the gate, George pulled him aside for a quick question. "When we hunt fox, it either gets away since we don't stop it from going to ground or, rarely, it's pulled down by the hounds and it ends very quickly. I've never hunted deer with hounds—what happens?"

"The huntsman dismounts and dispatches the stag with his hunting sword, breaks up the quarry, and rewards the hounds."

George thought of the long specialized knives, almost small-swords, used in German hunting. "I've never used one."

"We didn't think about that. I'll make sure one's added to your saddle gear."

"I've read about the old proper division of spoils to the hounds, but we don't do that in any formal manner any more."

"I'll help you with that," Rhys said. He turned to run the errand to the stable and armory.

George stood by the hounds they would be using in the temporary pen and did a quick refresher with Ives on their names. The rest of the hounds were expressing their disappointment at being left behind, loudly. "Keep it down," George called, and the volume diminished appreciably.

He went into the huntsman's office for one more brief look at the map. Coverts on the near right, far right, and three on the left. It was unclear what lay beyond if they got that far.

When he came back out, Rhian came up, already mounted. "Angharad's outside the gates ready for us."

Rhys returned, leading Mosby. "Owen the Leash and his men are ready." This, with a frown.

Benitoe, on a small white horse this time, was standing by. George looked at Rhys. "Is it time?"

"That would normally be for Gwyn to say, but for these three hunts I believe that's your choice. Now would be timely."

"Alright, then." George looked at the scabbard next to the saber. It contained two blades, a longer one in back and a shorter hunting knife on top of it in its own slot. He drew the hunting sword and examined it. The hilt was the base of an antler, crosshatched across the back for a better grip. The blade was about one and a half feet long, and an inch wide at its base, sharpened along one edge only, with a blood groove along the back, until the last five inches, which were sharpened along both edges. He resheathed it and looked at the hunting knife mounted on top. Also antler hilted, this was a style of hunting knife he recognized, with a three-inch blade good for butchering and other general uses.

He mounted up and patted his vest through the coat to check for the horn tucked between the buttons. Ives was standing by the pen with today's pack. George gave a brief startup signal on the horn, and Ives released the hounds who boiled into the yard while their packmates protested from their pens.

All four of the mounted staff counted the hounds. George tested Benitoe. "How many hounds?"

"Twelve and a half couple, sir." The others agreed.

Rhys stood mounted by the kennel gates and checked on Owen's men and the one member of the field today, Angharad. "All ready."

"Pack up," George called and the hounds fell into place behind him, Dando in the lead.

He nodded to Rhys who asked the kennel-man standing by the gates to open them. The pack left the kennel in good order. George touched his hat to Angharad as he went by and she fell in behind the pack.

This time there were no pack control problems as they descended the front yard to the manor gates and turned left at the road. George kept his instructions to the pack quiet and calm, and the whippers-in were more a dignified accompaniment than a necessity.

Owen's men kept up a surly argument behind him on the road. "Keep it quiet, please," George turned and told them. Owen gave him a contemptuous look but suppressed the conversation.

He glanced beyond them at Angharad, his hunt field for this morning, and she smiled at him. Don't screw this up, he thought, as he turned back to his work.

~

George spotted the ford on the river and took the path down and across. After ascending the other side and crossing the main road that ran along the east side of the river, he entered a large open hay field, with patches of woods around it. He looked at Rhian to confirm. "This is the spot, yes?"

At her nod, he held up his hand and cried, "Hold up." The pack stopped calmly behind him. He turned to Rhian."Alright, show me the search."

She hesitated, then said stoutly, "You try first. That's how I learned."

He settled himself on his horse and let his senses expand out to the land before him. The most vivid impressions were small and quick. He felt Rhian watching over his mental shoulder. "Those are predators?" he guessed.

"Fox on the ground, raccoon, and 'possum in the trees."

He could feel the horses around him and pressed out for something closer to that size. He felt one group of animals, bulky but not tall, in the far woods on the left and couldn't determine what they were. He projected a wordless question to Rhian.

"A sounder of boar," she said.

Ah, he thought. I didn't think of that. They were getting up and moving off quietly, having heard or smelled the arrival of the hunt. He tried again, using the sonar metaphor that helped him identify the ways. Off to the right, in the woods, were three cautious animals, medium-sized, and a heavier one, all together, lying down.

Deer? he asked Rhian, silently. She nodded.

He concentrated on the largest of the deer. He felt the heaviness of authority, the suspicion of rivals. These does and this territory belonged to this buck, and it was just about the season for the rut to start in earnest. Yes, he thought, this is our quarry.

He glanced at Rhian. "Would you like to try the first cast?"

Rhian looked apprehensive, but moved her horse forward. She gazed at the nearest covert on the right rather than the hounds, but she directed her thoughts to the pack, and George tried to listen in. She showed them the excitement of following something fleet-footed, musky, and confident, ready to defend or flee, both. The hounds responded with eager whines.

"Loo in," she told them, pointing at the woods, and they poured into the covert silently, heads down, seeking scent. George and Rhian cantered in with them, looking for paths to keep up. Rhys galloped over to the far side to look for deer fleeing and watch for hounds, and Benitoe stayed out of the woods on the near side to do the same.

Riding single file on the narrow trail, George paid attention to the hounds fanning out and moving forward in front of him, their noses to the ground. With his expanded senses, he could feel their eagerness and determination. No inexperienced young hounds these, to be distracted by the scent of squirrels or rabbits.

As they trotted and walked forward, George kept up an occasional low patter to the hounds. "That's it, puppies. Hunt 'im up. Good hounds." What he said didn't matter. It was the quiet voice identifying his presence and location that encouraged their work. An occasional blip from the horn had the same effect, and helped the whippers-in on the outside know where he was when they couldn't see him.

It was hard to see all the hounds in the undergrowth as they spread out, but he found he could keep a mental thread attached to each one. As one on the near side drifted too far away from the others, he called to him by name and encouraged him to return back to the pack.

With a sudden eruption, the three doe bounded across the path ahead of him, their raised tails flashing white with alarm. The hounds lifted their heads and leaned forward, but George's continued "Hunt 'im up" reminded them this wasn't the desired quarry and held them back. He could sense the deer as they fled the moving hounds behind them. Just like a canny old buck to send his harem out as a distraction while he sneaked on out of there, he thought. Rhian refreshed the thought of the proper quarry for the hounds and their noses dropped again.

They reached the end of the covert without finding, though a weak line of scent was holding the interest of a few of the hounds as they emerged into the gap between the patches of woods. Sudden laughter behind them caused them to raise their heads, and they lost their focus on the faint trace.

George told Rhian curtly, "Stay with the pack," and without waiting for her acknowledgment he galloped over to Owen, drawing up hard at the last instant like a slap in the face.

"If you can't keep your men from distracting the hounds, I suggest you wait over there until we're done," pointing at a small distant hillock where they had entered the field. Maybe they'll challenge me and I can deal with it today instead of two days from now, he hoped.

Owen opened his mouth in surprise to protest, but George overrode him. "Now." They went off sullenly.

He gestured to Angharad and waved her up. "The wind's coming up from the north. I'm going to try and hunt from the outside edges of these coverts in, so that anything we find might be encouraged to flee across the open space upwind, like those doe. If you stand quietly on the edge of the field behind us, you might get a view."

He returned to Rhian who had held the pack firmly for him, between the woods. "Thanks," he said. She looked relieved to have him take over again.

"Let's try that next covert. Look for a path on the outer side, and I'll try putting them in this time."

He waved them into the woods and rode along just inside the outer edge. The hounds came across a large tulip tree with rub marks on it from generations of deer scraping velvet off their antlers. Cythraul and Dando feathered at one spot, and then Cythraul opened his mouth and sang his joy at the find, striking out quickly to follow the trail. The zeal of the strike hound rang through the connection George had with him and pulled him along, too. The rest of the pack followed Cythraul and checked the scent for themselves, then shot off in his wake, raising their voices in confirmation and flowing over the brushy obstacles like a white river above the ground. George cheered them on, doubling on the horn.

The hounds burst out of the woods back into the field intent on the line, and George and Rhian scrambled to get to them as quickly as they could though the branches. For now, Benitoe was in the best position and he rode alongside them keeping contact. The horn and cry would've told Rhys to abandon his post and catch up, but he would now be well behind.

As George reached the open field, he glanced at Angharad, who had turned her horse to face north and was pointing in that direction. Good—she'd seen the stag leave the woods and sensibly kept silent so as not to disturb the deer or the hounds, using the line of her horse to indicate the line the deer had taken. He brought Mosby to a gallop to close the gap with the pack and had almost reached them as they dove into one of the northern patches of woods and slowed their pace. He waved Benitoe to a position on the far side of the woods and went in after them, Rhian close behind. Rhys, when he arrived, would follow the near edge.

The scent was clearly strong, and the lead hounds whimpered eagerly as they worked out the twists and turns the buck had taken. This took a little time, and George encouraged them quietly with his voice, praising them for their work.

The line took them to a small stream inside the covert and on the far side, the hounds checked. George sat his horse without moving and watched, wanting them to work the puzzle out for themselves before interfering. They cast up and down the far bank without success, then Rhymi turned back, recrossing the stream to the near side and running up the bank. George listened in with his expanded senses and could almost feel the cunning and suspicion in her thoughts, as though she said out loud, "This way, I bet he went out this way."

Several of the frustrated hounds on the other side were watching her with interest. They were rewarded when suddenly she struck the line and gave tongue. The whole pack dashed back across the stream and honored her find, and the hunt was on again.

The stag had gained ground on the hounds by his maneuvers and the scent was starting to dissipate. It held well in the sheltered woods, but each time the hounds burst into an opening, they found the wind had dispersed much of it and only traces remained on the grasses, the whole scent line, like a tunnel of invisible smoke, drifting downwind and rising as the air warmed under the morning sun. When the scent rose above their heads, George knew the hounds would be unable to follow anything other than the traces in the vegetation. Any hope of success depended on closing the distance with the quarry as quickly as possible. The buck had all the advantages at the beginning, being faster than the hounds and in his own territory, but if the hounds could keep contact with him, they would eventually wear him down and bring him to bay.

As the hounds followed the ever more faint line back out into the open field, they lost it altogether in the warmer air and checked. George looked back at Angharad to see if she had seen the buck emerge, but she shook her head.

He turned to Rhian, "I assume it would be considered unsporting to look for the stag here, to redirect them," he said, tapping his forehead.

"No, you mustn't do that. It's cheating. The hounds should use their own judgment as much as possible."

"Alright, I'll cast them forward and see if we can't find the line again."

He waved the pack forward into the next covert, hoping the more sheltered air would bring them another trace of the line, and Cythraul struck the trace again with joyous cry.

This stretch of woods and meadows didn't hold them for very long. After the buck had circled in and out three times, trying to confuse the track for the hounds, he headed off for fresh territory to the east, and George was off the map with regard to his preparations the night before. He'd been thinking of the smaller circles made by fox, not about taking a stag across country, and hadn't looked far enough ahead. Nothing for it but to settle in for the long haul and try to account for the quarry.

He hadn't yet seen this buck, following behind his hounds, but as they burst into open land he finally caught sight of him far in the distance, bounding down toward a flock of sheep whose heads were raised at the commotion of the hounds far behind him.

Rhys and Benitoe were galloping hard on each side to get close enough to control the hounds, and George pushed Mosby to do the same, Rhian trying to stay close. Worse than losing the stag would be for these hounds to run riot and kill someone's livestock.

There were no fences around the flock, so George looked for the shepherds or dogs that must be accompanying them. There they were, one shepherd and two outraged herding dogs with a fine view of a stag and a pack of hounds bearing down upon them at top speed.

The quarry was hidden from the pursuing hounds by the low folds of land and they hadn't yet caught sight of him, intent on the scent as they worked it out on the fly. George on horseback, however, could see it all from further back and higher up. He winced as the stag ran deliberately right through the flock, scattering sheep in all directions, and bounded out of sight into another patch of woods beyond them.

The hounds saw the running sheep and heard the furious shepherd dogs at about the same time, and a few of them hesitated, but Rhymi and Cythraul dove right into the flock before anyone could stop them. George broadcast the thought of the quarry as hard as he could and bellowed "'Ware riot" in a ferocious voice that promised severe consequences to any hound that disobeyed. The rest of the pack followed their leaders into the flock, where they milled like colliding galaxies spitting out woolly white stars.

The chaos that ensued was all on the part of the sheep. The hounds stuck to their work, ignoring both the panicked bleats and the futilely barking shepherd dogs. The buck had deliberately tried to foil his line with the scent of the sheep, and they were having difficulty working it out. Rhymi cast a wider circle hoping to strike the line again and found the buck's exit point. Her voice lifted the rest of the pack over to own the line and they tore off again in pursuit.

George arrived just as the hounds left, and he waved Rhys and Benitoe on to stick with the pack. "Do you know this man?" he asked Rhian.

"Yes."

"I don't see any injured sheep, but maybe there's a broken leg or some other damage. Please convey our apologies and listen to any complaints, then catch up as best you can."

Without waiting for her response, he touched his hat to the stunned shepherd and galloped off after the hounds.

The hounds stayed with the buck for another hour or so after that, checking occasionally but never for long, giving him no time to rest. Rhian and Angharad reappeared at the first pause, after the hunt doubled back in the direction of the original woods at Two Pines. The buck seemed to be seeking familiar territory as he tired.

Crossing one open field headed west, George caught sight of him again as the distance between them closed. A good-sized animal with a nice rack, he was clearly laboring, trotting rather than bounding. The sudden roar from the hounds brought his head up—they'd viewed him, and their voices changed as they raised their heads and pursued him by sight.

He made for the nearest covert with the hounds not far behind, and all the riders pushed to close the distance. Once in the woods, instead of the typical twisty trail through the brush, the buck pursued a clear path, and George rode hard on the heels of his hounds as they followed it.

Suddenly the voices of the hounds changed again to an excited high cry, pure as bells. They've bayed him, George thought. He broke through into a small clearing and saw the buck backed up against a stone outcrop, facing the hounds defiantly as they clamored before him. He had chosen to fight rather than flee further and be torn down.

Most of the hounds were cautious about getting too close to the flailing feet and threatening antlers, but some darted forward to draw his attention while others tried to snap at something vulnerable, Rhymi and Cythraul in the forefront of the daring ones. George knew he had to end this quickly before any hounds were hurt, and to be merciful to the deer. He dismounted, wrapping the reins loosely about a branch, and drew his hunting sword.

The buck's concentration was on the hounds before him, his natural wolf-like predators, and not on the man walking up from the side. George judged his moment and thrust the long thin blade into his heart. The deer collapsed.

"Good hounds, brave hounds," he cried, standing in front of the carcass and barring the hounds from overrunning it. He blew the *mort*, the death, and made a proud fuss over them, praising each one by name as they quivered with excitement. Then he drew them up to the far side of the clearing and with a stern "Pack up" he put them in Rhian's and Benitoe's charge to hold in place. Angharad sat her horse off to the side and watched.

George looked down at the carcass. What would Tristan do, he wondered. "Rhys, I'm hoping you don't have some elaborate custom for breaking up a deer, because I would have no idea where to start."

Rhys dismounted and tied up the reins of his horse. "We were never all that ceremonial in the old country, and the white-tailed deer isn't the red deer. We just gut it and give the hounds their reward on the spot, then we bring it home and hang it on a frame to drain the rest of the blood and cool the meat."

George cleaned his hunting sword with some leaves and resheathed it. He removed his coat and rolled up his sleeves, Rhys doing the same, and drew the shorter hunting knife. First he removed the scent glands below the tail, working very carefully so as not to pierce them and thus spoil the surrounding venison. He tossed those far into the bushes. Then, with Rhys's help, he turned the deer onto its back and opened it.

"Do we bring home any of the organ meats?"

"No, just the venison. The large intestine and the meat around the exit is the corbin's gift, and the hounds get the rest."

"The corbin's gift?"

"For the crows."

"What about parasites in the meat?" George asked.

"I'll get a fire going. We roast the meat for the hounds before they get it."

Rhys busied himself with a fire, setting aside some sticks for threading the organ meats while George turned his attention to the gutting.

While the fire was creating a good pile of embers for cooking, Rhys helped George with the basic dressing of the carcass. They worked for a few minutes in silence. George had done this work when deer hunting with a rifle as a teenager, and later when helping the Rowanton huntsman break up dead horses for the hounds, so he knew his way around an animal carcass.

"When we foxhunt, we can give an award to a field member who was in at the death, or who saw his first blood."

"Yes, we do that, too."

"For a fox, it's a pad or a mask. Isn't it a front foot, for a deer?"

"That's right."

George paused to wipe his blade on the grass, then he cut off both the front feet just above the joint. They were surprisingly bloodless, and all too reminiscent of Iolo's severed hands. He put them aside in a low tree crotch out of reach of the hounds and returned to help Rhys with the gutting.

By severing the organs at strategic points and taking care, they were able to pull a fairly tidy pile out of the carcass without making too much of a mess and began to roast the organs on sticks over the fire. The outdoor exercise in the crisp air made the aroma appealing enough to stir everyone's appetite and the hounds whined to be released to feast.

The gutted deer would still need to be drained of residual blood, but now they could tie it on one of the horses. Rhys volunteered his, since Mosby wasn't used to the task, and they lifted it up to tie it on behind the saddle with rope from his saddlebag. The trickiest part was turning the head of the carcass back on its shoulders and securing it so that the antlers faced backward away from the rider and didn't dangle over the horse's haunches. The horse snorted at the smell, but stood still for it.

Rhys picked up the large intestine and attached meat with a long stick, and draped it high on a bush in the clearing, then pulled up some grasses to wipe his hands. Crows had already gathered, watching with interest.

Only about half an hour had passed since the death and the hounds were eagerly awaiting what came next. George and Rhys pulled the tidbits off the sticks where they'd been roasting and made a cooked gut pile on the ground, then George stood in front of it and called the hounds to their reward, blowing and cheering them on the horn as before. They snarled over the spoils and contended for their favorite bits, but there was enough for everyone to get a taste.

He thought about the awards and went in search of some large leaves from a sycamore on the edge of the clearing. Let's hope they'll like this, he thought, as he wrapped each foot tidily in leaves.

He went on foot first to Rhian, who had moved up with the hounds. "I'm sure this isn't your first award since you've been hunting for many years, but this is your first time with me, and I would like to recognize the excellent work you did here today with this hunt." He presented her with the trophy and her face lit up.

"Thank you, huntsman. I'm very honored." He was pleased to see that she hadn't expected this.

He then walked over to Angharad. "I wouldn't presume to guess how many years you've hunted but today you are first in the field, for my first deer hunt, and I wish to honor you for it." He bowed and gave her the trophy.

She said, amused, "First in the field, and the entire field indeed." George could see that she appreciated the gesture nonetheless as she reached down and accepted it.

~

George mounted up and turned back to the west to hit the road and the river, calling "Pack up" to the hounds. They fell into place in front of him, and the whippers-in spread out to either side. Angharad turned to follow as they passed.

As they pulled out, George thought, this wasn't so different from foxhunting. The strangest part was the enhanced senses with both hounds and quarry. He was sorry he hadn't thought to see how the sheep felt about the whole affair, and chuckled privately.

The paths leading to the road were clear enough, and they reached the river soon. The hounds splashed in and drank their fill, and the riders let the horses drink. George and Rhys dismounted to do some cleaning up. Rhys scooped some water onto his horse's hindquarters to wash off the blood slowly draining from the carcass, and wiped the dampened area down with some pulled grasses.

Eventually they reached Two Pines from the north, on the road. George called up to Owen, where he sat dismounted with his men, killing time with some dice.

As they passed by, Owen and his men mounted and swung into place, wedging themselves between George and Angharad, so that she had to rein in to let them by. George could see the deliberate rudeness behind him but let it pass for now. He was working on the rest of his plan to evict them altogether in two days.

Humiliation, he thought, that was the key. Public laughter would be best.

CHAPTER 18

Ives greeted them at the kennel gates with a broad smile. "What a fine buck. And from Two Pines?"

"That's where we started him. What happens to the carcass?"

"We'll hang him to finish draining and cooling. The hide and shoulders properly go to the huntsman, the neck and shanks to the hounds, and the rest of the meat to the manor for its use. The head goes to the hounds, and the antlers to you."

"What am I supposed to do with all that meat and goods?"

"Well, if you're not eating the venison yourself, the shoulders are usually donated to staff or others that have done well for the hunt. The skins and antlers are useful to us in kennels and the surplus can be sold or traded to others. We do that all the time with the leather craftsmen and armorers."

"What did Iolo do?"

"Since he ate in the great hall, he gave the shoulders to the whippers-in or the kennel-men, sometimes others."

George had a thought. He didn't want to present a hunt award to Benitoe as he had Rhian, since Benitoe was operating as a professional, but this gave him an idea. "I'd like to do something special for Benitoe. Would he like the rack, as a trophy, to memorialize the first time a lutin has served on the staff of the great hunt?"

"That's well thought of. It would be a special honor for him to show his friends."

George called over to Rhian. "What happened with that shepherd?"

"Angharad and I calmed him down. He looked over the sheep and decided none was actually injured, just shocked. Normally Gwyn makes a payment for damaged goods or property, or sends someone to repair it. In this case, I don't think he has a real claim for compensation."

"Still, I'd like to keep good relations with everyone. Does he own the sheep, or does he work for someone else?"

"They're his flock. He grazes common lands."

He turned to Ives. "Can I give him a shoulder in compensation without disturbing anyone?"

Ives pursed his lips for a moment. "He'd be surprised, but certainly appreciative."

"Then let's do that, on behalf of the hunt." Ives nodded.

George turned his horse to face the kennel yard and asked Ives, "Please call all the kennel staff over."

Ives passed the word for a hasty assembly in the kennel yard. George waved Benitoe to him, waiting for all of them to quiet down.

He pointed at the deer still on Rhys's horse as the last of the hounds had just been cleared from the yard. "We were fortunate today. I wanted to thank all of you for the hard work you've done for Iolo and for all the help you've provided to me as a stranger, for the sake of the hunt and the hounds. This was my first hunt with you, and I have a lot to learn. But it's also the first hunt with this pack for Benitoe, and I wanted to welcome him formally, both for the work he has done, and also as a symbol of what else can be achieved. The rack's his, as a reminder of this occasion."

He turned from the surprised and flushed whipper-in and leaned over his horse to talk privately with Ives, "Think you can make use of the other shoulder as a gift to the kennel staff?"

Ives smiled broadly. "We'll have our own private feast on it in a few days, after it's aged properly."

After everyone had cleaned up at the kennels, George joined Angharad, Rhian and Benitoe for the ride into Greenhollow. Benitoe and Rhian rode together discussing the morning's hunt from their different views of it, leaving George with Angharad to follow behind. Mosby had been left at the stable for a rest and George was trying out Iolo's mare, Llamrei, in his place.

Angharad looked over as they cleared the manor gate. "Thanks for letting me come this morning. I quite enjoyed myself. You seem to be doing well building a rapport with the pack."

George was still excited and couldn't help bubbling over enthusiastically. "It's different from what I'm used to, feeling the hounds and quarry so directly, but very illuminating, too. I can't wait to do more of it and experiment."

Reining himself in to more formal matters, he continued, "I wanted to thank you for helping Rhian deal with that shepherd. I couldn't leave the hounds, and this is something she'll need to learn to do anyway. In a foxhunt, the protocol would usually be for a master or other prominent member to pull aside for that purpose, but I don't know the custom here."

"You did the right thing. She had him well in hand, and with two of us, there wasn't much he could do except give us the truth of the damage. He was still too surprised to bluster."

He thought about the plans he'd been considering on the way back from the hunt. "I suppose you noticed Owen the Leash's, um, behavior issues?"

"I was pleased to see you challenge him. He's gotten away with far too much these last many years."

He glanced at her. So, she apparently didn't approve of him, either. Good.

"I mean to be done with him in a couple of days, with Gwyn's blessing. What can you tell me about him, and how it all started?"

"About twenty years ago, the hunt staff for the great pack was as reduced as I've ever seen it. Iolo had always had two or three of the family in hand as whippers-in, some on a permanent or long-term footing, and others passing through as part of their training, as Rhys is doing now. This was reduced to two, when Rhodri completed his time and took to his travels, then just one when Islwyn was unexpectedly killed. That left only Merfyn, and Iolo had trouble controlling the hounds with just one whipper-in."

Angharad was letting her horse pick its own way into town as she settled into telling the story.

"How did Islwyn die?"

"His horse took him over a cliff. It was a great mystery, since he was an excellent rider and looked to grow into a great huntsman somewhere. No one was around when it happened."

George raised an eyebrow, and glanced at her skeptically. She returned the look with a shrug.

"What happened when the the staff was reduced to one whipper-in?"

"Creiddylad spilled word after word into her brother's ear about how dangerous it was that there should be only one, how the hounds were likely to harm someone without more control, and other such pointless warnings. Gwyn was preoccupied with other affairs, and he let her give him assistance in the form of Owen the Leash and his two cronies."

"Uh-oh. And how did Iolo take that?"

She regarded him earnestly. "You must understand that Islwyn was his great-great-grandson, and he was still stunned by the death. He was dismayed about the invasion of these uncouth and unnecessary strangers, as were all of the regular hunters like me, but he didn't have his heart in the fight about it. Gwyn's always had a soft spot for his sister, and she manipulates his guilt like the viper she is."

George looked at her. "What's he guilty about?"

"That's a long tale for another day. The short version is that he kidnapped her from her husband Gwythyr many a long century ago. It's why she has no home of her own, other than her modest dwelling in this new world. And she enjoys milking the grievance most thoroughly for maximum advantage."

She gathered up her horse as they approached the bridge.

"With Owen in place, for a while the situation restabilized, and when Rhys came and reached the age Rhian is now, we had two whippers-in sometimes, but that didn't last long. A sudden attack on his father lost us the services of Merfyn, and we were back to one."

George frowned. "Again? Who attacked? What happened?"

"I'm not sure. It was unexpected and there was some mystery about it."

"And then we lost the huntsman," George said.

"Yes, and then we lost the huntsman. No huntsman, only one temporary whipper-in, and Owen the Leash with his lads in place," she agreed. "There were smiles on their faces that morning, I tell you. Then you showed up."

"And spoiled what seem to have been some very long-range plans."

'Yes, I think that's right, that there were schemes in place operating too slowly for us to notice. If that's true, then you're now the number one obstacle in the way. When the news of this morning's successful hunt gets around, along with Owen's exclusion, you're going to become the prime target, to get them back on track."

"That's the plan," he said.

She looked hard at him. "Ah. You and Gwyn want them to expose themselves more plainly."

"Yes. But Rhian's a concern. I've warned her about the danger but it doesn't feel right to have her in the midst of it."

She smiled. "Don't worry about Rhian. She'll surprise you, I think."

The riders pulled up in front of Mostyn's house. George turned to Angharad and said, "I won't be long, just dropping these two off for a fitting."

"I'll go on ahead and get lunch ready," she said.

George knocked on the door with Rhian and Benitoe in tow, and Mostyn let them in.

Rhian walked over to the wall of shelving with cloth and began fingering materials.

"I'm not here for my fitting just yet," George said, "not till after lunch, if that suits you. But these two need livery as well, at Gwyn's request."

He looked at Rhian and Benitoe. "Both of you will be pioneering versions of the standard hunt staff clothing. Remember that you'll be a model for others when you tell Mostyn what you want, and don't request anything too extreme."

"If you can," George told Mostyn, "use the same colors as for mine, but they don't have to be identical otherwise. I'm looking for a similarity of look that marks us all as hunt staff together, not for complete uniforms like soldiers."

"When do you want this?"

"I need all three of us clothed appropriately before the hunt on Tuesday morning next, even if we have to come back for adjustments afterward. Is that possible?"

"Easily."

"Alright, then." He looked seriously at his two companions. "I'll see you all back at the manor. Travel home together, though—I don't want you riding alone. Understood?"

"I'll make sure of it," Benitoe said.

CHAPTER 19

George rode into Angharad's work yard and dismounted. Angharad stepped out of the kitchen door and called, "Put her away in the nearest empty stall."

He led Llamrei to the stable, into a loose box with fresh straw next to the horse Angharad had been riding this morning. He removed the saddle and saddle cloth, hanging them on a wall mount in the corridor to air out, and brushed her down lightly to make her more comfortable. Hanging the bridle on a hook outside the stall, he left her to a bit of grain and some hanging hay, with a bucket of water.

At his knock on the kitchen door, Angharad summoned him in. Cabal wagged at him from under the table and bounced up to give him a greeting. Ermengarde tumbled out of her basket with a high-pitched "yip" and wriggled over to be admired.

He hadn't expected a cooked meal, since Angharad had been out all morning with the hunt, but clearly she'd kept something heating slowly the whole time for the kitchen smelled wonderful. "What is that?" he asked, delightedly sniffing the air.

"A rabbit stew, with apples and dried fruits. I fried up some corn cakes to dip in it which are just ready now, so come and sit down. Tour afterward."

"Yes, ma'am," he said, taking his hat off and running his fingers through his hair. He hung the hat on the back of a chair post, and she took it away to hang on a hook near the door.

"Sink's over there, if you want to wash your hands."

He cleaned the dirt off from the ride, looking around the tidy kitchen while he did so. The kitchen stove was providing plenty of heat.

They sat at a table across the room from the stove, surrounded by windows with a view of the Blue Ridge on a bright autumn day, and the dogs lay at their feet. The stew steamed unpretentiously in an iron casserole on a wooden trivet, a large spoon alongside, and the fried corn bread lay crisp on a platter next to it, with butter and honey for condiments.

George paused to admire the plates, sturdy stoneware with stylized game animals running along the rim. "Yours?" he asked, looking over at her.

"Yes. I wanted to see if I could blend the different sizes of animals into a rhythmic line."

George could see what she meant; the line went from small game to large in a pleasing but unpredictable flow. It had the lively feel of Celtic art with running animals, but the stylizations were different, more natural. "I like it very much."

He spooned some stew onto his plate and added a piece of the bread. Taking a bite while it was still warm and crunchy, he smiled. "Fried in bacon fat?"

"What else? You like fried corn cakes?"

"They're a favorite of mine. Whenever we went camping, we brought along the makings, along with a rasher of bacon, and cooked them up in an iron skillet. We have a name for them, I wonder if you use it."

"What's that?"

"'Hush puppies' we call them, 'cause that's what the leftovers are used for."

She laughed delightedly, and the dogs at their feet kept an eye out for every crumb.

~

After lunch, Angharad offered George a tour of her workshops. She carried Ermengarde and Cabal joined them. "You're not worried about the puppy getting into trouble?" George asked.

"Cabal will keep an eye on her if I ask him to." And, indeed, when she put her wriggling armful down on the floor in the first large building, on the left, Cabal did his best imitation of a herding dog.

This was clearly where Angharad did her heaviest and dirtiest work. At one end wood-working and stone-carving benches with tools were covered under cloths. "I haven't done much three-dimensional work for a while, other than clay," she said. A woodstove in the middle of the long wall provided heat in colder weather for the entire building, but it was at the other end that George saw active work in progress.

Here there were low covered pans on work counters with various liquids, wrapped bundles that he suspected contained raw clay and other materials, and two different potters' wheels. He could smell the distinct earthy scent of clay, catching a bit at the top and back of his mouth. Shelving along the walls held unfired pieces, still dull. Two dusty aprons hung next to the doorway, along with a basket of rags for wiping hands. A standing broom showed how the shop stayed clean.

George had never worked with clay, but he knew it was a dusty, drab, business until firing brought out the strong colors and depth of the various slips and materials. Then he turned his head to the right and saw the end wall, illuminated by some of the many windows, shining where it would catch her eye every time she entered the building. Here, away from most of the dust, were shelves of finished works.

He walked over to it and worked his way down slowly, trying to let it all sink in. There were display plates ranging from fine porcelain down to deceptively primitive forms full of what the Japanese call *wabi-sabi*, that quality of subtle imperfection and randomness that characterizes all material things. He looked back at Angharad. "May I handle these?"

"Of course. That's what they're for." She stood by the door composedly and watched him.

He picked up a simple handle-less cup. The black slip covered the surface of the stoneware unevenly, revealing the raw texture of the material underneath. The glaze showed that variation in color that only use, age, and lots of hot water could cause. It fit the hand perfectly, with the unglazed portion touching the palm just reminding the holder that nothing is perfect.

He set it down and lifted a thin, translucent, porcelain plate. It showed a woodland scene of deer grazing before a backdrop of the Blue Ridge, painted in a naturalistic style. When he held it up to the window, he could see light glow through it around the shadow of his fingers. A light tap on the rim with a fingernail raised a faint clear chime attesting to the fineness and purity of the material. He marveled that a single artist could encompass both extremes.

As he moved along the shelves he lifted one piece after another for closer examination, shaking his head in admiration. When he reached the mid-section, he stopped. Here were statues and other medium-sized forms. The range of styles and subjects was overwhelming, from small abstract animal figures to full-sized realistic busts, some painted, some not.

He stepped back several feet and let his eye survey the whole display. He tried to see it as not just the output of one artist, but of one artist across hundreds of years, with all the time necessary to explore one style after another. He could dimly perceive a unity across the work, not just the unity of a single culture which, after all, did change over hundreds of years, but the unity of one mind, of one point of view, not inflexibly fixed but in a dialogue with the material and the subjects and its own experience playing out over endless possibilities.

He turned to Angharad. "I'd need days and days of looking at these, a few at a time, to begin to do them justice. I can't tell you how wonderful they are. But then you obviously already know that."

She colored faintly and looked down. George anticipated a conventional acknowledgment but she surprised him with a more personal statement. "We all like beautiful things, but I find the challenge of trying to create what I can see, and the certainty of falling short each time, to be a spur to further attempts. Each piece there is a failure to reach an impossible ideal."

"Yes, I can understand that, but how close you must come, or they wouldn't glow in the mind this way."

The color rose higher on her cheeks. Why, I've pleased her, he thought. After all these years, she cares what a human thinks about her work. Well, good, because I meant it. He was genuinely stunned to see the lifework of a artist like this, laid out over the centuries.

She picked up Ermengarde and went outside. Putting her down in front of the stables with Cabal on guard, she pointed to a clearing behind the workshop. "The kilns," she said. There were two of them, carefully sited in the open. "I used to have a third small one for metal work, but I've put that aside for now."

Her voice became a bit distant as she thought out loud, "I've been considering getting into glass for some time which would mean another building."

"Yes, please," George said. "I'd like to see what you could do with that."

She smiled, taken aback at the interest he was taking, but pleased nonetheless.

As she closed the door of the first workshop, Angharad was surprised at how moved she was by George's obvious sincerity. It's been a long time since I had an apprentice, she thought. I've forgotten what that feels like.

It's become too easy to just fall into the habit of loneliness, of talking only to herself, or of keeping quiet lest she bore her rare visitors with her actual thoughts, focused on problems of composition or execution, of how to manifest some vision in recalcitrant physical materials.

I need someone I can talk to about these things, it's been too long. Maybe it's time to seek a new apprentice. I'll write to Bleddyn in a few days and see if he knows of anyone.

She showed the kilns to George and spoke of doing glass next, all the while turning over the image of him, standing in the shaft of light at the end of the workshop, surrounded by colorful objects and holding the simple black cup. It would make an interesting subject for a painting, wouldn't it?

I wouldn't have expected someone like him to pick up the black cup first, holding it in those large hands and feeling the weight of it, its reflection of imperfection and impermanence, of life. He seems to understand that. Few do. Maybe it's the human perspective, the short life. He's clearly not a maker himself but he is… perceptive, I suppose, would be the right word. Unexpected, in one so young. It's as though I keep glimpsing an old soul inside, and I forget it's just not so.

But then, he's no boy. He thinks before he speaks, and he sees clearly. Clearly enough that he's beginning to see me, not my face, but me. It's been a long time since that's happened.

On the far side of the stable stood another workshop. When she opened the door for George, his senses were assaulted. The layout was similar, with a woodstove dividing the far long wall, opposite the entrance, but here there was painting on the right at one end, with a strong smell of oils and turpentine, and textiles to the left, with two looms, a large and a small. Everything was clean, well swept, and a blaze of color from one end to the other.

The looms were empty and covered with cloth. "More of an occasional practical craft than serious art, for me," Angharad gestured to the textile end of the building on the left. "I haven't got the patience for tapestry."

The shelving, bins, and walls at both ends were painted in long irregular blocks of color which got smaller as they moved toward the middle of the building, making an abstract match for all the paintings on the right. Both watercolors and oils, many were hung not only at the narrow end, but up along both sides for almost the same length.

George was again drawn to the display walls, densely packed with completed work, little of it framed. The watercolors were mostly landscapes, but they weren't all of the local area. There were winter scenes, almost Japanese in their spareness, with just a hint of an alpine forest that seemed somehow European. One quiet woodland scene stabbed at him, reminding him unexpectedly of his Welsh childhood.

"I've always admired those who can draw," George said. "All my life I've had a vision I wished I could render." He'd never told anyone this, and wasn't sure why he was telling her, perhaps because she was still a stranger, and an artist. It was something 'painterly' he could offer. He still faced the painting of the Welsh woods, too shy about what he was going to say to watch her while he spoke.

"There's an upland meadow and near the top, all by itself, is a great oak tree, hundreds of years old." His hands sketched the scene and placement. "The oak is strong and its boughs are wide and solid, stretching out evenly in all directions. I can't see them, but I know its branches shelter animals, and there are more on the ground as well."

Angharad was silent behind him.

"Ever since my childhood I've seen visions of it, and more frequently lately. The weather and the seasons change—sometimes autumn leaves and sunlight, sometimes heavy storm, sometimes a snowy moonlit night—but always it stands strong with roots reaching deep."

He cleared his throat. "It's silly, I know, but I can't help looking for it whenever the lay of the land feels right. Your landscapes have something of the feel of it."

He risked a glance back over his shoulder, trying to make this all sound casual. Angharad looked at him soberly, not laughing or making light of it.

He moved past the moment and turned his attention back to the wall.

The oils were altogether different from the watercolors. There were landscapes, with a concentrated boskiness that revealed a deep fondness for forests, but most of the oils were portraits, both busts and full-length. George could see that the styles changed over time, judging age roughly from the form of the clothing, and that the artist moved from an admiration of surfaces and composition, to experimentation in dramatic shadowing and three-dimensionality, to a sophisticated suggestion of depth and expression, and then a return to surfaces and form. Each area of concentration was an entire school of art in its own right, with variations and elaborations on the core concepts.

Why, long life changes everything, he realized. And isolation. He didn't see the influence of one artist on another, so obvious in an art gallery. These were her own schools, not someone else's used as a foundation. "How did you learn? Do you have apprentices?" he asked her over his shoulder, not taking his eyes off the work.

"For all the work except painting, I've learned from skilled craftsmen all my life, and shared my findings with them as well. We have another potter in this village who makes most of the domestic ware, and we chat frequently and share firings."

"But for the painting and drawing," she said, "my childhood masters showed me how to make materials and prepare surfaces, and how to see, to really see. Then they had me work largely on my own for twenty years before they would discuss their own works with me. That was all a very long time ago."

She looked at him. "Now and then I meet another painter, a few in my life, and occasionally one comes here for a few weeks or months. It's been many years since my last apprentice, but if one comes with the requisite fierceness for making a version however inadequate, of what he sees, why, then I'll have another one. I'm a master now, and that's my duty. And pleasure—teaching apprentices always clarifies my own understanding. I was just thinking about that a few moments ago."

This must be how Ceridwen operates, he thought. What a life for an artist or a scholar. All the time you need for your own studies, and an expectation that you will teach anyone serious who asks.

More than ever George was aware of the distance between them. He was drawn to her, to the mind which focused on the ever deeper understanding and realization of her vision. This was the dedication of a serious artist, but honed over centuries of existence. The work hadn't gone stale for her. I'm just a child next to this, he thought, not just in years, but in my expectation of mortality before this level of achievement in any field, much less several.

Gwyn's long life and vast powers didn't affect him in the same way, though for all he knew perhaps he was just as disciplined. Angharad's life was more vivid for him, and more impressive. Worse, he felt something resonate within him for the woman herself. She filled his eye, standing there, and her low voice soothed like velvet, but there was more than that to her, and it intimidated him. He assumed the feeling could only be one-sided and grieved unexpectedly over what he couldn't have.

In the grip of that emotion, he spoke his thoughts candidly. "I don't understand how you can bother wasting your time with me this way when you have so many better things to be doing."

Angharad looked at him, genuinely puzzled. "But I'm not pressed for time. If the older ones among us spoke only to each other, we'd never speak to our descendants at all across the years, and then what would be the point of life?"

"Besides," she continued, "you've nothing to be shy about. You came to a world you never knew existed, bearing our blood and maybe more. You're kind to our young folk and take them in charge. You fight bravely with unfamiliar weapons in loyalty to a family you don't know, defending them against their enemies. You take on a pack of hounds of fearsome reputation in pursuit of a goal you only partially understand, in front of strangers, not all of whom wish you well. And yet you seem to have no fear of failure and, indeed, have succeeded so far most wildly beyond Gwyn's expectations, if I'm any judge."

"All this in just a few days," she said, shaking her head in wonderment. "If all humans were like this, who would mind a shorter life?"

George was taken aback. This was a point of view he hadn't considered. He hadn't suspected there was anything about him she might admire.

Embarrassed, he looked away back to the wall of paintings. His mind shifted from regarding them as specimens of mastery to looking at the people portrayed, and he realized he knew some of them. Here was Rhys as a young man coming into his maturity, and there in another was a face he recognized, though younger in form and in an older style of Angharad's.

"Is that Gwyn?" he asked, standing in front of it.

"Yes, a great many years ago."

Long life surprising me again, he thought. These weren't miscellaneous Rembrandt subjects, to be appreciated just as art; these were also still living breathing people, most of them. Many are family, no doubt. An ancient portrait gallery, but of the living.

He found a chair behind him with a view of the wall and sat down abruptly as his knees suddenly weakened. "I can see I'll be needing some introductions to the family."

She smiled at him sympathetically. "I suppose this isn't what you expected?"

"You have no idea. The paintings we admire are memorials of the dead, by and large. Yours are more like snapshots of the living. Nothing here is what it seems."

Culture shock, he thought, dimly. It's finally hit me. He roused himself, under her gaze. "Tell me who's who, and I'll try to remember as much as I can."

"The oldest in your lineage here would be Beli Mawr, Beli the Great. He's Gwyn's grandfather. I've only met him once, when I was Rhys's age, and painted this many years later."

She pointed at a stern dark face, long and lean. His hair was entirely white, but the strength of his will was evident in his tense features.

"He was ancient and ageless then, and by all accounts he hasn't changed. He holds himself aloof from the doings of his descendants and isn't often seen. Ceridwen can tell you more about him, if she will."

She moved along to a ceremonial portrait, two strong men who resembled each other seated in adjacent throne-like chairs surrounded by a well-dressed crowd. Despite the formal tone, the two were individualized by different postures, the one on the left leaning forward to speak with the man bending his knee before him. Angharad had made of this painting a study of color and gorgeous materials, focused on the kneeling man who was dressed more soberly in dark greens. Two of the great shaggy Cŵn Annwn hounds, a dog and a bitch, were standing prominently, one on either side of him.

"These are two of his sons, Lludd Llaw Eraint, ruler in Britain, and Llefelys, ruler in Gaul. Pledging fealty before them is Gwyn ap Nudd, as Prince of Annwn. 'Nudd' is the older name for his father."

"Were you there, in the crowd?"

She smiled. "Better—I was court painter at the time. I'm not in the crowd because I'm in front of it, sketching furiously. I've made three versions of this scene: the large one requested by my patron, a later one for Gwyn, and finally this one, for myself."

She walked over to an informal painting of Gwyn in a recent style. "I've done many portraits of Gwyn since I came to live here. This is my current favorite." Gwyn was seated in the foreground on a rocky ledge, leaning forward with a hand on one of his hounds, gazing off across a valley to the Blue Ridge.

Angharad then pointed up to a group portrait of Gwyn and and another dark-haired man with a strong resemblance to him, standing together behind what could only be Rhys and Rhian, the latter a very young but determined child standing next to her more relaxed teenage brother.

"The fostering of Rhys and Rhian. That's Edern, Gwyn's brother and their grandfather. It's his room you currently occupy at the manor." Gwyn's expression was suitably paternal. Edern's was closed. Perhaps he was remembering his dead son, their father, George thought.

She moved now to a much older portrait of a young dark-haired woman, her lovely features subtly marred by discontent. She was walking alone across the picture, with her body leaning forward in one direction, but her head looking back the other way. The painting was full of tension, of influences from offstage.

George asked, "Is that Creiddylad?"

"Yes, the youngest of Gwyn's siblings, and my contemporary. She was never a happy woman, and hasn't changed."

"You promised to tell me this tale. Come, sit down." He patted the chair next to him.

She joined him, sitting in front of the wall of paintings but looking off into the distance of memory to compose her thoughts.

"As I said, Creiddylad's the youngest of Gwyn's siblings. Unlike his brother Edern, between them, he never knew her as a child and so, when at last they met, he saw her as a beautiful young woman, not a sister. Gwyn wasn't yet Prince of Annwn, but he was no longer young himself, and just coming into his mature powers. It isn't unknown for siblings separated by so many years to consort together or even bear children, though it isn't common." She looked at George to see if he understood.

"Their father didn't exactly approve, but neither did he concern himself about it. Then, in a rare intervention, their grandfather Beli Mawr decreed a betrothal between Creiddylad and Gwythyr ap Greidawl, as a more suitable relationship for his granddaughter. Gwythyr was a powerful lord, older than Gwyn, with many strong allies, and it wasn't a bad match."

She continued. "Creiddylad, still very young, was flattered to be the center of so much attention. She's always cared too much for the opinions of others, and she spoke to me about it once at the time, to boast about the disturbance caused by this betrothal. It was unseemly in her to glory in the ill-will between rivals with herself as the cause.

"Gwythyr was acceptable to her, and she did marry him. He was a proud man and thought her the jewel of his possessions. It might all have ended there, but Creiddylad was discontented that calm should follow all the excitement of her betrothal. She wrote to Gwyn frequently, taunting him alternately with her new happiness or with the latest outrage she claimed against her, at random. I don't know if she really meant him to act, or if she just enjoyed the power to torment, but she proved powerless to stop the events that followed."

George was paying rapt attention, sneaking a sideways look at her face from time to time. "Gwyn assembled his band of warriors, and stole Creiddylad back from Gwythyr. She went willingly enough, for the thrill of it. I was told by one who was there that she left on her own horse, with her favorite possessions, and took her time gathering them.

"Gwythyr pursued them, whether to recover what was his or out of love I cannot say. His own nobles and some of his guests accompanied him, and the two groups engaged in a running series of skirmishes. Gwythyr's group was divided, in the dark, and Gwyn captured many of his retinue, taking them all back to his lands under his father, planning to go on as before, with hostages."

She paused, and shifted uncomfortably in her chair.

"Soon enough Gwyn discovered that his sister wasn't truly committed to breaking her marriage, that her letters had been at best misleading and at worst provocative lies, and that he had already dishonored himself in attacking, unprovoked by any real grievance."

Sorrow crept into her voice. "Then, out of his frustration and dismay, he committed vicious acts which have echoed long afterward. Instead of just ransoming his captives, he began to kill them, one by one, since he couldn't kill her.

"This was bad, very bad, but worse followed. There was one hostage, Nwython, who had been captured with his son, Cyledr. Gwyn killed the father, and forced the son to eat his heart. The young man broke, raving, and Gwyn was brought to his senses. He released the remnant of his prisoners and sent them back to Gwythyr, but Cyledr Wyllt, that is, Cyledr the Mad, escaped to the forest and vanished."

George said, "Did it stop there?"

"Of course not. Gwythyr gathered an army and prepared to assault Gwyn, and then Beli Mawr intervened and admitted himself partly responsible. Gwyn bent his knee and offered recompense for his actions, but Gwythyr wouldn't accept. So Beli Mawr imposed a compact, that the two of them would fight yearly, at the turn of the seasons, until the ending of the world, Creiddylad to live with the winner. Gwythyr, as the more injured party, sought and was granted a boon. He repudiated Creiddylad, and would fight solely for the honor of the fallen.

"So it was decreed that Creiddylad live with Gwyn when he wins, and with her father otherwise and so it's been for now these many centuries."

"What sort of fights are these, between Gwyn and Gwythyr?" George asked.

"On Nos Galan Mai, the first night of May, they meet, unweaponed but for their powers, and strive for mastery in contests witnessed and judged by their peers. Gwyn usually wins, but not always. His reward is to do it again in a year."

"What about Creiddylad?"

"She's very bitter. She's never remarried and has no children. Living with her father is uncomfortable for both of them, and so she avoids it if she can. Her power over Gwyn as consort is gone, but she's still his sister and understands how to manipulate him better than he knows. He allows her to treat the manor as her home and has granted her Pencoed, that is, Edgewood, a small domain nearby for her own private use, most unwisely in my opinion."

"You think she still stirs up trouble."

"I know that she does. I don't like this Madog that she brings with her, these last many years, but Gwyn won't press her about him." She rose. "Ah, well, events will unfold as they will."

George took the cue not to outstay his welcome. He stood up and took one more long look at the wall of paintings, and his eye was caught by a large, off-white horn. Walking up to it, he saw this was a portrait from the side of a huntsman wearing a carved ivory horn at his back slung on a baldric around his chest. I used to know the medieval term for that, he thought. Oh, yes—an oliphant. Roland blew one to summon Charlemagne's army before his death. "Is that Iolo? I never saw him living."

"It is indeed."

He admired the stern, masterful features. That's a lot to live up to, he thought.

They turned to walk back toward the door, passing an easel with a canvas, draped in a cloth. "Your current work?" he asked pausing. "May I see?"

"I try never to show the subject the unfinished work," she demurred.

"I'll promise not to tell him," he said, raising an eyebrow hopefully.

"I don't know if that's a promise you can keep," she said, smiling. She gestured at it, "Go ahead, if you will. I just started it yesterday."

He lifted the protective cloth carefully and froze, the cloth still in his hand. The sketch, in charcoal with bits of background painted in, showed a mounted man from behind, his right arm stretching out a long garment, an arrow just coming through the cloth toward the viewer. The archer in front of him still raised his empty bow, and there was a clear area of different landscape behind him.

"I had no idea," he said.

"How could you? I don't often do action scenes but I found the composition an interesting challenge and, after all, I was there."

She took the cloth from his hand and draped it back over the canvas.

On his way back, George mulled over the ancient tales he'd heard, all of which were also family stories. Hard to keep both those things in mind at the same time.

What would happen if the great hunt weren't successful? Would Gwyn lose his realm, as others feared? If he did, would the family survive, these new kin of mine? Would I be able to get back home or would I be trapped here?

Or if the great hunt failed, for the first time, maybe getting back home would be the least of his concerns. You have to survive to worry about it.

If you don't succeed, a few days from now, he thought, everything may be at stake. It's not just the hunting and the killing of human quarry to be squeamish about, there are also real enemies, and you don't know who they are. You've been leaving too much of that to Gwyn.

Man up and quit wasting time. You need to take this seriously. You need a plan.

He considered. Alright, first get the hunt into a shape you can manage as fast as you can. If you can't lead the hunt, nothing else will matter.

Then find out what really happened in the last few years and see if you can get to know the enemy better, by his actions.

Finally, you've got to see what these new powers of yours can do, the beast-sensing, the way-finding, all the rest of it. It's no different from learning to fight for real, no doubt—awkward while you're getting started and frustrating, but if they can learn it, so can you. Quit holding it at arm's-length just 'cause it's not what you're used to.

Satisfied with this plan, he let his mind drift as his horse carried him smoothly along. And there's no reason I can't slip in another date or two with Angharad while I'm at it, he thought, and smiled.

CHAPTER 20

Alun found George at the stables, as he handed Llamrei over to a stable lad. The skies had darkened all afternoon and a light drizzle was beginning to fall.

"There's been a development," Alun said. "Edern ap Nudd is arriving, unexpectedly."

"That's his room I'm in, isn't it?"

"Not any more it is. At Gwyn's request I've moved you to Iolo's place."

George checked his pocket watch. He had an hour before the afternoon session with Hadyn. "Shall I come see my new quarters, then?"

They walked up the lane between the kennels and the stables. There were a few workshops on the right opposite the kennels, and then a high wall with a gate facing the lane, before the row of buildings continued. Entering at the gate, George discovered a two-story house fronted by a small tidy yard, much of which was garden. Two hollies, a male in dark green and a female forming berries, flanked wide steps to a veranda, and a tall tamarack larch provided shade over the whole house while leaving the garden's southern exposure open. The walls of the neighboring buildings rose windowless on either side to provide a private sheltered haven.

There were benches in the garden, and seats on the veranda, with tables. "Iolo liked to spend his time outside whenever he could," Alun said.

It was peaceful here, George thought. You could hear the kennels faintly, but separated by the garden wall, the lane, and then the empty kennel yards, it was a pleasant background noise rather than a nuisance. A neighbor's barking dog is an annoyance, he thought, but fifty of them was music.

"Easy access to the kennels, isn't it?" George said.

"There's a door across the lane there. His own corridor to his office. They call it the huntsman's alley."

They climbed the steps to the veranda. George could see that the house stretched almost from one side of the space to the other, with a narrow way around. "Does it go all the way through?"

"This is the back entrance. The other side's grander and fronts on the lane."

It's bigger than it seems, he thought. More deep than wide. As he entered, he confirmed his prediction, seeing three rooms on each side of a wide central hall to a double door in front. "Iolo lived here all alone in this space, with you? You must have rattled about like two peas in a pod."

"They tell me he raised families here, before my time. His great-great-grandson Islwyn lived here with him for several years before he died, but he was already grown. Since then we've kept rooms closed upstairs, and there have been few guests."

Alun took George on a brief tour. Kitchen to the left, followed by dining room and a front parlor. On the right, George could see Iolo's personality more clearly: a workroom with hand tools and materials that seemed to be an overflow from the kennels, a library in the middle, and a study at the front of the house that appealed immediately, with its worn leather chairs, fireplace, and books.

Upstairs, Alun showed him the guest bedrooms in front, furniture draped in sheets. The middle room on the west side was smaller and currently given over to storage for furniture too large for the attic. Beyond that was a corridor leading to two small rooms with windows fronting the garden side, above the kitchen. "My room is there," Alun said, indicating the outer room, "and years ago there was a maid in the next room."

The end of the hall held a bathroom with a view of the garden over the veranda roof. Next to it, over the workroom, was the main bedroom.

Alun opened the door for George. "I've packed up Iolo's clothes and stored them. Your things from Edern's room are here."

There'd been a woman's touch here once, thought George. The bed was backed by the eastern outer wall, leaving the windows all along the garden wall free for window seats, with a fine view of the Blue Ridge marching south on the right, over the outer palisade. Three wardrobes stood against the wall, mostly empty now, and two chests of drawers. A comfortable pair of armchairs with a table between them completed the picture of a little private world, where two people could lock themselves away for a time. "What does that door lead to?" he asked, pointing to a door opposite the garden windows.

"That was the nursery."

"Ah." The location made sense. He opened the door. This was a small room, over the library. The furniture was draped in cloth. "How long since it's been used?"

"I don't know. Many, many years."

It seemed melancholy to George, this empty nest sort of life played over and over again. I suppose you get used to it, he thought, but the constant reminders must be depressing. Or maybe family visits would fill a house like this with life and compensate for the ebb and flow of grown children.

"Thanks for making me at home here," he said. "I must be off to the training. Should I eat at the manor generally?"

"Breakfast here. Lunch or dinner or guests, just let me know."

"Who takes care of the garden?"

"Ifor Moel has the grounds men see to it. The rest of the place, that's my job."

"I'll see you before dinner to change, then." A thought occurred to him. "While I'm gone, I'd like you to choose something or two of Iolo's, to remember him by. I'm sure he'd want you to do that."

Alun flushed. "Aye, I shall do so."

George spent the earlier part of the evening in the huntsman's office, listening to the rain fall.

He'd been surprised at dinner by Gwyn's public congratulations on the successful morning hunt. Gwyn then upped the ante by announcing that he would accompany him on Thursday's excursion to see for himself, forbidding anyone else from joining him. This afternoon's conversation with Angharad had made Gwyn's political position clearer to him, and his public praise just ensured that his opponents would be motivated to act lest their long plans fall to nothing. He wondered if Gwyn recalled the plan to bring the relationship with Owen the Leash to a conclusion on Thursday.

George had hoped to meet Edern but he hadn't yet arrived. He had the stern face from Angharad's portrait of him still vividly in mind and wanted to see the original to form his own opinions.

The post-dinner session learning the hound names had gone well. In another night he and Benitoe would have touched all the hounds once as a group and would be ready to cycle back around till they were reliable with all the names.

Tomorrow's hound walk would take them to Eurig's place. He was eager to see it and to use the opportunity to strengthen his bonds with him. He was sure Eurig would prove to be a valuable guide to the politics, if he could keep his interest and goodwill.

Moved by the portrait of Iolo with the oliphant horn, he'd asked Ives for the key to the cupboard, but Ives told him it was among the personal effects that Alun had taken charge of. This left him grappling with a good task to sink his teeth into for the remainder of the evening, and he decided to start researching the events preceding the coming of Owen the Leash.

He walked over to the shelves of hunt journals. He needed the ones from more than twenty years ago, starting with a healthy staff of Islwyn and Merfyn. He picked out a volume from about thirty years earlier, and flipped through it looking for those two names. Merfyn was mentioned throughout, and Islwyn made an appearance near the end, so this seemed to be a good place to start. He pulled the handful of volumes from that point to the present, added the current one from the desk, and put them in a buckskin sack to protect them from the weather.

No point lighting a fire in here tonight, he thought. Let's look at these in my new study, in comfort, and then toddle off to bed nice and early.

He took the private exit Alun had shown him, down a roofed walkway between kennel yards, unlatched the gate at the lane, and latched it behind him again. A quick dash across the lane to the gate in his garden wall and then up the path to the huntsman's house kept him relatively dry, but he was glad for the warmth of the house. This rain seemed to mark the turn of seasons to true autumn, putting a chill in the air.

He stripped off his boots on the porch—still his only shoes until Mostyn's work arrived—and padded in stocking feet into the house, carrying them. Alun appeared out of the kitchen to take them away but paused, his eyes riveted by the toes beginning to poke holes through George's much abused socks. "I can fix that," he said. "Go on in to the study. I've laid a fire there."

Oil lamps were lit in the hall. Walking carefully in his stocking feet so as not to slip on the polished chestnut floor, George carried his sack of books into the front room and put it next to a worn leather chair by the unlit fire. By the light from the hall he found a lighter on the mantle and lit a wood splint from a holder there, touching the splint in turn to the oil lamps along the walls and then to the kindling beneath the logs, leaving it there to catch.

The sound of the rain outside on the lane intensified, coming down in sheets and making the fire and lamp-lit room more appealing by the moment in contrast. He took off his somewhat dampened coat and collapsed with a whoosh of pleasure into the seat by the fire.

Alun reappeared with slippers and socks in hand, and a robe over his arm. "These slippers were never used. They should fit, and the socks, too. I'll take those you are wearing." His look invited no disagreement on the subject.

He draped the robe over a chair. "This robe is little used. It's for sitting, when the hunt coat comes off."

George changed his socks and tried the slippers. It felt odd to wear a dead man's shoes, but the fit was fine. He was amused to see they were moccasins, not moccasin-styled, but the real thing: one-piece, ankle-high, stitched together at the top with leather thongs, and made of a heavy buckskin. He stood and lifted the robe, holding it out to look at it. It was more of a dressing gown in dark burgundy wool, with pockets and cuffs, suitable for appearing before other people if they called. He could see the point of such a garment to supplement the fire as the weather grew colder and tried it on. It was tight across the shoulders, and he could see Alun making note of it. "I'll tell Mostyn to make a robe to your size. What color should it be?"

"Any dark sober color will be fine. Perhaps not green, to make a change from hunt clothing. Don't forget pockets. Will I also need a robe for the bath?"

"No, a loose one hangs upstairs for that. Try it and let me know if it's suitable. Or not."

Alun straightened up a few items around the room that didn't need it. George remembered his suggestion to choose keepsakes of Iolo's, and thought Alun might be working up his courage to mention it. He asked, "Was there something you wanted to say?"

"Picked two things, I did, for remembering Iolo. Shall I show you?"

"Yes, I'd be very interested."

Alun returned in a moment. He carried in one hand a small framed portrait of Iolo, looking down fondly at a hound who was returning the gaze. George thought he recognized Angharad's work. "Very fine," he said, "and an excellent choice." Alun looked relieved.

"The other's just a little pocket momento." He held out a jointed snaffle mouthpiece, two bits of polished brass without rings. "Iolo used to fiddle with this in his pockets, he did, whenever he was thinking about something. I don't know where it came from."

"Very suitable, and a good reminder."

He continued, "Where do you spend your evenings, Alun, when you're not on duty?"

"I have friends, of course. There's work I turn my hands to, also. Iolo would let me use his workshop here in the house."

"Alright by me, too. What do you make?"

"Oh, small whimsies, is it? Birdhouses and the like."

"Will you show me sometime?"

"Yes, if you wish."

"I do indeed." He sat back down reluctant to move again.

"Will there be anything I can get you?" Alun suggested.

Ah, tempting thought. He'd need to take notes. "Something to take notes on." What else? "Do you know where the pipe and tobacco went? And an ashtray, of course."

"And I'll bring you something to drink, shall I? Mild or strong?"

"Good idea. Mild, please."

Alun took a bound notebook from a drawer of the desk in the room, larger than the one still in the breast pocket of the coat. "Iolo kept a personal journal of his own, here. The older volumes are in the library," pointing at the next room. He brought an ashtray from the mantle and the notebook over to Alun's table, leaving to fetch the rest of the items.

A personal journal—that will be a help, he thought. Sorry, Iolo, but I'm going to have to read your private words to help solve your murder.

The notebook Alun brought him was new. Herein starts my own journal and permanent notes, he mused. Not much casual use of paper for temporary purposes here, to be chucked in the fire. Think of it as a discipline to organize my thoughts before writing them down, then. And remember, it may not stay private; how hard would it be to come in when Alun was out and just read a journal sitting on that desk? Circumspection will be required.

He laid the full-sized journal aside and rose to fetch the pocket notebook and pen from his coat and bring them back to the table. He picked up the new unused journal again and wrote on the first page.

George Talbot Traherne

He turned to the next full leaf, and began, inhibited by the thought that, just as he was planning to read Iolo's private journals, someone someday (if not sooner) might be reading his own.

Tuesday, October 20,

I arrived Saturday, four days ago, apparently at the moment of the death of my predecessor, Iolo ap Huw. Such a short time for so much to recount. I will not attempt a full account of my experiences in this journal, but will use this for occasional reflections and for notes.

He paused to think. I should use this as bait, truthful but incomplete or misleading. I can use my pocket notebook for truly secret notes, and only transfer important things to a permanent record.

I am reading Iolo's hunt logs for the last three decades, to form a quick understanding of the customs.

He didn't want anyone to form an impression that he was looking into Merfyn, Islwyn, and Owen the Leash as part of a deliberate plan. He wanted Owen's discomfiture in the next two days to look coincidental and personal, not part of a tactical defense for Gwyn. This provided a reason for looking into these years in the hunt logs and had the added virtue of also being true.

Pulling the hunt logs out of the sack, he found the oldest one and opened it on his lap. Alun returned with a mug of hard cider, and the new pipe with its fixings, and took the coat away for a good brushing.

George filled the pipe with the fragrant tobacco, packing it loosely with his thumb. He took a long sip of the cider, lit up, and began reading, kept company by the crackle of the fire.

CHAPTER 21

As the full pack milled around them in the kennel yards in the dark chilly morning, George was grateful for the warmth of a hearty breakfast inside. He'd slept well in the strange bed and was ready for mischief.

He turned to Rhian and said quietly, "Be prepared for a bit of theater and follow my lead," then walked Afanc over to Rhys and repeated the warning. To Benitoe he said loudly, "Please tell Owen the Leash that his services and those of his men won't be required this morning." Ives, on foot, and Benitoe both looked sharply at him, and he gave them a private wink.

"You heard what he said, lad," Ives said, with a grin. "Get on with it."

Benitoe nodded and went through the kennel gates to Owen's band, sitting their horses. Both George and Ives positioned themselves quietly just behind the gates to listen.

Benitoe on his small tidy roan pulled up in front of Owen on a great sprawling brown horse and crowded a bit into his space. Owen was in mid-joke with his men and broke off to stare down at him. "What do you want, squab?"

With an expressionless face, Benitoe told him, distinctly enough for anyone loitering about to hear. "The huntsman bids me tell you he won't need your services this day." He nodded politely and turned to go.

Owen swelled with wrath like a toad. His face reddened and he spat out, "He can't do that." The men behind him stopped talking, and Benitoe ignored him. "Come back here, you ill-gotten spawn of a weasel…"

Benitoe turned and interrupted him. "Please clear a path for the pack," he said, his face smooth, and returned to the gates, while Owen sputtered impotently behind him.

"Well done," George said to him quietly as he came back.

"It was a great pleasure, sir." Benitoe grinned, now that his face couldn't be seen by Owen.

"No doubt, but make no mistake—he was dangerous before, and more so now. I mean to be rid of him altogether shortly, but walk carefully the next few days while this sorts itself out."

To Ives he said, "Quick, now, while they're unprepared. Open the gates."

The pack and staff walked calmly and under control past the stymied Owen, and headed out. From the corners of his eyes, George could see a small casual audience which had certainly overheard the exchange between Benitoe and Owen. He thought he detected satisfaction on some of the faces.

North of Daear Llosg the road led along the slope just a bit above the river, still paralleled by the larger road on the other side. As they came left around a spur of the ridge with the pack, George saw cultivated fields, and then an unpretentious cluster of stone buildings surrounding an old house, two stories high, whose original symmetry had been modified by several additions.

"Where do we go?" he asked Rhys, who waved him over to a gated field near the house. The pack spilled in and George dismissed them to Rhian's care as he saw Eurig approaching on horseback in company with a young man he couldn't place for a moment.

"Welcome, huntsman," Eurig said. "I think you know my young kinsman, my great-nephew. Certainly he's full of tales about you."

"Brynach, is that you? I didn't know you were a relative of Eurig here." It was his teenage sparring partner from a few days ago.

"I extend my uncle's welcome, sir." He said it shyly, but proudly, looking over at the hounds with longing on his face.

"Would you like to see the pack more closely?"

His face lit up. "May I, sir?" he asked, looking over at Eurig.

Eurig waved him forward, and George called to Rhian, to alert her to a guest. He used his extended senses to monitor the hounds attentively for any alarm, in case his read of the danger they posed to strangers was wrong.

While Brynach negotiated the gate, Eurig said, "No Owen this morning?"

"Indeed not."

They both watched the young man approach the pack calmly. The hounds came over to sniff his boots, and he leaned down from his horse to pet the ones he could reach.

Eurig said, noncommittally. "I never thought Owen was necessary. It would be good to see less of him."

"Or none of him at all," George said. They looked at each other with understanding.

"I see that you and Gwyn have something in mind. Good—it's past time he bestirred himself about this. You'll have heard that Edern's expected?"

"Yes, I've moved into the huntsman's house to free up his room."

"He's a rare and unusual visitor. You know the history of Gwyn and Creiddylad?"

"Angharad told me the story just yesterday."

"Edern's visits are infrequent because he doesn't care for the company of their sister. For him to come now, well, I think Gwyn's called him in to help." He looked straight at George. "Gwyn knows he has my support. If he, or you, can use it, just call for it."

"Thank you, sir. I'll be sure to pass that along to Gwyn."

"I'll see you then at dinner. Tegwen's still in residence, but I came back with Brynach yesterday to sort out some matters at the farm. We go back and forth like this in the weeks at year's end, since we live so close. Send Brynach back when you're done with him."

He turned his horse and trotted off.

George returned to the pack to find Rhian conducting maneuvers and Brynach paired up with Rhys. He watched for a few moments before approaching.

"Nicely done, Rhian." He waved Brynach and the two whippers-in.

"I know you all can sense the hounds directly, one way or another, but I don't want that to be the only tool in your kit. I don't know how Iolo liked to proceed, but I recommend you learn and use the ordinary, um, head-blind methods, too. There may be a time when you're too busy to do anything else other than fall back on that. For example, the hounds should be accustomed to avoiding whippers-in, as part of the packing-up process. When they see you approaching, they should think 'am I in the wrong place?' and look for the other hounds, where security lies. If you're preoccupied with a dangerous situation, if you need to turn them away from a bad place, like a cliff, simply getting in front of them should do the job."

"But if we can tell them directly, why not do that?" Rhian asked.

"You might not have enough time to tell all of them, you might not see all of them, you might be avoiding another peril at the same time—any number of reasons. You want the hounds to think for themselves, when they can, not always to be telling them what to do."

Rhys said, "So, you want them to do the task for which they're bred, to hunt, and you bring them to a place to do it, and maybe a starting point, but you want them to do the real work, as hunting hounds."

"Right, not as animate tools at the end of an extended pair of arms. So, as we work, let's listen in, as it were, but do as little 'push' or 'ask' as possible. I'm not saying give it up, it's far too useful for that. I'm merely cautioning that too much will weaken the skill and independence of the pack, just as much as not giving them time to work out a line on their own."

The staff nodded in acknowledgment.

George looked over at Brynach. "So, you like the hounds?"

Brynach grinned. "They're lovely."

"Up for an experiment?"

Brynach nodded.

"Please dismount and give the reins to Rhys."

Brynach hopped down.

George extended his senses to monitor this carefully. "Would you mind walking through the pack? You'll likely get a bit muddy."

Brynach looked delighted and waded right in. The hounds were eager for a closer sniff of him and crowded around. George couldn't feel any aggression from them at all.

Rhys said, quietly, "Looking to see if the whole excuse for Owen the Leash is a lie?"

"Yes. I was already convinced of it, but I'm just making sure."

"I could've told you that. I think the only people that the hounds menace are Owen's men."

"Really?" George called out to the others. "Have you seen the hounds growl at people?" When they nodded, he continued, "Anyone other than Owen or his men?"

There was a pause, and comprehension dawned on their faces. Rhian said, slowly, "I wonder what they're doing to make that happen."

~

When they returned from the hound walk, George and Benitoe picked up some food to take with them to eat on the road, since they would both miss lunch, and set off as planned to buy mounts suitable for a lutin.

As they rode through the village, George asked, "How do you like the work, so far?"

Benitoe answered without hesitation, "I'm very pleased with it, better than I'd hoped." He looked over at George with a crooked smile, "I particularly enjoyed this morning's conversation with Owen the Leash."

"Yes, I could tell."

There was silence for a moment, then Benitoe said, "There are always a few who think of us as children, because of our size. I'm not a child. I won't be treated as insignificant, especially by the likes of Owen."

This seemed like a good opportunity to George. "I've hesitated to inquire, not wanting to be rude, but perhaps you'll help me understand some of the customs?"

Benitoe nodded. "Ask whatever you will."

"Where are your folk from? How do you come to be living here?"

"We come from the realm of Gwyn's uncle Llefelys, in Gaul. When Gwyn became Prince of Annwn and moved it to the new world, he asked for volunteers to help settle and build, and he didn't restrict it to his own kind. A number of our ancestors wanted to travel, and Llefelys granted them leave to join his nephew."

"Do you live long lives, as Gwyn's folk do?"

"More than humans, but not like the fae. Two hundred years is a good span."

"Ives told me that most lutins work with animals."

"Yes, or small crafts. We're mostly scattered about the farms and villages. We have workers and tradesmen, even a few overseers and farm managers."

"Do you all live with the fae, or do you also have your own places?"

"Independent groups exist throughout this land, especially in the north. Most of us here, at the heart of the realm, work with the fae."

They rode quietly for a while south on the main road, having crossed the river at the village bridge some time ago. The day was still dark and chilly, with more rain threatening.

George said, "The work you're doing right now will get more dangerous. I believe there are people actively trying to sabotage the great hunt, and the easiest method will be to disable or kill the staff. I expect to be the primary target, but I may not be alone. Are you trained in fighting, at least in defense?"

Benitoe pursed his lips for a moment, and George thought he wasn't going to respond, but then he said, "We don't like to let it be known, but some of us do train with weapons."

"Would you like to carry weapons during your work, as I carry a saber? I can make that be my command, to help keep your secret." He looked directly at Benitoe. "I think it would be wise."

"I'll consider it. You may be right."

"Another matter… What are your skills with animals, exactly? For my part, I can sense the hounds as individuals, and ask them to do things. Perhaps command them—I haven't tried that. It was the same for the woods creatures in yesterday's hunt. This was new to me, here. I don't know what's normal for Gwyn's folks."

Benitoe said, "Like most of my kind, I can feel them, like glowing lights. I know when they're in pain or uncomfortable, when they're well-fed and content. In general I can't distinguish individuals, but I find that some of the hounds are more distinct than others. Cythraul and Rhymi, for example."

"Those two are different from the rest of the hounds," George said. "Iolo's journals say that he got them 'from the usual place' and brought them back to suckle one of the dams. Do you have any idea where he meant?"

"No. I didn't know how new blood came into the pack."

They compared notes, and the hounds that felt different to Benitoe all seemed to be outsiders.

"What about creatures other than hounds?"

"Well, horses, too, of course. Your Mosby's different from Afanc and Llamrei, as though they aren't quite the same kind of horses."

"Right now, as we go alongside these fields, name what you can detect."

Benitoe said, "Mice, dimly. Hawk. Groundhogs."

George continued, "Fox, rabbit, something… chipmunk?" He paused. "Man."

They looked over together and saw someone working in the field.

"It's all there if you look for it," Benitoe said.

"We should develop this further, as far as we can, each in his own way."

They played the game for a while as they rode along.

In the distance, on the left, they could see farm buildings. Small horses or ponies began to trot alongside them inside the paddocks.

"What can you tell me about Iona and Brittou?" George asked.

"I've never met them. Iona's raised stock for generations of young folk, and for those lutins who can afford them or who inherit the castoffs. Her manager, Brittou, has a good reputation for fair dealing."

"I like the look of these, certainly." The small horses showed the typical conformation of larger horses, just in a smaller size, but the large sturdy ponies had their own distinct grace and presence.

~

As they rode into the farm lane, a couple of yellow dogs came barking out to greet them. George's "hush" quieted them down. They looked like blackmouth curs, typical all-round farm dogs.

The stables and farm buildings were wooden, not the ubiquitous stone that George had become used to seeing everywhere. The house, too, was a medium-sized clapboard building, painted white, with a wide porch, sited to get a clear view of the Blue Ridge. Paddocks lined the lane and the yard, and curious heads popped over every fence.

"Quite a greeting," George said quietly to Benitoe, who chuckled. They dismounted.

The noise of the dogs, suddenly stopped, brought a groom from the nearest stable out to look. He went back in to announce the presence of visitors.

A middle-aged lutin stepped out, wiping his hands on a rag. "I'm Brittou. Are you the new huntsman Ives told me to expect?"

George shook his hand, introducing himself and Benitoe. "We need mounts for my whipper-in and if other lutins decide to give it a try, we'll need mounts for them, too. But today, we're looking for three. I'd like to introduce myself to Iona, if I may."

"Come along up to the house with me, then. We'll take care of your horses for you." He waved the groom over to take the horses into the stable.

As they talked, a woman had walked out onto the porch. She was below average height, slender, and gray-haired, like Eurig. *She's of a size to ride her own stock*, George thought. *Maybe that's what got her started.*

Brittou brought them up the steps and introduced them. "So you're the new huntsman," she said, looking him over. "I'm Iona, of course, and I hear you want some of my ponies. I asked Brittou to gather a few for you to take a look at."

They walked together to one of the paddocks and leaned on the fence. There were seven ponies in a small herd. George had helped find mounts for children in the Rowanton Hunt, and these all looked like Welsh types to his eye, with the refinement you would expect from that breed, but still sturdy and strong like all ponies. "What a wonderful quality," he said to Iona, who smiled appreciatively.

"I take it you won't be trying them out yourself," she said dryly, surveying him from bottom to top, crimping her neck to do it.

"Hardly," he said, smiling at her quip. "That will be Benitoe's task. They'll need to keep up with the rest of the staff horses, but I assume that won't be a problem?"

"They're faster than they look, and they'll outlast your horses in a long hunt."

"I believe it. Just look at them." The pony herd was racing around the enclosure out of sheer exuberance.

Brittou returned with the groom and tack, and pulled a pony at random out of the group that immediately trotted over to inspect them. This was a bay mare with a white blaze who stood quietly to be tacked up while Benitoe held her head and made a fuss over her. George extended his senses to her and found her calm and decisive.

Benitoe mounted and tried out her gaits, impeded somewhat by the curious herd that followed along behind them. He asked Brittou to set up a jump for him.

George turned to Iona. "Ifor Moel said he would settle with you directly once we made our choices. Is that agreeable?"

"That's how we usually do it, for business with the manor."

"Don't embarrass me now and charge me double, just 'cause I'm new," he joked.

"It'll be a fair price. I hope to get more business from you, if more lutins follow his lead," she said, nodding her head at Benitoe. "I'd like to see more of them as coachmen, too, like that young Isolda. Some of my cobs would work well in harness."

"I don't see how you can bear to part with these lovelies. The way that herd follows along to watch, they're the most amusing personalities I've ever seen in ponies. I'm more used to the ones named Viper or Deathwish, not these sunny specimens."

"I won't sell a stubborn pony for a child, and the mean ones don't get a chance to breed."

They watched Benitoe take the bay mare over a three foot jump to confirm her basic suitability as a hunt mount. There was nothing to fault.

"Will I see you in the hunt field?" he asked.

"Yes, most of the time. I was there when Iolo was killed and saw you come down from the woods. Look for me next week when hunting resumes."

Benitoe had moved on to the next pony, a dark bay gelding with black points.

"Would you like to see some of my other stock?" Iona asked.

"Certainly."

She took him on a tour of one paddock after another. The small herds in each trotted up to greet them, then wheeled along their enclosures like flocks of birds. There were two smaller paddocks with a single pony stallion in each. "These are two of my studs who don't live well with other stallions." They were magnificent, with heavily muscled necks and bodies, and a proud carriage, their manes long and flowing.

"You must've been doing this for a long time to become so expert at it."

"For hundreds of years. Even so, each foaling season brings new surprises. I bring in new blood from time to time, of course.

And then, my ponies travel everywhere, so I get news from everywhere, too, from the parents who buy them and from the children who learn on them, after they've grown. Ponies live a long time, you know, longer than horses."

"So, not such an isolated country life as it seems, eh?"

"Only when I want it to be." She pushed off from the fence of the paddock they had reached at the end of the lane. "Let's see how your lad's doing."

They walked back up the lane where the maples were showing their last bit of color before losing all their leaves. Benitoe was trying a white mare. George took a closer look; he was distinctly more mud-covered than when he started.

"Had a spill?" he called.

"That gray one there had her own opinions about the suitable height for a jump and I wasn't adequately prepared for her reaction."

"Ah." The gray looked pleased with herself, but George could sense no vice in her.

"She did eventually take the jump," Benitoe was quick to add.

"I was sure of it," George said, with a straight face.

Benitoe dismounted and Brittou and the groom untacked the pony. "That was the last one," Brittou said.

"So, what do you think of them?" George asked Benitoe.

"They're all rather wonderful," he said, including Iona in the response. "Any of them would be fine. If I must pick my three favorites, they would be the first bay mare, the white gelding, and the gray mare."

"The gray that dumped you?"

"It wasn't really her fault. They have nice gaits, good temperaments, and great willingness."

"Iona, what's your opinion?"

"I think those are good choices. The gray would be a boss mare in the right circumstances, but she's cooperative as well as smart and strong. That sort of independence could be useful for a whipper-in. The bay is absolutely steady, and the gelding's a joy to ride."

"What are their names?"

"The gray is Gwladus. The bay mare's Eleri, and the white gelding is Halwyn."

She had Brittou remove the other four, and put halters on the three chosen ones. "Do you have lead ropes?"

George paused as an idea struck him. Could he treat these ponies like a pack of hounds and make a showy splash to attract attention and draw out Iolo's murderer?

He said, "I was thinking of conducting an experiment. Do you have a larger field we could use? Doesn't matter if it's already occupied. We'll need to mount up ourselves." He explained what he had in mind to Benitoe, in front of an amused Iona.

They waited for the groom to return with their horses, then they opened the paddock gate to the larger field beyond. George picked up the mental threads from the three ponies, and bonded them into a little herd, with Benitoe's mount and Afanc included. He treated Gwladus like the boss mare and tried to guide them as a herd the way he wanted them to go. It worked better than he would've thought. By using the gray's natural inclination to lead he was able to treat them almost like a harnessed troika, with the other two horses trailing behind.

Benitoe watched what he was doing, with all his senses. "What will happen when they want to stop and graze, or if they get spooked going through the village?"

"I don't know. Let's try to cut through the herd over there."

Like all the fields, this one had a pony herd, but it had kept its distance, so far. They headed for it at a trot, and the herd swept out of the way and circled around the back to keep an eye on them. Their three ponies didn't seem to care.

"Alright, let them graze for a few moments without separating, and we'll see if we can start them up again."

They dropped their heads to the grass, and the other herd came in curiously to sniff them, now that they weren't behaving so oddly. After a few mouthfuls, George picked them up again as a group and encouraged them away from the herd. They went willingly.

"Will this work as they go through the village and into the manor yard?" Benitoe asked.

"I have no idea, but wouldn't it be a fine show if we can pull it off?"

Benitoe grinned with him, and nodded. "Let's give it a chance."

They brought their three back to the paddock through the open gate and closed it behind them.

"You're going to try that, all the way home?" Iona asked.

"Might not work, I grant you. I'd like those lead ropes, just in case."

"Well, I admire your ambition. I imagine I'll hear all about it, one way or the other."

George smiled, "No doubt."

They brought the three loose ponies up the front yard of the manor and through the curtain wall at a brisk trot and came to a showy stop in front of the stable. Grooms poured out to take charge of all five mounts while George and Benitoe dismounted and walked up to the three ponies, taking them by their halters and making much of them for their cooperation on the long journey.

They had gone through the village at a prudent walk. Riders passing them in the direction of the manor had clearly spread the word, because quite an audience had appeared to watch their arrival. Isolda and Ives joined Benitoe who was pointing out the good points of the ponies, and some other lutins came by to comment. Rhys and Rhian were on hand, to support the hunt, and Brynach and Eurig stood nearby, Brynach with a broad grin on his face. Ceridwen came over to greet George.

"Putting on a show?"

"Can't hurt any. The more competent I look, the better a target I make of myself. I think this should be a good attention-getter."

"Even Gwyn came to watch." They walked over together to him.

"Nice ponies," he said.

"Yes." I can be just as laconic as he can, George thought.

"Good recruiting lure for other lutins."

"I thought so."

"A big entrance."

"That was the idea."

Gwyn looked at him and smiled slightly in appreciation of the verbal volley. "I heard about the summary dismissal of Owen the Leash this morning, at the hand of a lutin."

"Don't forget the showdown coming tomorrow morning," George said. "I'll make it as public and humiliating as I can, and you should blame it all on me."

"I haven't forgotten. You might want to take special guard for the possible consequences."

George smiled fiercely and leaned forward on his toes. "Let him try something. I'd like to know who he really reports to."

They watched the ponies being admired for a moment.

Gwyn said, casually. "I may bring a guest hunting tomorrow."

"Oh?"

"I've asked my brother Edern to join me."

"We'll do our best to show you sport, but you know it's going to be all about training, still," he said.

"We'll be spectators only. Don't worry about us."

CHAPTER 22

At dinner that evening George finally got his opportunity to meet Edern. He was interested to see that Edern was seated to Gwyn's right, after Idris. It was a place of honor, certainly, but also well separated from their sister on Gwyn's other hand. Eurig's comments about Edern's dislike of her were borne out by the stern countenance he maintained throughout the meal whenever she spoke, and the effort he made to confine all of his own conversation, what there was of it, to the immediate family seated to the right of him.

George swapped places with Rhian so that she could be nearer her grandfather, and Rhodri joined him at the end of the table on the same impulse.

"Does he ever smile when he isn't looking at his grandchildren?" George asked Rhodri quietly.

"Not always then, either. He used to smile at their father, but they remind him too well of what he's lost. No blame to them for it."

"What happened?"

"We can't talk about it here, we'll be overheard. After dinner."

George caught Edern studying him occasionally during the meal, and once he leaned over his grandchildren to speak to him directly.

"How are you enjoying your stay, kinsman?"

Interesting. He calls me 'kinsman,' unlike his sister. "I'm enjoying it very well, sir. The challenge is absorbing, the people are welcoming, and I'm very pleased to discover family here. It'll be hard to leave when my job's done. I'm only sorry that my opportunity came at such a cost."

Edern nodded soberly. "My brother has invited me to join him tomorrow. We'll try not to interfere with your training requirements."

"I look forward to it, sir. We'll try to give you good sport."

At the end of the meal, as things quieted down, Eurig rose from his seat with Brynach, and walked up on the dais to stand in front of George, drawing all eyes.

He spoke loudly so that all could hear him. "Huntsman, my kinsman Brynach tells me he wishes to study the hunting of hounds. I seek your permission to apprentice him under your mastership, to employ him as you see fit in this learning until such time as he may be released by you or relinquish the work himself. I pledge to maintain his costs, in horses, in clothing, and in such expenses as may arise until this term is completed. How say you?"

There was dead silence in the hall. George had risen when Eurig's speech began, and glancing down at the seated Gwyn, he could see by his stiffened body that this was a surprise to him as well. Eurig had played his own political card in the game, in strong and public support of Gwyn. George felt compelled to warn Eurig about the danger Brynach was getting into, but not in public like this and besides, looking at Brynach's shining face, he couldn't spoil this glorious moment for him with mere prudence.

He replied, projecting his voice clearly, "I am pleased to accept Brynach as apprentice to the study of hunting with hounds, to guide and support him to the best of my ability until such time as I release him or he relinquishes the work himself."

He turned to Brynach and extended his hand across the table. "Welcome, Brynach. Please join us in the kennels after dinner."

Brynach clasped his hand, stammered out a reply, and followed Eurig off the dais, unmindful of his footing.

George sat down abruptly in his seat as murmurs rose in the room. "Is this how it's usually done?" he asked Rhodri.

"The last apprentices were Rhys and me, and those weren't formal, just part of our family's diverse training. Before that, it would've been Islwyn, who was Iolo's family so again no formal apprenticeship… No, the most recent time something like this has happened would've been Merfyn's apprenticeship, perhaps thirty or more years ago, and I would've been too young to witness it. I don't doubt that Eurig made up the wording on the spot, just now."

"The sly old badger. Glad he's on our side," George said. He thought about the tangle he would leave behind in a few days. "What'll happen after the great hunt, when I return?"

"That will be for the two of you to work out with a new huntsman, I imagine."

"So I should just make it up as I go along, is that it?"

Rhodri shrugged.

George considered, then turned to Rhian on his left. She and her brother had been as startled as anyone. "Please come, both of you," looking past her at Rhys, "to kennels this evening."

Rhodri surprised him. "May I come, too?"

"You're always welcome."

"Good." He grinned. "We can have a party."

Rhodri filled in the story of Rhys ab Edern for George as they walked over to the kennels.

"Rhys was Edern's youngest son, and the younger the child, the closer the parent. He was still young when he sired Rhys Vachan, less than a century, I believe, and the birth of Rhian so soon after was an even stronger blessing, so close as they are in age."

"What happened to him?"

"Remember, this was only about twelve years ago. Rhys and his consort were summoned to Edern's father's court. They were to bring their children, but Rhian wasn't much more than an infant, so they decided to ignore that part of the invitation and bring the children another time. They left them in the care of a nurse in Rhys's household and took the way that would send them to Rhys's grandfather. Only it didn't."

"I don't understand," George said.

"The way entrance they used was in the correct spot, and the token activated it, but it was a false way, one that had been overlaid on the real one just a few feet in front, and they were sent with all their companions to a place unknown. Some of the group had traveled with them just to see them off, and it's by their accounts we know what happened."

"Gwyn was brought in to look at the situation, and I helped him, as best I could at the time. The invitation enclosing the way-token was shown to be false. When we tried to find the false way, it was gone or hidden."

"No wonder Gwyn didn't want to linger on the other side of the way at Daear Llosg."

"Right. He didn't want to spring a similar trap."

"So, were they killed?" George asked.

"No one knows for sure. None of them have been seen again, and we must assume the worst since if they were being held merely as hostages we would've heard by now. Edern put a steward in charge of his son's estate to hold it for Rhys, but he couldn't leave the children there, subject to some other hostile act, and he wanted to devote himself to pursuing the villains who had attacked his family. So Gwyn offered to foster them."

"Is that what usually happens to orphans?"

"Yes, but there's more to it than that. This was no random attack but the act of an enemy who took time and care with the plot and had special abilities with the ways that are unfamiliar to us. Enemies we have in plenty, but Rhys ab Edern was too young for it, so they must be enemies of Edern or his close kin. None of those, so far as we know, could have made that way-trap. The best speculation I've heard runs that this was an old enemy allied with a new or hidden power, whose trap only partially succeeded."

"And everyone's lived with that uncertainty for twelve years?"

"Yes, and they're now very alarmed at recent events, of hidden ways with unknown owners, of sneak attacks on Gwyn, of tunnels through our palisade, and, most of all, of the mysterious death of our huntsman, preceded as now seems clear by successful attempts to weaken our ability to conduct the great hunt that go back twenty years or more."

"So you think it's all connected," George said.

"Wouldn't you? I have my own partial theory. I think the only person who seeks the failure of the great hunt is Gwythyr ap Greidawl, for the ancient grudge. I think he must be behind the loss of Islwyn and Merfyn, beginning twenty years ago. I'm less sure, but I suspect he was also behind the attack on Rhys ab Edern and his family twelve years ago, since there was no one accessible to him in Gwyn's direct line equally vulnerable, and he hates us all. But I don't know where the way knowledge is coming from, I can't see how the murder of Iolo was managed, and there are just too many loose ends. I could suspect Creiddylad of almost anything, but not of working in combination with Gwythyr who repudiated her, nor is she skilled in these areas."

"Someone told me Edern isn't usually here, that he was probably called. What about you? Would you normally come back at this time of year or were you summoned?"

"Gwyn called me to come immediately. I believe he sent an urgent summons to Edern, too. Edern hasn't been here for years, and I was surprised to see him. Perhaps he senses the hand of whomever killed his son, and wants to be in on the fight. If anything, he's more suspicious of Creiddylad than I am, blaming her for whatever plot resulted in the loss of his son."

They had lingered outside the kennel gates for this conversation, for privacy. George saw Rhys and Rhian headed their way, with Brynach, and tapped Rhodri on the shoulder to call his attention to it.

He turned to wave at the others and opened the gate for them all.

There were so many people in the huntsman's office for the evening meeting before a hunt that Ives and Benitoe had to bring in additional chairs of their own. Alun, with excellent forethought, had supplied sufficient mugs and beer to get them started.

George began with introductions. "Ives, Benitoe—you may have missed the news that I've just accepted Brynach here as an apprentice for learning about hunting with hounds." Brynach smiled shyly at them across the room. "This raises interesting questions about everyone's status, and I wanted to sort that out first."

He continued, "This will be old hat to some of you, and please correct me if I'm suggesting something that doesn't sound right or proper, since I don't know what you're all accustomed to. Just bear with me.

"First, Ives is kennel-master. His word is law here in kennels, and you'd be well advised to heed it anywhere else, too. Doesn't matter if it's 'your job' or not. We all in agreement about that?"

Heads nodded all around.

"Alright, then. Rhodri has graduated from this particular school and doesn't count." Rhodri took a comic bow and Rhys found something to throw at him, which he ducked.

"Rhys, like Rhodri before him, is going through an accelerated course of exposure which will be followed by some other form of learning altogether, all of this to fit him for rule. Or so I understand."

"That's right," Rhys said. "I've been whipping-in under Iolo for two years, and this great hunt was to be my last. Next will be history and politics under Ceridwen and my foster-father, and my outdoor work will all be related to farming." This last with a grimace.

"Now, Benitoe. You've joined as what I would call a professional, someone who makes his living at this. You have some experience, will be learning more, and expect to stay for the long-term. That's not an obligation on your part, just an assumption on mine. Do I describe rightly?"

"Yes, that's how I see it, too. Just as Ives is a professional."

"Alright. Rhian, now, is what I would describe as an amateur, someone who doesn't currently make their living at this, though that could change. She is, in any case, not of age to make that decision. Our newest member, Brynach, falls into that same category, but he's an official apprentice. The only difference in status that I see between Rhys, Rhian, and Brynach is that the first two are amateurs who are not apprentices because they have additional obligations and may be short-timers, whereas Brynach will be treating this as his primary responsibility for some time. Correct?"

Rhian objected, "This is my primary responsibility, too."

"Agreed, but like Rhys you'll probably have a series of temporary roles to fit you for estate or domain rule, not so? In which case, this is just the current one and I should expect to either lose you later, in this role, or for you perhaps to make a different decision when you're of age."

"I suppose so," she said.

"Alright, then. Here's what I intend. Rhys and Benitoe, you're free to participate or not, as you choose, but I encourage you to come. Starting next week, I'll begin a course of study for Rhian and Brynach. It will include reading and discussion, kennel management and hound maintenance, hound management and hunting, and breeding and training. Since so much of this will be practical rather than theoretical, I want to see all of you at the meets, doubled up as appropriate. For now, that means Rhian with me and Brynach with Benitoe. We'll change that around sometimes."

Rhian asked, "What will happen after the great hunt…?" She stopped, awkwardly.

"You mean, when I leave?"

She nodded.

"None of that's been decided for sure. If I must go back, I'll urge the continuation of this with my successor. For now, let's just assume it's permanent."

He looked at each of them with emphasis. "One more thing. As you all must realize by now, we have enemies among us. Iolo's dead and more attacks are threatened, aimed at disrupting the great hunt anyway they can. All of you will take basic training with Hadyn for self-defense and become comfortable with some weapon you can carry with you while hunting. I won't have anyone harmed for loss of a knife at the right moment or reluctance to use it. Are we clear on this?"

Rhian and Brynach nodded.

"Starting immediately, mind." Looking around the room, he tried to make them see the importance of this. "We're a team and must train like one and act like one, helping each other with our tasks and prepared to handle emergencies together. I won't insist that you travel in pairs everywhere, but at least consider it when you go to the village."

This time, everyone nodded.

"Alright, then, let's work on the plan for tomorrow."

George pulled Brynach aside before he left and spoke to him about ordering livery from Mostyn. "You can go down tomorrow when Rhian or Benitoe go in for their second fitting. See them to set it up."

George dropped in on Ceridwen before turning in. "I was glad when you asked for this meeting today," she said as she came to the green door of her house. "We have much to discuss."

They made themselves comfortable in the deep armchairs in the study George had seen on his last visit, and Ceridwen began.

"You asked about some of the investigations I've been doing for Gwyn. You remember the parchment note that came with Iolo's hands?"

"Yes. I thought it might be a palimpsest."

"You were right—older writing was scraped off for this scrap. The topic wasn't relevant, and I couldn't identify any obvious source, but the word choice and spelling was more old country than local, for a few words that have changed over the centuries."

"Doesn't that match what you thought about the words on the spell-stick?"

"Yes, it's consistent. Along with the hempen twine, all three items point to an old country source, not one of our own," she said. "Or else it's very clever misdirection."

He stared into the fire for a moment, the lamp light making visible rays from the traces of smoke and dust in the air.

"Weren't you going to be taking a look at the hole in the palisade, with Creiddylad?" he asked.

"Yes, and wasn't that interesting. You know, she grew the palisade herself, when first we came here? That's the area her skill lies in, plants and herbs."

"Idris told me the story."

"I had the hardest time getting her to come with me but finally, yesterday, we approached it from the outside and, I hope, in secret. I think it shocked her." She picked up a small wooden bear from the low table between them and toyed with it.

"You've seen me eating with her at meals?"

He nodded.

"It doesn't do much for my appetite, but someone has to stay close to her and try to monitor her activities. I don't trust that Madog fellow, never have. One benefit of my spoiled meals is that she really can't deceive me well. All of this to say that I don't think she expected the damage at the palisade. I won't say she didn't expect something—after all, we told her about it—but I'm sure she didn't anticipate such a poisoned tunnel as we found. She wanted to try and heal it, on the spot, but I persuaded her to leave it alone for a while."

"Do you think she can heal it?"

"Surely. She built it in the first place and the damage doesn't seem to be spreading."

"Has anything tripped the alarms at the small hidden way?" He waved his hand to the west.

"Only wild animals, so far. The clearing shows no other sign of use, and the way you sealed at Daear Llosg is undisturbed, as near as I can tell."

Ceridwen rose and walked to the door, bidding a servant to bring some tea.

George said, as she came back, "Thanks for bringing me up to date." He leaned forward in his chair. "But now I need to hear about the rest of the theories and actions that only the people in the inner circle know, which must remain secret from Creiddylad, since she's suspected of being involved in some way."

"Besides her," he continued, "I'm finding out more and more about the events of twenty or more years ago with Iolo's staff, with Merfyn, Islwyn, and the coming of Owen. Add to this the mystery surrounding the death of Rhys and Rhian's parents that Rhodri told me of, and I find it hard to think it's all coincidence."

"Yes, I see enemy action as well," Ceridwen said, "and so do Gwyn and Edern."

"And Angharad, who told me some of the history. I presume many others have suspicions."

The tea arrived and in a few moments, George was leaning back comfortably in his chair with a hot mug, and Ceridwen had put hers aside so that she could gesture while she talked.

"Let me tell you a tale," Ceridwen said, "and we'll see if we can build a framework that can bear the weight of our suspicions."

George settled in to listen as she set the stage.

"About twenty years ago, the hunt staff for the great hunt were thus: Iolo, Rhodri, Merfyn, and Islwyn. Rhodri was the youngest, having just joined for the limited traditional training of a scion of the house. Merfyn, about your age at the time, was the son of Ithel, from Gwyn's father's court. He intended to stay indefinitely, having been given leave to do so in order to help his father build kennels and maintain a hunt when he returned. At that time, he had been working for Iolo, oh, about ten years."

"Twelve. I've been reading Iolo's hunt logs and personal journal."

"Ah. The third whipper-in was Islwyn, Iolo's great-great-grandson, the youngest of his current descendants. He was a rising master, then in his twenties, and had been working with Iolo for about six years." She looked at George, who nodded to confirm the dates.

"Islwyn looked to become another huntsman under Iolo, with excellent control over horses and hounds, and growing experience with the cunning of the wild beasts in the field. He lived with Iolo. I hadn't seen him so happy in a great many long years."

She paused to take a sip of her tea. "Rhian may be another such as Islwyn. It's too soon to know."

"This is how it stood when I think it all began." She set her mug down. "Rhodri departed for the next phase of his education. This was the start of his travels to learn music, something he's still doing, combined with his diplomatic training.

"So, now Iolo had two seasoned whippers-in with one of them, in his own family line, looking like a new young huntsman-in-training. At that moment it seemed to us that all was well, that the hunt was assured of continuation. Looking back, I think instead that this was the spur to strike, before this stability became unbreakable, while there was no one in the family of an age to serve as a replacement."

She looked at George as if to make sure he had been following closely. "Who has most to gain from damage to the hunt?" she asked.

Like an obedient student, he replied, "Gwythyr, I imagine."

"Yes. This has the smell of Gwythyr who would love to see Gwyn bested at the great hunt. Gwythyr's strong but not subtle, and the first action taken that we can recognize is the death of Islwyn, the sort of violent action which is just his style."

"Islwyn and his horse went over a cliff?"

"Unlikely as that sounds for a man with full control over hounds and horses. It was during a hunt, just before the Nos Galan Gaeaf, so he was alone, as a whipper-in usually is. We heard the cry as he fell," she tapped her forehead, "but nothing of any use to us about how it had happened. We went over the ground very carefully afterward, you may be sure, but we could find nothing."

"You assume the horse bolted, too near the edge for Islwyn to stop it?"

"We know from his cry that he was surprised so, yes, that seems the most likely thing."

"What could scare the horse so? A bear or wolf?"

"This was a hunt horse, trained to such things, and in any case Islwyn would have been aware of it. And we found no tracks."

"So, something Islwyn couldn't sense popped up out of nowhere and scared the horse off the cliff."

Ceridwen nodded.

"When you put it like that, could it have been a way opening?" Ceridwen stared at him. "Well, couldn't it? Unusual use of the ways seems to mark many of the events we're talking about."

"That's something I never considered," Ceridwen said slowly. "Gwythyr has no special skills with the ways, much less than even I have, so no one would think to look for that."

"Maybe he has a friend or ally. Or maybe it isn't Gwythyr."

"No, I like the notion of an ally skilled in the ways. Gwythyr's had strong partnerships before, to serve his will."

"How did the great hunt go, that year? Iolo's notes don't elaborate on any difficulty."

"We went forward with just Merfyn in place, having no other choice. It was grim; Iolo was sunk in grief. But the hounds stayed under control and we fulfilled our task."

"So if someone was looking for a quick disaster for Gwyn, they would have been disappointed."

"Indeed. But we couldn't be sure it was an attack, and there was no immediate followup." She cleared her throat. "Except that Creiddylad began her campaign for a different hunt management arrangement. She argued for a guard staff as a line of secondary whippers-in. It roused all our suspicions again, but she painted it for Gwyn as her way of helping in his time of trouble. Gwyn was… susceptible… and Iolo was too preoccupied with his loss to resist much."

"And so Owen and his men arrived."

"From her own household, or so she said."

"You don't believe that?"

Ceridwen pursed her lips. "You've heard the story of her marriage and its aftermath?"

"Angharad told me."

"She would know. They're of an age, though never friends."

She continued, "Creiddylad was always weak and feckless, and when her mischief-making caused so many deaths, Beli Mawr punished her with this absurd internal banishment, her father's domain or Gwyn's. I fear she never felt herself responsible for the carnage, but bitterly enough she resents the result. Gwyn, in pity, granted her Edgewood from his own realm, here, so that she might have some independence."

She sipped her tea. "I understand his motivation, but it removed her from under his eye, which was a mistake."

"What's it like, in her domain?"

"No one knows. Gwyn sent craftsmen to help her build it, and she recruited some farmers, but they don't travel. She doesn't invite her family. In the early days, the families of those who left with her petitioned Gwyn to visit their relatives, but he bowed to her wish for privacy and supported her refusal."

George straightened up and leaned forward in his chair. "But they were his people. How could he let them vanish, possibly to death or disaster, and not check on their well-being?" He couldn't keep the incredulity from his voice.

"Over the years, especially at the beginning, many of us said the same thing. It was too near the disastrous slaughter of the abduction, and Gwyn's guilt over his own actions left him open to her manipulation. So it was done. Now we know little of her domain, except what I can gather with each seasonal visit, from her or her entourage."

"What do you think it's like, then?"

"I think she's a little tyrant, in her way, but she's not clever and, like many such, doesn't understand her own limitations. Her bodyguards, like Mederei, do her bidding honestly, and so do many of her staff, but there are some whom I think have their own agenda. I can't believe that Owen the Leash and his men are truly hers—they don't pay her that sort of respect, and why would she have had such men in her pay so handily? For what use of her own? I believe she fears them, a little, for all that she pushed them on Gwyn as an aid for the hunt."

"So, where would they have come from?" George asked.

"I don't know."

"What does this Madog fellow do?"

"Officially he is to her what Idris is to Gwyn, a trusted second. I've often wondered if he's really in charge; he says very little but he's ferociously intelligent, however he tries to hide it with lowered glances and pleasing manners."

"Where did he come from?"

"He won't say, and Creiddylad answers no questions about him. Whenever she first took up with him, she first brought him here on her visits, oh, about fifty years ago. Gwyn hasn't been rational on this topic, perhaps because he suspects Creiddylad has taken Madog as a secret consort."

George steepled his hands together. "Let's look at this analytically. Creiddylad's original farmers and crafts-folk may have thrived behind her closed walls, but how do they trade? Where does she recruit people of her own class or any other outsider?"

"She had one way at Edgewood which Gwyn restricted her from but she closed it against all but Gwyn, who had higher authority over it, and he respected her privacy. This satisfied the terms of her exile. That doesn't mean she hasn't found other means of travel. She could have her own trading arrangements, though I've never heard anyone speak about them, and it's the sort of thing one hears in gossip—who's buying or selling what, what's the latest fashion, and so forth."

"Still," she continued, "it seems clear that she must be communicating with complete outsiders, or even traveling herself. Else it's very difficult to explain Madog or Owen."

"So much for exile, then." George tried to bring the problem back to its fundamentals. "What does Creiddylad want, really?"

"Not to be under her father's control nor her brother's," Ceridwen said. "To let the past by bygone."

"How could she get that?"

"Earn it by a demonstrably changed character." She raised an eyebrow at George's skeptical glance. "Yes, I know. Not likely."

"How else?"

"Make it worse to hold her than to release her," Ceridwen said slowly. "Embarrass Gwyn, or her father. Appeal to Beli Mawr, her grandfather, perhaps."

"And the best way to embarrass Gwyn would be for the great hunt to fail, for the first time. That would put her on the same side as Gwythyr," he pointed out.

Ceridwen waved her hand. "There's no love lost between them any more. But she's not above attacking Gwyn for her own private purposes, even if it furthers Gwythyr's cause. I don't think she would want her brother to come to actual harm, but she wouldn't balk at humiliating him if it won her her freedom. It might even please her better that way."

"So she might have been behind the attack on Islwyn, instead of Gwythyr."

Ceridwen shook her head. "She has no more facility with the ways than Gwythyr does. If it was way-based, and the later attacks certainly were, then we're still missing an important player."

They both paused to consider that.

"What was the next event?" George asked. "The disappearance of Rhys and Rhian's parents?"

"About twelve years ago."

"Rhodri told me. That happened in the British domain, right? Does that rule out Creiddylad?"

"Not if we assume she has her own travel ways by now. But again, this was a strange and unexplained use of the ways."

"If Creiddylad doesn't want to harm Gwyn, would she kill Edern's son? It's just an accident that the children weren't included."

"It doesn't ring true," Ceridwen admitted. "It's not related to the great hunt. It's a direct attack on the family."

"So, maybe we're back to Gwythyr?"

"Edern's not sure. He sees their sister clearly, where Gwyn does not. Ever since the disappearance of his son he's been scarce at Nos Galan Gaeaf, preferring to spend his time away from her."

A servant stuck his head in the room to see if anything was needed, and Ceridwen requested more tea.

"Then something happened to Merfyn. Can you tell me the details?"

"Two years ago, just after Rhys had started his service as whipper-in, Merfyn's father Ithel was attacked and killed. The murderers were never caught. Merfyn was called home to take charge and that ended his time here with the hunt."

"Is it known who killed him?"

"No, but there's no particular necessity to invoke the use of travel ways to do it."

The fresh tea arrived and they sat and sipped it for a few minutes staring into the fire.

George stood up and paced in front of the fire. "So, let me see if I have this right. Islwyn's killed, cause unknown, use of travel ways possible. Owen's put into place by Creiddylad. Hunt limps along, Iolo holds it together. Eight years pass. Rhys the elder is presumably killed, way technology is definitely involved. Ten years pass. Rhys the younger begins as a whipper-in, and Merfyn's removed. Coincidence? Two years pass. Iolo's murdered. Ways are not involved directly, but two secret ones are found."

Ceridwen nodded at his summation.

"What a mess," he said. "It's possible that not all of it's a part of the same plot, for example, Ithel's death, but this all reeks of intent. What surprises me is the long passages of time between events."

"I disagree. You must understand we take the long view. To my mind, this supposes a patient enemy or enemies, but not unusually so. This is a long strategy of undermining the effectiveness of the great hunt. In that context, what's twenty years out of close to fifteen hundred?"

"What would've happened if I hadn't shown up?"

"We might have tried to hunt with Rhys as huntsman. It might have worked, but not indefinitely. Or Owen the Leash might have been in a position to sabotage it directly."

"So my presence wrecks this long slow setup. Why haven't they attacked again?"

"Too soon, perhaps. We've disrupted the plot and they haven't responded yet. I think they will. It would be too frustrating to get this close and walk away."

"Alright, then," George said. "What can we do? I don't want to just wait for it."

"I've set in motion some serious investigations about Madog. You plan to summarily dismiss Owen and publicly humiliate him, which should dismantle a long term stratagem. Iolo's not been dead a week—give them a little time."

George waved her counsel away. "That reminds me. What about that servant of Creiddylad's, the fellow who looked so pleased to see Iolo's hands?"

"Rhian spoke to me about him, too. His name's Meuric. He keeps out of everyone's notice, more than seems normal. I haven't yet determined a way to find out more without making it obvious."

"Does he have any friends among the other staff?"

"Not that I can see. I think he avoids it. I think they're also a bit unnerved by him, as you and Rhian seem to be."

"I wonder if Alun could find out more about him," George said. "Maybe I'll give that a try, if he's willing."

CHAPTER 23

On Thursday morning Ives had a large pack prepared. By Saturday, George wanted to have worked with every hound at least once, and that meant a large pack today: twenty-two and a half couple, including all the young ones. He looked over the mounted staff in the yard and sighed that only Rhys was yet in livery, but that would change and soon they'd look a lot less motley.

He walked Llamrei over to Brynach who was mounted on a handsome buckskin gelding and trying to stick close to Benitoe while staying out of the way. "It's a long story, but there may be a confrontation at the gates with Owen the Leash, and I may call on you to demonstrate how friendly the hounds are. You alright with that?"

"As you wish, sir." He straightened with pride, keeping any apprehension off his face, and George nodded approvingly.

"I'm putting you with Benitoe for a while because his methods of sensing and handling hounds are different from Rhys's and Rhian's, and mine, too. I think you can learn from him. Drop by the huntsman's office this evening after dinner, and we can have a private chat about everything."

"I look forward to that, sir." Brynach touched his hat.

Looking round at Benitoe, George noted with approval that a small-sword was mounted on his saddle on the left, with two small axes on the right. "For throwing?" he asked, as he rode up to him.

"Yes. I may add a bow," Benitoe said.

"Good. Be sure Rhian and Brynach get a look at what you've arranged. For the next few outings, I want you to show Brynach what you can of how you monitor the hounds, and keep him close."

Rhys, too, was armed, carrying a saber. He was keeping an eye on Brynach and Rhian, clearly taking George's words about protection to heart.

"Everyone ready?" George called. They turned to face him. "This morning we expect to be followed by Gwyn and Edern, both. Be prepared for some excitement before we move off."

He turned Llamrei to Ives at the kennel gates. "Hold them for a moment, Master Ives."

He walked his horse through the gates, alone. To his left were Gwyn and Edern, sitting their horses and waiting for him. Around them an unusual number of spectators for this early in the morning were loitering including, George saw with interest, Creiddylad and her entourage. An open space had been left in front of the gates for the pack.

Owen the Leash and his men were lined up on the right, somewhat wary and silent, remembering yesterday's treatment.

No time like the present, George thought. Before greeting Gwyn and Edern with the pack, I will set my own house in order. He rode over to Owen and spoke to him directly. "Owen, thank you for your service. I dismiss you and your men from this duty."

Owen purpled, but reined in his wrath under Gwyn's eyes. He appealed directly to Gwyn. "My lord, this cannot be. We are needed to protect the people from the hounds."

George responded before Gwyn could speak. "No protection's required."

He turned to the gates. "Brynach, please come out." The kennel gates cracked open and Brynach rode over to George.

"Dismount, please, and stand before the gates." Brynach handed his reins to George, and walked to the middle of the open space, facing the gates, looking young and very much alone.

"Master Ives, please release the pack," George called. He could hear a few indrawn breaths from the audience and ignored them.

The gates opened wide and the pack with the hunt staff walked out in an orderly group, surrounding Brynach and stopping there. The hounds crowded around, fawning on him for attention. The staff kept them packed up.

"Brother, you can't permit this," Creiddylad said, urgently, looking up at Gwyn on his horse. "It's not safe." There were a few chuckles in the crowd as they watched the hounds dancing around Brynach. She cried out more loudly, "Owen, show him."

Owen walked his horse to the hounds, and the nearest began a threatening growl. The muted laughter stopped. "There, you see?" she said, triumphantly.

George used his horse to crowd Owen back from the pack and the hounds quietened. He spotted Alun on the edge of the crowd and waved him forward. "Trust me?" he said. Alun nodded. "Then go say hello to a hound."

Alun steeled himself and walked over to the pack, extending a hand carefully. A couple of hounds trotted over to sniff him, wagging as they came.

With a snort, weapons-master Hadyn made his way through the crowd and strode right into the pack, remarking loudly, "Always fancied a well-mannered hound." At that, several others came to the edge of the pack and made a fuss over any hound that approached.

George said, across the rising noise, "What I see, sir, is that the only ones threatened by these hounds seem to be Owen and his men. Why is that, do you suppose?" The crowd quieted to listen.

Creiddylad was silent.

"I can't do my job with them about," he continued.

Gwyn looked down at his sister. "What can I do? We need his help for the great hunt. We'll find some other task for your men."

She muttered, "No, this isn't right. We have to have them." She turned and walked off, Madog supporting her.

Owen drew aside, stiff and glowering, and took his men around the crowd to join her.

George let the crowd enjoy the hounds for a few more minutes, surveying the scene from his horse, while Brynach waded out from among the eager noses and remounted. Edern looked at George with a considering expression on his face. Eurig, on the other hand, had no such restraints and tossed him a broad smile and an appreciative wink.

"Alright, pack up," George said to the hounds and staff, waving the crowd back. He rode over to stand in front of Gwyn and Edern and doffed his hunt cap. "My lords, please pardon the delay. We're ready to begin."

Gwyn cleared his throat and waved him toward the gate in the curtain wall. "Please proceed, huntsman."

George took the pack south of the village, staying west of the river, then crossed at the ford. Just below the crossing and across the main road was a series of fields, in particular a hay meadow and its surrounding woods, with no visible dwelling. This was the Riverwind fixture, and it looked like good deer habitat to George.

He brought the pack to a halt on the edge of the field, near the woods on the left. The younger hounds were restless and kept the whippers-in busy pushing them back into the pack.

Leaving the pack in Rhian's charge, he rode over to Gwyn and touched his cap. "We're ready, sir."

Gwyn looked over at the lively pack. "Brought a few of the young entry, did you, huntsman?"

"Yes, sir."

"How many?"

"All of them." George broke into a grin and shrugged. "They have to get experience somehow."

"Indeed."

"Any instructions?"

"As you will, huntsman."

George touched his cap again to Gwyn, and nodded at Edern, who nodded back, then cantered back to the pack.

The plan they had discussed last night was modeled on the hunt of two days ago. Rhian and George agreed there were deer in the the woods on the left, and George sent Benitoe with Brynach around on the outside ahead of the pack.

This time George cast the hounds into the covert instead of Rhian, giving them the target of a heavy musky buck. They streamed in and almost immediately struck a line. George both heard and felt the first hound to voice his find. "That's Goronwy, isn't it?" he asked Rhian, and she agreed. One of the outsider hounds from Iolo's journal, George thought. We've got the other one of his year, Elain, out today, too.

The hounds boiled all over Goronwy's find, honoring it with their own voices and following in his wake until the pack was in full cry, and George and Rhian were fending off branches trying to keep with them. At a sudden check in a clearing, the pack milled around one corner trying to unravel how the buck had exited. George saw another group at the other end, which included most of the youngsters.

Uh-oh, he thought, and sure enough that group tore off on its own following a line out into the meadow. George could feel that it didn't really smell the same to them but they were too excited to care. They had shifted to another buck and the pack was split. He couldn't be in two places at once and had to trust to his whippers-in to comprehend the situation and fix it. He used his voice to help the rest of the pack settle back to their work and soon Elain struck the trace of the original buck as he left the clearing. The main pack headed east deeper into the woods, and George followed, with Rhian.

He could hear, through the trees, the pounding of hooves as Rhys sped to get in front of the hounds in the meadow and turn them off the wrong line, but he had to dismiss it from his concerns and concentrate on the main part of the pack, still on the track of the original quarry. The scent quickened for his hounds and they burst out into the open of the main meadow at its far end, still headed east.

They checked at a small stream that ran through the field headed for the river, and George took a moment to look back. Guilty hounds were headed his way at speed, with Rhys in the distance rating them loudly and cracking his whip in the air to give point to his displeasure at their mistake. He turned further in his saddle and spotted Gwyn and Edern on a little rise between them, watching the show and talking together.

He had no more time to spare as Goronwy picked up the scent again and the pack was off, most of them giving tongue. George blew them on with his horn, and the youngsters from the split ran up from behind to join them, giving George a wide berth as he told them sternly exactly what he thought of them.

Rhys followed at a gallop to take up his position on the right again. "It was a squire, a spiker," he called, as he went by.

Benitoe, with Brynach, popped out of the woods ahead of them on the left. "All on," he called to George, who had done his own count and agreed, raising his crop in acknowledgment. Well, at least we didn't lose any of them, he thought. Cunning of that buck to cut across his young understudy's trail in hopes of diverting the hounds, and it worked for him, with the young and stupid ones, anyway. I dare him to try it again.

~

The buck kept them going for almost two hours, but George and the re-united pack finally brought him to bay deep in the woods, a good distance from the river.

Gwyn and Edern had the hunt in view most of the time, watching the hunt staff deal with the challenges of a pack overweighted with youngsters.

"He's been keeping them relatively in hand, I think," Edern said, "after that first split." They were sitting mounted together off to the side observing the breaking up of the deer.

"I agree with his decision at the start to let the young hounds be properly rated so they could learn, rather than just overrule them by command," Gwyn replied. "Better that they learn to think for themselves by discovering what's wrong. That part reminds me of Iolo."

He looked at his brother. "Thank you for coming when I sent for you. You can see the situation."

Edern nodded.

Gwyn asked, "So, what do think of him, in general? What is he?"

Edern pondered that question. George was certainly Gwyn's descendant, but neither of them could believe in the timing of his arrival as coincidence. "Friend or foe, you mean?"

"Not exactly. I want to know who sent him. He could be a friend but sent by an enemy in innocence, after all."

"I don't know what to make of your relationship with Cernunnos. I know you think he's involved, but why now?"

"Because now things are in jeopardy for the great hunt, more than ever before, with Iolo's murder. The strings pulled by our enemies are all too visible, but not the exact pattern that they make."

Edern looked impatiently at his brother. "I'll tell you what I think, after that show with Owen this morning. I don't think he's going to be controlled. You and Cernunnos between you may have bred him, but he's not your tool, and I don't think he's likely to be Cernunnos's either. Make your alliance with the man, and bind his loyalty to you. Take that leap of faith in his honor."

Gwyn nodded and considered his brother's words.

Brynach was delighted to receive a deer foot trophy for his first successful hunt as staff, and almost as proud to be selected to bear the dressed carcass across the rump of his horse, while George and Rhys concealed their smiles at not having to carry the messy weight on their own horses.

George trotted up to Gwyn. "I think this is a good time to stop, sir, if that's alright with you, while they're flushed with success."

"Agreed. Well done, huntsman. Think these youngsters learned anything?"

George looked at him sharply. He might have been referring to the hounds or to the entire hunt staff, including himself. He could make nothing of Gwyn's bland expression. "I imagine we all did," he said.

He turned to go, but Gwyn stopped him with a raised hand. "Do you think this Scilti character's still at the inn, kinsman?"

"I don't know, but he was there two days ago when I was last there." He waited expectantly and watched both brothers. Clearly they had something in mind.

"I think we should stop by the inn on the way back, huntsman, and drink a health to the hounds. What say you?"

The clever old tactician, thought George, bearding a possible enemy agent in his own lair under the pretext of a celebration. Well, why not? Keep 'em off balance. "I think that's an excellent notion, sir."

~

The hunt returned to Greenhollow on the main road. Unlike the last time George had led the pack through the village, at Iolo's death, the people in the street weren't avoiding the hounds and dashing indoors. Word must have spread about the confrontation with Owen, and people held their ground as the hounds went by.

At the Horned Man, Rhys rapped on the gate of the stable yard and vanished inside to make sure the interior gates were closed, then he returned and opened it for the pack and George led them in. The hounds clustered around the horse troughs eagerly, but were agreeably tired from their morning's work and well fed from its successful conclusion, happy to nap for a while or otherwise relax.

Gwyn and Edern had already handed off their horses to the inn's grooms and entered the inn. The hunt staff did the same, giving the carcass over to be hung under cover, but George and Rhian lingered a moment. There were people looking through the bars of the gates at the hounds and George didn't want to miss an opportunity to begin repairing the decades of fear that Owen had built up.

"Rhian, tell them inside I'll be a few minutes yet. I want to let a few people in to meet the hounds"

"I will, huntsman."

George walked over to the gate and spoke through the bars. "You're welcome to come in and see the hounds. They're very friendly, though a little tired and dirty now. They'll do you no harm."

Some older children came in readily, followed by a few adults after a bit of hesitation. At George's instruction, they kept their voices quiet but walked easily among the hounds who were pleased at the attention. After everyone had had a few minutes to get a good look and pet some hounds, George thanked them and sent them away, closing the gate. He spied Maonirn at the stable door. "Will you keep an eye on that gate so people don't just wander in and let the pack out?"

"Indeed I will. Fine beasts, aren't they?"

"Thank you," George said. "By the way, where's that Scilti fellow, do you know?"

"His horse is in the stable. I'll bet he's in his room, hiding from your lot."

"Any news of him to tell?"

"No, he's that slippery. I'll keep my ears open."

As George entered the main room of the inn and let his eyes adjust, he found three tables had been shoved together, and the whole group, Gwyn and Edern included, were well into their second drink, judging by the glasses. An empty chair had been left for him, next to Gwyn.

He waved at Huw Bongam as he went by and took his seat. "Hard cider, please, and water."

Gwyn said, "Rhian tells me you had another impromptu hound tour in the stable yard."

"Can't hurt. We have a lot of damaged reputation to repair."

"I'm very pleased to be rid of the immediate cause of that. I'd like to know how Owen was making the hounds growl at them."

"Speaking of unwelcome people, I have news of our suspicious visitor here," George said. He relayed the information from Maonirn.

Gwyn replied, "We haven't seen him, but there's something unwholesome upstairs. It was mostly to get a closer look at the situation that I proposed this stop."

"I assumed as much. What can you do from here?"

"We can… taste him, my brother and I. We'll know him again, whatever appearance he may carry."

"Handy, that." He tried to see if he could sense anyone above him, but wasn't successful.

The room had been empty before they arrived, but by the time they finished the second round, several people from the village had joined them. George recognized a few of them as hound visitors from a few minutes ago. One of those stood and proposed a toast. "To the hunt." All rose and raised their glasses, shouting, "To the hunt."

After they had taken a drink. George, still standing raised his glass and called, "To the hounds." Anyone who had sat down rose again and echoed him.

Huw Bongam surprised him by walking out into the room and crying out the concluding toast, "To the master." That one raised the loudest response. Everyone drank and sat back down.

Edern leaned over to Gwyn. "When's the last time that happened?"

"I can't recall, it's been so long."

"Think he heard, upstairs?" George asked.

"Oh, yes. I could tell that he did. And wasn't he unhappy about it." Gwyn smiled.

The first thing George did in the huntsman's office after dinner was to take the key he'd gotten from Alun and open the case holding the horn used at Nos Galan Gaeaf.

He knew from Angharad's portrait of Iolo that it would be an oliphant, but seeing it in person was a different experience. He sat at the desk and admired the densely carved ivory, with its smoothly molded running beasts. It was the end of a tusk, less than a foot and a half in length, with a flattened natural curve. At some point it had been fitted for a removable mouthpiece, also in ivory. Two metal bands served both as reinforcement and as attachment points for a baldric. George had seen large brass horns strapped across the backs of French huntsmen worn the same way.

He intensely wanted to try out the sound, but knew he'd have a kennel eruption if he did. He'd have to find some location far from the hounds to practice. Perhaps he could bring it along on the next visit he made to Angharad. He'd sent her a note thanking her for lunch and hoped for a reply.

He looked up at a tap on the open door, and Ives came in with Isolda. "Wanted to see if there was anything else you needed tonight," Ives said. "Ah, you've got it out, I see."

Isolda walked over to admire it. "May I?" she asked, and at George's nod picked it up and began to look over each animal in turn.

"What's the history of this?" George asked Ives. "It's in good condition for something used out of doors annually and casually stored. I would expect lots of cracks with the changes in humidity."

"The horn came with the hounds, I always heard. It's part of the trappings of the hunt. I don't know who carved it or what protections they used, but I've never seen a crack."

This was true, George discovered, when he took it out of Isolda's hands and examined it again carefully. There were minor scratches and signs of wear from use, but no cracks. All in all, it looked less than a hundred years old, not many centuries.

At a knock on the door, Brynach stuck his head in. "You wanted to see me this evening, huntsman?"

"Good, come on in."

Ives stepped back from the desk. "I forgot why I came in. You and all the hunt staff are invited to a dinner tomorrow, courtesy of the kennel staff. We're celebrating the departure of Owen the Leash. That deer shoulder from Tuesday will be put to good use."

"I'd be delighted," George said. "Where and when?"

"Well, that's just it. Our usual location won't do when we include big folk, so traditionally we, um, use your house for mixed events."

George snorted at being invited to his own house for dinner. "Have you mentioned this to Alun?"

"Certainly. He's never happy to be a guest in his own kitchen but he's used to it by now."

"Not to be indelicate, but what do you use for chairs?"

"You clearly haven't looked through all the house yet. There are chairs just for our use at that table, and steps we use for the kitchen."

"I see." George smiled. "Who am I to stand in the way of tradition? Brynach, will you come?"

"Yes, thank you."

Ives nodded. "Good. I'll get an invitation to the others this evening." He walked to the door, and Isolda followed, closing it behind her to give them privacy.

George pointed Brynach to a chair. "How are things working out here for you, so far?"

"It's really interesting," Brynach said. "I like the hounds. They each have their own personalities, and they way they work together as a pack is something I've never gotten to see this closely before. I've heard you've been mixing them up with each group you take out."

George nodded. "Some hunts I know keep separate packs, such as a dog or bitch pack, and hunt them independently. I've been told that these hounds all hunt together for the great hunt, and so I want them all to be used to each other in these ordinary hunts as well as in the hound walks, even if I don't take them all out for each hunt, to make it easier to control them in smaller groups. We have several leaders, and I want them cooperating, not concentrating on trying to prove who's better. I want the middling hounds willing to follow all the leaders."

"The young entry, too?"

"I want them all ready for Nos Galan Gaeaf, if they can be."

"It was scary the way the pack split this morning. I was glad it was Rhys who had to pick them up and not me."

"It's not too hard to fool the young and the dumb." He glanced at Brynach to see if he took offense at that, but he seemed to have missed the tease. "You have to rate them strongly and shame them into not repeating the mistake, and it has to be done the instant they do wrong—timing is everything. Did you notice that Rhys galloped to the front before stopping them, instead of running after them cracking a whip?"

"Yes."

"Can you tell me why?"

"You can't yell at them from behind to make them turn, you have to turn them from the front. Otherwise they're just going to run away from you faster."

"That's right. You have to become a barrier they bounce off of, back in the direction you want. Once you break their concentration on the wrong line, they'll want to rejoin the main pack anyway."

"Do you know why we walk them as a big pack, all together, for exercise?" he continued.

"Because it's more convenient that way, to make sure they all get some work?"

"That's a side benefit. The main reason's to get them used to thinking of themselves as a pack, to encourage them to stay together as one. They're housed in separate groups to reduce kennel fights and unwanted breedings, but whenever they're out working, they should become one unit, working together to follow one quarry, until they account for it."

Brynach sat in silence for a moment. "It's a very pure sport, sir, isn't it?"

"I've always thought so. Hunting just for the table is different. With nets or pits, bait, arrows and ambush—it's still a skill, of course, but it seems less noble to me. We're not just directing a pack of wolves either, for real wolves are practical and would concentrate on the easiest prey, the young and the weak. Instead, we ennoble the hounds as well, seeking the strongest and most cunning beasts. We make it hard for ourselves, and hard for the hounds, out of respect to the quarry who will escape us if he can or fight us if he must."

He continued, almost speaking to himself. "To be successful, we must forge an alliance with the hounds that unites and expands all of our senses. That alone is exhilarating, even if the quarry escapes or we find nothing at all. It's like waking up on a bright morning after rain has washed the air—that exciting feeling, just for an instant, of having new eyes and using them for all the right reasons. The hounds don't chase and sometimes kill just because they're a bit hungry, but because it's in their nature, and we yearn for that same sense of rightness for ourselves."

Brynach cleared his throat. "Is that why you and Rhian don't just sense the quarry and set the hounds on it directly?"

"That's right, it would be cheating. The rules are important. If you just overpower the quarry, where's the nobility in that? If I'm starving and must kill to survive, well, alright then. But that's not sport."

George shook his shoulders and changed the mood. "Sorry, I didn't mean to go on like that. What I really wanted to know was, how do you communicate with hounds and horses? It's new to me and I don't know the different nuances for others."

"I think you were right to put me with Benitoe to start, sir. I'm not like Rhian or, I guess, like you. Rhian and I talked about it, afterward. She sees detail for each hound, and the quarry, too. I see the pack, or parts of it, in groups. It's like I can tell it's hounds, and she can tell which ones."

"Some of that may change with experience, once you can match up what you know with what you can sense and see individual hounds working."

"Rhys said the same thing. He told me he's much better now than when he started."

"I suspect it's like learning another language. The sounds are all one long undifferentiated stream until, one day, it starts to click and your brain begins to hear words and phrases instead."

Brynach nodded excitedly. "That's what Rhys said. He said 'I can speak hound now' and I didn't understand what he meant."

"Alright then. You let me know if anything bothers or puzzles you, now."

"Yes, sir. I will."

He left, and George sat for a moment alone in the huntsman's office, feeling not just the weight of the hounds and the great hunt looming ahead of him, but also his responsibility for the young folk who had put their lives and training into his hands on a moment's acquaintance.

CHAPTER 24

Returning from the hound walk Friday morning, George found Isolda waiting for him in the yard with a broad smile.

"When you've disposed of your hounds," she said, "come join me with all the hunt staff in your office. We have a surprise for you all."

A few minutes later, when George ducked through the doorway into the building, he discovered Isolda standing in the entry corridor outside his office door steering him into the office where he joined the rest of his staff. He was surprised and pleased to discover Angharad there, too, chatting with Rhian.

"What's this all about, then?" he said.

He was the last one in and Isolda had closed the door behind him. Now she opened the other door to the back corridor, and stood in the doorway expectantly, looking at Angharad who walked over to stand in front of the huntsman's desk and addressed them all. "I heard from Mostyn that your new livery was to be delivered today, and made arrangements for Isolda to come pick me up and bring it along. Yours, too, Brynach."

There was excited chatter from everyone except Rhys, who leaned casually against a bookcase already wearing the customary uniform and preening just a bit over it.

"Out there in the back corridor you will discover packages with your name. I thought you all might like to try on some of the clothes, so we'll give Rhian here this office for privacy, and the rest of you will just have to use the corridor."

With that, Isolda held the door open ceremoniously and Angharad shooed all the men into the back corridor and closed it again. Alun stepped up with a smile and showed them the array of goods, still wrapped, and sorted into piles by name.

After exchanging a few words with Alun, Rhys stepped forward. "I am to be a model of good taste, Alun says, and stand here as a comparison." He spun about theatrically and struck outlandish poses, while Brynach struggled to keep his dignity and not giggle. Benitoe was under no such constraint and snorted loudly.

There was a general unwrapping. Alun pointed out the chairs he had brought to keep their clothing, new or old, from the floor. He came over to George and said privately, "This is all Angharad's doing. I thought to put your evening finery away already, but she said she wanted to see that, too."

George was struck by Angharad taking the trouble to arrange this. He chewed on that thought, and what it might mean, while he removed his coat and breeches, sitting to pull off his boots, with Alun's help.

Benitoe and Brynach were ahead of him, with Rhys helping Brynach explore all the pockets in his new hunt coat. George saw that each of them had two coats, as he did, and a kennel coat for dirty work.

"What's that?" Brynach said, pointing at the revolver in its holster at the small of George's back, exposed now that his vest was off.

Alun had seen it before, during Mostyn's measurements, but George hadn't intended for this to become widespread knowledge. He decided to make the best of it and go into details.

He took the gun out of its holster and held it up for them to see. It was a small stainless steel revolver, with a 2-inch barrel. "Where I come from, this gun's a deadly weapon. For hunting, it's just another tool. Sometimes we find an injured animal that must be finished off, or a horse breaks a leg and must be put down."

"Why not use a hunting sword?" Brynach asked.

"We hunt fox, mounted, not deer. Usually the fox gets away. If he doesn't, there's nothing left to worry about. Nothing to butcher, no meat to bring back. So we don't wear hunting swords."

"But gunpowder doesn't work here," Rhys said.

"Yes, so everyone keeps saying. It's just a habit, part of my hunting gear. Here, take a look. It's quite safe if I take out the cartridges, just like a bow without arrows."

He emptied the five cartridges into his hand and passed the S&W Model 60 .38 Special around for them to handle. Benitoe wanted to see how it opened and closed, and to look at a cartridge in detail, so George took a moment to show him everything and explain the parts—casing, primer, bullet, and gunpowder. Benitoe inspected the fit and finish of the revolver components, as if he wanted to see how difficult it would be to make.

"You use this for defense, then?"

"Yes, like a small crossbow, but more powerful and much faster and easier to use. We have long versions," he held out his hands to indicate the length of a rifle and mimed holding one to shoot, "which can cover great distances. Then there are large ones, with wheels, for military uses against fortifications. I use this particular gun for dispatching animals at need, but I also use it when not hunting, with a much more practical holster, for self-defense, and I've got several other guns, too. This one's rather small for my hand, but easy to wear."

Rhys said, "Like a knife, this can be carried hidden or not, yes?"

"That's right. Our soldiers and guards carry them visibly, as you would a sword, but many ordinary people, and villains, too, carry them concealed."

George reloaded the gun and returned it to its holster. He finished dressing and looked down the corridor at the others. "Let's go take a look in daylight."

Out in the kennel yard they discovered that Rhodri had joined them, wearing his own ancient coat from his service days which still fit him, more or less. He grinned at the peacocks emerging blinking into the sunlight. "Alun slipped me a note this morning with Angharad's suggestion that I join the fun. I must say, you're all looking rather splendid."

It was true. Rhian wore breeches like her companions, with a long hunt coat. The bright new coats contrasted with the two older ones on Rhys and Rhodri, but all were double-breasted, similar in cut, and the color and material of the new ones were clearly a match for the old, just fresher. The boots, being new, gleamed.

"Let's see those hats, now," Rhodri said, and they settled tricorns on their heads, to everyone's amusement.

They milled about in the yard inspecting each other, with Isolda laughing at Rhian's clothes and the kennel-men popping out to take a look. The hounds contributed their own commentary. George found himself wishing for a camera for a group shot. Hearing a scritching noise behind him, he turned to find Angharad standing well back of him, sketching with charcoal on a pad of paper.

He complimented Rhian, Brynach, and Benitoe each on their choices and teased Rhodri about the fit of his old coat, then made his way back to Angharad as the group began to disperse.

"It was very thoughtful of you to arrange this," he said.

"It was no bother at all. I had other business to attend to at the manor." She put away her charcoal sticks and closed the pad.

"Alun said something about wanting to see the evening wear?"

"Yes, I'd like that."

"Why don't you come back into the office and I'll put on the coat, at least."

They walked in together, and he left her there to change coats. The material had a lovely hand to it, not too heavy nor too soft in its drape. Like the hunt coats, it was double breasted, but elaborate detailing was worked over the lapels and altogether it was much finer.

He wore it into the office to Angharad's admiration. "Yes, that does suit you well. It shows your size to its best advantage, with nothing clumsy or over-large. I do approve."

It was clear—the next move was up to him. "I wonder if you'd come to the huntsman's home for a quiet dinner Monday night, before my first public hunt? I'd be glad to provide an escort home, or to arrange a guest room for you."

She looked down a moment with a small smile, then glanced up again. "Only if you promise to wear your new coat."

George had asked Ceridwen to meet with him this afternoon for an extended catch-up session on his newly discovered powers, to find out what he could actually do and what the rules were. He was a man who liked to understand his tools completely, someone who actually read the manuals. This incomplete knowledge made him deeply uneasy.

Sitting comfortably in her study, he leaned forward to explain what he was after. "I'd like to understand more about the way things work here, the way they're different from my world." He was reluctant to use a word like "magic."

"For example," he continued, "why is it that so much, um, power seems to be associated with wood? There are spell-sticks, and way-tokens, and what's with those icons on wood in the stables?"

Ceridwen happily took on the role of teacher, George just another in a long line of students.

"That's because wood's an in-between material: dead but once living, hard but easily shaped, part of something large but small enough to hold, and so forth. Such ambivalent materials are valuable as storage devices or holders of power."

George automatically looked for apparent exceptions, to test this reasoning. "What about limestone or chalk? The shells that make those up were once living, too. Even marble, which is limestone transformed. Or coral."

"You make an excellent point." She walked over to a bookcase, searched for a moment, then pulled out a large thin leather-bound volume. "Edneved ap Gwilt, in his work on 'The Sources and Uses of Bindable Materials,' talks about this."

She laid the book on a table in front of the book case and leafed through it. "It's right about here, somewhere… Ah, found it. See?" She beckoned him over. "He claims that the accumulations of shells in limestone, which he could see clearly with enhanced vision, occur after death, and so don't share the large-small part-of-a whole set of properties."

George enjoyed this sort of game and countered with relish. "Alright, what about large individual shells, such as conch, which make nice carved cameos?"

"Edneved spoke to that as well. He held that shell and pearl in any case were an extruded but non-living artifact of a living organism while the cells of wood were the organism itself. That's why bone and skin are also useful, when shell is not."

She reached for another book, this one small and thick. "There's still ongoing debate about horn, antler, and tusk. I don't agree with Iorwerth Goch who claims that they are essentially as living as bone and just contain some additional scaffolding, making them less pure but still useful for power purposes. Other vegetal materials like straw or paper, or other animal residues such as hair or wool, fail as either non-living or aggregations of individuals or parts."

George threw up his hand in mock surrender. "I'll concede defeat and accept that wood's an especially appropriate material for the purpose. That doesn't explain what's happening in the stables."

"Icons are used to mark ownership and help with finding and sorting lots of items, some of them mobile, like horses, for lots of owners. It's to reduce mistakes. Your sign…" She looked at him quizzically.

"A lion rampant, from my grandfather's Talbot arms."

"Your lion is on the stalls of your horses and on your stable chests. When tack has been cleaned, if there's any confusion about who owns it a blank piece of wood is laid upon it, and your lion will appear. It's a simple household spell; storage in a marked container, like your stable chests, imbues the object with a sort of mark that can be made visible. It wears off over time, so that ordinary purchases aren't confused with, say, recent theft. A horse in a stall is residually marked in the same way."

"Like a brand that can wear off and be replaced. Or a linen mark for laundry."

"That's right."

Alright, that was at least consistent, even if its underlying basis was unknown. He could just think of it as highly developed technology and call it magic for now, as long as he could understand how it worked and how to use it.

"Here's another one. People keep telling me to 'just ask Ceridwen' so I'll follow their advice."

She nodded expectantly.

"Let me start with guns. No one can explain to me why gunpowder doesn't work. And is it only gunpowder, or also the newer smokeless powders?"

"You have a gun, then?"

For the second time that day, Gwyn reached under his coat and pulled out his revolver. He unloaded it and handed her the empty weapon.

She held it in both hands and examined it from all directions. "The last time I saw one of these it looked very different. It was in one piece, made partly of wood, and had an ignition mechanism that used a piece of flint."

"That's, um, a bit out of date. Flintlocks went out of fashion almost two hundred years ago."

He quickly outlined for her the development of percussion caps, primers, cartridges, and smokeless powder.

"I haven't dared fire this, since I only have a few rounds with me, but everyone assures me it won't work." He looked at her quizzically.

Like any good instructor, she composed her response carefully before speaking, laying a foundation for her explanation.

"As you've noticed by now, we do trade with the human world. We don't maintain an industrialized society, and thus make do without many of the products of your world, but there are some items that we simply don't want to do without and so we make exceptions. We buy lamps and lamp oil, lighters, cotton, and so forth, because they're too useful to forgo and too laborious to make on a non-industrial basis. We reach for those few things from your world that allow us to keep our lives comfortable without risking exposure or pulling our culture in undesirable directions."

She continued, "Some of us make visits—Gwyn, most notably, but others, too. The travelers bring back many things. Some have been interested in gunpowder and its military uses, and several have studied how it's made as well as brought samples. We have books and treatises." She waved her hand at a shelf on one of the bookcases.

"But it doesn't work for us. In the open air, on a dish, it burns feebly, even when fresh, while we read that it should flare up and burn brightly or with sparks. Enclosed in a firearm, it burns no better. We've tried making it here from raw ingredients according to the instructions, but it makes no difference."

"It may be," she said, "that none have tried your new smokeless powders in the last hundred years and perhaps those will work, but I doubt it. I imagine that my colleagues have looked into it, perhaps secretly, and failed, or else we'd have seen the results by now. The utility of firearms for war and hunting is obvious, and the rest of the metal technology is sufficiently within our reach, or our ability to trade, as to make it feasible."

"I'd be happy to sacrifice a cartridge, to take it apart for an experiment," George said.

"Perhaps later. I confess I'm curious."

"I must warn you, I'm no chemist," he said. "If it doesn't work, I'm not going to be able to do much about it. I'm sure there are books in my world that would help."

He stopped, struck by an idea. *There's no reason air guns wouldn't work, the ones that allow you to pump them manually instead of using compressed air. I wonder if that's more practical than small crossbows, though. Might be a lot of technology* dependency for not much better results, with concomitant support difficulties in the field.

Ceridwen looked at him quizzically. He laughed. "I just thought of an experiment for another day, that's all."

She interrupted their session to order some fresh tea.

Armed with a fresh cup, George steeled himself for a more uncomfortable discussion, not about external objects but about powers within himself.

"Part of what I really came for today was to set a formal course of study with you, as I am trying to do with Hadyn for physical defense."

"What is it you want to learn?"

"Everything, like an ordinary student, but for right now, I need to understand the ways and glamoury and discover at least what's possible in general, and what I can do. I'd also like to know more about communication with animals. There seem to be several different methods."

"I can give you books to read about that, but it's Gwyn you want as a practical instructor for speaking with the beasts, because much of it's in the blood. For glamoury, there are also books but it's really all direct guided practice and observation— I can help with that. For the ways, I can guide you but I already know you can do things I can't. There are many books to study, there."

"Where would you like to begin?" she said.

"Can we start with a reading list?" He spread his hands hopefully.

"I'll do better than that. Let me think for a moment."

She walked over to one of the cases about midway down the wall opposite the fireplace. "I'll empty this shelf here and refill it for you. The books will be in four sections: general knowledge, bespeaking others, glamours, and the ways. You'll read the books in order within each section, but you may skip among the sections as seems most urgent to you."

George could see her pedagogical instincts take over.

"For each book you will make notes in a journal—this journal," she said, walking over to a shelf behind her desk and taking out a new journal, like the one Alun gave him from Iolo's desk. "You will record the book's author and title, a brief summary of its contents, any important facts you'll wish to recall later, and any questions you may have. I'll set aside time to discuss those questions with you."

She handed him the blank journal. He took it with his weak left hand and it dropped into his lap. He picked it up again with his right hand and put it on the table. He wiggled the fingers of his left hand and massaged it with his right unconsciously.

Ceridwen continued without noticing. "This is for your own benefit, you understand, to lay a foundation. When you've digested each book, I'll show you where it lives on the shelves normally and explain to you a bit about its neighbors."

George appreciated the thoroughness and orderliness of her proposed program. "It's most kind of you," he said, "to take all this time for one student. I'm grateful."

"Nonsense. It'll be refreshing to discuss these things with an interested adult instead of a reluctant young captive.

"Mind you, these books mustn't leave the room. You may come here at all hours and not disturb me, whether I'm at work at my desk or asleep in my bed. I'll let my staff know to admit you and, if they're not awake to do so, please let yourself in quietly.

"As a practical exercise in what's left of our time today, let's work on some elementary glamoury. Basic rules: a glamour once achieved can be maintained indefinitely by an expert, as the story of Pwyll tells us. A glamour affects any who can see the wearer, and the glamour caster knows his own glamour while he casts it."

George said, "I raised the question with Rhian about Scilti, is it a mental effect on the beholder, or a physical change? Either way, what about other senses—hearing, smell—and physical remnants, especially for smell? Can it fool a hound, for example? If the glamour's released, does the scent while glamoured still fool the hounds?"

Ceridwen looked at him sharply, but with approval. "A well-cast glamoury affects both sight and hearing, but not touch. It reflects properly in a mirror. For the caster, it's like operating within a shell, and a bit oppressive for long uses which is how many glamour casters are revealed, when they take a little ease. Not many have written about smell or taste, and the ones that did say those senses are not glamoured, which is why we warn girls away from wearing scent during a glamour. I doubt a glamour would fool a hound, who relies on his nose before his eyes or ears."

"For someone to be fooled by a glamour, they must be within a certain range, and so casters tend to keep the lines of sight restricted to reduce the risk of someone far-off seeing something wrong.

George said, "This all implies it's a mental power rather than a physical one. Smell residues are physical. A distant view would be the same as a closeup one, if there were a physical change."

"That's right." She drew him over to stand next to her desk. "Let's make a practical start now. Picture someone of your own gender whom you know very well. The more vividly you can bring him to mind, the better."

George thought of his grandfather, his erect posture, the white hair, the wrinkles on his face, his frame on which the muscles were getting thinner. He drew himself more upright to help with the impersonation, but the rest he shaped with his mind. As he concentrated, he could feel a soft sort of film settle upon him, and his eyes were caught by edges to his view, as if they peered through a domino mask. When he tried to look at those edges directly, they fled to the side of his vision, always just barely glimpsed.

He looked down at his hands and saw the veins raised and exposed, the padding of fat under the skin thinner and worn. The surface of the skin was softly wrinkled in all directions, like crepe, and the joints of the fingers were swollen.

Ceridwen handed him a small mirror and he raised it to his face. It looked wrong, and he realized he rarely saw a mirror-image of his grandfather's face, just the normal view. He used the mirror to look down and saw that he was much thinner in frame, and that his coat had changed to match.

"Now walk about a bit, remembering to 'be' this person, not yourself."

He took a few steps, mindful of stiffened knees and slower stride. He felt his posture change to match.

"Now remove it," she said.

He pictured his hands, cupped sideways and facing inward, raising to his face, joining, and running down the front as if he were pulling them through a join in a stage curtain, then tugging them out to the side at chest level to 'take off' the glamour wrapped around him, opening his hands wide at the end to dismiss it. The ghostly shapes at the edge of his vision vanished and, when he glanced at his hands, they looked normal.

"Well done, for a beginning. You moved awkwardly and it was a bit thin and wavering, but not bad," Ceridwen said.

"Can you cast on the look of an object as a glamour?"

"Yes, an object's not uncommon, for concealment. But remember, an object doesn't move."

"What about something of a different size, a child, for example?"

"That's much harder. Height and weight don't really change, just the appearance of them. You could be a woman, but you'd be very tall for one—if you made yourself seem shorter, you wouldn't be able to provide the correct stride and reach. So the more different you are from your natural form, the easier it would be to be revealed by accidental touch or by inconsistencies of movement.

"Practically speaking, you want to have similar garments in your glamour to what you're actually wearing, and choose a similar height, and similar weight. There are some who cross genders in glamoury, but I think you're too large to try that. You'll also want to avoid letting people touch you. Sometimes you can spot a caster just by that automatic careful isolation in crowds, even when not glamoured.

"One more practical exercise before we stop for today. You notice that it took time for you to assume that glamour of an old man?"

"Yes, I built it up from steps as I recalled them."

"That lack of speed can be deadly in an emergency. You must always have a standard form, not your own, that you can call up quickly, without thought. There are experts who have several such forms available at need, but we'll begin with just one for you."

"How do I build that up?"

"Most students start by taking their current form as a special case, and trying to find the untouched version of it as if it hadn't lived their particular life. Then they add a different life history to that base version to build up their variant form. So the first step is to construct a sort of proto-glamour. Project who you really are, at bottom, without the accidental incidents of your life."

He understood what she meant, but not quite how to go about it. He stood, centering his body carefully on both feet and resting his arms at his side. He stared off into space, trying to distance himself from his normal body image, and called forth whatever would come.

He felt himself grow taller, but his head became much heavier and the weight pulled it forward from his shoulders and down, then up again in a new posture as he compensated by tilting forward and lifting, his neck oddly curved. His lips pursed and he felt the front of his face extend narrowly, and his vision expanded to include much more of the room on either side. Unlike the previous glamour of his grandfather, this time his vision was unimpeded.

He could smell the smoke of the fire, the burning oil in the lamps, the leather covers and quietly decaying books on the shelves, the ink on the desk, the mice in the walls, the shock of the woman standing before him as her skin chilled. He tilted his head to check the smells, and the unexpected weight of his head made him brace his neck muscles and his whole body to support it. He flared his nostrils and more of the scents in the room rushed in to overwhelm him.

A falling ember in the fireplace startled him in the silence of the room, and he felt his ear twitch to focus on it, not a simple vestigial movement along the top of the jaw, but a live swiveling sensation, of just the one ear.

He regarded Ceridwen. The color had faded from her face, and from the room around her. She stood stock still, her hand raised to her mouth and her eyes wide. He held up a hand and it seemed ordinary to him, except that the color was muted.

Ceridwen groped for the mirror and gave it to him, her hand trembling slightly. As if compelled, he raised it slowly to his face.

Rising above his human shoulders the head of a great antlered deer stared back at him.

CHAPTER 25

George recoiled from the mirror in his hand, then brought it back into view. The antlers were enormous and nearly scraped the tall ceiling in the room, even at their natural slant. He noted, somewhere behind the shock, that they were shaped as red deer, the great deer of the west that the Celts and Scythians were so fond of portraying.

He shifted the mirror to his left hand and raised his right to touch the antlers. They were cool and smooth to the touch, and longer than he could reach, stretching back above and behind him with many tines. He brought his hand down to the top of his head and felt the strange ridges where they joined his head. Some distant part of him wondered if they shed every year and grew back in velvet.

He ran his hand further down his head and stroked the short, coarse fur on his forehead and cheeks. If he didn't look at it, he could imagine it as a well-trimmed beard, but when he watched his hand on his face, the disconnect between what he felt and any human face made him shudder. Worst was the narrow muzzle with its alien nose and mouth. The face was expressionless, showing neither smiles nor frowns.

He rather liked the ears and his ability to move them about. He held one and twisted it, testing its pliability.

He reached out and grabbed Ceridwen's hand, and she jumped but didn't resist. He laid it flat along his furry cheek under his own hand, and then leaned down so she could reach and laid it on an antler and released it.

She drew back and recovered her poise. "Can you speak?"

He opened his mouth, but casual speech seemed impossible, just a disconcerting series of bleats and grunts. He moved his head side to side, slowly, trying to keep his top-heavy weight under control.

"This can be touched. It's not therefore a glamour," she said.

He raised his hands palm up and shrugged his shoulders.

"You could be touched before, so that wasn't a glamour, either."

Another shrug.

"This is wholly out of my knowledge. By the form, this is clearly part of your father's heritage or, perhaps, of he who summoned you, if they're not indeed the same."

He wanted to know how to change back, most urgently. He mimed lifting his head off and stamped a foot.

"Yes, you're right. The first thing is to restore you to your customary form. Can you reverse the process?"

Could he? He tried to stand straight and still again, with his arms at his side. His stance was wider than normal and his chest and neck still bowed forward to support the unaccustomed weight. He visualized the form he had seen in fragments in the small mirror, trying to make a complete picture, and pulled it back inside himself, stopping part way as he felt his human face return. He knew from the weight that the antlers must still be there.

Pleased by his partial success, he winked at the shaken Ceridwen, and then pulled again and the weight relented, letting his posture change to fully straighten up again.

He reached up to confirm that his face was back and the antlers gone, then staggered over weak-kneed and collapsed in the nearest armchair.

Ceridwen took a bottle and glass from behind her desk and poured him a stiff drink. He reached up with both hands and she wrapped his fingers around it. He sniffed—brandy, with apples. But oh how dull a smell. His view of the room had regained full color as his human vision returned, but the scents had dimmed to almost nothing, and he stopped trying actively to pick them up. What must it be like to be a hound, he thought. He took a good swig from the glass and sat in silence listening to the fire, letting the liquor warm his blood.

After a moment, he finished the brandy and cleared his throat. "Well, that was… interesting," he ventured. "Not the sort of default form you had in mind, I take it?"

"Hardly."

She stood over him, then backed off a bit and tilted her head sideways to contemplate him. "Did you know, when you paused in the change back and winked at me—you horrible man, and me worried you might be stuck—your face wasn't your own?"

"Oh?"

"It was thinner, rougher, hairier, the chin was pointed, and the brows lower, with a peak."

He felt the tremors in his hands relaxing as the brandy had its effect. He was exhausted, either from reaction or from the change itself.

"Well," she said, "I think we'll leave further trials for another day."

She pointed her finger at him. "You're not to seek out Hadyn today. You are to go home and sit for a while."

"Yes, ma'am." He wasn't inclined to disagree with her about the stupidity of pursuing dangerous physical activity just now. He put his glass down and rose, a bit unsteadily.

"It's been an intriguing lesson, today," he said. Some devil made him give her another wink as he turned to leave.

The brisk air outside hit George in the face like a dive into a pool. It refreshed him for a moment, but he was overtaken by an irresistible yawn. Ceridwen was right. I should stop by the house, maybe take a quick nap.

He let himself in to the quiet house. Dinner was sometime off and Alun didn't seem to be around. He pulled off his boots and left them near the back door, then climbed the stairs in his stocking feet.

He opened the wardrobe and discovered all the new clothing, neatly hung. He added his current coat and vest.

The room was quiet, even in mid-afternoon, and the bed looked soft. Draped across the foot of it was the new dressing gown, in a deep shade of dark red, warm and welcoming. A yawn and then another seized him and he thought, I'll just lie down for a few moments.

Gwyn sat behind his desk and listened to Ceridwen's description of George's transformation.

"Not a glamour? You're sure?"

"I felt the fur on his face, the antlers in my hand, not that my hand could go all the way around the base of them."

"We know his regular form's no glamour either. Either that, or Mostyn's the most unperceptive tailor alive."

Ceridwen choked. "This is no joke, Gwyn. This was Cernunnos, in the flesh."

He patted the air to slow her down. "But you said George remained himself throughout the transformation."

She calmed down. "Yes. You could see he was shocked, but he recovered enough to explore the form with a mirror, and he remembered our conversation about touch not being something that could be glamoured, which is why he had me feel his face and antlers. And then there was that awful wink as he pulled partway back to an antlered human head. I can't see Cernunnos winking at me, can you?"

Gwyn agreed. "So really there were three forms unglamoured, yes? Cernunnos, the Horned Man, and George."

She reluctantly confirmed this.

Well, well, well. How very unexpected, he thought. And here I was worried that Cernunnos had some subtle plan. Looks instead like he's planning to take a starring role. What does he want? What will happen to my kinsman if he gets it?

Ceridwen asked, "Did anything like this ever happen to Iolo?"

"No, not that I ever knew. I don't think he would have tried to hide it."

"I've never seen him, but you have. What did Cernunnos look like?" she asked.

"A great red deer's head on the body of a man. Strange and terrible." Ceridwen was nodding in recognition before he finished.

Gwyn said slowly, "You know, when all's said and done, Annwn is really Cernunnos's kingdom. He just lets others rule it, until they prove unworthy, as Arawn did. My father may have invested me," he nodded to Angharad's painting of it on the wall, "but it wasn't really his to give, only Arawn's to lose, and Arawn owed fealty to my father. It's ridiculous to think that my father has the genuine disposition of Cernunnos's realm at his disposal, but it's been so long since he's been seen that people forget the truth."

"What do you think his appearance now means?" she asked.

"I don't know," he said. But he did know, or suspect. He would never be rid of his dishonor from that ancient fight. Iolo, too, and now Iolo was dead. Perhaps I've finally been found unworthy myself, and Cernunnos was preparing a successor. Was that George's role?

And what if it were true? He no longer believed that George had any ill intent and he wouldn't harm his kinsman deliberately, just to keep him from being a pawn for Cernunnos. There was no honorable way back from that sort of action.

~

The rattle of pans somewhere downstairs roused George eventually. He found a coverlet had been thrown over him and the door closed. His watch told him two hours had passed, and the daylight was starting to fade.

Guess that was more of a shock than I realized, he thought, lying lazy and comfortable, disinclined to stir. I don't imagine Iolo manifested in quite this way, judging by Ceridwen's stupefaction.

So, why am I not more frightened by it? Because it still feels like "me" somehow, he answered himself. My body recognizes the form, and I'm still in charge. It's not like a possession, with me watching, more like an unanticipated physical skill, as if someone threw a ball at me for the first time and I just reached up and caught it, not knowing I could. Strange.

But what kind of monster am I, then? Was I always this way, and didn't know until I came here, or has this world done it to me?

A horrifying thought struck him. Are there more forms inside me like this? How could I find out? What if I stand there all receptive like that and something less highly evolved shows up? The world's first six-foot lobster, say.

Going along with this uncritically doesn't sound like such a good idea after all. Can I get stuck? Can I become something that can't think well enough to return? Or someone that doesn't want to return?

This is getting me nowhere, he decided. Just don't lose control. After all, it took deliberate effort on my part to create this manifestation. Don't do it again.

~

He heard more noise outside his room, and rose, cracking open his door to peek into the hallway. He found Alun, wrestling with chairs from the storeroom. He had half a dozen out in the hallway, smaller and higher then the usual sort. Despite the unusual size they looked to match the chairs in the dining room, where George hadn't yet eaten a meal.

He stepped out in his slippers and picked up two of the chairs. "Where do you want them?"

"There's no need for that, sir," Alun said. At George's look, he said, reluctantly, "Down in the dining room, then."

One after the other they brought four of the chairs down into a swirl of activity. The dining room was well lighted and airy. George saw that someone had opened windows in the front parlor, and in the kitchen behind, so that a fresh breeze swept through. The fire had been laid but not yet lit, and everything was clean and gleaming.

The table was arranged to seat twelve, with six larger chairs remaining in place and the smaller chairs they carried finding a place among them, one at the head of the table. Alun returned upstairs for the last pair while George stood in the kitchen doorway to survey the activity.

A large pot bubbled quietly at the back of the stove, the source of a most delicious smell. One of the kennel-men was just peering into the oven after checking on the contents of the pot. The counter held several loaves of crusty bread. George noticed three footstools placed in strategic locations, one in front of the kitchen table where the other kennel-man was using it to reach a pile of greens, chopping them up with a large knife suited to his smaller hands.

George ducked out of the doorway without attracting their notice and helped Alun place the last two chairs. "I see Huon and Tanguy are hard at work in there."

"Must make a change from cooking for the hounds," Alun said. "At least, I always hope so before taking a bite of the result."

"Hard to have your place invaded, is it?" George hoped to tease him out of his pique.

"I have to admit they clean it up well, after." Alun relented and smiled. "And it makes for a pleasant evening."

He regarded George for a moment, with some hesitation. "This is an informal meal, and they will be doing what serving there is."

He paused, and George ventured a guess, "So, I hope that means you will be joining us?"

Alun looked relieved. "Yes, so I will. I wasn't sure you would like that."

"How's it any different from our quick breakfasts in the kitchen?"

"This is formal entertaining, with guests."

"You're a guest same as me tonight," George said. "Which reminds me, I've invited Angharad for a quiet dinner Monday night, so perhaps that's the sort of occasion you had in mind. Can you provide us with a simple meal, nothing elaborate?"

"Indeed I can." He cheered up visibly.

George said, "It'll be a late dinner, right after the pre-hunt meeting which I'll keep short. I've invited her to sleep in a guest room, if she wishes to stay, so that will also need to be prepared. She'll be hunting with us the next morning, so breakfast, too. I'll be getting up earlier than she does, of course."

"I'll see to everything," Alun said. "It's been such a long time since there were house guests here."

George looked in the mirror on the dresser as he completed dressing. He swung it on its frame to point down and then tilted it progressively up to get a piecemeal impression of his appearance.

Alun had advised him to wear the less formal of the hunt coats, so as not to outshine the kennel-men. He was trying out his new low shoes with the breeches and hoped to break those in with a minimum of blisters.

He transferred his pocket watch to the weskit, took one last look and headed down the stairs to join the assembly, a guest in his own house.

He found the fire lit in the dining room and guests milling about in the kitchen getting in the way. Rhys and Rhodri were old hands at these events and harried their hosts with jokes as they prepared the finishing touches, but Benitoe was the worst, knowing best how to bedevil the kennel staff. Ives in the role of host finally roared at the intruders and chased them out to the dining room or hall, depending on which doorway they were closest to, closing the doors in their faces.

George took charge of the guests, collecting them all in the front rooms and finding seats for them. Isolda came out of the kitchen a few moments later and brought a platter of small savory bits of meat and dough. Benitoe volunteered to help her, and they came back together with a tray of glasses and two pitchers, one each of cider and beer.

Brynach and Rhian hung back a bit as Rhys and Rhodri crowded around the food, and George walked over to talk to them. "First time at one of these?"

Rhian nodded. "Rhys would tell me about them, but I never hoped to see for myself." Her eyes shone.

"My first time, too, but I know even less than you do about what to expect."

"Oh, that's right. I'm sorry, but it seems like you've been here forever," she said.

Seems like that to me, too, sometimes, he thought. Aloud, he said, "Easier to be guest than host. All we have to do is not drink too much, break anything important, or tell any stories that we would regret in the morning."

He could see Brynach taking this much too seriously. "Relax, both of you. It'll be fun, I'm sure."

Their appetites restored, they helped empty the platter, and Alun brought it back to the kitchen. He returned with Ives.

Ives announced, "My lords and ladies, please do us the honor of joining us in a meal." He bowed them into the dining room, where Isolda took care of the seating.

George found himself placed at the foot of the table, with Ives at the head. On George's right were Isolda and Benitoe, followed by Rhodri, Huon, and Alun. To his left were Brynach, Rhian, Tanguy, a young lutine introduced to him as Armelle, and Rhys. The lutins were dressed in tidy red jackets and light breeches, except for Benitoe who wore one of his new green coats, like the rest of the hunt staff. Armelle and Isolda were in dresses that stopped mid-calf, with red bodices and light skirts, blue and gray, respectively.

A grand tureen in the middle of the table was accompanied by serving dishes of root vegetables and greens on either side, and small loaves of bread on platters at each end. More pitchers of beer and cider squeezed in with everything else.

As the last person sat down, Ives rose and raised his glass high. "To a successful hunting season." All rose to join him, and drank. They sat down again.

Tanguy, the senior kennel-man, rose. "To our huntsman, who provided the meat for the feast." This time all rose to the toast but George, who nodded in acknowledgment.

The younger kennel-man, Huon, rose for his toast. "To the hounds." All stood up for that, and gave a cheer.

"Let's eat," Ives said. "Rhodri, you're in charge of the stew. We'll pass the plates up and back."

George's plate returned heaped with a savory rich venison stew soaking into the potatoes and carrots. He raised his glass in a private salute to that first deer from his first hunt here, and fell to with vigor after everyone had been served.

Tanguy and Huon were kept busy with occasional forays into the kitchen to refill the serving dishes, but eventually everyone slowed down and began looking for those last morsels to tuck in before complete satiation. The kennel-men started to clear platters and plates.

George had chatted genially with his nearest seatmates, Brynach and Isolda, but when not called upon to converse he observed with interest the couples that had been seated together and were talking to each other. Tanguy and Armelle were clearly a pair already. They laughed at each other's jokes, and touched each other to draw attention to items of interest.

On his right, Isolda was ten years Benitoe's junior, yet she was an adult and the two seemed to find each other engrossing. Certainly they never lacked for conversation. From time to time, George caught Ives at the end of the table surveying that situation with a fond eye.

On George's left hand were a couple of young folk, not quite fully grown. Brynach was clearly fascinated by Rhian, but shy about it, while Rhian seemed oblivious. George noticed that Rhys, not well placed to supervise, yet managed to find a way to glance down the table every so often to watch his sister. On one occasion, Rhodri caught George watching Rhys watching Rhian, and winked at him. George grinned back.

As everyone awaited the final course, George was momentarily abandoned conversationally by his seat partners. He looked down the table and felt the glow rising from the people there, not from the crackling fire. *This is very like a family dinner at any holiday, warm and welcoming. But I'm not really part of it, am I? I'm temporary, a guest in this place. They're the real participants.*

They've been very good to me, but what would they think if I transformed again, as I did this afternoon? How would it be then? Who befriends a monster? No, it's better if I return. No horned man in the human world, I'll bet.

Isolda caught the pensive look on his face. "Anything wrong?" she asked, quietly.

George shook it off. "No, no, my dear. Just some silly thoughts, poking at a sore place. I'm enjoying myself tremendously, and very grateful to be invited." He smiled down at her.

I may feel like a stranger, he thought, but I'm a part of this for the moment. I have a clear duty as huntsman and if I must be an outsider, still these people have need of someone like me.

Huon interrupted this brooding by bringing in a large baking dish with a great clamor. The smell of apples and cinnamon rose wonderfully as he put it down. There was a big letter "O" made of dough superimposed on the crust. He laid the great pie on the center of the table and Tanguy brought out more plates.

Ives stood and cried out, "All rise. To the destruction of Owen the Leash and all his works." There was a great clatter as everyone hastened to stand and raise a glass. They turned in a body and bowed to George, who nodded back.

"My pleasure, believe me," he said to them.

They sat back down and carved into the pie. Everyone wanted a piece of the "O" on the crust, to do it justice.

George pulled out his watch to check the time while waiting for his piece. Isolda said, "This tracks the hour of the day, doesn't it? Could you show me how?"

He unfastened the watch from his weskit and placed it down on the table for her to see. He showed her how it opened, and explained why the outer case had an inset window in the middle so that it could be read one-handed on horseback without having to actually open it up. She held it up to her ear and giggled at the tick-tock sound. He opened up the back case to show her the delicate mechanism with its wound spring, gears, balance wheel, and the escapement that made the ticking noise.

"What's the meaning of this?" she said, touching the elaborate engraving on the back cover.

An old girlfriend of George's had found the antique watch and given it to him several years ago for his birthday. She told him she couldn't resist the St. George and the Dragon engraved on the back, with St. George on his horse pinning the head of the writhing beast to the ground with his lance.

"We have stories of heroes from long ago, and one of them is named Saint George. He was famous for killing dragons. This watch was a gift, and the picture's a reference to my name."

Then he showed her the compass, at the other end of the watch chain where a fob would normally be. This was as much a wonder to her as the watch. He tried to explain magnetism and the spinning planet to her, but made little headway and gave up, contenting himself with showing her what it could do.

His end of the table had fallen silent as he talked with Isolda, Benitoe looking on as well, and George glanced up and realized he had a larger fascinated audience. "Pass them around," he told her. "Just be careful of the watch—it's easy to damage when the case is opened up."

The commemorative pie was well and truly consumed while the watch and compass made their round and came back to George.

The cheerful conversation continued around the table until the fire burned low and Ives called a halt. "We have hunting in the morning, and work still to do this evening to clean up. Time to let these good folk retire and send them on their way."

With some laughter, he conducted Rhys, Rhian, Brynach, and Rhodri to the front door and bade them goodnight, waving them off to find their way back to the manor house. Alun and George were forbidden to help with the cleaning, while all the lutins stayed behind to pitch in, singing boisterously and laughing in the kitchen behind closed doors.

George looked at Alun standing in the hall listening to every noise from the kitchen with a look of distress on his face. "Never mind, time for bed," he told him. "You can hear them from your room just as well as you can from here. Besides, you've had just as much to drink as they have. Let them bear the blame for any dropped plates."

Alun smiled slightly at the tease, and together they walked a bit unsteadily up the stairs.

CHAPTER 26

Someone's laughing at us, George thought. This last private hunt Saturday morning wasn't going well, and here they were, soaked to the skin and chilled, in their brand new livery. He was grateful for one thing, however—the water running off his tricorn behind him ran in two channels instead of right down his back. The lack of any observers for this fiasco was also a blessing.

The skies had been dark and threatening when they set out, but Rhys's counsel that this would normally be considered hunting weather made him persist anyway. By the time they reached Eagle's Nest, the fixture just a couple of miles southwest of the manor, a steady drizzle had obscured the view up the heavily wooded slope.

The stag they had been following was moving slowly across the slope, the hounds behind him having a hard time holding the line. While they were stopped for a moment to puzzle it out, Rhys rode back to George and Rhian.

"If he reaches the top and crosses over, he's lost to us."

"I don't understand. Why can't we just follow him over?" George asked.

"Do you know what's over there?" Rhys said.

"I do. The lovely Shenandoah Valley, the Valley of Virginia."

"This isn't Virginia. The west country is closed to us. People who go there come back damaged or not at all. Hounds, too. All hunting stops at the ridge line."

"It's a big country out there," George protested.

"I've been told that the ridge marks the boundary all the way. Ceridwen can tell you more about it."

But the Appalachian mountains don't form a continuous barrier, he thought. It's not all one mountain seam, and there are plenty of gaps. He looked at Rhys's sincere and worried expression and decided now wasn't the time to discuss it.

"Alright, I'll take your advice. See if you can get to the front, then, because that buck's headed for the top." He pointed in the direction of the stag.

"Rhian, go with him. If the hounds don't break off, he may need you. No matter what, you two stick together. I'll stay with the main pack."

They rode off to his right, their horses making heavy going of the steep wet ground.

He blew his horn to halt the hounds and reached out to monitor their response. After several recalls, most of the pack had returned. Benitoe and Brynach arrived a few minutes later and sent in two more couple that had been slow to obey. A quick count showed they were still three hounds short.

"Who's missing?" he asked. "I don't see Cythraul."

"Aeronwy and Rhymi, too," Benitoe said.

George reached out. He felt the deer hesitate at the top, then move forward. Behind the buck, he could feel the three hounds, with horses coming up behind them. The hounds crossed over, and the horses stopped. There was a sort of flare that he suspected was Rhian trying to stop the hounds directly, but he couldn't tell if it succeeded.

George turned to Benitoe and Brynach. "We have a situation now. The deer has crossed to the other side, and all three hounds after him. Rhys and Rhian are near the top trying to get them back. If we're to get them any help with that, we're going to have to bring the rest of the pack back and return."

The two whippers-in waited for their orders, serious and attentive.

"We're going to bring the pack in quickly. Brynach, you'll stay on my left. Benitoe, take Rhys's usual spot. If you have any problems, sing out."

"Pack up," he called and pushed them out ahead of him. He let Afanc find his own footing and concentrated on making sure the pack stayed together down through the thick woods.

When they reached the road, he pushed the speed, bringing them back through the manor gate and up to the kennels at a trot. They poured into the kennels, the hounds milling about excitedly.

"Brynach, you stay here, sort out the hounds, and tell Ives what's happened. I'm headed right back. Benitoe?"

"I'm going with you."

"How's your mount holding up?"

"We haven't gone far today, she'll be fine."

George nodded, and the two of them clattered out of the kennel and cantered back down through the manor gates and down the road.

He could still feel Rhian, somewhat distantly. She was moving downslope, and he left the road with Benitoe short of the original opening into the woods to try and meet her partway. Benitoe pointed out the entrance to another path and they both headed that way. Before they reached it, Rhian and Rhys emerged, with two of the hounds, Cythraul and Rhymi.

Rhian was distressed. "We can hear Aeronwy but can't find her, and these two kept wanting to go back over whenever we took our attention away from them."

"You did the right thing to stick to the hounds you had." Looking at Rhys, he asked, "What happened?"

"All three went over the ridge after the buck. We could hear them baying on the other side but couldn't see them. She called and I blew. These two," pointing at the hounds, "finally returned but Aeronwy didn't follow them. I thought we better return these and go back."

George reached out. The buck was gone but he could dimly sense one hound. "I feel her. You two go back with these and get cleaned up. Shouldn't take long to pick her up."

Rhys nodded and moved off with Rhian, pushing the hounds along.

George sent out a call to Aeronwy and thought he felt a response.

He told Benitoe, "She's on our side but I don't think she's moving around. She may be injured."

They walked up the steep slope on the wet path cautiously, George in the lead. The ground was churned with hoof prints from Rhys and Rhian's descent, but Benitoe, closer to the ground, leaned down with interest. "I think I see prints leading up, and they don't match ours. They're just a bit earlier. Someone else came up here a little while ago."

"In the rain?"

"Or just before it."

The path opened to a shallow gap created by a fallen tree, and George paused. Benitoe waited behind him. George sensed ahead for the hound, and was surprised to find a horse, closer and approaching. He couldn't hear it yet. Remembering how near they were to the manor, he decided he wanted to see this person without being seen, if possible.

"Back up into this gap by the tree and don't make a sound. Don't move. I'm going to try and identify this guy and I don't want him to see us."

They backed both horses up, George calming them into stillness with one part of his mind. The trees and the rain, along with their green clothing, partially hid them, but George wanted better camouflage. He looked across the path to a tree draped with fox grape vines, and used that as a model to build a similar glamoured wall in front of them that he could dimly see through. It wavered badly under his uncertain control, but he hoped it would be adequate in the bad visibility. He ignored the sound of Benitoe stiffening beside him in surprise.

Moments later they heard a rider descending the path, bits of the tack rubbing, and hooves thudding slowly as the horse found footing. It snorted as it smelled their own mounts.

The rider was impatient and in a temper. He paid no attention to his horse's alert. His head was down, ducking out of the rain, but he raised it level as he passed by their blind, and George widened his nostrils, damping his flare of excitement as best he could and trying to keep his glamour under some kind of control. It was Scilti, wearing his false form. George still couldn't tell what was behind it.

The horse and rider continued down the path and out of sight. George thought, I could probably have suppressed his horse's reaction to our presence. I'll have to try that, next time.

George waited until he was sure they were beyond hearing, then dropped the glamour. Benitoe looked at him cautiously.

"I didn't know you could do that."

"Me, neither. I've just started experimenting with Ceridwen." He thrust away the thought of how that experiment ended.

Benitoe looked down at Scilti's horse prints. "That's the one who came up here earlier. You know who he is, don't you?"

"He's a stranger at the Horned Man, calling himself Scilti. He wears a glamour." He looked directly at Benitoe. "Gwyn knows about it. This mustn't be talked about with anyone else, since we're not sure who his friends are."

Benitoe nodded.

"I want to know what he was doing here," George said.

"Let's get the hound," Benitoe said, "and I'll let you know if our path diverges from his as we go."

They continued climbing on the path until, at one fork, George was pulled left by the hound sense, while Scilti's path went right.

"Hound first," George said, "then we're coming back to this spot."

They found Aeronwy not far away. She had come back to this side of the ridge and had no apparent injuries, but she was exhausted, as if she had run back as fast as possible and couldn't take another step. With some maneuvering they managed to get her lifted to George's arms so he could carry her draped partially over his lap across the saddle.

When they came back to the fork, they took the other branch and continued to follow Scilti's trail. It came out onto a rock outcrop forming a ledge in front of an overhang, almost a cave, nestled near the top of the ridge, framed in front with trees reaching up from below that masked it from sight. One gap in the trees allowed a spectacular view down the slope, showing the village to the right, and the manor to the left, fully visible.

"Well this is a convenient spy hole, isn't it?" George said. He stayed on Afanc to hold the hound, but Benitoe dismounted to look inside. He didn't walk in, afraid to leave muddy footprints where the rain wouldn't wash them away, but it was quite shallow, providing shelter from the weather and not much else.

"Nothing inside that I can see," he said.

Continuing along the ledge, he found another path out. "There are different prints here, a man on foot."

"So, two of them meet here, then go their separate ways. Do you know where that path goes?"

"Could go anywhere. If you stayed at this level on the ridge side, you'd intersect the route from Daear Llosg, not far from the top. I've never heard of this overhang, but I haven't explored all over the slope. It may be well known."

"I want to follow the other fellow, but we need to get this hound back."

Benitoe said, "We're probably closer taking this path than going back down the way we came. We can come in at the postern gate."

"Agreed." Benitoe remounted and took the lead to make tracking easier. The path led gradually downslope, directly toward the manor. After several minutes, George called out quietly, "Hold up." This was the general area of the small hidden way he had found earlier, and he cast about again looking for it. He located it, not far in front of them.

"Alright, continue." The path they were on took them straight to it. They passed through the slight widening of the path without effect and continued on. "We're not far from the back gate," he told Benitoe. Benitoe gave him a glance, as if to wonder how he knew that.

At the next fork, George recognized the left branch as leading around to Daear Llosg, having come that way a few days ago. They stayed to the right, headed for the manor, and at the next branching, the footprints they were tracking turned right, gradually going down toward the palisade. The riders followed the straight branch down the slope instead and came out at the clear space before the palisade, facing the rear sortie gate of the manor. The other path would have emerged to their right.

The guards were on the alert, having heard them on the path.

"We have a hound we need to bring in," George told them. "Has anyone else been here before us, this morning?"

They shook their heads and opened the gates for him, looking skeptically at their horses, made nervous by the palisade and reluctant to enter the tunnel despite its stone shielding. George reached for the horses and his hound to calm them, and they quieted, walking through the tunnel and out the other gate.

"Benitoe," he said, quietly, "we're going to ride casually to the kennels, following the perimeter close to the palisade. I want you on the outside. As we approach the balineum, take special notice of the ground and see if you can find those tracks again. Don't let anyone notice what you're looking for. There's a secret way through the palisade beyond the baths that we're not supposed to know about, and we don't want to alert our enemy."

Benitoe nodded seriously and began surveying the wet ground, with George on his larger horse blocking him from the view of the rest of the manor yard.

Past the balineum complex, Benitoe paused to fiddle with his tack. He muttered, out of the side of his mouth, "The prints are visible here, coming from the palisade. It's a well-hidden spot."

"Alright, let's follow them as if just taking this route to the kennels by chance. I don't imagine you'll be able to track them far, though, with all the usual activity in the yard."

They turned left and made another twenty yards before Benitoe muttered, "Lost him."

"To be expected. Will you know him again, if you see the prints?"

"Yes. Medium weight, male, right shoe nicked on the inner heel."

"Excellent. Keep an eye out for him. We think he lives inside the gates." He looked at Benitoe directly. "Be careful, these are dangerous people."

"Good," he said. "So am I."

~

What's the point of climbing up the ridge in all this rain just to be told to wait? I can get him any time, I can. He doesn't know me, none of them do. They just go around with their little jobs while I sit and watch.

Makes me hungry, all this creeping and waiting. Like the little animals in the woods. You have to sit still, still, and not let them see you move. Until you're close enough to grab them, till they're in your hands, hearts pounding, throbbing under your fingers, eyes shining. Then they're yours, and you can stop them whenever you want.

~

"What's wrong with her?" George asked Ives. "Cythraul and Rhymi seem none the worse for wear, but she's a wreck."

They looked down at Aeronwy, lying on a bed of straw in the infirmary pen, away from the other hounds. She had taken water and some broth after they cleaned her up but wouldn't eat anything else.

"I think she's just exhausted and worn out from fright. If she crossed the ridge, there's no telling what she found."

"She feels cold and lonely to me," George told him. "I wonder if she has a couple of kennel buddies we could let in to keep her company and warm her up?"

"You stay here. I've an idea, I'll be right back."

George sat down stiffly along the wall next to the tired hound and lifted her head onto his lap, running his large hand down her side and rubbing her neck. Her tail beat feebly on the ground at the attention.

Ives returned with two bitches. "This one's her littermate, and the other's their dam. They all get along fine."

Both hounds walked over to Aeronwy and sniffed her all over. The older one lay down next to her with a sigh and was soon joined by the younger one, eager to burrow into the only corner of the pen that was covered in straw.

"That'll work," George said. He stood up carefully, feeling every ache and the chill of a cold wet morning.

George walked across the lane to his gate and up the path to the porch. He couldn't walk in, dripping and filthy like this.

He knocked on the door, and Alun opened it, took one look, and held up his hand with a "stay put" gesture. He returned in a moment with an organized kit. "Sit there," he pointed. The hat and gloves were first, then the boots came off, reluctantly, the leather wanting to stick to the wet socks. Then he peeled the socks off, giving George dry wool socks to put on instead, and slippers.

He stood up, emptied all of his pockets into a basket Alun provided, then with Alun's help took off the wet wool coat he'd been wearing, shivering in the sudden chill in his shirt sleeves, since the coat had been keeping him warm, even soaked. Alun reached for the weskit, too, draping it with the coat on the back of the porch chairs. He sent George ahead of him into the house, walking carefully to avoid any puddles in his slippers, and bade him stand on a towel in the hall, next to the door. He stripped off the rest of his clothes, dried off, and put on clean warm undergarments. Before putting on his dressing gown, he walked into the kitchen to wash the dirt and hound grime off his hands and face and towel them dry.

Alun returned with a hot mug of tea and he sat down in front of the kitchen fire, beginning to recover as he warmed up inside and out and listened to the rain fall. Poor Alun, he thought, all those nice new clothes.

CHAPTER 27

The rain falling lightly but steadily after lunch inclined George toward study. He'd been quite surprised at his partial success with the camouflage glamour earlier in the woods, and wanted to explore the subject and see what else was possible.

At lunch he kept an eye out for people coming in with wet feet on the stone flags, to see if he could spot the prints Benitoe described, but without success. Of course, if the unknown were already inside, he could come to the meal dry shod or even in different footwear, and George would never know. Frustrating, he thought.

He hadn't yet seen Ceridwen or Gwyn to report to and decided to see if Ceridwen had set up the shelf of books for him yet. That way he could learn something, and if she was there maybe give them more information to chew over.

At home, he put together a little bundle of his slippers, a couple of apples, and the new notebook Ceridwen had given him, and dashed across the lane, trying to stay dry. A knock at her door produced a servant who let him into the library and went to fetch tea while he looked over the shelf she gave him, now populated with several books.

The first two at the left were general reading. The leftmost one was titled *First Principles* and looked like a basic work for students. He pulled that one out and skimmed the rest. There were two books in the next section on the subject of glamours, three following, about ways, and two on talking to beasts. Excellent, he thought. This should hold me for a few days, assuming I can read them. Both the books in the first section were printed, but at least three of the others seemed to be manuscript.

He had shed his wet shoes at the door and walked about in his slippers, comfortable and dry. The servant brought in the tea and placed it next to an armchair near the fire, which he freshened up with a couple of logs before leaving.

George added his apples to the tray and sat down, keeping an eye on the doorway. Ceridwen wasn't at home at the moment, but expected soon.

As she had bidden him, he opened his notebook and started a section on his first assignment. According to the front matter, the book in his hand was printed in 1838, and claimed to be the 23rd edition of a work first produced in Cor Tewdws, wherever that was. No author was mentioned. He was relieved to find it legible, in a language he could follow. He began reading.

A crack as an ember broke off a log in the fire finally caught his attention and he looked up to find Ceridwen in the doorway, watching. The tea was cold, and his finger marked his place more than halfway through the thin volume.

He rose to greet her. "Thanks for putting these books together so quickly for me. This is fascinating." He held out the first book and waved it, finger still inside.

"It's good to have an eager student." She walked over and perched on the arm of the leather chair across from him. "Were you looking for me earlier?"

George found a scrap of paper from the kindling basket to hold the place in his book more permanently and put it aside as he sat down again. He recounted the discovery of Scilti in the woods, and their tracking of whomever he met back to the manor. Ceridwen listened attentively.

"Come here and show me where you were."

She pulled out one of the scrolls behind her desk and rolled out the same map George had seen before when he showed her the ways. He bent down and used his finger to sketch out the various paths. "We came right through the spot with the small way. Can you tell that? Are your traps in place?"

"I felt passage up the slope this morning, and back twice. There was no indication that the way itself had been used, no delays or interruption in movement. The first two were a man on foot, the last was two on horses."

"Sounds right to me," he said.

"It's the first time the traps have been activated since I set them, by anything other than animals alone."

George straightened up and stretched. "That overhang may be a common meeting space. It probably takes less than half an hour to reach it from here on foot, so almost anyone could vanish for an hour and not be noticed. No one keeps track of Scilti and the woods are broad. He could enter that network of trails from anywhere and make his way over to the ledge."

"How would he get a message to his partner to meet him?"

"I should think that depends on who his partner is. There may not be any regular need for messages anyway. There might be a standard time for Scilti to meet with this spy within the walls, and they're just sticking to a schedule."

"If that's true," Ceridwen said, "then we might learn something just from that. Who isn't otherwise available from one point to another of a Saturday morning?"

She sat down at her desk and drew out a piece of paper. "All the instructors like Hadyn and the craft-masters, and their students, would be tied down. The manor house staff would many of them be preparing the lunch meal and starting on dinner, or doing other household duties. In any case, they'd be well supervised. Same for the stablemen and, for that matter, the guards."

"That leaves kennel-staff, which I can look into, outdoor workers, people who work in the out-buildings..."

"All the primary residents, the guests, and their staff," she said.

They looked at each other. George said, slowly, "I can't see one of the highly visible residents or guests taking this hike unnoticed and coming back filthy and wet, but what about their staff? What do they do every day?"

"Whatever their lords ask for. Other than helping serve at meals, they have no other fixed duties."

"So, let's add them to the list. There can't be that many," he said.

George considered. "You know, Maonirn at the inn said Scilti was out every day. Where does he go? Does he just come to this one spot and hope that his partner can meet him, or does he have other spies to talk to?"

"We need to know," Ceridwen said, "You can't follow a rider on foot, and a horse would be too visible. We must intercept him instead."

"What about more traps? We could set something up at the overhang and at potential entry points in the west woods"

"The problem isn't making them," she said. "It's monitoring them. There's a limit to how many I can pay attention to. They also can't tell us identity very well. I won't know for sure it's Scilti who triggers them, or whom he meets."

"But we can learn a lot about what's going on just from that little bit of information, by comparing the times."

"True." George saw her mentally weighing her choices.

"I know the overhang you found and how to get to it. I'll set traps at the paths there, and also at the entrance of the trail across from the palisade hole. Just before dinner tonight would be best, when most people are here and Scilti is known to be at the inn."

"But it'll be filthy wet and getting dark," George said. "Let me go with you, at least."

"If you like, but it won't be the first time." She waved her arm at the cozy library with its warm fire and gleaming shelves. "I'm not always the well-groomed scholar in her tidy den."

She placed her hands on her thighs and stood up. "Come tell me about the glamour you cast when Scilti went by. I want to hear all the details."

"Are you sure this will work?" Alun said.

He stood under the dripping roof before Ceridwen's door while George knocked.

"It'll be fine," George said. He hoped he was right.

The door was opened by Ceridwen's servant and they entered the hall trying not to make a mess. It was only a short distance across the lane, so they were still relatively dry, barring their footwear which they wiped.

Ceridwen, dressed in boots, breeches, and coat, met them in the study. "You've been here before, Alun, haven't you?"

"Yes, my lady, but not for some time."

George saw him looking ill at ease. He pointed him to a chair by the fire. "Sit down. You're going to be here for a while. Might as well be comfortable."

Alun reluctantly sat down, and George and Ceridwen joined him.

"Tell Ceridwen what you told me, about Meuric," George said.

"You asked me two days ago to see if I could find out more about him. I talked to some of my friends in the manor and heard some strange things."

"Such as?" Ceridwen said.

"He doesn't have any tasks to do. He's always there to help with the dinner service, but otherwise they see little of him. Guests who bring servants, why they keep them busy, especially with clothing and little errands, and so the staff get to know them, but my lady Creiddylad uses the house staff for that, not Meuric."

"What does he do all day, then?" Ceridwen asked.

"They don't know, but they like to make up stories about it. Some hold he's not natural, that he stalks small animals to eat them."

Ceridwen gave him a look.

"Well, there's this giggle he has which will send shivers down your spine, it will. A few think he must be a bedmate of his lady, but most think that couldn't be hidden from the house staff and dismiss the notion."

"Anything else?" Ceridwen said.

"They know he's in and out of the house at all hours and that he keeps out of the way of the lords. Except for young Rhian and Rhys. His eyes follow Rhian, and the house staff are outraged by it and united in wishing him ill."

"I've asked Gwyn, and he doesn't recall seeing his face. That's strange for one living in the house," Ceridwen said. "It must be deliberate avoidance."

George said to Ceridwen, "I suggested to Alun that one of the lords could have glamoured himself and come in from a wet day like today secretly, but he tells me that's impossible."

Alun said, "Someone would notice him wet, his clothes would need to be cleaned, the servant straightening his room would have seen evidence—there's just no way it could be hidden, even if no one saw him leave or come back. The staff would know, there are no secrets there. Plenty of servants come in wet, for their work or from errands, but not the lords, not without notice."

Ceridwen nodded. "You're probably right."

She looked out at the windows where the light was getting darker and stood up.

"It's time we were going. Stand up, now," she said. "Let me get a good look at you."

George watched Ceridwen standing across from Alun and taking in his clothing. She was dressed as he was, to make things easier.

Ceridwen, in a single instant, shimmered and reformed as Alun's copy. She gained slightly in stature but otherwise was changed mostly in face, hair, and clothes. When she spoke, it was in Alun's deeper tones. "This is easy enough, especially when you start with similar clothing."

Alun looked deeply uneasy to see such a duplicate of himself. "Is that what I look like, then? Surely I don't sound like that."

"Everyone asks that," Ceridwen said, in the same voice. "Don't worry, I'll take care for your reputation while I borrow your form."

"We'll make better arrangements next time," George said to Ceridwen as they came in, soaked, a couple of hours later, to the relief of the anxious Alun.

"Did it work, then?" he asked.

"Like a charm," George said. "We bickered in the stable about going to town in such bad weather, and you could see the lads hiding their grins. If anyone was paying attention, I think they were satisfied. We took the route up along the palisade once we were out of sight of the gate guards."

Ceridwen had dropped her glamour the moment she reached the study. She stood with George in the doorway, to minimize the mess she was making with her sodden garments. "Thank you for the borrowed form, Alun. I hope you found something to amuse you?"

He looked down at the small book still in his hand, caught up when he rose. "Yes, my lady, very interesting it is."

"What have you got there?" she asked.

George glanced at the book and thought it looked relatively recent, compared to most on the shelves.

"It's about a lad raised by wolves in a far country with strange beasts," Alun said.

Good heavens, George realized. It's Kipling's *Jungle Books*. "Where did that come from?" he asked Ceridwen.

"Gwyn brings back books when he travels, and they tend to end up here. Sometimes I wish I could get more of some of the authors."

She waved at one of the shelves, but George couldn't make out the details from the doorway and didn't want to cross the carpet, wet as he was. He vowed to look more thoroughly at his next opportunity.

"Take that one with you and bring it back when you're done," she told Alun.

"Thank you, my lady." He closed it and put it carefully inside his coat, and accompanied George to the door.

"Try to look wet," George said, as they dashed across the lane. "It seems highly unfair that you're not."

"Ah, but I'll get to clean a second set of clothes for you when we get home."

"There is that," George said, with a grin.

CHAPTER 28

What if I can't keep this under control, George thought, in the huntsman's office after lunch on Sunday. That glamour in the woods was all external, but now he was trying to change his own appearance again. The last thing he wanted was to trigger that horned man form.

He was afraid to try it alone, but yesterday's excursion with the glamoured Ceridwen made it clear how much this was a basic tool. He'd have to learn to master it.

He was taking a break, interrupting the selection of materials for his apprentices to study with practice on his glamours. The internal window to the dark nursing pen that still held Aeronwy served as an adequate mirror.

His most recent attempt had yielded an implausibly tall female who strode about like a man and had only the faintest understanding of how skirts should move. Alright, no women, he thought.

The man I know best is grandfather, but I need someone in a younger age range so I can fade into the background—there are few elderly fae. I'd best make up a persona for myself and learn to know it well. The first thing to eliminate is whatever makes me stand out in a crowd from a distance. Then I can work on the face and surface appearance.

My size is the big problem, so to speak. The height's not so unusual, but it makes me obvious and a few inches shorter would be good. Breadth was worse, he thought. They're all rather lean here.

Alright, think "narrow." He envisioned Rhys and Gwyn, tall but lanky. His appearance changed in the reflection, drawing in at the shoulders and chest. Now let's try for shorter. He saw his reflection shrink by three or four inches. Not bad, he thought, turning around and checking from other angles.

A rap on the door startled him, and he walked over to open it. He watched his shorter arm reach for the knob but his real hand was already there, and he rapped his knuckles badly with the careless thrust.

"Ouch," he said, dropping the glamour and successfully turning the knob with his other hand while shaking the fingers on the damaged one.

Isolda stood there, looking puzzled. "I was walking by after talking to my father and couldn't make sense of what I was seeing through the window."

George shook his head ruefully. "I'm doing my glamour homework. Ceridwen set me the task of developing a standard alternate appearance. My first try with her didn't go quite as expected, and I wanted to surprise her for next time."

"Benitoe told me about yesterday in the woods. Can I watch? Maybe I can help."

"Why not," he said. "You'll have to keep it a secret, of course. I wouldn't want it to become generally known."

She nodded and sat down.

This time he tried the thinner and shorter body without the benefit of the mirror. Isolda's eyes widened, but she nodded to show he had succeeded.

"Walk around and pick things up," she said.

He moved about the office, weaving around the furniture, and found that he stumbled easily, misjudging distance. When he went to pull a book off the shelves, he almost dropped it, then recovered and opened it awkwardly as if to read. He walked to his desk and sat down, reaching for a pen to write with and knocking it to the floor.

He dropped the glamour and sat back in his desk chair. "Not quite a success, is it?" he asked Isolda.

"I would imagine that changing size is a real challenge," she said, thoughtfully. "You move around like a larger man, which you are. The stride length doesn't match the apparent length of your legs, so you look very odd as you walk. When you reached for that book, your eyes probably told you one thing, but your sense of your own body told you something else."

"That's about right. I wanted to mask my size and height to blend in better."

"I can understand that, but movement's giving you away," she said. "Can you make yourself actually smaller, to match the new dimensions? I mean, could you hunch over a little, slump, and hold your upper arms closer to your body, to effectively shorten your reach and narrow your chest?"

He was nodding as she spoke. "Maybe keep my knees bent, too. That way, the body and the appearance will be closer in synch."

He stood up again. His appearance didn't change much, but now he moved less clumsily around the room.

"Yes, much better," she said. "If you practice that way, it should work. Keep thinking about taking up less space."

"Uncomfortable, but doable," he agreed. "It'll never work on a horse, though. Better not need to fight, either."

He glanced at her. "Now I have to choose a face. Let me try this without a reflection." He closed his eyes and concentrated on feeling his jaw wider, his cheeks hollower, his hair shaggier.

Isolda's bright laughter made him open his eyes. "No good?" he said.

Wordlessly, still laughing, she covered her mouth and pointed at the internal window to tell him to see for himself.

Sigh. His reflection looked like a zombie, stiff and lumpy.

A knock sounded on the door and Benitoe opened it. "I heard noise…"

He broke off and stiffened, seeing Isolda sitting there laughing at a stranger in hunt livery with his back to him.

George dropped the glamour and straightened up. "Just practicing," he said. "It's not easy."

Benitoe relaxed. "Let's see," he said.

George resumed the body portion again. "I'd gotten this far and we were starting to work on the face when this young lady here lost her composure," he said, with mock severity.

"I couldn't help it," she said to Benitoe. "Try again," she told George.

This time he widened his mouth and held it open, and narrowed his chin. He browned his eyes and lightened his hair to a medium brown, fading his eyebrows to match.

He looked at Isolda to see her reaction. This time she gave him a sober appraisal. "Much better. Looks like a real person, and not quite you," she said. "Go look."

His reflection showed him an ordinary, unremarkable man, very much the effect he was looking for.

He raised the timbre of his voice from baritone to tenor. "What do you think, Benitoe?"

Benitoe startled at the change of voice. "Very odd, sir, but effective."

George considered Alun's usual clothing and added that change.

Isolda clapped her hands once in approval. "Now walk around," she said, and George obeyed, while both lutins scrutinized the performance.

"If you can return to this appearance at need and practice it, I think it will mask you well enough," Benitoe said, and Isolda nodded her agreement.

"There were fewer here last year, this far ahead of the great hunt," Gwyn said to Edern at Sunday dinner, shaking his head.

"You know they've come to see your new huntsman, and they're making an effort to see him at work beforehand. There will always be more come to watch a potential disaster than to applaud an ordinary victory."

Gwyn's mouth quirked at that piece of wisdom.

Edern continued. "I predict there won't be many arriving tomorrow, that this is just about everyone."

"As each one comes to greet me, I can feel the same old alignments. The same people profess to be friends, the usual subset of them smile to cover their enmity—no surprises."

"And you expected to sense particular enemies this year?"

"Well, they're here, aren't they? We know that." Gwyn clenched his fist on the table.

"Brother, they've probably been here every year, since this particular plot started." He tried to encourage Gwyn. "It's a good thing that you sense nothing different. I believe you have special enemies, indeed, but they've been scheming for several years, by the evidence. If there were a general uprising planned, you'd know it from the changes in their less adroit peripheral allies, excitedly anticipating success."

"Instead, you think it's just a long conspiracy hoping to finish. I suppose that's better, but we may all end up just as dead either way."

Edern looked at him as he watched their guests dine in his hall morosely. "It's not like you to be down-hearted in this way."

Gwyn was silent for a moment. Then he said, even more quietly, "I fear Arawn's fate, the withdrawal of the favor of Cernunnos."

"For the old… actions?"

"For the old crimes, yes," Gwyn bitterly corrected.

"That was a very long time ago."

"And it's never been properly paid for." It was even rewarded, he considered, when he received Annwn partly in compensation for ending hostilities with Gwythyr. He started his reign from a position of dishonor, and how could he remove the shame of that?

Edern objected. "They were your enemies, fighting against you."

"They were my prisoners, my hostages, and their care was in my hands." And they had good reason to fight—they were obeying their lord, who had a sufficient cause. He didn't want to dwell on the familiar thoughts.

"We know Cernunnos is taking a hand," Gwyn said. He had brought Edern up to date on George's strange manifestations two days ago.

"But it may be on your side, in support. He's provided a huntsman for you, after all."

"Yes, but Iolo's gone. Did he help with that, too?" He hadn't forgotten that Iolo was tainted by the same cruelties so long ago. "Iolo was less guilty than I am, and I'm still here."

He glanced down the table at George, laughing with his deep voice at the punchline of one of Rhodri's elaborate stories.

"I can't help but wonder if young George there is being sponsored as more than huntsman, as…" he broke off.

"As your replacement?" Edern supplied.

"Clearly Cernunnos is working within him. To what end? The fact that he's of my blood only makes me the more uneasy; what more natural to legitimize a transition of rulers?"

Edern frowned. "He's done well by you so far. What do you intend?"

"What can I do? The hounds must be hunted, and he's the only practical choice."

"Well, but afterward?"

"If we're all still here, you mean." It may be too late by then, of course, he thought. "I don't know yet. We'll have to see how much of a threat he poses."

Monday evening, George slipped inside the house gate eagerly, and paused in the yard. Light streamed through the windows, and he could smell the cooking inside.

He'd hastened his staff through the pre-hunt meeting, raising some surreptitious smiles when they saw him dressed for dinner in his new clothes, since he hadn't attended the meal in the great hall. They knew about Angharad's visit, of course, but everyone carefully avoided the topic.

As he came into the house, he heard voices in the front room and walked through quietly to join them. Alun and Angharad were bent over the small painting of Iolo that Alun had chosen for a keepsake.

He paused to look at them before interrupting. Angharad was wearing a charcoal gown with crimson touches about the cuffs and collar. Her long hair was coiled in elaborate braids like a coronet, and she looked positively regal.

"Sorry I couldn't break away sooner," George said, and they lifted their heads.

"Alun's taken great care of me," Angharad replied. "He was just showing me an old painting of mine. I remember this one. The hound's name was, let me see, Rhyfelwr. Warrior. He was one of Cernunnos's hounds, I believe."

"You know about those? Do you know where Iolo got them? He keeps it obscure in his logs."

"Gwyn should know. Whenever he won on Nos Galan Mai, Iolo would leave and return with the year's new whelps for all to see. No victory, no pups."

Alun picked up the painting to put it away.

"Have you been settled in your guest room?" George asked.

"All fine and comfortable," she said. "How did you spend your day?"

"After the hound walk, I rode out with Rhys to see tomorrow's fixture for myself, to check the lay of the land. Then I read about the old hunts there in Iolo's logs, to get a sense for what to expect."

"Hunts from the Dale are usually quite good," she said.

"That's what I'm afraid of, the comparison."

Alun reappeared to shoo them into the dining room. The table had been reconfigured to seat two, and set with plates George hadn't seen before, clearly of Angharad's manufacture. She smiled faintly to see them.

Alun brought in wine, and busied himself in the kitchen, delivering courses but otherwise making himself scarce.

"How has your week of practice hunts worked out?" Angharad asked, as they ate.

"I think it's gone about as well as I could have hoped, but it's an absurdly short amount of time to take over a pack. Don't misunderstand me—I'm not that worried about embarrassing myself tomorrow; if it happens, it happens. It's just that I gather the stakes on Saturday will be higher for everyone than I realized when I accepted the job, and I've only got these next two hunts to rehearse."

She nodded soberly. "That's so. You'll have seen the many new arrivals in the last couple of days?"

"I skipped dinner in the great hall tonight, but I saw them yesterday. A glittery bunch, and some seemed to have their knives out for Gwyn."

"And for you, too. For some, it's personal; they don't like Gwyn to have so much power, or he's done them some wrong. For others, it's just a taste for change, destructive or not." She took a sip of her wine. "Long life brings boredom to some. It's a great vice, to not reckon the consequences, or simply not to care."

"I don't imagine they like the idea of a human huntsman much, either."

"That's part of it, certainly, but not the main issue. Much of it's envy, I'd say. They remember how Gwyn got his position." She put her fork down. "How much do you know about his predecessor?"

George leaned back in his chair to listen. "Very little."

"Arawn was the Prince of Annwn, for, well, I don't know how long. Hundreds of years, anyway. Annwn is really Cernunnos's realm, but he doesn't rule it directly. That's why Arawn was titled prince, not king. Beli Mawr, I believe, understands this, but his son, Gwyn's father, king in his own domain, has come to think of Annwn as his to bestow, that Gwyn is a prince under his kingship, as a son and heir. Gwyn understands that he holds this title from its real king, and not his father."

She picked up her glass again. "They've fought over this and it's estranged them, that Gwyn should not feel beholden to his father for his rule. It's why he removed Annwn to the new world."

"But your painting of the investiture shows a different view," George said.

"It was done for Gwyn's father, not for Gwyn. The version in his council room is a constant reminder of their disagreement."

"What happened to Arawn?"

"That begins with the tale of Pwyll Pen Annwn."

Before she could start, Alun brought in some fruit for dessert and they concentrated on that for a few moments, before she started the story.

"Pwyll was the lord of Dyfed, in the old country. He originally offended Arawn by driving his hounds from a deer kill and claiming it as his own. They agreed to exchange places for a year and a day, taking each other's appearance and slaying each other's enemies, which they did. At the end of the time, they changed back, and Pwyll earned Arawn's friendship for having slept chastely for that year in the same bed as Arawn's wife. Pwyll returned to Dyfed with the title Pwyll Pen Annwn—Pwyll, Head of Annwn—for the year's exploit."

George thought to himself, so Pwyll's a byword for maintaining an undetectable glamour for a long time. That explains the references I keep hearing.

Angharad said, "When Gwyn stole Creiddylad back, some of the men in pursuit belonged to Pwyll, visiting Gwythyr, and were among the prisoners mistreated and slain by Gwyn. Pwyll's fury became Arawn's as well."

"Gwyn made many enemies that day, it seems."

"It's haunted him ever since," she agreed. She toyed with an unused piece of silverware. "Arawn, in that year's great hunt, hunting the hounds himself, turned from the starting way he had opened with all assembled, and cast his hounds directly at Gwyn. I was there."

"What happened?"

"Gwyn fled through the way—what else could he do? It was that or be torn down on the spot."

"But he survived."

"Cernunnos was angered that the great hunt should be so misused for personal enmity. He led Gwyn through the ways in the form of a great red deer and at last, when Gwyn was brought to bay, Cernunnos cast off Arawn's control of the hounds and turned them on him."

She continued, "Gwyn and Cernunnos returned together through the ways, the hunt accompanying them. It's the only time I know of that Cernunnos was manifest in the great hunt."

"So Beli Mawr thought it might be a good idea to turn Annwn over to Gwyn, I take it," George said.

"Well, Cernunnos had clearly shown him a mark of favor, and it seemed his public apology for his treatment of the prisoners had been accepted."

"Is that the only time the great hunt has failed?"

"The only time I've ever heard of."

~

In his study after dinner afterward, George showed Angharad to a comfortable armchair by the fire and sank into another one himself. They sat in silence for a moment, warm and replete with a good meal. They could hear the clatter of dishes as Alun cleaned up.

"I miss my dogs," George said. "They'd be sitting here, something to do with my hands."

"And you with a whole kennel full," Angharad gently teased. "What are they?"

"I have two, both males. Hugo's a coonhound, an old-style blue-tick. The other one, Sergeant, is a yellow feist. No squirrel was safe." He smiled fondly.

Alun poked his head in. "Something to drink?"

They agreed on brandy, and in a few minutes he reappeared with a bottle and two glasses. "Will you be wanting anything else?" he asked.

"No, and thank you for a wonderful meal." George turned to Angharad. "You know, that's the first dinner he's made for me. Now I understand what I've been missing in the great hall."

Alun nodded in acknowledgment. "I'll be leaving you, then. Don't forget you'll be rising early tomorrow."

Killjoy, George thought. Here he had Angharad in the house and he wanted to enjoy it. Oh, well, the next topic would probably kill the mood anyway, he sighed.

"I've been wanting to tell you something," he said, putting his glass down on the table between them. "I've learned a bit about glamours since I last saw you, from Ceridwen. Have you heard?"

"No. That's a good idea."

"Well, maybe. She was trying to show me how to create a default glamour for emergency use…" he looked at her and she nodded in understanding, "by reverting to an unmarked version of my true self as a foundation."

"And did it work for you?"

"Not quite as she expected." He hesitated. "I need your advice."

"On aesthetics? Whether you'd be better as a redhead?" She chuckled.

He smiled ruefully. "No. I want to know if you'll recognize it."

"As you, you mean," she said.

"Maybe I better just show you."

He stood up and faced her, spreading his feet to steady his balance in anticipation of the weight. The brandy helped remove his inhibitions, and he quickly brushed his everyday body image to one side. This time he briefly felt the horned man form appear, succeeded by the full red deer head, bowed forward under the antlers.

Angharad had risen as the change began. She showed no shock, nor could he smell it on her with his newly altered senses when he flared his nostrils. Just intense interest.

She walked up and placed her hand on the antlers and stroked his furry cheek. Then she backed off and, with a gesture, asked him to turn around.

He obliged, slowly, trying to manage the top-heavy mass as smoothly as possible.

"Yes, that's the form of Cernunnos as I saw him last, which is what you wanted to know," she said. "But you're still George?"

He nodded.

"So, his form but not him. And not a glamour, of course, since I can touch it."

He nodded again.

"Fascinating." He could see her fingers twitch as her eyes went over his form, tracing its lines.

He hadn't expected this. It wasn't so disturbing this time, since he knew what was coming, and Angharad's lack of shock removed much of the horror of it.

He held up a finger to get her attention.

"What, there's more?" she asked.

He nodded, then tried the partial pullback that gave him a primitive human head, horns still attached. This time he paused in this form and held it. He felt the neck muscles of the full red deer form adjust to compensate for the changes.

He tried to speak and found his voice much deeper, and hoarse. "This seems to be an added bonus."

"The Horned Man," she said, in wonder. "Oh, you lucky man."

That's not how he would have put it, he thought.

"Are there other forms?"

"Boy, I hope not." He found the sound of that voice unfamiliar, as if someone had turned up his bass.

She laughed. "Is it hard to maintain them?"

"I don't really know. This is only the second time, and the first time all I wanted to do was get back to normal. It doesn't seem to be a strain, except for my muscles."

He thought more about it. "These shapes are very strange. My body stands differently, because of the weight and I haven't learned how to move well." He gestured at the antlers. "The senses are completely altered. In deer form, they seem to match the animal, and in this form, they're somewhat intermediate, with better sight than the deer, but a weaker nose. Still better than my normal sense of smell, though."

He withdrew from the horned man and returned to his human form, dropping into the armchair. She sat back down with him.

"How did this happen?" she asked.

He told her the story of his childhood and his Welsh father. Like Ceridwen, she agreed there must be a connection between his father and Cernunnos, though what it was she couldn't say.

"Could your father do what you just did?"

"I have no idea. I never saw anything."

He steeled himself and asked the question he'd been wanting to. "It's me inside those forms, for now. What if they're just preparation for, for someone else."

"You worry that Cernunnos might possess you."

"Yes. And that would be it for me."

"Or he might let you go again afterward," she said.

"Does he do that?"

"Who would know? I've only seen him once before. I don't know of anyone who can speak about what he might do."

He slumped his shoulders in the chair and she laughed at him. "Come, now. What will be, will be. Don't take it so hard. Revel in the splendor of it."

She stood up and waggled her hands at him. "My fingers have been itching since you showed me these grand things. Would you mind if I did some sketches?"

"Why not," he said, shaking his head.

"I'll just fetch something from my room."

It was bracing the way she took this for granted, he thought. Just another manifestation of the marvelous. He took advantage of her absence to sip a bit more brandy for courage, anticipating the lack of a suitable mouth shape soon.

She returned with a sketchbook and sticks of charcoal, and soon he was walking about and posing in the full form with the red deer head, and then as the horned man, his coat removed and shirt opened so she could see the transition better. Good exercise for my muscles, anyway, handling these antlers. Already the posture changes were becoming more comfortable as he got accustomed to them, though he kept a wary eye on the height of the ceiling.

After half an hour or so, she relented and put down her sketchbook. He pulled back the horned man form and returned to normal.

"I'm sorry to keep you up so late, before your big day tomorrow," she said. "I'm afraid I'm used to living alone and I can get obsessive when exploring a new project, if there's no one to stop me."

"I'm happy to oblige. Could I, um, take a look? As the deer, my eyes don't see very well in mirrors."

Silently, she turned her sketchbook so he could see. Page after page was filled with quick, expert impressions.

He took it from her hands and sat down to look at it, turning the pages carefully by the edges. The full deer form was not quite what he expected, a monster head on a human form. Instead, the human body changed smoothly at the chest into the musculature to support the stately head, a deep pelt covering most of it below the neck, denser and shorter above.. It looked almost natural, except for the human dress. He knew from touch that there was fur below his neck, but these sketches showed non-human musculature under it. He wondered what it would look like, nude.

The horned man was another revelation. The head was a bit larger than human, as it must be to hold those antlers, but the posture was more upright.

The face was a great surprise, despite Ceridwen's description. It was indeed thin, rough, and shaggy, the chin pointed, and the hairline in a widow's peak. He could see no resemblance to himself in it. This was no blend of his own features with the deer; this was a separate person, as distinct in form as the deer itself.

He mentioned this to Angharad.

"The Horned Man is one of Cernunnos's manifestations. I think that must be his face, in that form, and nothing of your own."

He handed the sketchbook back to her. "And what if something should come along to fill those forms, I wonder?"

She patted his hand as she took the sketchpad and badeid him good night.

As he undressed for bed, George tried to forget that Angharad was just a few rooms away, down the hall. Too soon, he told himself. But still, how wonderful to have her there.

What a clever woman, to laugh at my worries about Cernunnos instead of indulging them. She's right of course, there's nothing I can do about it anyway. Might as well get used to it.

Concentrate on doing my job and keep an eye out for danger, that's all I can do.

He paused, holding a sock, and chuckled. How about that, bringing a sketchbook with her for the visit, just in case.

Artists. I bet she'd stop to sketch a tornado as it approached, and wait for a good close up view.

CHAPTER 29

Inside the kennel gates, George turned Afanc around to get a good look at his staff, ready to go. Alun had worked miracles with the rain-soaked clothing from Saturday, and everything looked clean and polished. Even the hounds were brushed. Alright, he thought, we look like a professional outfit. Let's see if we can perform like one.

Ives opened the kennel gates and George led the pack into the yard and straight through the curtain wall, passing stragglers still getting mounted near the stables. The larger crowds of the full hunt field were gathered and waiting near the manor gates in front. He was about a quarter of an hour ahead of the planned departure and intended to wait quietly off to the side until he received Gwyn's signal to depart.

The hounds and staff trotted in an orderly manner behind him as he brought them down past the hunt field, raising his hand and halting them twenty yards from the open gates.

The first group of hunters was just in front of him, off to the left. Gwyn was there, of course, and all the family—Edern, Creiddylad, and Rhodri—joined by Ceridwen and Idris from the household, and Madog and Angharad. He smiled briefly at Angharad, recalling their pleasant breakfast which seemed like hours ago, and she returned the smile.

Behind them was a mixed group of Eurig and Tegwen, Iona, and some of the other local powers, as well as many of Hadyn's people, and the man himself. He expected they would pick up some of the villagers as they went south down the road.

There were also new faces, people he'd been introduced to on Sunday, or heard about from Rhodri. Some nodded at him in a friendly, or at least neutral, manner. The expressions of some of the others varied from stonefaced and unreadable to disdainful or hostile.

Benitoe, the whipper-in nearest to them, began to attract muttered remarks about the unsuitability of lutins in the hunting field. George looked back at him and raised an eyebrow in silent apology for putting him in this position, berating himself for not thinking to switch Rhys to that side this morning. Benitoe gave him an almost imperceptible shrug and maintained an imperturbable expression. Brynach beside him, however, wasn't so successful at hiding his indignation. George shook his head slightly, and he subsided, but his anger at the continuing slurs was transparent.

Rhian next to George started to turn in sympathy, but he said to her quietly, "Eyes front. Ignoring it's the best policy."

She swallowed and obeyed.

Then they started in on him. The voices were louder on the subject of humans and their proper place in the hunt, in front of the hounds indeed, but fleeing. The comments were meant to be overheard, and George kept his eye on his staff to make sure they didn't react to any of it.

Rhys left his position on the outside of the pack to come up and identify some of the speakers for him, and he filed them away for later consideration.

Glancing over the hunt field that was starting to come together, he was pleased to find many faces, local ones, mostly, indignant on his behalf and looking to Gwyn to put a stop to it. Their support was comforting.

Then the bottom dropped out. The speakers with their ostensibly private conversation began to speculate luridly on Iolo's death and his own probable role in it. He clamped down on his self-control and straightened in his saddle, determined to disregard the blatant provocations. Rhian stiffened at his side and he looked down at her quellingly. "We're professionals. Ignore it. It's just another weapon."

Gwyn faced the crowd and raised his hand for silence. Looking over at George, he said, "Huntsman."

George nodded and led the pack through the manor gates and south down the road to the Dale. His people had passed the first test, and he was proud of them.

Walking his horse back along the road, the manor gates just coming into view, George looked back with pleasure on the bucks tied behind both Rhys and Brynach. His hounds and staff had done well, providing sport for the field. All of them had seen some action, and most had made it to one or both of the *morts* to watch, with approval, the hounds receive their rewards.

Even better, two of the visitors had failed their jumps in the pursuit, resulting in what the Rowanton Hunt members referred to as "involuntary dismounts." Their mud-stained clothing gave their friends something else to talk about instead of his staff. He felt that he had earned some goodwill from a few of the skeptics behind him since they'd set off some hours ago.

He wasn't sure when it started, but he had begun keeping a sense of the ways and their locations always in the back of his mind, like an internal compass tied to points of reference. The Guests' Way outside the gates was looming up on his right as he led the pack home at a tired trot. Looking at the way as he rode past, he sensed a man, invisible in the way mouth, not moving, and his hackles raised involuntarily as his subconscious mind painted him as a threat before he could think about it.

He started to lean to his left and reach over with his right arm to pull out his saber, Afanc dancing under him at the sudden move. Wham! Fire exploded in his right thigh as it took a blow that staggered the horse, and Afanc bucked under him and spun.

I've been shot, he thought. "Rhian, take the hounds," he cried. He could feel the horned man pushing to emerge and fought with it while trying to stay on his horse. Not now, damn it. He reached out to quell Afanc and soothe him, then wrestled the partial manifestation back down.

He was infuriated to sense the shooter vanishing back into the way in the few seconds all this had taken. Gwyn and Idris with several others came galloping up to the chaos, and he waved them toward the way. "He's in there, he's getting away."

Gwyn led a group to the way, at speed. Just before they charged in they were met by a late-arriving party of guests, dumbfounded to be greeted by an angry mob. By the time the confusion was sorted out, the attacker was long gone.

Rhian had taken the hounds off the road to the left and the staff stayed with her. George could feel a pounding throb in his leg but he couldn't bring himself to look at it yet. It was taking most of his attention to hold Afanc quiet. He must've been hit, too, George thought.

Not until Angharad and Ceridwen came up to him with a look of serious purpose did he finally glance down and see the quarrel, buried up to its vanes in his thigh, pinning him to the saddle, the blood dripping down Afanc's side and pooling in the dirt.

It worked! Not dead yet, but maybe he'll bleed and bleed. Let's see him take the great hunt now.

Too bad he moved and there was only time for the one shot, but you knew you wouldn't get a second one. There was no way to conceal a longbow. That's alright, it should put him down for a while, if not for good, and then it'll be too late.

Won't be long now. I'll just creep on back through the palisade once I've circled through the ways. Plenty of time to get back before I'm missed.

They've forgotten me, but I haven't forgotten. I'll never forget.

"Let's get him down," Angharad said to Ceridwen, "before he makes it worse.

Ceridwen stood by his trembling horse and looked at the volume of blood running from the wound. "It's starting to slow down so I think he was lucky, it missed the big artery."

"Lucky?" he said. "I'm pinned to the damned saddle."

Angharad's mouth quirked. If he was swearing it couldn't be that bad. "Let's take you off the horse, saddle and all."

"Be careful. I think it goes right through and into Afanc. You must lift the saddle away from him there, not drag it."

She summoned Hadyn over who unfastened the girth. Iona came up to hold Afanc steady. With the help of several men, they hauled George off his horse and laid him on the ground, still straddling the saddle. He swore the whole time under his breath, whenever the twisting saddle tore at the wound.

"How's my horse?" he asked.

Iona called over. "It went in about an inch. He'll be fine, once it heals. I'll bring him up to the stable for you."

"The pack?"

"Rhian took them back to the kennels, and the hunt staff with her," Angharad said.

"Good for her." He lay back in his awkward position, exhausted.

A painful wound and he still worries about the things in his charge, Angharad thought. *A man in control. I like him in this mode, even flat on his back.*

Meanwhile, Gwyn had dismissed most of the field. She saw he'd appointed Idris with some of Hadyn's people to mount an impromptu guard, in case of another attack. At Ceridwen's request he'd sent a rider up for her bag with medical supplies.

Ceridwen took charge. "The first thing is to cut the quarrel where it enters the saddle. We're lucky it's wood, not iron."

"Lucky, again, is it?" George muttered sardonically from the ground. Angharad chuckled.

Hadyn knelt over George and shoved his left hand in between his leg and the saddle to hold the shaft still, George swearing quietly all the while but trying not to move. Hadyn used his sharp knife to cut quickly through the ash shaft and pulled the saddle away as soon as it parted.

The rider returned with Ceridwen's bag and Angharad helped her prepare for the next step. "We'll need to pull this bolt out straight, and there's not a lot of it here to grip." Once again, Hadyn stepped up. "Not yet, though. First we have to cut away the cloth." She took a very sharp knife from her bag, and sliced away the breeches above and around the wound, pulling the lower material down to the top of his boot.

George rolled his eyes rhetorically. "Leave me some modesty, ladies."

"Don't worry," Angharad told him. "Nothing we haven't see before." That got a smile from him under his cold sweat.

Angharad stood ready with materials while Ceridwen nodded to Hadyn to pull out the bolt. His fingers tightened on the shaft and vanes and he drew it out with steady force. Blood followed on both sides, but without the spurting that she had feared, just a flesh wound.

Ceridwen cleaned it, placed absorbent padding on each side, and bound it tight. George closed his eyes and slumped back a moment in relief.

Recovering, he propped himself up on his elbows. "Let me see the saddle."

Hadyn brought it over. The head had gone completely through an inch and a half of padded leather, and a good inch of it was visible on the inside, where it had cut Afanc. Hadyn tried to pull it out and couldn't get a good enough grip. "You'll need pliers for that," he said.

Gwyn had watched them work on George, his face and body rigid in the way that Angharad recognized as controlled fury. His voice showed no sign of it, however, as he asked lightly, "How shall we get you home, kinsman?"

"I'll walk," he said, from the ground.

"You'll do no such thing," Ceridwen said.

"Well, I won't be carried. It's not that bad."

Privately, Angharad doubted that. He was pale and still sweating. That was a good bit of blood to lose, and it had to be very painful.

"Let me suggest riding," she said. They looked at her skeptically. "It's his right leg, but he only needs his left to mount. We have enough folk here to boost him into a saddle for the short trip."

"Let's give it a try," George said.

Eurig came up with his heavy horse and volunteered it. With a certain amount of shoving George managed to swing his wounded leg over and settle gingerly in the saddle, letting the leg dangle loosely on that side while he used the stirrup on the left for balance. Eurig led his horse on foot, Tegwen riding alongside him.

Ceridwen rode on ahead to prepare the infirmary for more serious treatment, and Angharad rode beside him, to try and balance him if he started to come off on her side. He swayed in the saddle but hung on grimly, silent now.

Rhian picked herself up from the ground behind the kennels and faced Brynach again, reluctance apparent in his every move. "Again. Show me that again." They circled around and she feinted to the left, then tried to hook his leg and topple him before he could close with her. It failed again, the leg out of her reach.

He's too tall for that to work, she decided as she disengaged. I'll bet he puts on a few more inches before he's done. It's just not fair, I'm almost done growing and I'm younger than he is.

Brynach stopped her. "I know Hadyn's been starting you with unarmed combat, and that's probably fine to lay the basics, but if you want my opinion, I think you should go straight to weapons work. You need a knife as an equalizer for your size."

He avoids looking directly at me when he mentions my size. Boys, she grinned. At least he's trying to help instead of just brushing me aside.

"I won't always have a knife," she said.

"Why not, if you make it a policy that you always carry at least one? You can always find somewhere to carry a knife."

She considered that. Knives were easy to conceal, even in girl clothes. The pocket slashes cut right through skirt and petticoat to the pockets tied beneath, and she could easily reach a knife strapped around her thigh that would never show. Or even two.

"There's no reach to a knife, though. That's a good idea for defense, but how can I attack with my smaller size?"

He lectured her in tones she could tell came from Hadyn. "A knife is for defense—it's all about cunning and determination. Arrows are for stand-off offense, staying out of reach. Sword, clubs, lances—that's man-to-man, where skill and strength are of equal benefit."

He broke off and looked at her. "I'm sorry, but you're going to have a hard time with heavy hand-held weapons against much larger, if slower, opponents. Even if you're quick, they can still take much more damage before it disables them."

"Benitoe has a sword, and he's smaller than I am. Throwing axes, too." She'd been surprised to see him turn up with them, strapped on his saddle, but glad, too. They were all in this together.

"You'll have to ask him, then."

She couldn't do that. He was twice her age, and she couldn't imagine how she would phrase it. It was a good idea, though. She glanced at Brynach. He hadn't said it out of pique, as some boys might; he made the recommendation straight, like a friend.

She nodded at him seriously. "I'll think about it."

I can't wait for Hadyn on this, she thought. "Where can I get some knives to use?"

"Take them from the house armory. You live there, don't you? Try some different styles—length, shape, weight—and see what works for you and what's easy to conceal. I've heard that real knife users handle three types, long-blades for defense against longer weapons, short knives for serious concealment, and throwing knives. Go for those last, they take a while to master."

"Thanks, I'll do that. What can we use for now?"

He clearly thought he had deflected her for the moment, but if he knew her better, he'd have realized that wouldn't work. She kept her face straight and let his good nature and his willingness to oblige her lead him her way. And it worked.

"You need dulled blades to learn on, but here's one of mine for starters. With sheaths on for both of us, or I won't do it." His face acquired a stubborn expression.

I guess I can only push him so far. She nodded.

They circled around each other and tested for openings. She liked the way the knife extended her reach. It lengthened his arm, too, but put the rest of his limbs at risk to her point.

She tried her feint again, but this time when she attacked she slashed at the other arm instead of trying to brush it aside for a hold. That worked much better.

They kept up the sparring for a few minutes, and when Brynach stopped one attack with the sheathed point at her throat, they were startled by applause.

Several people were standing about, with smiles on their faces. "What's the matter, boy? Won't she have you?"

Rhian straightened up, her cheeks flaming. Where had this audience come from, back behind the kennels? Worse, she saw Hadyn approaching with determined strides and a black look on his face. She put herself in front of Brynach and faced him.

"This was my idea. I made him do it," she said.

"Did you now, lass?" he said, with visible restraint.

"No, Master Hadyn," Brynach said, coming around her to stand directly before him. "I was helping a friend practice." His face showed no willingness to apologize or explain, and only then did Rhian realize the difficulty she had put him in.

"You two are coming with me," Hadyn said. Squaring their shoulders and trying to make the best of it, they followed him, and the bystanders moved aside, laughing, to let them pass.

George squirmed in his armchair, trying to find a less uncomfortable position for his throbbing leg. He was grateful to be back in his study after the morning's disaster. Ceridwen had stitched the wounds shut and sealed the skin but she'd warned him the deep muscle injury would ache while it healed. Ache, is it, he thought. Doctors everywhere make the same understatements.

He planned to take it easy the rest of today, but he was determined to ride on Thursday, the day after tomorrow. Alun was off searching for a cane he could use. Iolo had a few, but he'd been a shorter man and they wouldn't work for him.

A loud knock on his back door drew his attention, and someone bellowed without waiting for a response. "You there?"

"Come on in," George called, recognizing Hadyn's voice.

He heard a clatter of more than two feet, and watched Hadyn enter with Brynach and Rhian, a hangdog look on the one, and defiance on the other. Behind them, Hadyn gave him a suspicion of a wink, and George settled himself with a dead-pan expression, expecting some theatrics.

"What can I do for you, Master Hadyn?" he said, feeding him a straight line to get him started.

"Are these yours, huntsman?" he growled, placing a hand on each of them at the shoulder, as if they were prisoners.

"They are. What seems to be the problem, master?"

"I'll thank you to tell them not to spar, with weapons, unsupervised," Hadyn said.

Ah. This was a bit more serious than he'd supposed. "Can you explain, Brynach? You're the elder here." Interesting. That made Rhian blush.

"Nothing to report, sir," Brynach said.

Rhian shrugged off Hadyn's hand. "Don't be silly," she told Brynach.

She turned to George. "This was all my idea. I was… worried about you." She glanced surreptitiously at his leg. "It looked very bad, this morning, and it's not right that we couldn't stay there and fight for you."

George was touched, but couldn't afford to let it show. "You had the pack to take care of, all of you, and I was proud of you for taking it in charge on your own responsibility. That was more important."

She looked surprised at that. "I've started work with Master Hadyn, and I understand why he sets the tasks in a certain order, I do, but I need to be better right now. There isn't enough time to do it his way." She glanced back at him in apology.

She paused a moment. "All those people in the field, they don't like you. They don't like Benitoe. Some of them may just be grumbling, but we have real enemies, they killed Iolo. We need to be able to defend ourselves."

Well, she wasn't wrong, of course. It still didn't sit right with him that a fourteen-year-old girl was worried about attacking deadly foes.

He glanced at Brynach and could see him drinking it in, admiration on his face. He's got it bad, he thought, but it's going to be a while before she's old enough to see it. He seems to have the sense to understand that though. Good for him.

He looked at Hadyn, and thought carefully about his official response.

"I commend you for your loyalty to your comrades and your zeal to make yourself a better warrior in their defense." She looked up, her face lightening.

"However," he said sternly, watching her face fall again, "my willingness to let you make your own choices about a dangerous line of work doesn't include unnecessary danger incurred deliberately in training." Looking at Brynach, he said, "You're the elder. I'm sure she was very insistent but you shouldn't have given way."

Brynach said, "It was just going to be unarmed combat, initially."

"I believe you, but you're much bigger, and not experienced enough to keep from injuring her by accident. You're used to being the smaller person in training, not the larger."

"You're right, sir," he said, abashed.

"That's not fair," Rhian said. "I made him do it. And he made us keep the knives sheathed."

"No, Rhian," Brynach said. "He's right. It's my responsibility not to give in."

He gave them a moment to repent, glancing at Hadyn to see his nod.

"That said, here's what we'll do, going forward. Weapons-master Hadyn will concentrate on some emergency coaching for both of you, for the next five days, after which he will return to his usual course of instruction." He glanced over at Hadyn to see how the proposal would be taken. "You won't do any sparring with uncovered weapons or unbated blades. None. Am I clear on this?"

They nodded, relieved that the dressing down was over.

"Despite what I said about the size difference, Brynach, Rhian will have to learn to cope, and so should you. If you must spar together, then Rhian must wear at least a padded vest until both of you are more expert. We all get knocked around in training, but I want no deadly accidents. Are we agreed?"

They nodded again.

"Now, about the hunt." They stood a little easier. "I will hunt the hounds on Thursday, I must. But would you do me the favor, Rhian, of taking the hound walk for tomorrow, if you will?"

"Yes, huntsman." She looked suitably solemn at the responsibility.

"That will be all." He regarded at them sternly. "Don't make me regret letting you both off with a warning."

They left as quickly as they could.

Hadyn stayed behind and looked down at George as he fell back in his chair, an involuntary grimace seizing his face as he relaxed and reacted to the painful throbbing for a moment.

"Feeling it, are you?"

"What am I going to do about this sort of thing?" he said, waving his hand in the direction of the absent youngsters. "I can't protect them like this," looking at his elevated leg.

"You can't protect anyone, in the end," Hadyn said soberly. "Death comes for us all."

"Not on my watch, if I can help it."

"Ah, but you can't help it. They're independent people, and you're not all-powerful." George shrugged in reluctant acknowledgment.

"You need to learn this," Hadyn persisted. "I train people to fight. Some of them die by violence, but many don't, and I hope that those that do lived longer because of what I taught them. It's the best I can hope to achieve."

"Yes, but I'm training them to hunt. Death should only come by accident, not deadly intent. The image of war without its guilt."

"Maybe in your world. Not in ours."

Reluctantly, George had to agree. He needed to toughen up and face the reality of this place, not a world as he might wish it to be. "You're right, of course. I just hate putting someone in harm's way, especially a youngster."

"As do we all," Hadyn said.

~

The hard chair at dinner in the great hall hurt his leg just as much as he had expected, but George knew that he had to put in an appearance in order to squelch any rumors that he'd been put out of action altogether by the morning's attack.

He used a simple cane Alun had found, he didn't ask where, to suppress his obvious limp as much as possible, but he avoided any other visible concessions, so his unelevated leg was pounding with every heartbeat and he shifted restlessly in his chair, trying to compensate. He pushed the food around on his plate to hide his lack of appetite. Rhodri seated next to him on the end fell in with his mood and didn't press him for conversation.

George pulled himself together and asked Rhodri, quietly, "So, how many of these new faces are actively wishing me gone, and Gwyn, too?"

"You know, I don't think that's where to look. Plenty are disapproving, of humans, lutins, or any other innovations, but that's just normal for them, it's not really personal. They don't mean Gwyn any particular harm by it. You earned some goodwill with that crowd this morning by giving them a good hunt, and showing up at dinner tonight helps."

Rhodri topped up George's glass of wine. George was under instructions by Ceridwen to drink to make up the blood loss. "The others can't be won over and you shouldn't waste your time with it. Gwyn doesn't. They come to see Gwyn fail, nothing simpler. They probably weren't even making most of the catcalls this morning, they're happy to let the blowhards do that."

"No," he continued, "I think these are the same enemies we've been discussing the last few days, just taking advantage of knowing your specific location at a predictable time. An opportunistic strike."

"They damn near succeeded," George said morosely.

"That's not the way to think about it. From their point of view, it was a failure, and that suits me fine. Look at it that way. You're leading a charmed life."

He has a point, George thought. He straightened up. Put on a tough face and force them to try harder. That's what you wanted to accomplish, wasn't it? Push them off balance?

Gwyn rose to address his guests. They fell silent. "Let's thank our huntsman for this morning's sport: two fine bucks, which you will be tasting before the week's out." He waved for George to rise to acknowledge the polite applause.

George could see he knew exactly what this would cost him. He pushed his chair back nonchalantly but carefully, and stood, casually leaning against Rhodri's chair as he rose, his face expressionless. He nodded his thanks and sat down again, taking his weight on his arms, his every move trying to maintain control while hiding the effort. Only Rhodri was close enough to see the sweat break out on his face once he was reseated.

He hissed and grayed out for a moment when his thigh took the weight again and Rhodri poked him. "Not now, not here. Hold it together a few more minutes." He nodded and opened his eyes as if nothing had happened.

Rhodri continued indignantly. "Rhys and I are going to walk you back to your house after most of the guests have left, and you're going to bed if Alun has to tie you down. Gwyn had no right to do that."

"No, you're wrong. We have to keep the focus on me. Gwyn knows this." He settled himself to endure for a little while longer. "If I start to look like I'm not worth taking out as a primary target, it might be Rhian next. I'm not going to let that happen."

Early to bed, and grateful for it, George tried to settle himself into a least-painful position. He expected tomorrow to be worse, as the bruises and stiffening really kicked in. Maybe I can try the steam baths.

Was today a net gain, he wondered. The hunt went well. Rhodri was probably right that the most vocal jerks weren't a real concern. One thing for sure, the hunt was successful enough that the enemy was worried. Forcing them to react was all to the good.

So, on balance, it was a good hunt and we're one step closer to the enemy. Cost, one damaged huntsman, hopefully still functional. On that basis, it seemed like a decent trade.

But the nerve of them. What if it's someone else next time, one of mine instead of me? This has got to be stopped. He clenched his fist.

Restless, he stared into the darkness of his room. Why did the horned man begin to manifest? I didn't invoke it. Can it do that on its own? That wasn't just distracting but downright sinister. What about the full deer form? How would the crowd have reacted?

As a curious parlor trick for Angharad, it was one thing. Rather different, if he had no control over it.

CHAPTER 30

"So you're sure about the timing, then?" George asked, Wednesday morning.

"Absolutely. The traps from the private way went off just about the time we were getting you onto Eurig's horse," Ceridwen said. "The inference is clear—the shooter exited via the guests' way and returned via that private one. I can't be certain, but I don't believe in coincidence."

George sat with his leg propped up in the huntsman's study, trying to ignore the ache. As he'd predicted, today he was sore everywhere, though the pain from the wound itself was more localized, a sign it was beginning to heal.

"Can you tell how much time elapsed? I was a bit occupied, myself," he said.

"Close to an hour."

"So you think he just exited one way and came back the other?"

"Perhaps," she said. "Or perhaps he took another way or two in between."

"They'd have to be close, wouldn't they?"

"It takes no time to travel the ways," she said, "only as long as to cross the few yards of the way itself. All the time would be spent crossing the ground between them, and you can cover a lot of distance in an hour, if there's any sort of nexus with multiple ways."

They heard voices in the hall, and Alun showed Isolda in, a long cane in her hand.

"Back from your morning trip already?" Ceridwen asked her. At George's look, she explained, "Isolda has started driving officially for the manor, running village errands morning and afternoon."

"Congratulations, I didn't know," George said. "I'm usually out with the hounds in the morning."

She looked at them seriously. "I have this cane for you from Angharad," she said, "and she passed along some news as well."

George took the cane from her with his left hand and promptly dropped it as the sporadic numbness in the hand kicked in. Isolda bent down and picked it up for him. He admired it for a moment, a straight clean shaft with a long hound's head at the end for a grip. Did she carve this for him yesterday, after she left at mid-day? That didn't seem possible, even if the shaft was already prepared. It looked brand new, though, with a soft oil finish, and he could smell the oils when he raised it to his nose.

He held it on his lap, his hands playing with it while he looked at Isolda expectantly. "Thanks. Her news?"

"A personal message for you, that she told Mostyn about the clothing replacements you'd need." Her face took on the demeanor of a professional messenger. "And a warning for Gwyn's council, which I give here to you now."

Ceridwen said, formally, "You are heard. Speak."

"Angharad sends word from Huw Bongam. This morning, the man Scilti departed the inn in haste, taking all his possessions. The groom Maonirn asked him where he was headed, and Scilti rebuked him with a slash from his crop. This was reported by another groom. When Huw Bongam went out to the stable to see for himself, Scilti was gone. And Maonirn's missing."

"What does Huw Bongam think happened to Maonirn?" George asked.

"He thinks Maonirn was angered and tried to follow Scilti, to see where he went. He expects him back after he tires of following a mounted man on foot."

"Is there more?" Ceridwen asked.

"No, my lady."

"Thank you, Isolda." The young lutine nodded formally to both of them and left.

"Takes her job seriously," George said.

"She's starting off well. Who knows what she can make of herself as she gets older?"

"What do you think of this? We know Scilti has a confederate inside the palisade. Was it Scilti who attacked yesterday, or was it the other one, the one who killed Iolo?"

Ceridwen said, "Why would Scilti panic now, unless it was him?"

"That doesn't feel right to me. I'd have bet on the other one." George paused. "I'll tell you what really worries me, though. I think

Maonirn went after Scilti partly because I asked him to keep me informed. I should've realized it would put him in danger."

"He made his own choices. Lutins are good at being overlooked. If he went after Scilti, I doubt Scilti spotted him. We'll hear back from him, soon enough."

I hope so, George thought. He had a bad feeling about this. And where did Scilti go? Was he gone for good?

This time Rhian was going to do it by the rules.

After yesterday's scolding she'd decided it wasn't fair to get Brynach into trouble. Besides, if she set it up right, there wasn't even any real reason to hide, except she didn't want people to look at her as she learned. It was alright for Brynach to see, he was learning, too.

She'd gone to the house armory yesterday before the afternoon training and taken a hard look at some of the shorter weapons in the bins and hanging on the walls. There'd been a pair of long slender knives, stilettos, she supposed, whose sheaths were pierced for straps that could work under a skirt. Two shorter unmatched knives, sturdy enough to slash with, seemed the right size for along her side under one arm and behind her back, like George's gun. Those she could wear under hunt clothing when the stilettos wouldn't work. She found two flat knives she thought could be used as boot knives and throwing knives. And there was one tiny blade, no longer than three inches with grip, that she thought might be a good hidden weapon to wear all the time, maybe under the root of her braid.

She'd felt guilty for a moment, looking at her haul. This room was usually locked and she'd begged the key from the housekeeper—the armorers always forgot that she had one. But then she considered, it's my family, these are mine, too.

She'd brought the whole pile of blades in a sack to the leather craftsman for strap and sheath work, and he worked up the two stilettos on the spot. It had felt so odd to wear them secretly at dinner last night under her gown where she could reach them through the pocket slits, but reassuring, too. She was determined never to be without a weapon again.

This morning, she'd arranged to meet Brynach back behind the balineum after the hound walk. No one would see them here, in the blind spot between the baths and the palisade, and it was rarely walked, the perimeter route being longer than the shortcuts from place to place. The strap work was finished and she brought the whole pile with her in the sack to show Brynach, including the ones she wore last night. She wanted his opinion.

While she waited, she took off her hunt coat and tried on the two she intended to wear while hunting. The one under her left arm had been tricky to arrange without the straps showing, but the one in the small of her back, easier to get at under the skirt of the weskit, worked fine. The boot knives would take more planning.

Brynach came around the corner of of the building, carrying a bag of his own. Good, he'd brought the padded vest she wanted, from the main armory. She didn't want to get it herself, under Hadyn's eye, and besides, she wasn't sure what to look for or where they were kept.

"Look what I got yesterday," she told him, handing him the sack. He emptied it carefully onto the ground and started to go through her selection while she took off her coat and hunting weskit to try on the protective vest and fasten it, making sure she could still reach her knives. It only covered the front, so the sheaths strapped around her shirt were still reachable. It was a reasonable fit. I guess they get young men of all ages, she thought.

She saw that he'd spotted the two strapped-on blades as she changed. "Let me see those knives," he said, and she handed them to him, one at a time.

He examined them and Rhian was struck, for the first time, by how much larger his hands were than hers. Why, he still has a lot of growing to do. Of course—he's likely to be as big as Eurig, or maybe taller, eventually. Her perception suddenly shifted, and she briefly saw him as as stranger might, as a young man of promise, not just her comrade.

"These are good choices. The flat ones will be boot knives?"

"If I can figure out how to wear them. Strapped to the calf or sheathed in the boot?"

"I don't know," he said. "You'll have to experiment. They could all use cleaning and sharpening. I'll show you how to do that, when we're done."

He showed her the contents of his own sack, dull knife-shaped iron blanks with grips, in several lengths, and a long practice sword with a blunt edge and point. They each took a practice weapon and began.

After several minutes they took a breather. Brynach was facing the palisade and when he froze, eyes widening, she spun to see what he was looking at. A man came through the bushes of the barrier. She'd forgotten about the hole there; she couldn't get that close to it, no one could, so how could someone get through? As he straightened up and saw them, she recognized Scilti, from the inn. He didn't know her. She wasn't wearing the glamour he saw a week ago.

He looked at them with their practice weapons and smiled coldly, drawing his sword.

"Get behind me, Rhian," Brynach said, swapping the iron practice blade to his left hand and picking up the dull sword.

At the sound of her name, Scilti focused all his attention on her and she felt the hair on her arms rise. He took his time, drawing a main-gauche for his other hand and ignoring Brynach. He began to stalk her, with Brynach trying to intervene.

Why did we leave our swords with the hunting gear? Why aren't we wearing them, Rhian cried out silently. If I go for help, he'll get Brynach. He's taller, he's experienced, his weapons are real. And Brynach won't run, I know he won't.

Brynach surprised her by backing up a few steps before Scilti was quite on them. He dropped the practice weapons and seized her two stilettos on the ground, flinging off their sheathes and running forward to prepare for Scilti's sword.

He'll be killed, Rhian thought, paralyzed. Then a cold wave washed over her and time slowed down. She dropped her practice weapons and drew both the knives strapped to her body. She drew up even with Brynach on his right and said, "I'll take the short blade."

"Stay back," he told her, but she ignored him. Side by side they engaged.

Brynach worked to trap Scilti's sword with his two shorter blades and Rhian concentrated on keeping the main-gauche occupied. It was clumsy work, but the coordinated attack from two directions confounded Scilti for a moment, too. He managed to slug Rhian in the cheek with the knife still in his fist, and in the seconds it took her to recover he beat Brynach back into a defensive position.

She picked herself up and concentrated on just his one hand, the one weapon, trusting Brynach to keep the sword engaged and off of her. She tried to move around his left side, to make him fight in two directions, but he was quick, able to drive her back and re-engage Brynach while she recovered. Only once was she successful enough occupying his attention for Brynach to get in a touch with a stiletto, but it wasn't deep.

She had to get help but she couldn't leave. The sound of clanging iron in the practice bouts a few minutes ago had brought no witnesses, so this deadly fight wouldn't either, and their voices wouldn't carry. The hounds! She could rouse the hounds. She used her link with them and called for aid.

Half the yard away a great cry rose up from the kennels and echoed off the stone buildings. The roar was frantic while the fight continued, Scilti gradually wearing them down by forcing them to alternate, keeping them too off balance to synchronize an attack. Rhian could feel herself slowing down and she knew it was just a matter of time before Scilti got in one good hit on either of them, and that would be it. Then, suddenly, two snarling hounds bore down upon them, with Benitoe running far behind them, drawing his sword.

Scilti coolly backed up and disengaged before the hounds reached him, then turned and ran for the palisade, sheathing his main-gauche as he ran and reaching into his vest with his free hand to pull out something small. He held it as he lowered his sword and entered the gap in the wooded under-story, vanishing from sight. The hounds whined as they got as close as they dared to the palisade, their blood up.

Rhian called them back to calm them down. Cythraul and Dando, she noticed, remotely, a good choice. The pack in the kennels quieted down.

Benitoe reached them and she realized, it was over. It had felt like she'd keep on fighting forever. Rhys came running up, sword in hand, and George hobbled some distance behind him.

Rhys gave them a quick look. "Are you alright?"

They both nodded, out of breath, and he ran on toward the back gate. "Stay with them," he called back to Benitoe.

Rhian and Brynach both bent over to catch their breath, and when she caught his eye, they grinned at each other. We did it, she thought, we're alive.

As she straightened up, she saw Ives pounding up with Huon and Tanguy. The kennel-men carried butchering knives but Ives had picked up a cudgel from somewhere. Brynach spotted them at the same time Rhian did, and the two of them broke out into a whooping laughter that was surprisingly difficult to control. With the arrival of George, skipping lopsidedly on his cane to make speed, the whole kennel and hunt staff were there.

Rhys jogged back. "I've sent the gate guards after him from the outside. Who was it?"

Rhian realized she was the only one who could identify him. "That was Scilti, from the inn." George's face tightened. "I don't understand how he was able to go through the palisade," she said, "but he clearly didn't expect to find guards here." She looked at Brynach, grinning.

"Good thing we were so well armed," he said, deadpan, looking at the pitiful little pile remaining of Rhian's knives and the useless practice weapons.

She couldn't help it, she collapsed into laughter again, the two of them leaning on each other, holding on by the shoulders. She felt her hand shaking and looked at it, wondering if the feeling would go away.

Her comrades laughed with her, and she was warmed to have them there, trying to protect them.

Benitoe remarked dryly, "The next time you two set up to practice, you might invite some of the rest of us. I'm sure we could all use it, and we're all in this together." Rhian and Brynach nodded weakly.

Rhys walked over and shook her, mock ferociously, then gave her a quick hug. "Don't scare me like that again."

By this time many in the yard had heard the hounds or spotted the running hunt staff and followed them. Of their seniors, Ceridwen was the first to arrive. She stood next to George. "I felt someone come through the traps down from the overhang and positioned myself to try and spy out who it was, but he didn't get this far. Was it our unknown?"

"No, Scilti, apparently," he said. "Now we know where he went.

"He's gotten as far as the clearing with the small way and hasn't left. I think we'll find he's gone."

Rhian was bewildered. She didn't know about any of this. What small way? What traps?

Her foster-father was walking up, and her grandfather, too, both of them with faces like thunder. She straightened up and tried to brush herself off, but if she looked anything like Brynach there was no way she could make herself presentable in time. She was in trouble, again.

Brynach spotted them and came to stand by her. "We did nothing wrong," he told her quietly.

That's right, she thought. Then he spotted Eurig on the edge of the crowd, and it was her turn to encourage him.

Gwyn stood silent, surveying the inner circle of hunt and kennel staff with the two hounds, and the rest of the ad hoc posse gathered around. He visibly mastered his emotions and the crowd around them quieted down to see what would be next.

He glanced at Rhian and Brynach standing straight before him. "I trust you two aren't injured?"

"We're alright," she told him.

Looking at Ives with his cudgel and the two kennel-men, he said, "Thank you, Master Ives, for your sturdy defense." He nodded at the three of them. "Please return these hounds to the kennels."

"The rest of you," looking at the inner group, "I will see you in my council room. Immediately." He singled out Ceridwen and Eurig with a gesture to join them.

"Find my sister and send her to me. Now."

Gwyn finished giving instructions to the servants as everyone settled down around the table, George limping in last and sitting next to Rhian.

Gwyn looked at her. She was still wearing the protective vest, and his breath caught to see that there was a deep slit on the chest over her heart, with stuffing popping out. A bruise was coming up on one cheek and her braid was a mess, but he reluctantly approved her shining eyes. A glance at Brynach told a similar story, but he seemed well enough, though Eurig's face was unreadable as he sat next to him.

Edern, on the other hand, couldn't restrain himself from speaking to Rhian. "This must stop. I won't have you putting yourself at risk in this way."

Rhian predictably bridled at this. "It's my choice. I was warned. I want to do this, it's all I've ever wanted to do."

Gwyn looked over her head at George and they exchanged mutual looks of parental despair.

"Enough," Gwyn said. "I want an orderly report of exactly what's happened, and then we will consider the consequences."

At this, Creiddylad entered and, hard on her heels, Idris. This would be tricky, Gwyn thought, not to mention too much in front of Creiddylad.

Ceridwen began, relaying Angharad's message from the inn that Scilti had left and Maonirn was missing. She continued with her description of the traps laid on the path from the overhang and how they had been triggered, down to the end of the path as it reached the palisade.

Creiddylad said, "This is why you left the gap in the palisade, so that you could catch someone like this?"

Gwyn nodded.

Eurig spoke, for the first time. "And how long have you known there was a passage through the palisade?"

"Since Iolo's murder," Gwyn told him. He saw Rhian nod guiltily. "We left it open to see what we could observe. Ceridwen was monitoring its use." Looking at Rhian and Brynach, he said, "Obviously we didn't expect these two to be caught in the middle. Perhaps if they had told someone…"

George spoke up. "In their defense, they came to me yesterday and received a stern lecture about sparring without the proper protections. I am very pleased to see that they listened," pointing at Rhian's vest. She looked down at it and seemed to realize for the first time that she had taken a cut there that might have been deadly. The blood drained from her face. "I didn't know where they were planning to meet next, if at all, or I would've prevented this."

Brynach spoke up while Rhian recovered from her shock. "We just wanted a place outdoors with some privacy. Both of us felt the need to get some experience with weapons quickly, after the attack on the huntsman yesterday."

Watching a flash of gratitude wash across Rhian's face, Gwyn suspected that Rhian had been the moving force, not Brynach, but he silently applauded his gallant assumption of responsibility. He could see that Eurig was drawing a similar conclusion.

Time to release some of the tension in the room.

"Foster-daughter, I notice that you were rather better armed than I would have expected for a sneak attack. Please stand up."

She rose. "Show me what you were carrying." She drew the two knives from their chest harnesses and put them on the table. "And in the sack?"

Gwyn watched George stifle a smile as he saw where this was going.

Rhian reached down and drew out the two stilettos and placed them on the table next to the knives. Gwyn looked at the bag, which clearly had more content, and back at Rhian, silently. She reluctantly reached in and drew out the boot knives, and tossed them onto the pile with a clank. "Is that all?" he asked.

"Close enough," she said, defiantly.

Good, he thought, she's got something small and private she doesn't want to reveal.

He let her stand there for a moment, then relented. "I approve." He saw the surprise and relief, before she straightened again before him like a soldier. "You will seek out Hadyn and get his recommendations on concealed blades, and the suitability of these. He will give you whatever he thinks appropriate and coach you on their use, immediately, on my word."

At Edern's aghast look, he said, "Brother, she must be armed. Better she become expert as quickly as possible. It's saved her life today." Looking at Brynach, he continued, "That, and a brave comrade."

Rhian glanced down at the seated Brynach, looking uncomfortable at the praise. "Scilti would have killed us if Brynach hadn't held him off with just those two knives."

Gwyn waved her to her seat again and asked Brynach, "Were you able to do him any damage?"

Brynach retreated gratefully into a professional report. "No, sir, our blades were too short. I caught him on his left arm once, but it was shallow, I think."

Gwyn asked, "How did it end?"

Rhian cleared her throat. "I couldn't think what to do. We couldn't hurt him and he'd get in a blow eventually that would end it. No one could hear us. Then I realized I could make the hounds be heard and tried that. It worked," she said, wonderingly.

Benitoe carried the tale. "Ives and I were in the kennels when the pack erupted. We didn't know what it meant, but they were frantic about something. I asked Ives to release two of them to see what they would lead us to. I thought they'd run to the gates but they went the other way, so I opened the huntsman's alley to them and let them out into the lane. They took off, growling, and I followed."

Rhys spoke up. "I was down at the stables and looked up at the pack cry. I saw Benitoe and the hounds racing up the lane, and took off after them. When I got there and heard what had happened, I went on to the back gates to send some of the guards after Scilti from the outside."

Idris said, "I can tell you what they found. Rhys told them where to start looking, and they located the spot where Scilti had tied his horse, but he was long gone by them."

Ceridwen finished, "The traps told of horse and rider making their escape."

Rhian started to speak, "But I heard you say something about…" She broke off and looked at George in surprise. He shook his head imperceptibly.

Gwyn assumed George had kicked her under the table. Good, they shouldn't let anyone else hear about the small hidden way.

Ceridwen asked, to cover the moment, "How did he get through the hole in the palisade? How did he even get close to it? Did anyone see?"

Brynach said, "He had something in his hand that he took out of his vest. I couldn't see what it was."

"So," Gwyn said, "This is the tale of the attack. Anything else to add?"

Eurig spoke for the first time. "Did this Scilti murder Iolo?"

"No," Gwyn said, offering no explanation, watching Creiddylad's face carefully. Eurig took the hint, canny old badger that he was, and didn't push for more. I owe it to him to fill him in privately after the meeting, Gwyn thought. His kinsman had been in peril, too.

Creiddylad changed the topic. "We must close the gap in the palisade, at once. I never would've agreed to leave it if I thought Rhian would be harmed."

Gwyn thought that this, at least, was sincere. He didn't think she knew much about Scilti, but she obviously was involved in this some way. Wasn't it interesting that she hasn't asked whether Scilti was the one who attacked George yesterday. Perhaps she already knows who it was.

What he didn't sense was any indication that she was directing these attacks herself. Someone else must be in charge.

Why would Scilti come in through the palisade? As far as we know, he hasn't done that before. It can't have been to attack Rhian; he had no way of knowing she'd be there. He must have come for some other purpose and simply seized the opportunity when he realized he'd been seen. Whatever it was, he'd failed, driven off by a couple of teenagers.

Something's happening to the enemy alliance. It's unraveling somewhere. Creiddylad seems genuinely distressed that Rhian might have been killed, and perhaps that'll weaken it further.

Let's close the palisade and push them some more by rubbing their noses in the failure.

By the time George, limping slowly, arrived at the palisade behind the balineum, a small crowd had gathered. It wasn't often they could see a serious magic working, and in broad daylight.

He braced himself on his cane near Gwyn, who was regarding the people with approval. A show of power, George thought, where all could see that he was protecting his people.

After a brief conversation with Ceridwen, Creiddylad crossed the no-man's ground to stand in front of the palisade gap, leaving Ceridwen behind with the rest of the onlookers.

George said to Gwyn, "She doesn't have any problem with the 'keep away' effect?"

"She made it, she can control it," Gwyn said, watching her.

"Or destroy it?" George said. "Good thing she's on your side, then."

That earned him a hard look and Gwyn's full attention. George wasn't sorry, it needed to be said.

"At least our unknown unfriend is probably shut up in here, too," George said. Trapped in here with us, he added silently.

Creiddylad bent her knees to lay both her hands flat on the soil in the gap. A subtle shaking of the soil resulted, magnified by the branches into a larger tremor swirling through the trees and bushes. She straightened and brushed off her hands absently while she looked hard at the gap. The leaves withered visibly and dropped, for three feet on either side. Some in the crowd gasped.

George realized that though the palisade was autumnally colored, all the leaves elsewhere were still firmly attached, where in the woods outside, in late October, they had started to fall. Did these leaves normally fall, or just renew themselves in the spring?

Daylight from the other side showed through the bare branches. Creiddylad stood, concentrating on her task, and nothing seemed to happen. Then George saw a green fuzz starting to overlay the bare wood. Before his eyes, leaves began to bud, twist, and then open, like a stop-action film. Other motion caught his eye, and he saw vines twisting across, branches extending from the bushes to support them. At ground level, spreading roots formed humps in the dirt, sending new shoots upward. The scent of fresh growing things drifted down to the crowd.

After no more than half an hour, she was done. The new growth showed green where the palisade on either side displayed autumn leaves, but otherwise the repair was undetectable.

She stepped away and came toward Gwyn, nodding and walking past him to the manor. She seemed tired, to George, but his sympathy was limited. She was connected to their enemies in some fashion, and they had almost killed Rhian today. He watched her stonily as she entered the manor alone.

CHAPTER 31

The stunningly hot water of the baths in the balineum was having an effect on the deep ache in George's abused leg. Alun told him no one used the baths in the middle of the afternoon, and he was relieved to find that true. The healed skin was still intact after the exertions today, but bright red in the heat, and the muscles were weak and painful.

He hoped to avoid meeting anyone. It would hardly inspire confidence for people to see him wounded like this. So far, he'd been lucky to have the place to himself for what must be half an hour. In the silent room, he heard nothing but the occasional lap of water, and lay there mostly submerged, half awake.

The noise of someone fumbling at the rear entrance door roused him, and he scrambled out to avoid detection, limping quietly to stay out of sight as the footsteps came all the way in to the main bathing area. He was about to duck into the changing room when he heard the steps head that way, and dodged out of sight around the doorway back toward the baths.

Whoever it was exited at the rear door again, back into the anteroom at the back entrance, and he seized the opportunity to dry off and dress hastily, assuming they'd be back. He was just buttoning his vest and looking for the contents of his pockets when he glanced down at the footprints on the damp floor. There was the imprint Benitoe had described to him on Saturday, tracking the unknown spy back through the palisade—right shoe nicked on the inner heel.

Excitement raised his hackles. Maybe he could finally see the fellow's face. He hastily grabbed his pocket contents in his left hand and his cane in his right and swung toward the rear door to follow, when it reopened to the sound of two voices. Reconsidering, he ducked back into the dressing room and froze.

One of the speakers came in and spoke back through the open rear door, "Are you sure no one's in here?"

That was Madog, George thought. No one else had such a round, self-sufficient, even charming voice.

The voice on the other side of the door, in the anteroom, said, "I walked all the way through. No one uses the baths this time of day."

George didn't recognize the voice. It was thin and jittery.

Madog said, "If you see anyone coming, tell me and leave as if you have an errand."

"I know what to do. They can't see me from outside," the voice said, sullenly.

"There's a reason we don't meet like this. It's too suggestive for us to be seen together."

Got that right, George thought. If only their positions were reversed, so he could see the other one and hear Madog. Well, can't have everything.

"Scilti's gone. That message you sent him in the saddle didn't cover enough," the other man said. "We have to talk about what's next."

"You were right, I'll give you that, when you said he was unnerved, trapped in the inn by Gwyn and Edern and the whole stinking hunting party. But what possessed him to start that fight today, and to not even win it?"

"Bad luck," the other one said. "I think he was coming to talk to you, and blundered, thundered into them." Then George thought he heard the oddest thing—a faint giggle.

If Madog heard it, he ignored it. "Now he's gone back through the way, I felt him. When I get back there, he better be gone. He'll be lucky to get work standing border watch. He's roused all their suspicions and accomplished little. Even Creiddylad's beginning to balk."

"Does she know how we were getting through the palisade?"

"No, and I don't intend to tell her. She knows too much already."

The outside voice became more frantic. "You're not thinking of stopping? We can't fail now, not when we're so close. You have to let me finish it."

"You? Look what a mess you made of your attack on that wretched human. I'm going to have to take other steps now. How could you miss like that?"

"He saw me and moved. You know I only had time for the one shot. I barely got back ahead of them, first to Creiddylad's place, then yours."

Madog sighed. "When I set these things up, there aren't any failures or loose ends. Rhys ab Edern isn't coming back."

The voice replied, with a sly poke. "But the children lived, didn't they?"

Shocked, George dropped the pocket knife from his left hand onto the bare floor, and the conversation stopped. He hastily picked it up and crammed everything in his pockets any which way and buried his cane in a pile of towels to free his hands.

He was unarmed in the baths and unable to run, so he quickly tried to calm himself enough to assume the glamour he'd been trying to make habitual. He changed the clothing to something drab and tried to shape his body language to fit a servant. At the last moment, as footsteps approached, he remembered Isolda's injunction to keep his arms tucked in to shorten his reach to match his appearance.

He grabbed a stack of towels and started to lay them out, as though delivering them. Madog turned the corner and glared at him. George straightened, then bowed.

Don't walk, he told himself. The limp will give you away. He's armed and dangerous. Concentrate on the glamour, if you drop the glamour, you're dead. "Sorry to disturb you, sir," he said.

"Been here long?" Madog said, with studied disinterest.

"No, sir. Just came in the other way to clean up after one of the gentlemen." He moved about carefully, hiding the limp, and put the towels he had snatched back into their places on the shelves. I could use some of Rhian's knives about now, he thought, for all the good it would probably do me.

Out of the corner of his eyes he could see Madog looking at him with suspicion, but then he could hardly be expected to know the faces of everyone in Gwyn's establishment. Madog spun on his heels without a word and left.

George retrieved his cane but concealed it with the glamour as he carefully walked to the rear door Madog had used. It took forever to walk smoothly without the telltale limp. By the time he opened it and looked outside, they were both long gone.

Madog shook his head, disgusted with himself as he walked back from the balineum to the manor. Well, he thought, what do you expect when your tools are the inept and the deranged?

What a botched job of checking for listeners. Did he hear anything? There was something off about him, like a glamour, but who would it have been, if so? How would they know about the meeting? What did they hear?

He glanced at the huntsman's house as he walked by. Damn complication, that fellow, he thought. The mad one wants to kill him, but he wants to kill everyone, and look what a lousy job he did, bad enough to make things harder for my plans but not enough to stop him hunting. I should never have let him try the ambush, but after that fellow got rid of Owen the Leash—complacent idiot—he had to go. I need the control at the end of the great hunt, if this is going to work.

We're going to do it my way now. It'll be easy to make them think of him as Iolo's killer. Just point them in the right direction and provide the evidence. The mad one can do that for me. No one will believe a human in this, I don't care what lineage he claims. If they keep him, I'll have cut off much of his support. If they don't, anyone else will be easier to topple. I'll be there at the end, and the mad one, too, if I can keep him under control that long. Too sharp a weapon not to use, but such a hard one to handle.

It's only three more days. We can stay hidden that long, surely.

Such weak tools, but it makes them easier to manipulate, at least the sane ones. Pompous Gwythyr gave me the way in, and making myself indispensable to Creiddylad was hardly a challenge. Any man who seemed to respect her despite her history could probably have done it. What a pair they must've made, way back when. It amused him to make the two of them, bitter enemies now, into unaware mutual allies of his cause. It would horrify them, he chuckled, if they ever had the brains to work it out.

Creiddylad thinks it's all about her—the death of Iolo and the discomfiture of Gwyn. She thinks it can stop there, and not kill anyone in her family. But she's dreaming—her nephew's already dead, and more to come. I wonder if she'll recognize her role in it, when it's all over.

Gwythyr's at least straightforward. He doesn't ask about my methods. He just wants Gwyn dead. I bet he wouldn't care that I'm using Creiddylad to do it, might even please him more.

Why don't they ever wonder what's in it for me? Why do they think I'm willing to do their dirty work? Who do they think will take over this domain when Gwyn's gone? Edern has no standing and he's far from home. Creiddylad can't do it, it's all personal for her. Gwyn's father will never grant it to Gwythyr. Why can't they see this?

They're too old, they've had it their own way too long. I'll shut the ways and hold it tight, just as I've done all along for my own lands.

They disdain the younger ones like me, these old ones. Let them slumber in ignorance just a little while longer, until they're forced to recognize a new power in the western lands. I've kept myself hidden long enough. Annwn and the great hunt will give me standing like nothing else. They'll have to come to me, then.

George hobbled in to Gwyn's council room when his knock was acknowledged. "Good, you're both here," he said, as Ceridwen looked up from her conversation with Gwyn.

"Didn't I tell you to stay off that leg?" she said.

"Wish I could," he said, "believe me."

He limped clumsily over to the table and collapsed into a chair. "I have news…"

After hearing his account of Madog's conversation, Gwyn and Ceridwen sat for a minute or two, rearranging their theories about the enemy alliance into a new shape.

Ceridwen was the first to break the silence, with an almost random observation. "However the palisade was breached, I'm sure Creiddylad didn't do it herself. Between that, and the ability of Scilti and the other one to get through it, I'll bet some part of her essence was tapped without her knowledge. That's the only thing that makes sense, magically. I think she's guiltless in this, at least."

Gwyn looked grateful, fleetingly, but he shook his head. "She still wishes us harm and can't be trusted. Edgewood's connected to Madog's by this conversation, and she's kept that hidden. He may be the driving force, but she's his ally."

"You were right, last week, about Scilti," George said to Gwyn. "You and Edern must've scared him silly at the inn."

"That's good, but I didn't expect it to rebound on Rhian."

"No one could've foreseen that," George said. "I think their theory that this morning's attack was just bad luck is probably right."

"This is a complicated alliance, and they're unraveling, but they've really only lost one weapon today" Ceridwen said thoughtfully.

George said, "Don't forget Owen the Leash. They had a plan for him."

"Yes, but we still don't know who this other fellow is, inside our home. He's a knife looking for a victim."

Gwyn sighed. "All we can do is hold out for three more days, and hope to identify him. Meanwhile, I hold myself responsible for not looking into Madog more when he first appeared in my sister's train. What do we know?" he asked Ceridwen.

"The only one of that name I could find came to this new world long after we did, eight or nine hundred years ago."

"Why did we never meet him then?"

"They say he settled with the Indians, to the west," she said.

Gwyn paused. "Could this be source of the barrier to the west?"

"Can't be, it was there before he came, if this is the same person."

"We've been fools to ignore this," Gwyn said.

Privately George agreed, but maintained a discreet silence.

Gwyn rose. "I must tell my brother what we've learned and seek his forbearance until after the hunt, so that we can capture them all. I don't know if he'll agree to wait, now that the worst is known about his son."

"Wait a minute," George said. "So, our only plan is to wait?"

"And not to reveal what we know."

CHAPTER 32

George sat at Angharad's table on Thursday and helped himself to a second piece of beef pasty. The crust was crisp and flaky around the meat and vegetables in their savory gravy. His leg ached with the morning's hunt exertions, but he was beginning to regain his appetite.

He asked Angharad about the hunt. "So, how was it from the perspective of the field?"

"I overheard many conversations. More were in your favor, and Gwyn's, than on Tuesday. Many were surprised just to see you out at all."

"It's not so bad, today," he said, kneading his thigh. "Thanks for the cane. It got a lot of use yesterday."

She acknowledge his words. "I thought Iolo's sticks would be too short."

"As indeed they were," he said.

She began to clear some of the plates from the table.

She said, as she moved about, "Madog was there this morning, smooth as silk. He's invisible when he wants to be, but always watching. I can't say I'm surprised to find him a major force against Gwyn, but I have it in me to feel sorry for Creiddylad, once she realizes how she's been used."

"She's a case of 'be careful what you wish for,' I think. That much malice doesn't get my sympathy," he said, "nor such treason to her own family."

She nodded. "Poor Edern, confirmation at last of what he's always feared."

She sat back down. "Scilti seems to be gone for good, then."

"That's what we're hoping." He paused before taking another bite. "Didn't I tell you? I stopped by the inn on my way in and spoke to Huw Bongam. No trace of Maonirn at all, and he's been gone overnight. They're all very gloomy over there, fearing the worst."

George finished his last few bites in silence. He leaned down and picked up the bag he'd brought with him, slung over his back, when he rode in.

"I confess I had ulterior motives in inviting myself to lunch today, though the charm of your company needs no excuse." George smiled at Angharad.

"And just how may I help you?" she said, falling into the game.

"I need to test my tools, for Saturday." He opened the bag and drew out the oliphant that he'd taken away from the cupboard in the huntsman's office, and her face grew serious. "I couldn't wind this where the hounds could hear me, but I have to try it out for myself before I need to use it for real."

"Also, this," he said, reaching behind his vest and pulling out his revolver and placing it on the table in front of him.

"Ceridwen says gunpowder won't work, but this isn't the same gunpowder she's used to, she's out of date. I need to try it, but if I'm right, it'll make a loud noise, and I didn't want to let the wrong people know about it at the manor."

At Angharad's suggestion, George stood between the kilns, aiming his gun at the soft dirt.

"Cover your ears," he told her.

He had no idea whether or not this would work, but his belief in the universe's sense of humor weighted the scale for him in the direction of failure. He cocked the hammer back and pulled the trigger. Click.

He sighed. "That'll teach me to doubt Ceridwen."

He removed the cartridge and showed Angharad the dimple in the primer made by the firing pin. He couldn't tell if the primer had gone off, but certainly the gunpowder hadn't been ignited.

"What does it look like before firing?" Angharad wanted to know. He showed her an unfired cartridge and explained how they worked.

"Would you like to take it apart for further tests?" she asked.

They walked to her woodworking shop just a few steps away. With two pairs of pliers, George pulled the bullet from the case and spilled the smokeless powder into a dish. He spread it in a thin line on the plate and put a lighter to one end of it. The powder burned very slowly, almost like an inert substance, rather than quickly with a tall bright flame.

He made a mock ceremonial gift of the steel-jacketed bullet and brass cartridge case to Angharad, then reloaded the intact cartridge and replaced the gun under his vest. "I guess having one fewer cartridge now isn't going to matter much, but I had to know."

He walked to the door. "Let's try the oliphant."

"I wanted to see this again, and compare," George told Angharad, standing in front of her painting of Iolo wearing the oliphant slung across his back.

What will it sound like, he wondered. Low and slow, like a cow's horn?

Raising it with both hands he put the strange mouthpiece to his lips and pursed them as for a simple straight hunting horn. He took a deep breath and blew.

It took a second or two to adjust his mouth and create the right vibration to generate sound, and then it came, echoing slowly from all directions in the enclosed space of her workshop, as if the voice of the earth itself rose straight from the ground and gained volume from some agency other than his own breath, filling the room.

Angharad's dogs howled and the hairs on his arms rose in sympathy. The breath seemed to last forever, and he felt the horned man rise to continue it. He couldn't break it off until his lungs had emptied, and then he spent the next few moments pulling the horned man back.

When he could speak again, he said, "It sounds like the end of the world." She nodded solemnly.

"Did Iolo hunt the hounds with this, like a silver horn?"

"No, he hunted by voice for the great hunt. The oliphant announces the start of the hunt, the *mort*, and the 'all home' when everyone returns."

"Did Iolo bear the horned man, too?"

"Not that I know of. You must make your own path with this."

The dogs began barking again, this time to announce a visitor pounding on the workshop door.

It was Huw Bongam. "We've found Maonirn. That bastard Scilti slit his throat and buried him deep in the hay loft."

He has plenty of nerve, I'll give him that, Gwyn thought, while he waited for Creiddylad to be found. Madog had just left the council chamber.

How could I not have realized what a facade that was, he wondered. I must be losing the habit of focusing on the younger ones, a dangerous practice I'm going to have to reform. No wonder he thinks he can get away with anything, no one pays enough attention to him to disabuse him of the notion.

Madog had stood there in front of him, with an affable look of concern on his face, and told him he was sure, absolutely sure, that George had had a hand in Iolo's murder. "Search his house," he said, "You'll find a weapon. He had something to do with it."

Gwyn was confident that Idris understood the game being played by the look on his face when Gwyn sent him off to the huntsman's house, but Madog didn't notice. He took Gwyn's urbane thanks with unconvincing modesty and left, having planted his barb.

Creiddylad knocked on the open door and entered.

"You sent for me?" she asked.

"Sister," he said, "I wondered if you could help me understand more about yesterday's events. Do you know anything at all about Rhian's attacker?"

He put it that way, instead of "our invader," to see if she would be more motivated to honesty by a reminder of the family she was betraying.

"I told you already. I've never met him."

Truth, perhaps, but she didn't say she'd knew nothing about him.

"How do you suppose he got through the palisade's warding effect?"

Ah, that struck something. She looked uneasy about that.

"How should I know?" she said.

Gwyn thought, it's her magic, she should know how to circumvent it. He tried a different tack.

"I was just speaking with Madog. Remind me, how did you meet him?"

"He came to me when I needed him, a long time ago." She surprised Gwyn with a lonely look of remembrance.

"Where's he from?"

"He showed up one day and stayed to serve me. I've never seen his home. You know how it is with the younger ones, he's probably embarrassed by it. He was too shy to meet you here until just a few years ago."

That rang true. This was the vain self-centered woman he remembered. It wouldn't be hard to use her, if you wanted to devote enough time to the project.

Gwyn made one more attempt to reach her, to give her a chance to restore her fidelity to the family. Softly, he said, "Sister, why are you trying to cause trouble here?"

She looked him straight in the eyes, fully committed. "It's not me. Look to that human huntsman you're so proud to claim as kin. He's no kin of mine."

Idris returned, putting two clawed sticks, like the ones thought to have been used on Iolo, onto the council table. "These were in the desk in the study," he told Gwyn.

"You see?" Her voice rose. "He did it, just like Madog feared."

Gwyn dismissed her. After she left his eyes closed in sorrow and he bowed his head for several moments. She was no sister of his any longer. Idris stood by quietly.

He raised his head again, his face smooth. "Interesting gambit, don't you think?" he said, pointing his chin at the two weapons.

"This is absurd, you know. George was there when the bloodhounds were searching, and they never identified him."

"Madog and Creiddylad probably don't know all the details of that, or have dismissed our understanding of it."

"Then there's the problem that Alun cleaned up the house. His first loyalty would've been to Iolo. There's no way something this trivially hidden would have escaped his attention, or our knowledge," Idris said.

"Yes, it's not very respectful of our intelligence, is it? I feel rather… underestimated," Gwyn said, with a wry smile.

"And, of course, the most obvious problem is that we, at least, know Cernunnos has taken an interest in George. He could hardly be a less likely suspect." Gwyn sighed.

"So, what will you do?" Idris said. "They seem determined to push this story."

"What can I do? If I don't uphold the accusation, lend it some apparent credence, I'll give myself away to them. I'll reveal that I know too much." He poked at the clawed sticks in front of him with a finger. "George will expect me to behave differently in public. He'll know I don't truly believe it."

"Will he? Are you sure?" Idris asked.

George sat alone in his study, in the dark. Alun was out on some errand of his own, not having expected him to return before dinner ended.

His thoughts were bitter and his stomach churned.

He understood why he needed to be the bait, and he agreed with the reasoning, but this, this foul accusation, discussed all around the great hall as if he weren't even there, this was too much.

He had come back from his meal with Angharad to deliver the news about Maonirn's murder, and noticed cold, evasive looks wherever he turned.

Even at Gwyn's table, there was an outcry, with Madog and Creiddylad maliciously slandering him and beseeching Gwyn to "do something about it." And with Gwyn so little defending him, the cries rose against him like a pack of wolves. He could see the hunt staff, indignant on his behalf.

He took it stone-faced as long as he could, then rose from his meal and faced the crowd in the main hall. When they quieted, he told them, in an expressionless voice that carried to the back of the hall, that it was a slander, and that he had nothing whatsoever to do with Iolo's death. He picked up his cane and limped heavily off the dais and out of the hall.

He thought he had detected sympathy on Edern's face, and Idris patted his arm as he turned to leave. This reassurance was welcome, but it was bitter to have his name blackened like this without defense, after all the work he'd put in, making the pack his own. To return after a successful hunt in the morning to an evening of strangers asking if he could be trusted to hunt the hounds in two days, this was a blow.

Sitting in the dark, he considered. Well, could he hunt the hounds on Saturday? After two more sleepless nights, dreading the dreams of the horned man emerging, out of control?

CHAPTER 33

Friday morning, Angharad sat out on the huntsman's porch, sketching a detail of the holly branches, and waited for George to return from the hound walk. He opened the gate eventually and took a few steps in, looking down at the ground with his head bowed.

Still limping hard when no one's looking, she thought, and then they pile all this, this dirt on top of him. Isolda's description of last night's dinner in the great hall must have been accurate, for all that she hadn't been there herself.

He looked up, and she smoothed her expression. His face lit up at the sight of her. Having that effect on someone never lost its charm, even now, and she was warmed by his regard.

The day was soft and balmy for late October, not too cold to sit outside with coats on. George joined her on the porch, and Alun brought out some tea for them.

"It's a pleasure to see you, but I didn't expect it," George said.

"I've come for the next two nights," she said. "I hoped you wouldn't mind?"

"Not at all, though I fear I might not be great company."

"I'll have to see if I can change that, then." She smiled at him, and he responded in kind.

She continued her sketching while they talked. "I had a nice long chat with Isolda this morning." Sliding her eyes to watch carefully, she saw his face fall and his body tense.

"Then you've no doubt heard about the change in my reputation," he said.

"What I heard was a great deal of indignation on your behalf by everyone who knows you. No one believes this slander."

He relaxed a little. "That's not how it seems, here."

"Well, never mind. You'll find plenty of support tonight at dinner, I promise you."

She could see him take a hold of himself and straighten up. "It was just too much for me, last night. I'll do better tonight."

She didn't like the circles under his eyes. Wasn't he sleeping?

"I didn't tell you what else I heard from Isolda," she said, with a conspiratorial air of gossip.

"Yes?" he said, willing to be entertained.

"All about Benitoe. Did you know this has been going on for a while?"

"I suspected something, but no one's told me."

"She's the one who recommended him to her father, as a whipper-in for you," she said.

"So Ives approves of this?"

"Oh, I think so. If Benitoe proves himself to you, he would make a fine son-in-law, don't you think? And well suited to Isolda, each with their own ambition to succeed."

"He's turning out very well," George said. "I'll make sure to mention it to Ives, casually, in case it isn't obvious."

Good, she thought. Get him thinking about someone else, and something cheerful.

She closed her sketchbook and stood up. "Come inside. I've brought you a present."

One of the chairs in the study had been moved to catch the natural light from the window. Propped on its arms, in a simple frame, the painting Angharad had been working on in her workshop several days ago gleamed richly.

Seen from behind, George on Mosby raised his right arm dragging the front of the midnight blue robe up with it. The arrow fired by the archer visible at a distance to the left was just bursting through the heavy satin, its yellow fletching drawing the eye like a flash of light. The background portrayed the river meadow landscape visible through the way as a discontinuity against the local landscape. The chaos of the startled people in the original scene had been largely cleared away so that the eye could focus on the main compositional elements, the muscled rear of the dappled gray horse and the glimpse of his head, the dark blue robe with its decorative borders, and the red menace of the archer's clothing, as he reached for another arrow. A jagged rhythm to the major color forms drew the eye round and round, accentuating the action and menace of the arrow, aimed into near perspective in the direction of the viewer. The point of the arrow gleamed, picking up the metallic glints of the horse's tack and mounted weapons.

George froze in surprise, then limped over and stood in front of it, keeping out of the light. It was awkward to bend down, and he pulled over a side chair to sit on while he bent forward, elbows and forearms on his knees, to give it a thorough scrutiny.

Part way through he broke his concentration with a chuckle and sat up. "I didn't mean to be rude, examining a gift like this, as if I were looking for a flaw."

She laughed at his absorption. "Do go on. I'm very pleased by your interest. An artist has to work for herself, but it's a great joy when her work speaks to someone else."

George wasn't sure he completely believed her, but he was drawn back to the painting again. The viewer couldn't help but see the arrow aimed, not directly at him, but close, about to jump out of the frame. No matter how the color masses drew the eye, you kept worrying about that arrow, trying to keep an eye on it.

It was remarkably alive as well as compositionally brilliant.

He straightened up solemnly and this time turned all his focus on Angharad.

"I don't know what to say. This is wonderful." He groped for words. "It makes my heart stop. Makes it sing, too."

She laughed at his incoherence, clearly pleased.

"Alun will be hanging this over the mantle, as soon as I'm done looking at it up close," he said.

How many hours did this take her, he wondered. To think of her spending that time, and gifting me with the result. He walked over to her, trying not to limp, and grasped her right hand in both of his. "I haven't the words to thank you," he said, embarrassed.

George welcomed Rhodri into the huntsman's office at the kennels. The hounds were quiet, snoozing in the afternoon sun.

"Thanks for coming. Glad to see you're still speaking to me," he said, sardonically.

Rhodri laughed. "You shouldn't take it personally. No one thinks you had anything to do with Iolo's murder. That's all for the politicians and the spies. And the fools, there are always some of those."

"You're right. I overreacted last night. Nerves."

"I can understand why you'd feel nervous, but honestly, you've done a good job getting the hounds this far," Rhodri said. "If you care for my opinion."

"I do care, thanks."

Rhodri looked gratified.

"In fact," George said, "you're the first person I thought of. I need to pick your brains for a detailed description of what to expect tomorrow night. You've hunted it, with Iolo."

"Ask away," Rhodri said, leaning back in his chair, "and I'll tell you what I know."

"Alright, how does it start?"

"The hunt assembles at the kennels two hours before midnight and heads in procession to the village, picking up more riders as it goes along. Gwyn opens a way in the middle of the bridge and it remains open while the hunt's away, so the people who stay behind have to choose ahead of time which side of the village they want to be on, for the end of year celebrations. There are always at least two parties, one based around the inn.

"When you get to the foot of the bridge, Gwyn will make a pretty little speech for Cernunnos and open the way. You'll enter with the hounds and the field will follow."

George asked, "Where will the way open to?"

"It's impossible to tell in advance. It's different every time. The hunt is sent to the quarry, and the hounds are cast at him."

"So it's quick, then?" George said.

"Not at all. The quarry runs, and ways are opened for him. Those ways stay open while the hunt continues. A rider who falls off or is otherwise lost must either seek the ways by himself, or wait for the hunt to return at the end to rejoin it, so you can see there's some risk involved. Anyone can ride in the great hunt, but it's not for children."

"What happens if they can't find the ways and also miss the hunt coming back?"

"Then they have to get back the hard way, round by the land. Since they might not be in our domain any longer, or even in the new world, you can see how that could be a bit… awkward." He smiled. "We have stories about getting lost during the great hunt."

George said, "Can the huntsman get lost?"

"Not if he keeps in contact with his quarry. The hounds will follow through the ways, and the huntsman can always find his way back. Iolo once told me it's the only time he could see the ways."

"How many ways will there be?"

"That's impossible to predict. I've seen a hunt that took a dozen, and I've heard of a quarry dispatched after three. One thing, though: the first way can open anywhere, but the rest seem to stay in the same rough vicinity, judging by the stars. It's always around midnight here at the *mort*, wherever you come out, though it may be anytime at night at the first way. I've seen the dawn rise, if we've gone very far east, before returning and sleeping through the same dawn again."

"What happens if the quarry escapes?"

Rhodri sat up in his chair. "The hunt pursues until the quarry's killed. If he escapes, justice has failed." He looked at George seriously. "It hasn't failed in Gwyn's reign."

What a change in the great hall from a couple of weeks ago, George thought. Every table and bench was pressed into use for dinner.

George was calmer than yesterday, determined to tough it out now that he was over the surprise. He expected it to be easier with Angharad at his side, and was grateful for it. He smiled at his friends as he joined them, and this time he was able to see the welcome in their faces. He avoided looking at the rest.

He was struck by the brotherly resemblance of Gwyn and Edern sitting sternly together. "They look like that painting of yours, of the fostering of Rhys and Rhian," he said quietly to Angharad. "They've mastered the imperious glare."

Angharad choked at his irreverent tone.

I can handle this, he thought cheerfully.

Then the malice started again.

Creiddylad said to Gwyn, in a carrying voice, "How can you expect us to eat at the same table as Iolo's murderer?"

George cared little for what Creiddylad thought of him, but he felt the horned man stir, here in public, and that alarmed him. He pulled it back down.

Madog chimed in, "I really think it would be wiser to make other arrangements for tomorrow night, my lord."

Again, the horned man started to rise. He clenched his teeth and kept his face expressionless, pulling it back.

Creiddylad continued her chorus. "Cernunnos would surely find disfavor with him, brother. You mustn't jeopardize the hunt."

Angharad felt him going rigid this time, and placed her left hand over his right where it clenched into a fist on the table. She squeezed it lightly in sympathy, with a look of concern on her face.

George was disturbed. He himself wasn't much moved by these insults, but something inside him, separate from him, seemed to be. It wasn't himself he was trying to control, but something or someone else, angered by Creiddylad's lies. As he choked it down he remembered old tales about the imprudence of insulting the gods. Settle down, he told whatever it was. This is aimed at me, not you. It subsided reluctantly.

Seeking a distraction, he scanned the hall, and spotted Creiddylad's odd servant, Meuric. He was out of step with his comrades, grinning when he thought no one was watching.

He pointed him out to Angharad. "That's the fellow I told you about, the one who watches Gwyn and Rhian."

She observed him for a few minutes. She shuddered with a sudden foreboding. "I hate the way he watches Rhian. There's something very wrong about him."

Eurig and Tegwen came up with George to wish him luck tomorrow, and all thoughts of Meuric were driven out of their heads.

In the huntsman's study after dinner, George and Angharad enjoyed a quiet drink. The painting still had pride of place on its chair, now turned so that George could admire it in the lamplight.

"I'm very glad you're in the house this evening," George said. "It's hard to believe this will all be over in a day or so."

"Will you be staying on, after?" she asked.

"I confess I've avoided thinking about it." He took a sip of his brandy. "It started as a favor done for a relative and an adventure in a foreign land."

She nodded sympathetically.

"I always assumed I would be returning. I put my life on hold, briefly, treating this like an exotic vacation." He put his glass down. "But now that life seems faded and dull. I can't picture what it would be like, returning. I have grandparents, and friends…"

"And dogs," she said, with a smile.

"Yes, and dogs to go back to. But then how much of this world's excitement would fade when it becomes a routine job? How many of these relatives think of me with family affection?"

Angharad said, quietly, "I think the affections of your friends and family here are very real, more real than you know."

He glanced at her quickly, to see if she meant anything more by that. "I've been slow to act, with some of them," he said deliberately, "not knowing how long I would be here."

She gave him an understanding look. Ah, message received. Good. If I'm still here in a few days, things will change, he promised himself.

Angharad said, "Have you thought about your heritage? These things are part of you, in either world, but how will you deal with them somewhere else?"

"You mean the horned man? I keep hoping that'll be gone after tomorrow."

She shook her head, "I doubt that. Remember your father—it's in your blood."

She was probably right. He desperately wanted to know what had happened to his parents.

"More than that," she said. "What if you're long-lived, like Rhodri, and this is just the beginning? You have other gifts, with glamoury and the ways, and the speaking to beasts. It's likely you have the years, as well."

"What would you do? How is it for you?"

She sat back in her chair and steepled her hands together. "The first hundred years are a burst of youth for all of us. We're invulnerable, in our own estimation, and the world's a fine and fascinating place. Most of us just live, building families, learning, enjoying ourselves. Then we collide with the nature of life. Most marriages cannot last for many decades of unchanging existence. We lose track of our children and theirs, eventually, many of us. And the dreadful sameness of 'just living' takes its toll.

"I was lucky, I had something to interest me, a striving that would never achieve perfection, that would never be satisfied. It's kept me young. Those without resources become monsters eventually. Look at Creiddylad.

"But I pay a price for it. My art keeps me sane, but I live solitary to do it. My arrangement here with Gwyn is an ideal compromise—I only hope it can last."

George asked, "Why must you live alone for your art?"

"Because my art is part of me and takes most of my time, it's what I'm passionate about. There's not enough left over to satisfy most husbands, however much I may care for them."

George looked at her consideringly. "They sound selfish, to me. Have they no passions of their own, with their long lives?"

She laughed. "Well, artists rarely marry artists—too much conflict of vision. Maybe a scholar or a poet would work. But you know how people are fascinated by opposites. I haven't found an answer yet."

CHAPTER 34

It was a quiet morning in the kennels, with no hunting or hound walking today. The break in routine felt strange to George.

Angharad had been a welcome presence at breakfast, calm and well-rested. Couldn't fool her about my sleeping, though. I've forgotten what it feels like to sleep through a night. Maybe I can rest tonight, after it's all over.

Ives knocked on his office door. George tried to read his face, now that they had a few minutes. Ives noticed the scrutiny and spoke up stoutly, "You're not thinking we believed any of that garbage they're trying to sell in the hall?"

George said, some of the tension easing, "I hoped not, but you weren't there for Iolo's death and would have every reason to be suspicious."

"I know you well enough to know an evil lie when I hear it. And you forget, Orry told me all about tracking the killer with his hounds."

Ives shook his head. "None of them are thinking straight. The hounds would know the killer, his guilt if not his identity. They'd never hunt for him."

George cleared his throat and asked Ives to sit and join him.

"Which hounds will be going out tonight? What's usual?"

"All of them, of course, including any youngsters that have seen hunting this season. Except for Aeronwy, she's still weak from her expedition across the ridge Saturday."

"I thought she was improving?"

"And so she is, but she'd never keep up tonight."

"Are they that eager to hunt at night, when they only do it once a year?"

"You won't recognize them tonight, not one," Ives said. "It'll take all you've got to hold 'em back. Just be grateful it's not the dark of the moon."

"Rhodri told me what to expect for tonight's ceremonies, and warned me people can get lost. Does anyone keep a head count? What should I be bringing?"

"Let Gwyn worry about the hunters. You'll need weapons, water, rope…" He thought a moment. "The oliphant, of course. Let the stable know which mount you'll use, and check the tack yourself."

That echoed George's list. "I'll warn the staff, too, but would you also check them when they come, to make sure? All but Rhys are new to this."

"I will." As he rose, he looked at George behind his desk. "You should try and get some sleep, lad. You're going to need it," he said, and closed the office door behind him suggestively.

Would if I could, George thought.

Well, I can leave a message about Mosby at the stable, but otherwise there's not much for me to do. He checked his pocket watch and thought about lunch. Seeing that crowd will just kill what little appetite I've got.

Maybe a nap here will work better than in my bed. If I kill the lights and draw the curtain, no one will look for me here.

He darkened the room and stretched out on the old sofa. He was so over-tired, he desperately wanted to sleep and tried to make himself relax enough to drop off.

Eyes shut. Silence. Hounds stir, far away. Leg throbs. Not bad, hard to ignore. Eyes open and scan the room. Vision pulses dimly, with the leg, with his blood.

Eyes closed. Hear the mice behind the wall. Smell the nest, the stolen grain, stronger now, head heavier. No, damn it, get back in there and let me sleep.

Horned man pulls back. All alone in his head. Floating, drifting.

Quiet.

A breath.

Eyes pop open.

How will I know the quarry deserves this?

I forgot to ask Rhodri. Do the hounds kill him, or is it me?

~

Rhian stood next to the wagon in front of the kennel gates and surveyed the piles of material they had to work with.

"Let's start with the evergreen boughs," she told Isolda, standing in the wagon bed, and began passing them up to her.

The cloudless afternoon was refreshingly chill, and they started to sing as they wound twine around the branches and tied them to the wagon's side-rails.

"Where's Benitoe?" she asked Isolda, just to see her blush.

As if summoned, Benitoe and some of his friends appeared from the direction of the stables.

"Afternoon, ladies," they said in chorus. Benitoe introduced them to Rhian as part of his club of riding enthusiasts. Most were young, Benitoe's age or less, but at least two of them were a generation older.

"We were just deciding who would follow the hunt tonight, riding which horse," he said. I'll only need one myself, and so we have two more than usual. Still not enough, though, so it's quite the debate."

Isolda looked down from the wagon bed. "How about drawing straws?"

"An excellent idea," one of the older ones said. He picked up a few pieces of straw from the pile on the ground. Selecting ten pieces, he broke two of them off short, leaving the others at a uniform longer length.

"Will you hold these for us, my lady?"

Isolda smilingly accepted, and held them out in her two hands, concealing the ends.

"And, my lady Rhian, will you kindly make each selection for us, since you can reach our fair arbiter of chance, and we can't?"

Rhian composed her face as best she could. As each lutin approached, she privately drew a straw on his behalf, and gave it to him, until all had been served.

The two with the short straws sighed melodramatically. One of them was the older fellow who had arranged the drawing. "You see how I am served for offering a fair solution. But at least this means I can claim a seat on the wagon next to blind fortune here, in compensation." He bowed theatrically to Isolda, who giggled and curtsied back.

They went off laughing, but Benitoe stayed behind and helped them decorate.

The bundling and placement of the the highly-colored autumn leaves went slowly, with pauses for mock hats and beards, and for sly attacks down the back of the neck.

Brynach walked up, a bit shy. "Can I help?"

"Of course," Rhian said. "See those piles of straw? Ever make garlands?"

Soon she had him waist deep in the middle of the stack, pulling out the longest strands for her, while she showed him how to braid and tie them.

The two pairs were busy for some time, then Rhian winked at Brynach and said loudly, "What do you suppose they're up to, over there?" She giggled, as Benitoe and Isolda suddenly realized how soft their conversation had become and how little work was being accomplished.

They were still at it when Rhys showed up, carrying a small sack of apples. "Alright, move over, everyone. Let an expert show you how it's done." He tossed apples all round and started hanging the straw garlands Rhian and Brynach had made.

Eventually, with the addition of a few ribbons on the edges of the seats to flutter as they drove, it was done. The last of the straw was distributed in the bed of the wagon to ease the bumps for passengers, since the benches along the sides would be overflowing.

Rhian, Rhys, and Brynach stood a few feet away to admire their handiwork, munching on apples. Benitoe leaned against the side of the wagon, Isolda standing over him and laughing at something Brynach said. As Benitoe looked up at Isolda, Rhian glimpsed his briefly unguarded expression and caught her breath. No, she thought, no more teasing.

Will someone look at me that way someday?

"We're all here," she said, suddenly solemn. "The start of a new year."

"Seems a pity for George to miss this," Isolda said.

Rhys said, "But he'll see it tonight."

Benitoe said quietly, "It's not the wagon she means. It's all of us."

The great hall was draped with greenery and garlands for the end of the year, the crowd within boisterous and noisy.

George watched them from his seat on the dais and found them remote and distant, like players on a stage. They straggled in, not making much of their light supper, but drinking freely. A steady stream of servants ferried in pitchers, and the noise on the main floor rose to become a solid wall.

Things were more decorous on the dais, but none of it seemed to penetrate George's attention. As the evening progressed, he stopped responding to Angharad's attempts at conversation on his right, and Idris and Gwyn on his left, until now he sat silently, not touching his food or drinking.

The noise in the main part of the hall began to recede, and he could hear a pulse in the air, languid and low. The lights dimmed in rhythm with it. He tilted his head ponderously trying to hear it better.

This isn't so bad, he thought. I just have to live through it, let it take me. Like getting drunk.

He shook himself. No, I won't lose myself. I'm in control, I must keep my judgment.

Something laughed at him, but looking at the faces around him, he realized they hadn't heard it.

He looked down at Angharad and saw worry plain on her face.

"It'll be alright," he said with difficulty, his tongue thick in his mouth. He wasn't sure she understood him.

The pulse was in his body now, and he moved slightly to its rhythm. Gwyn spoke quietly to Edern, looking at him, and his ears twitched, listening.

No, my human ears. Not your turn yet, he thought.

He heard Gwyn say, "It never took Iolo this hard."

What was he talking about, George wondered absently, as he tracked the pulse of the world.

~

George found himself standing at the kennel gates, holding Mosby's reins. Rhodri, next to him, said something he couldn't make out. Looking closely at him, Rhodri stopped talking and began to check Mosby's girth and look over the gear he carried.

"Up you go," Rhodri said, and George understood. He mounted Mosby and walked him over to join his hunt staff.

They looked proper to the occasion, well dressed and solemn. He nodded his head, lowering it heavily, to acknowledge the respect they did to the occasion.

They looked at him in concern but it meant little to him. The horse would carry him, he thought. All he had to do was stay on and listen. He tilted his head again, moving it to hear better. The slow throbbing was in the air, in the ground, he could feel it through his horse. The heartbeat of the world echoing in his blood and his skin and his gut, slowing ever so slightly, preparing for the year to turn.

~

Rhian looked at George, so strange and grim, as if he doesn't see us at all. She glanced uneasily at Rhys, who looked as disturbed as she felt.

As she saw her foster-father and grandfather approach, she straightened up and moved next to George, taking her official spot. She might have to take care of him, in this strange mood.

Rhys came up close behind her, and Benitoe and Brynach on the other side. They spread around the huntsman in support. George didn't acknowledge them. He seemed to be trying to identify a sound, by the way he turned his head, his movements measured and slow.

From her position next to him, she noticed his fingers twitching on the reins in a slow rhythmic beat, and a tic on his face kept time. The hair on the back of her neck rose.

Stretched out all the way to the stables, the field finished assembling and approached the kennel gates, leaving a space free around the hunt staff for the pack. Gwyn walked his horse to the head of the field, nearest the curtain wall.

There was a pause. George hadn't asked for the pack, Rhian realized suddenly. He's lost in there somewhere. She turned to the kennel gates. "Please release the hounds, Master Ives."

George roused a bit at the sight of the pack, and relieved her by smiling faintly down at her. She glanced over at Isolda's wagon waiting to the right of the kennel gates, Ives hastening over to join Isolda on the seat. Isolda gave her a merry smile to lift her heart, and she was herself again.

The field was quiet behind them. Gwyn called, "Huntsman," and George led the pack forward through the curtain wall.

~

Coming through the village, George was vaguely aware that the number of riders had grown significantly, and more waited for them off to the side of a cleared space in front of the bridge.

Gwyn cantered ahead of George and the pack, turning his horse to face the field on the ground before the bridge, to the left. He waved George and the pack over to the right. The revelers who would be staying for the party pulled off on either side and along the river banks, out of the way of the riders. Isolda drove her wagon straight past the pack up to Rhian on the right for a ringside seat. Rhian on her horse was level with Isolda on the wagon seat, and they were close enough to talk to each other quietly as they waited for the crowd to settle into silence.

As the noise diminished, George was again caught by the low, slow pulse around him, slower than before, the air thick. The moon above him, nearly full, throbbed to the same beat.

Gwyn raised his arm under the torchlight and the moonshine until all the voices had stopped and only the creak of leather, the shuffle of hooves, and the spit of the torches could be heard over the quiet flow of water.

He gestured toward the center of the bridge and a way opened across the middle. A view of a moon-lit meadow surrounded by woods perched incongruously over the running water. The village's other celebrants, on the other side of the stream, were blocked from view.

The open way called to George, but he held himself in check. No, not yet. Soon.

~

Gwyn faced the crowd, prepared to give the invocation, but as they watched him, his own eye was caught by a man coming forward from the crowd on the river bank over near Ives's wagon of lutins. He was the only man moving in the silence.

His face came fully into the light of one of the torches and Gwyn's stomach clenched before he could place him. The face reminded him of someone. A sense of cold dread descended.

Why does his face alarm me? It's something very bad, something about a father and a son. Nwython! This is his son, the one they call Cyledr Wyllt, who got away. The heart, I made him eat his father's heart.

Frozen, he watched him grin and reach inside his coat.

Gwyn tried to turn his horse to reach him, but he was too far away, and there wasn't enough time.

~

A catch in the pulse of the world startled George to awareness. Swinging his head to the right, he saw Meuric walk out of the crowd by the river before Gwyn could speak. The movement of Meuric's hand to the inside of his coat clashed with the regular beat George was moving to, and it jarred him. It was wrong.

Meuric's hand emerged with a knife. He shouted to Gwyn, before the silenced crowd, "Now I take your heart as you took my father's."

He threw the knife, not at Gwyn, but straight at Rhian, just a few yards away. George and Rhian couldn't react quickly enough, but Isolda launched herself from her wagon seat into the path of the blade and intercepted it.

She fell to the ground and didn't move.

George stared at her in horror, then watched Meuric turn to the foot of the bridge, and run to the open way. He sprinted through it and the way vanished.

Wrath, outrage, implacable judgment—with a feel of rushing wind, Cernunnos erupted within George as the fully antlered red deer, and George welcomed him. He smelt Isolda's death on the air, and turned his head ponderously toward the bridge where Meuric fled, lifting his muzzle and sniffing the air for his scent.

One ear twitched as Gwyn cried, "He can't close the way, it's not possible."

The crowd around the huntsman began to fall back as they saw his altered form, until a space was opened up all around him. Only the hunt staff stood their ground gamely, Rhian weeping for her friend, gathered up on the ground into Ives's arms.

~

Gwyn felt the shutting of the way like a physical blow.

Am I about to lose everything? Rhian lives, but at the cost of another innocent.

He looked with sorrow at Ives, sitting keening in the dust, stained with blood, Isolda in his lap. This is my fault, too, for the old sin.

He looked back at the crowd. Why are they all backing away? He looked at Idris, facing him, and followed his gaze to… his huntsman, crowned with antlers that gleamed in the torchlight.

~

Rhian thought, Meuric means to kill me. Why?

No, Isolda, don't!

She heard the awful, hollow thud of the blade striking home. She knew with certainty that she'd never be able to forget that sound, that it would haunt her all her life.

She looked down. Move, please be moving.

That faint awareness of her friend that Rhian always carried was gone, and she cried out, even as Ives leapt off the wagon to kneel by his daughter and lift her up.

The movement of the crowd backing away caught her attention. When she looked left she saw George? Cernunnos? beside her, starting to kick his horse forward. He was moving slowly but relentlessly toward the bridge.

Her skin prickling, she turned to accompany him, taking refuge in her duty. She heard Ives behind her, choking out to Benitoe that he'd take care of Isolda, that he should go on now and help kill him.

Oh, no—Benitoe. How horrible.

Ives was right, Meuric must die. The huntsman will show us how.

George watched through Cernunnos's eyes, or it may have been the other way around—it was very confusing. He paused next to Gwyn before setting foot on the bridge and turned his heavy head to him, watching silently through the deer's brown eyes.

Gwyn said, abashed, "But the way can't be reopened now."

George pulled the manifestation back to the form of the horned man so that he could speak.

"It can be opened by me." The voice was hoarse and deep, and the words were not his own. "Your sins were great, but this," gesturing at Ives weeping over Isolda, "this was not a sacrifice that justice required."

He passed Gwyn and brought the pack forward onto the bridge. He could smell Rhian's tears, and felt her, anguished and fierce, beside him.

He reached for the oliphant strung across his back and sounded one long, low note that filled the river valley all around. He felt the pulse of the world slow as the way re-opened.

The antlered huntsman led the pack through the way, and the field followed in silence, flickering in the torchlight.

CHAPTER 35

George fought for control, or at least accommodation, as soon as the pack cleared the way, moving them off to the right to let the field come through. He tried to pull back the horned man, while Cernunnos pushed for his full form. In compromise, they settled for the horned man in form and surface control for George.

Dazed no longer, George was seized by grim purpose. He could still feel the slowing pulse of the world, but it was in the background now.

He adjusted his seat to rebalance his top-heavy weight on Mosby, wondering in passing what had happened to his tricorn back at the bridge.

He looked down at Rhian. "Don't weep, my dear, that's for later. We have work to do." He felt Cernunnos echoing his words.

All this while the field was still trotting through the way.

He turned his head slowly and found Gwyn standing by, watching him warily.

"Kinsman," he said, "his real name is Cyledr Wyllt." George dipped his head in acknowledgment.

George finished settling himself, glancing around at the moon-lit field surrounded by woods. Nothing indicated the direction his quarry had taken. He turned to his hounds and waiting staff. Benitoe's face was frozen, and the rest nodded to him formally.

He cast around him on all sides for Cyledr, giving the hounds a mental image of grinning malice and a reek of rot from within.

The hounds exploded with anger and fury, even Dando, he noted, remotely. They, too, are possessed. Doesn't matter, he thought, as long as they can do the job. Same for me, I suppose.

It took them but a moment to locate his trail, and then they had him fixed in their minds. They charged forward following the scent, Cythraul and Rhymi in the lead.

As they galloped straight across the meadow to the woods on the edge, George had little time to wonder where they were. He could feel another way flashing open before they hit the trees. The old way behind him was still filled with riders coming from the bridge but he had no time to wait for them.

He followed the baying pack as they plunged through the new way after Cyledr, Rhian at his side and the whippers-in trying to catch up to the hounds.

They rode out onto a stark and chilly boulder-strewn field that stretched featurelessly in all directions, low ridges miles away visible in the moonlight. The moon was still rising but had shifted oddly in the sky. The far north, George thought. Tundra? The ground was mossy and soft underfoot, but harder underneath with ice.

There were no trees or landmarks.

He looked back, turning his heavy head slowly. Most of the field still seemed to be with him, but he expected to shed stragglers at each location if they couldn't keep up. This would be a cold place to pass the time and possibly deadly to be lost in.

As the hounds checked and cast about for the scent, the whippers-in passed him and got to their proper positions on either side. George was beginning to understand the balance of the rules. Cyledr was fast, even on foot. The hounds were faster, but each way they crossed would slow the hounds down, for the transition and to reacquire the scent. The contest was roughly balanced.

Rhymi picked up the line and was honored by the rest of the pack which roared off along the trail. The field tried to stay with them, fearing to be lost in this place.

George felt the flash of a new way opening, and when the hounds reached it, they poured through.

An unexpected thunder of hooves on packed dirt, and they popped out onto a street in some village, right into a crowd of people. By the torches and the inn sign, it seemed to be another end of year celebration.

With cries of alarm, the crowd tried to get out of the path of the pack and riders in their midst, scrambling to either side of the road. George had to clear space for the riders behind him and had no choice but to bring the pack forward to find room.

The hounds split around people stranded in the road, ignoring them as they swept through. He brought them to a halt near the edge of the torchlight, wondering how they were going to pick up scent in this mob.

Now that he was stopped and the people had a moment to take stock, his great crown of antlers suddenly became the focus of attention, and the crowd grew quiet. People poured out of the inn as word spread of the spectacle in the street outside. Riders were still coming through the way and being directed off to the side.

At the cry of "Huntsman!" George turned his head ponderously. A young boy had climbed one of the posts of the stable gates of the inn and looked him straight in the face from that height over the heads of the crowd, his eyes shining. "He went through there," pointing along a cross street that ended at the edge of a stream.

As well as his heavy head would permit, George bowed in his saddle to him for the news. "My thanks, young sir." He directed the pack into that road, the crowd parting before them. Cythraul and Goronwy began to feather as they tried to pull the thread of scent out of the tangle.

Behind him, Gwyn rode up to the space he vacated and called to the bystanders. "What village is this?"

From the doorway of the inn, a voice cried out, "Danderi. We know you, Gwyn ap Nudd."

Gwyn spun to face him. "All are welcome. We will return this way."

Already a few bold celebrants had left their drinks and emerged mounted from the stable yard, seizing the opportunity, and at Gwyn's words others rushed to join them.

George heard the augmented field behind him, but focused his attention on the hounds. As one would work the trail, others dodged ahead to see if it continued and, as the overlay of other scents diminished, more and more of them cantered head-down on the line until finally, near the shallow river, they burst into cry.

It took only a few moments to determine where Cyledr had crossed and to pick up the trail again. George felt the flash of the next way in the distance and, after a hard gallop, they popped out into a woods, careening downhill in darkness and trying to check their speed before crashing into something.

~

The wild ride down through the trees shed a number of the riders. The path, what there was of it, zigzagged back and forth down the slope, in almost complete darkness.

George was relieved to see that they were coming to a clearing lit by the moon. The hounds ignored the terrain, hot on the scent, and all his staff were still with him, swinging around him to reach the hounds again as the ground opened up away from the trees.

Then he saw Brynach's horse stumble and go down, throwing him clear. He raised a hand from the ground as the horse got up and waved George on as he went by.

George didn't stop, he couldn't stop. They'd lost time at the village and working through these trees, and the flash of the next way was far ahead, on the other side of the clearing. Other dismounted riders would help him, he hoped.

The hounds ran silently, heads down and certain.

Rhian rode as well as she could, barreling through the woods next to George. She saw Brynach get thrown in the clearing and looked to George, but couldn't read the expression on the face of the horned man.

She knew he couldn't stop, and Benitoe couldn't either. They'd have to leave Brynach behind and pick him up, returning. She marked the spot carefully, so she could find it again.

Maybe Eurig will see him.

This way took them to an open upland meadow, peaceful and quiet under the moonlight. There was no sign of movement, but in the distance a great oak stood alone near the top of a gradual slope, its leaves fallen, majestic.

The hounds checked. George moved forward from the gate and let them work out the trail. A quick look round showed all his staff except Brynach, and he could hear the field leaving the way and lining up behind him, catching their breaths.

After a few moments, the hounds picked up the line, whimpering with eagerness, and cantered loosely up the hill toward the oak.

Halfway up, George felt the flash of another way opening, next to the tree. He looked up at the oak just in time to see Cyledr step out from behind the trunk and dash through it.

The hounds broke into furious cry as they finally viewed their quarry and tore into pursuit, abandoning the scent trail, their bodies low to the ground as they stretched into a gallop. George and all his staff charged after them. Behind him, he could hear the heavy thunder of many riders, pounding up the slope.

The hounds poured into the way, the whippers-in beside them, while George and Rhian brought up the rear, but before the two of them reached it, another way flashed open downslope right beside them. Cyledr sprang out like a leopard and pulled Rhian from her horse.

George wheeled Mosby as quickly as he could, but Cyledr had backed up to the oak, his strong wiry left arm wrapped around Rhian's chest, pinning her arms to her sides while she struggled. He held a knife to her throat, and she stopped moving.

The knife winked in the light. A small trickle of blood ran down Rhian's neck where the point had pricked her, black in the moonlight, the only thing moving in that tableau. George flared his nostrils at the smell.

He froze, a few yards below them.

The hounds started to pour out from Cyledr's last way, snarling and intent on their now unmoving prey at bay. George roared, "Hold," and stopped them all in their tracks by direct command. It was like trying to keep back a runaway coach with dozens of horses and he didn't think he could hold them for long.

Cyledr snuggled Rhian's back up tight against him, and giggled.

~

Cyledr grinned at the frustrated hounds. Made you run in circles, didn't I. Too bad, he'll never let you get me while I have my lovely girl here. Such a nice warm squirming girl body. Smells good.

Told them I'd get their heart. It's just about here. Ah, soft.

I've got plenty of the way-sticks left he gave me, I can keep this up all night long.

Do it here or take her with me into a way and close it up tight, tight, tight?

~

George struggled to hold the hounds in check. The whippers-in had exited the last way and returned to the silent tableau. They sat motionless while the hounds snarled and struggled for release.

Cernunnos pushed hard to manifest and George lost his control of the form. There were gasps in the silent field behind him. Loose the hounds, he commanded, loud in George's head.

George shook his head, their head, and resisted. I won't hurt her.

He must die, Cernunnos insisted in a cold, implacable voice. George's hold on the hounds wavered, and he concentrated to maintain it.

I'm not one of your hounds.

Are you not?

George's temper flared and he pushed back hard, driving Cernunnos all the way back and resuming his normal form. We're going to do this my way, he told him.

What was left of the field spread out directly behind him. They formed a semicircle in silence to see justice done, attention divided between the threat at the oak tree and the struggling huntsman.

George, focused on the hounds, ignored them. He could feel the world waiting, the beating pulse almost stopped.

CHAPTER 36

George looked up the hill at Rhian's face, separated only by the pack and a small margin of ground. She didn't move, but she couldn't keep the fury from her face. No room for fear.

He began to push Mosby slowly through the quivering hounds, up the hill, getting closer.

"Go back home where you belong, human," Cyledr said. "There's no place for you here. I've waited a long, long time for this, and I'll be gone before you can blink, you stupid bumbling half-wit."

"And you, old man," he called over to Gwyn standing with the field, "you'll be next." His voice carried in the waiting stillness.

Cyledr grinned more widely and his knuckles tightened on his knife. George strained to keep a hold on the hounds. He's going to do it, he thought. He'll just sidestep into the way afterward.

He rolled his eyes to the heavens in desperation. The stars were dim with the nearly full moon, but one of them winked at him, moving slowly across the sky.

A plane!

George reached under his coat, and drew his gun. In one smooth motion he swung up his arm and shot Cyledr through his exposed right shoulder, hard against the oak.

"We're not in your world any more, we're in mine," he cried.

Rhian tore herself free and reached for a knife, but Cyledr was already down, writhing on the ground. Rhys shouted, "No!" and galloped to her, reaching down an arm to swing her up behind him and pull her away from the tree.

George released the hounds.

When it was over, witnessed in grim silence by the assembled field, he called the hounds back. They came to him, willing and obedient, back to normal.

He lifted up the oliphant again and blew the *mort.* The sound seemed to echo to the ends of the earth. He felt the spinning of the world hanging suspended, like the end of the swing of a pendulum.

Rhys dropped Rhian by her horse. As soon as she mounted, she rode back to George, relieved to see his normal face.

"Brynach," she said, "We left him behind."

George turned and called to Rhodri, behind him with the field. "Can you find your way back without me?"

"Yes."

"Go with her, then, and see if Brynach needs help."

Rhodri joined her. "At your service, my lady." Then seriously, "And very glad indeed to see you well, cousin."

She'd think about Meuric/Cyledr later. She had a terrible feeling about Brynach and wanted to get to him as quickly as possible. She galloped down the hill, Rhodri at her side, and he guided her through the way.

George brought the pack down the hill to the assembled field, and passed Ceridwen coming up. She dismounted at the body by the tree and bent over it.

Behind him, he felt the two ways used by Cyledr and the pack wink out, the last one first. Was that Cernunnos cleaning up after the hunt, or had they been made by Cyledr and affected by his death?

"We must go," George said to Gwyn.

Idris came up. "Where's Madog?"

Someone in the field spoke up. "Madog left just now, back through the way, and our lord's sister followed close behind."

George looked at Gwyn, alarmed. "Rhian and Brynach are in front of them."

Gwyn waved him forward and pulled the field together to follow.

George paused at the way and looked back to make sure everyone was following. Ceridwen had remounted and was cantering back, and the oak tree stood alone again, on its hill in the moonlight.

Suddenly he realized—this is the oak I dream about, the one that protects. And here it is, in some spot in the human world, not in the otherworld at all. I may never find it again, but that's alright. It's real, and now it's mine. He caught Angharad's eye and pointed at it with his chin. She looked back at it, and nodded her understanding.

He turned forward again and rode through the way with the pack.

~

George emerged into the clearing to find Brynach on the ground at the far side holding a sword, and Rhian standing over him, a knife in each fist. As he cantered up, Madog tried to attack, but was warded off by Rhodri, still mounted. Creiddylad stood by, watching.

He heard the thunder of Edern, Gwyn, and Eurig riding past him, metal scraping as they drew weapons. Rhian was preventing Madog from closing by directing his horse away. George could feel it. Clever girl, he thought.

Madog looked up at the noise as the charge started from the far end of the clearing, and shrugged. Without ceremony he turned and galloped into the woods, slowing to climb the hill back to the entrance way, Creiddylad at his back.

George brought the pack over to Brynach and Rhian. "Alright, you two?" Rhian, breathing hard, nodded and called her horse and Brynach's over.

Brynach said, "It's just an ankle, I think. I can't stand on it."

Tegwen and Ceridwen rode up and dismounted to take a look.

George looked for Gwyn, circling back with Edern and Eurig. "I know you want to go after him—me, too—but we can't until we collect everyone. We'll have lost several people here in the woods."

Idris set up a hue and cry, and half a dozen stragglers made it down into the clearing after a few minutes. George stopped them to listen for a moment, and they could hear one other in the woods, shouting as he came. This proved to be one of the villagers from Danderi who had joined them along the ride. He was leading his limping horse.

George checked around with a mental call and turned up no one else. The way behind him, to the oak tree meadow, winked out. Rhodri felt it, too, and gave George a look of alarm.

"Alright, that's everyone. I've checked," George told Gwyn. "Madog and Creiddylad aren't here, they've probably already gone through ahead of us. We have to leave."

Eurig helped get Brynach lifted to his horse, where he rode with one leg loose. The villager rode double with a friend, leading his horse. They climbed through the woods back to the entrance way following George and the pack, as quickly as they could manage.

~

As he rode out of this way at the top of the field, he picked up the pace, alarmed at the lead Madog was gaining and worried about the ways closing behind him. Danderi across the river below gleamed, still lit for the new year celebrations. The villagers who had joined the hunt field here raised a shout as they saw their home.

They crossed the river and clattered down the street back to the inn. There they found their entrance way in the middle of the road had been marked off with benches, to prevent anyone accidentally going through. Someone helpfully shouted, "Two passed through ahead of you, several minutes ago."

Drinkers in the doorway of the inn spotted the hunt returning and called to their comrades inside. Half a dozen riders pulled out of the hunt field, saluting Gwyn as they passed him, and crying, "Well done, huntsman," to George.

The innkeeper, standing in his doorway, offered drinks to everyone. Gwyn and Edern, grim in their pursuit of Madog and Creiddylad refused, but two of Gwyn's guests decided to stay for a while, declaring that they knew where they were and how to return home through more conventional ways.

Behind them, George felt the way across the river wink out. Can we be stranded here, he wondered.

We've wasted enough time. Without waiting for Gwyn, he waved a couple of the men in the streets at the benches blocking the way and they hastened to pull them back, just in time for George to send the pack streaming through.

~

George expected most of the stragglers to have been lost here in the boulder field. The entrance and exit ways, both, were in unmarked and undistinguished patches of ground, and only a very lucky rider would be likely to find them without landmarks.

Not far from the entrance way the wiser people had dismounted and gathered together without wandering off, afraid of missing the hunt on its return and being left behind.

They cheered and remounted as they saw the hunt come through at the other way. Idris rode into the group to question them, and they reported the flight of Madog and Creiddylad a few minutes ago. Some had tried to follow them out, using Madog as a guide, but he threatened them off.

They rejoined the hunt field as quickly as possible, and George led them to the entrance way just as the other way behind him vanished.

~

As George popped out of the woods into the open field, still glowing in the moonlight, he found it deserted. Any stragglers here had already found their own way out, in one direction or the other.

He brought the pack down to the entrance way with its dim view of the bridge at the village, and held them there, off to one side.

Gwyn sent Idris through ahead for news of Madog and stood next to George, with the hunt staff, to let the hunt field go by.

As the last one crossed, the way behind them at the other end of the field winked out. George and Gwyn rode on together last through the way and brought the pack out, their horses' hooves rattling on the wooden bridge surface.

Gwyn paused at the foot of the bridge to let the pack go by, and George brought them back to the spot they started from, marveling at the size of the crowd that had returned to cheer their arrival. Isolda's wagon was gone, and all traces of her death with it.

A moment after Benitoe with the last hounds exited the way, it closed.

George reached for the oliphant and sounded it, for the third and final time. The low lonesome echoing note silenced the crowd. He felt the world start to spin again into its new year, and then he could no longer hear the beat of it.

The parties on both sides rejoined each other across the bridge. A girl ran up to George, shyly, holding his tricorn up to him. He bent over his saddle and thanked her gravely.

Idris made his way back to Gwyn through the crowd as the hunt field broke up. Gwyn brought him to George, standing with the pack, and waved Edern over to join them.

"Madog's headed in the direction of the manor, with your sister," Idris told them.

Gwyn looked at George. "He's going to try for the ways. We'll need you there, kinsman."

George took in Rhian beside him. She was running on nerves but still alert. "Can you take the pack home? Slowly?" The hounds were tired and dragging.

"I can do it, huntsman," she said. Benitoe and Rhys nodded.

Tegwen came up and said, “Brynach and I will ride with them.” George thanked her.

An impromptu posse formed up. Gwyn, with Edern, took the lead, and Idris, Ceridwen, Eurig, Rhodri, Angharad, and George joined behind them.

With a loud cry of “Make way” to clear their path through the celebrants, they cantered up the road in the moonlight, breaking into a gallop as they left the crowd behind.

CHAPTER 37

Their pursuit was in danger of being blocked for a while by clusters of riders back from the hunt making their slow way home, but they pulled off the road to let them by as they heard them come up behind them.

George felt Mosby tired beneath him, and knew the other horses were also worn out, like their riders. But Madog and Creiddylad were no better off, and they had to try and catch them, if they could.

Mosby wasn't built for speed and fell to the back of the group. Angharad slowed down and waited for him, so that no one rode alone on the dark road.

Gwyn and Edern barely hesitated at the manor gates. The guards waved them on up the road and the chase continued, a bit more cautiously now, to spare the horses.

By the time they reached Daear Llosg, George and Angharad were a couple hundred yards behind. Madog had clearly been there for several minutes trying to open the way George had sealed. George could see that it hadn't worked. The seal felt intact, almost glowing in response to Madog's attempts.

As Gwyn's group approached, Madog gave up on it and turned his horse west, toward the ridge. Gwyn and Edern halted below them, letting their horses recover. George and Angharad caught up and made their way to the front with Gwyn.

Creiddylad sat her horse between the the parties and looked at her brothers. Then she looked up to Madog, about to send his partially recovered horse up the slope. She said nothing, but Madog, hesitating, held out his hand to her and beckoned. She turned to follow and they both rode off into the woods.

George told Gwyn, "They're making for the small way, behind the palisade."

"Can you shut it?"

"Not from here."

Setting themselves to one more effort, the posse followed as hard as their horses would allow.

~

Madog swore in frustration as he heard the hooves approaching. That damned human's seal held the way closed against him and he couldn't break through. It was outrageous—he created this way in the first place. It belonged to him.

Well, too bad for Creiddylad, that was her way home. He'd planned to ride though with her and close it behind them.

Damn that Cyledr. Wrong girl at the bridge. If he'd just acted quickly instead of taunting them at the end it might still all have worked. The transported way-loop ambush did its job, just as planned. He'd got that part right.

He'd been surprised when Cyledr's way-token successfully closed the way at the bridge, he hadn't expected that to work, a token-based claim-and-close on a new way. Didn't work long, though, once Cernunnos got involved. Didn't expect to see him. That vision still dried his mouth. Glad he wasn't after me.

Must be his fault that none of the ways closed for me on the way back. I wonder how he did it? Maybe he's the nominal owner, so he has the prior claim. That killed my backup plan, to trap the rest of the hunt behind one of the temporary ways on the return. Now they're breathing down my neck instead of being lost somewhere coming back overland

Time to regroup and get back home, through the hidden way. I bet they don't know about that one, and my horse has had a few minutes to breathe.

He turned to climb the slope, and saw Creiddylad poised below him. She held onto her dignity, but her eyes held a mute appeal. Abandon her to her brothers or take her with him? She could never go back. Well, he'd seen worse. She'd held up her end of the deal, after all.

He reached out his hand and beckoned to her, oddly pleased to see the gratitude in her face. Together they cantered up the hill.

~

Before they could reach the wide place in the trail, pushing through the dark paths in the woods, George felt the two they pursued take the way and vanish. When they arrived a few minutes later, the spot was empty, and they started to crowd into it, until George at the rear called them to stop.

"You can't see it and might blunder through." They made a space for him to bring Mosby to the front.

The open way remained invisible to everyone except George. He dismounted, handing his reins to Angharad to hold, and walked over to it, marking its line by dragging his boot along the ground in the moonlight as he had done before. The rest of the riders filed in and took their places around it.

Gwyn and Edern sat their horses directly in front and sat silent and grim.

"What would you have me do, kinsmen?" George asked, looking up at both of them. "We could follow them."

Idris behind them said, "Never, into an enemy way, prepared for ambush."

Gwyn and Edern looked at each other for a few long moments, coming to a silent agreement. Gwyn said, "Close it, kinsman, destroy it utterly."

George looked to Rhodri for guidance. He seemed uncertain but nodded. So, a way could be eliminated, not just sealed. But how? He studied it until he thought he understood. A way through space was something like the parting of the Red Sea by Moses. The waters, held back precariously, wanted to rush back in and so here did space press on all sides to crush the tunnel into oblivion.

So he let it do so.

He felt a gentle breeze on his face as some of the trapped air puffed out, stirring the leaves at their feet. The way was gone, as if it had never been. Rhodri stared at George, his face pale.

Gwyn and Edern joined hands on horseback, facing where the way had been. "We, Gwyn ap Nudd and Edern ap Nudd," speaking alternately, "had once a sister, Creiddylad ferch Nudd. We renounce her, now and forever."

Gwyn intoned. "I, for her part in the murder of Iolo ap Huw and Isolda, daughter of Ives, and Maonirn, servant at our inn, and for the attempted murder of my foster-daughter Rhian ferch Rhys, and my kinsman George Talbot Traherne, and Brynach, kinsman of my vassal and friend Eurig ap Gruffyd."

Behind him, Eurig nodded.

Edern responded solemnly. "I, for her part in the murder of my son Rhys ab Edern and his wife and retainers, and the attempted murder of my grand-daughter Rhian ferch Rhys."

The words fell into the night's darkness and resonated there with a feeling of breaking bonds. George felt something stir within him, as if Cernunnos had heard and noted it.

Idris led them all out, in silence, down the paths to the back palisade gate. The guards were surprised to see them there, so late at night, but cheerfully wished them joy of the new year.

It will be good to get home, George thought as they made their way together to the stables in what was left of the moonlight.

~

At the stables they found people waiting for them.

George dismounted stiffly and walked over to Benitoe, standing alone on the edge of the group. His face was desolate, and George grasped his shoulders and bowed his head in sorrow. There was nothing they could say to each other that would do any good.

Eventually, Benitoe said. "I must go now, to Ives, but I wanted to report. All the hounds are back safe, and Rhys and Rhian have gone to bed."

"Please tell Ives how deeply I grieve with you two," George said, as they parted.

Tegwen had waited for Eurig, but there was no sign of Brynach. Eurig was telling her about the renunciation of Creiddylad as George approached.

"How's Brynach?" he asked.

"He'll be fine," Tegwen said. "He rode with Benitoe all the way back."

Eurig bowed to George formally. "We are very grateful for his preservation."

"Tell Rhian. She did most of it, when Madog threatened, and against Scilti before that."

"Indeed I will do so." He looked at his wife and smiled. "I hope we'll be seeing ever more of her, in time."

He put his arm around Tegwen and they walked quietly off toward the manor.

That left Angharad, next to him. "I'll see you back at your house," she said, touching his shoulder, and turned up the lane.

He looked in on Mosby, and found him already drowsing, brushed down and comfortable in his box. When he came back out, he found he was the only one left.

He walked slowly, still limping, over to the kennels and was stopped in his tracks by the sight of Isolda's wagon, standing abandoned outside the kennels on the far side of the gates, its decorations torn and drooping. He felt the blow in the pit of his stomach. His head bowed, he opened the gates to the kennel yard.

Quietly, he entered each of the pens from the corridor side, looking at the drowsy hounds on their benches and telling each of them how good they were, how proud he was of them. The occasional resonant thump of a tail was the only noise he heard.

No one else was in the kennels.

He stepped inside the huntsman's office and put the oliphant away, locking the cupboard. He couldn't think of anything else that needed to be done. He walked out down the huntsman's alley. All was quiet in the lane, no one was about and no lights were visible until he opened his own gate to see lights on in his house.

He walked heavily up the porch stairs, and there was Alun to greet him at the door.

"You shouldn't have stayed up," George said.

Alun waved that aside. "Angharad returned a little while ago. She may be asleep by now."

George took a chair in the hall and Alun helped him off with his boots and provided slippers. "Can I get anything for you?"

"No, go to bed."

Alun showed no intention of leaving until George went upstairs, so he reluctantly stood up again and climbed one last flight, leaning on the banister.

It was too much work.

George, dead on his feet, fumbled with the buttons on his shirt. His bed looked soft but somehow he'd gotten himself tangled up after he got his coat and vest off. He remembered putting his gun on the chest of drawers and emptying all his pockets, but he kept reaching into pockets, expecting to find more, until he made himself stop, holding onto the furniture.

Something was missing. What was it? What had he forgotten to do?

He turned around, and things went blank for a moment.

He found himself in front of the door to Angharad's room, down the hall. He raised a heavy hand—odd, was that his hand?—and knocked softly.

She came and opened it. He looked past her into the room and could see that she'd been reading.

"I wanted to make sure you got back alright," he said, his tongue clumsy. She waited for more, but he swayed, and she reached out to him.

"Let's put you to bed, my dear," she said. She led him by the hand over to the far side of her wide bed, and made him sit.

He focused on her, confused.

She bent over and unfastened his breeches, removing them with his delayed assistance and then addressed him, sitting there, her hand on his shoulder.

"Lie down," she said, and pushed sideways.

He collapsed bonelessly on top of the covers and kept falling, into a dreamless sleep.

CHAPTER 38

George rolled over, comfortable in his bed, but the smell of bacon was proving hard to ignore.

Something was wrong with the light, though. Too bright for early morning. He opened his eyes. It's late, I've overslept, he thought in alarm.

Wait, where am I? This is Angharad's room. He looked down. He was on top of the covers, mostly dressed, but someone had thrown a blanket over him. He had only the vaguest recollection of last night, tapping on her door. A flush crept up his face. What must she think of me?

Well, can't have been too bad. At least she gave me a blanket, he chuckled.

He stretched, wincing at the wound in his right leg, and took stock. He felt much better, not exactly well-rested, that would need much more sleep, but cheerful and ready for action.

Better clean up and get downstairs before they eat all that bacon.

~

After a late breakfast, George shy in front of a placid Angharad, he walked to the stable to check on Mosby again. Finding him well, he went on to the kennels and stopped, frozen in place.

Rhian was there, alone, trying to take down the decorations on Isolda's wagon. She went at it wildly, tearing the garlands into heaps at her feet.

She heard George's involuntary protest and turned to him defensively. "I want to clear it all away. I don't want Ives and Benitoe to have to look at it."

George opened his arms in pity and she fled into them, weeping against his shoulder. He wrapped her up against his broad chest and rocked her, crooning, "Hey, now, hey," and other soothing noises. He concentrated on being a warm comfort, a shelter from the world of sorrow she was growing up into. He thought of the oak tree standing solid on its hill.

Eventually the sobs broke down into coherent words and he released her enough to let her speak, muffled, into his coat. "It's my fault she died. She did it to save me. Now I have to be worth it, and how can I be?" She started wailing again, and he tucked her back in against his chest thinking about what to say.

He looked down at the top of her head. "You know, it's one of the finest things anyone can do, to give their life for their friends. It's the death of a hero."

No reaction. "She saw the threat, faster than anyone else, and she decided, I can save my best friend. And she did."

Still no response. "When my time comes, I hope I can be as brave and as selfless. What she did was glorious and you'll always remember her for it. It's for those she left behind to honor her and not grieve, as best we can."

Hiccups, now, against his chest. "All of us must die, but how we face it is up to us," he said. "And how we handle the death of our comrades."

Over her head he saw Rhys approaching, concerned about his sister. George released Rhian and tilted her face up, one finger under her chin. "This will hurt for a long time, but eventually you'll carry her here, I promise you," laying his hand on his heart over his dampened coat, "and she'll be a comfort, always."

Rhys glanced at the wagon and his sister's face with understanding. "Let me help, Rhian. We'll get it all taken care of, and I'll have the wagon put away so no one needs to look at it."

They turned back to the wagon, Rhian's breath still catching as she calmed down. As they worked, Rhys kept up a steady conversation about how brave she was fighting for Brynach and resisting Cyledr. As she visibly took hold of her emotions again, she started to ask about Cyledr, what his story was. George and Rhys filled in what they knew.

When the wagon was finally stripped, and all the trimmings piled back into it for disposal, Rhys went off to arrange for horses and a wagoner to take it away. Rhian looked at it and choked up again.

"What is it, my dear?" George said.

"Isolda wanted you to see all of us together decorating it yesterday. We had such a good time."

He hugged her from the side with one arm, while she stood tall, tears running down her face.

~

George and Angharad were enjoying a more substantial mid-day meal with Alun, when they heard a knock at the back door.

Alun brought back Tanguy, the kennel-man, his face saddened.

He bowed formally to George and Angharad, and they rose from the table to return the gesture.

"Master Ives has invited you, all three, to attend our farewell to Isolda at Daear Llosg, at sunset."

George glanced at Angharad for agreement, then said, "We'll be there, to stand in sorrow with her friends and family."

Tanguy bowed again and left.

"I can't picture her given to fire," George said, dismayed.

Angharad shook her head. "That's not what happens. We all use that spot for ceremonies, but the lutins will take her on and bury her afterward."

"I didn't know. Will there be anything at graveside?"

"Their burial ground is private. We don't intrude upon it. I'm not sure just where it is."

Angharad turned to Alun. "I'll leave after the ceremony this afternoon."

George would be sorry to see her go. He invited her out onto the porch, the day being too mild to waste indoors.

"About last night…"

"You were very tired," she smiled. "Nothing to be embarrassed about."

He shook his head ruefully. "I feel like I was on a new year's binge, and not a drop taken."

"You should go take a nap," she said. "You have a lot of catching up to do. I can look after myself."

A nap sounded like an excellent idea, his stomach full and the temperature just right. "Alright, I will. Please ask Alun to make sure I'm up in time to dress for the ceremony." He rose and went in, up to his bed, opening the windows wide to let in the air, and adding blankets next to him on the bed in case he got chilly.

~

Alun leaned over and shook him. He opened his eyes, drowsily.

"Sorry to wake you, but Rhodri's here."

How long had he been asleep? He checked his watch and found he'd been out about an hour and a half. He rubbed his face and reached for his shoes and outer garments.

What did Rhodri want?

Walking downstairs, he found Angharad and Rhodri laughing together in the study. Rhodri looked up as he heard George's steps.

"What a wonderful painting she's done of you," he said.

George smiled. "Yes. I love it."

The simple declaration gladdened Angharad's face, and Rhodri raised his eyebrow as he caught the look between them.

Reluctantly, Rhodri stood up. "Sorry to intrude, but we didn't see you at lunch and were concerned. Gwyn is convening an initial meeting to deal with things after last night, and he wants it over well before Isolda's funeral. He sent me to summon you both."

Angharad said to Alun, before they left, "Would you arrange a seat in a wagon for me, for the ceremony, so my horse can rest a bit longer before I leave tonight?"

George added, "I'm down to just Llamrei myself, with Mosby exhausted and Afanc wounded."

"I'll take care of it," Alun said, shutting the door behind them.

As they walked toward the manor, they encountered departing guests clustered in the yard in family groups, sorting out horses and belongings. One fellow caught sight of George, and bounced over to shake his hand, giving a respectful little bow over it. "Thank you, huntsman."

Soon there was a steady stream of them slowing him down. George recognized some of the blowhards from the earlier hunts who had had a lot to say about Iolo's death and human huntsmen. They all thanked him, often with a little ritual gesture. George murmured something polite to each one and kept on moving.

Rhodri laughed at his bewildered look as the last walked off. "It's not really you they're thanking, you understand."

He laughed again as it finally dawned on George what they wanted. Of course, it was Cernunnos they were trying to impress. His lips quirked. Lot of good that'll do them.

"They think you might be staying and they want to be in your, um, his, good graces for next time," Rhodri said.

He paused as they approached the manor doors. "Are you staying?" He looked straight into George's face.

At his side, George could feel Angharad waiting to hear his answer.

"I don't know," he said, slowly. "I have some decisions to make."

~

The three of them were last to the council room. George took a seat between Angharad and Rhodri and looked around. This was Gwyn's inner council and family, as well as members of last night's posse.

Gwyn and Edern, with Rhys, Rhian, and Rhodri represented the family. I suppose I do, too, George thought, with a bit of surprise. Ceridwen and Idris were there, of course, and Eurig and Angharad as special guests.

Gwyn greeted George. "I'm pleased to see you well, kinsman."

Before George could murmur a reply, an irrepressible yawn made its way out. "Sorry, sir, still a little short on sleep."

A chuckle traveled round the table.

Gwyn called the session to order. "I would like to start by thanking our huntsman for a successful hunt under difficult conditions."

Gwyn and Edern were content with nods, but everyone else around the table rose and bowed to him, before reseating themselves. George's face flamed with embarrassment.

Gwyn said, "I also wish to especially thank Eurig and Angharad for their help last night. I want all of you to know what will result from that, and what we have discovered."

He paused to order his thoughts.

"Today we opened the way that Creiddylad had caused to be closed against all others and took back the estates we had granted her from our domain. Her way is now restored to public access."

George leaned over to Rhodri. "You've been busy," he whispered.

Rhodri's mouth quirked.

Gwyn said, "Idris has made an initial inspection." He nodded to Idris to report to the group.

"This morning, Mederei Badellfawr, Creiddylad's bodyguard, came to me as spokesman for Creiddylad's party here. She's offered to help by easing the transition with the people in charge at Edgewood. I believe she's ashamed of Creiddylad's actions and wants no part of it. I've left her at Edgewood with some of my men and Ifor Moel, who will give us a full report.

"Our initial impression is grim. It will take a long time for this estate and its people to recover. Not only does Creiddylad seem to have been an untalented ruler from the start, but Madog has been there for hundreds of years, we think, and made it worse. Her people are isolated, hungry, and mutinous. They've been cut off from trade."

Rhys asked, "What about the lutins that settled with them?"

"They've vanished. We think they're in hiding, not dead, and have reverted to their old hidden customs with the humans, only coming out at night, and so forth. We're going to need help from their families here to lure them out into the open again."

Gwyn said, "I well remember the counsels of some of you that this might come to pass when I gifted Creiddylad with Edgewood, and I grieve to learn my error has cost so much pain."

There was a moment of silence.

Well said, George thought. It's a confident ruler who can admit a mistake and own the results.

Gwyn said, "It will take years, many years, to restore Edgewood to health, and I must set a steward there. I intend to place my foster-son Rhys in this position, for his education, as a pledge of my determination to repair the damage, and for the good of the people."

The look of surprise on Rhys's face amused George. Well, I knew I would lose him as a whipper-in.

Rhys stammered a reply, thanking his foster-father. Rhian squeezed his hand and Edern looked gratified.

"Rhodri will work closely with him, to finish sorting out all the issues with the ways, and to give him some practical experience with diplomacy at its most basic level," Gwyn said.

George leaned over to Rhodri again and whispered, "Ouch."

Rhodri choked and kicked him under the table. Then he nodded to Gwyn in acknowledgment.

"These are our preliminary plans, and more will become clear once we have Ifor Moel's report."

He paused and looked around the table before continuing.

"Now, here, with our family and close friends, I want to tell you all what we think brought us to this point. Much of this story seems correct to me, though there's much we can't confirm.

"We believe Madog's home is west of the mountains, and that he claimed it several hundred years ago. We know he's a way-master of unusual skill. He has appeared at several courts in the old world, as if he were just another lesser fae, and at some point he met Gwythyr and formed an alliance.

"Gwythyr wanted what he always wants, but Madog wanted more. We think Madog covets Annwn for himself. It would make him one of the higher powers, if he were successful. He thought of Creiddylad as a way of getting close to us, and he sought her out.

"She had kept her one way restricted and her boundaries secure through her control of the tokens, under mine, but Madog showed her how he could do much, much more for her. We don't yet know how he gave her access to other ways, but she became his companion and partner, and he took her with him on his travels, under a glamour. Her annual appearance here, well-clothed, deflected concerns about the damage she was doing to Edgewood in its isolation, since we assumed that it must be on the trading routes somewhere.

"We don't know when this partnership began—we'll find out from the staff at Edgewood—but we first learned of Madog when Creiddylad began bringing him with her each year, about fifty years ago. I believe that marks the starting point of the plans that culminated last night. That's when they began trying to move the pieces around to make the great hunt fail.

"Eighteen years ago—you remember, Rhodri—our kinsman Rhodri finished his two years with the hunt and left for his music travels. He'd done his rotation early to free up time for this study. Soon after he left, Iolo's promising kinsman Islwyn was killed, hunting. Ceridwen and George now think, and I agree, that Islwyn may have been ambushed from some unknown way, arranged by Madog. There's no evidence for this, but it makes perfect sense as a first move on the part of the enemy.

"They may have hoped that a sudden loss of two whippers-in would cause the hunt to fail, but it didn't work as planned. Merfyn was the sole whipper-in for several years, but Iolo made do, and it must have seemed that no progress had been made.

"At this point, Creiddylad took an active hand and petitioned me to bring in Owen the Leash and his men, and I foolishly allowed it. Madog supplied them to her, of course. In retrospect, this was the setup for their second try at the hunt.

"Madog was clever. With each move he made, he allowed things to settle again afterward so that we would not detect the noose tightening. It wasn't until twelve years ago that he next showed his hand, partnering with Gwythyr. While Madog wanted to make the hunt fail, to capture Annwn, Gwythyr just wanted the destruction of my family by any means, as an end to itself.

"We now believe that Madog set up the false way that ambushed my brother's son, his wife, and all his retainers. We have reason to believe they're probably all dead."

Gwyn reached for his brother's hand with both of his and bowed his head over it. Edern's face was stony.

George caught the dismay on Rhys and Rhian's faces. This is the first time they've heard any of this, he thought.

Gwyn straightened up. "Luckily, the children were safe and, as soon as Rhys Vachan would let us," he looked mock-sternly at Rhys, "we brought them both here to be fostered. We thought Edern was the object of the attack and this would make them safer. It did remove them from Gwythyr's direct reach, but it gave Madog all his eggs in one basket.

"For all of this time I could not believe that Creiddylad would harm the family directly, that she would have anything to do with the death of her nephew or the attempt on the children. I was wrong."

Rhian spoke up, "It was the strangest thing. While Madog was attacking us in the clearing, where Brynach fell, she was looking at me in the oddest way, as if she were sorry, and not sorry, both."

It was a moment before Gwyn resumed.

"Since Rhys Vachan survived, Madog continued to bide his time with Owen the Leash in place, waiting for Rhys to join the hunt for the family stint, two years ago. Shortly thereafter, Merfyn's father Ithel was slain in a senseless fight, and he left to assume his father's domain. Was that death also part of this tale? I'm suspicious of coincidence and I think it was within Gwythyr's power to accomplish.

"Now the time was ripe to destroy the great hunt. All the pieces were in position. Gwythyr gave Cyledr Wyllt to Madog, as a weapon. Cyledr had found his way back to him long after his father's death. Madog gave him to Creiddylad, as a servant."

He paused. "To this day I don't understand if Gwythyr and Creiddylad know that Madog's used them both for his own plans.

Do they know of each other's involvement?" he said, looking at Edern.

"Who can tell?" Edern said.

"Madog sent Scilti in, independently, as an outsider. Scilti's job was to control Cyledr and cause any other mischief he could. Madog also provided spell-sticks and some form of way-tokens, whatever they needed."

Ceridwen spoke. "We think that Madog took from Creiddylad the personal traces needed to breach and nullify the palisade. She might not have known about it."

Gwyn nodded in agreement.

"Madog launched the final plan by having Cyledr kill Iolo, using a distracting disguise. It removed a piece and muddied the waters, both. Two weeks before the great hunt, with one whipper-in. What could we do?"

He looked at George, who tried to keep from squirming.

"At that very moment, Cernunnos took a hand. I don't know how he knew, thirty-odd years ago that we would need him—perhaps that's when Madog's plans to take over Annwn reached some particular point—but George's parentage raises many questions."

George was shocked. Was I bred for this, like a hound? What about my mother's marriage? Was my father Cernunnos himself or some sort of… avatar?

Did Cernunnos put me into place as a piece, to counter Madog's pieces? Cold-blooded bastard.

Gwyn said, "George came to us at Iolo's death, and all their plans began to unravel. When he brought the hounds back successfully, it must have unnerved Madog to think we might have found a substitute huntsman, and thus the attack at Daear Llosg the next day. We haven't unsealed that way yet to confirm it, but I think we'll find it leads to Edgewood. The fighters, of course, were probably provided by Madog. It must have made him particularly angry for his ambush to not only fail, but to be thwarted specifically by George."

Clang, George thought, another part of a higher plan slamming into place. He thought he could almost hear Cernunnos laugh.

Ceridwen said, "We don't know when the two hidden ways were created, but we've found many traces of the methods used for all of these things. Cyledr's possessions in the servants' rooms included unused spell-sticks which we're still studying, and unusual way-tokens. I searched his body at the end, and he was carrying more of them. I don't know how many of the ways at the great hunt were opened or tampered with by Cyledr, using these tools, but we know at least that he closed the first way that Gwyn opened for the hunt on the bridge."

Gwyn said, "We don't know exactly why Scilti killed Maonirn and passed through the palisade, but he may have been trying to get orders from Madog when he couldn't meet with Cyledr. He escaped, back through the same way that took Madog and Creiddylad late last night. That way is gone, now, destroyed by George."

Rhys asked, "Where did it lead?"

"I think it went to Madog's own lands," George said.

Gwyn said, "This is where we are today. Cernunnos seems to have assented to our continued rule, but our enemies are very much alive and currently unreachable. We have a great deal of work to do to heal what's ours at Edgewood."

He looked at George. "And we have a question that must be asked. Kinsman, will you stay and lead the hunt for us?"

You knew this would come. He shifted in his chair uncomfortably. "I'll tell you my decision, soon."

Gwyn persisted. "I want you to stay." Edern nodded.

"Soon," George said, stubbornly.

As the meeting began to break up, Edern came up to George and bowed. "Thank you for the life of my grand-daughter."

"Tell that to Ives," George said, and then was surprised at himself. Where did that come from, he wondered. Isolda's death wasn't Edern's fault.

~

George rode Llamrei alongside the wagon carrying Angharad, Alun, and Brynach as they entered Daear Llosg. Not much had been said as they came up the road from the manor. George was lost in his own thoughts about Isolda, her wonderful promise and the price she paid.

In the light of the setting sun, he was stunned to find so many people. It seemed that over a hundred lutins must be there, as well as most of the tall folk from the manor and much of the village. He took a position behind them and said to Rhys, who had ridden over to join them, "I had no idea there were so many lutins here."

"Many more will be at the interment, almost everyone who could travel here in time."

George recognized Brittou, from Iona's place, up with Ives at the front, as well as both the kennel-men, and Benitoe, his face desolate. Less than a day ago, he had a future all planned out, soon to be buried in the coffin lying before him.

The coffin seemed tiny, suitable for a child. It lay deep in a bed of autumn leaves in a wagon.

So much life, so much heart, in such a little space, George thought.

Gwyn stood in the first row, his head bowed.

Rhys said to George, "My grandfather asked me to make sure that the lutins at Edgewood are well taken care of, for the sake of Isolda and my sister's life."

At that George looked up sharply to Edern standing next to Gwyn, and their eyes met. Edern nodded formally, and George acknowledged him with respect. I was sorry I snapped at him when he thanked me, and here he's gone and done the right thing, George thought.

Ives stood forward and the crowd silenced.

"We will return to the soil, the mother of all. My daughter, Isolda, will shine within our hearts, until we join her there."

A hum rose up from the lutins, eerie in the still air.

Benitoe stood next to him.

"She was to be my wife. When I tracked her murderer-to-be I wished him worthy of a fight. My words have turned to ashes, and my strength to nothing."

Another hum saluted this.

Rhian walked to the front and stood next to them, nervous but determined.

"We were each other's best friends. She gave her life for me, and for all of mine I will remember and try to be worthy of it."

This time the hum sounded for a longer time, and George felt the pull to join in. To judge by the increased volume, he wasn't alone.

When it died down, Ives mounted the wagon with Benitoe, and Rhian stepped aside. The procession of lutins followed them, north up the village road.

~

On the road back to the manor, George rode up to Gwyn.

"I've been meaning to ask. Where do the whelps come from, that Iolo got each year? No one seems to be able to tell me."

Gwyn laughed. "It's very simple. When I win at Nos Galan Mai, if I do, I find I can open a temporary way, like the one at Nos Galan Gaeaf. Iolo would go through and bring back two pups, male and female, before the way closed."

"Where did he go? What's it like?"

"I don't know. I've never known what he sees or if it's the same every time. Or if anyone else is there, or if there are any choices of other whelps. I can't hold that way and go through it, both."

He looked at George. "This is the blood that keeps the pack going. We try to keep all the hounds in the pack within three generations of an out-blood cross like this. Persistent losses at Nos Galan Mai would weaken the pack, and then they might fail the hunt."

George rode in silence next to him for a moment, then said, "It seems to me you pay a heavy and somewhat precarious toll for your domain, sir."

"All things have a price," Gwyn said.

Instead of turning in at the manor gates, George continued with the villagers for a while and turned off to the west, ascending the meadows until he reached the start of the woods. The sun had almost vanished, only the afterglow still shining from the ridge behind him. He looked down the slope eastward, the direction of his home a couple of weeks ago, just a few miles and another world away.

Greenway Court's lights were visible to his left, behind the dark wall of the palisade, and to his right below him, along the stream, the lights of Greenhollow shimmered. Beyond them, to the east, was darkness.

He reached out and felt for the ways. The one he destroyed last night was truly gone, but he could still find the one he arrived through, unchanged. I could go home and visit, he thought. I'd have a lot to tell Grandfather.

The stars were coming out, the rising moon not having washed them all out yet. He looked up—no planes, of course.

A world without electricity. But does that really matter, he wondered. It's a world with strong ties, with a juice and sweetness to it. He could make a difference here, settle down to it.

His family needs him. Yes, this is his family, it feels like one now, not a group of strangers. They have enemies, and they need a huntsman. After all, he thought with a quirk to his lip, accepting it, I've been bred for the job.

He tried to single out Angharad's house in the village below. Maybe I can even form a family of my own.

What would happen if I went back? What if I'm long-lived, as Angharad suggested? And what place is there for my other new-found skills? Wouldn't I feel more out of place than ever?

We must take the world as we find it, in this life, but I've been given a choice.

He sat there for a few minutes more, until Llamrei stirred under him.

The moon's rising, he thought. Time to go home.

CHAPTER 39

George removed his hunt coat and vest in his bedroom and hung them up, taking out the red coat with its gold collar and the canary yellow vest he'd arrived in.

The hound walk this morning had been short and uneventful, the hounds still tired from the hunt on Saturday. Brynach's ankle didn't prevent him from riding in Rhys's spot, now that Rhys was trying on his new responsibilities. We're going to need some more recruits, George thought distantly.

As he came back downstairs, Alun faced him, distressed at his change of clothes.

"Don't worry," he said, patting him on the shoulder and walking out the door.

~

George halted at the top of the hill on Llamrei, and looked back down the slope toward the manor across the stream, the village hidden in the folds of land. This was where he'd first seen Gwyn's hunt, where Iolo had been killed.

I'm sorry I didn't get the chance to meet him, he thought. He could've taught me so much. But then, if he hadn't died, I probably wouldn't be here.

He checked again to make sure he had his entering way pinpointed, and rode into the woods, just as a fresh breeze brought a hint of the chill of winter coming.

He knew where he was going and sought out paths that took him there directly. The clearing with the way on its margin was just as he remembered it, in his first moment of panic, but this time he knew how to find the way itself.

He dismounted and hung Llamrei's reins on a bush. This way wasn't transparent, like the one on the burning ground or the one Gwyn opened on the bridge. Not until he took a step in could he see what was on the other side. He hit the fallen trees immediately, all the way across, and backed up again into the clearing.

I'll never be able to set Llamrei at that directly, he thought. She'd have to be already jumping to clear it, and she can't see it.

He stuck his head back in and saw that the uprooted base of one of the trees created a gap beside the trunks, to the right.

Back in the clearing, he gave this some thought. Alright, if I can just expand the way in that direction, we can go around. Now how would I do that?

He set his mind to it, put metaphorical hands to the right hand margin, and tugged. The opening resisted, and then began to move slightly. He stopped. No, that's not right, I want to leave the left edge in place. This time he added an imaginary foot anchoring the left hand margin, and pulled against it.

The opening refused to move for several long minutes, but George persisted. Finally, it seemed to stretch to the right, growing in size horizontally to do it, keeping its original height. When he had extended it sideways about six feet, he stopped, maintaining his hold.

The feeling of elasticity started to fade and, when it was completely, gone, George released his hold. He moved over to the new right side of the way and looked in again. Perfect. He could pass through here with Llamrei.

He was pleased with himself. I wonder if this is how it's supposed to be done? He hadn't gotten that far in Ceridwen's books.

Unhitching Llamrei from her bush, he remounted and walked her through, stilling her alarm at walking into apparent bushes. She was fine once she saw the ground properly on the other side.

He found the weather just the same, a fresh chilly breeze stirring the leaves. Something was different, however, something hard to pin down.

Ah. He could hear farm equipment, a faint sound of diesel engine. An air brake from a truck on the distant highway. The general almost subliminal sound of civilization.

George set his course for the back roads to his grandfather's place.

George approached his grandfather's house, riding over the back fields. Monday wasn't a hunting day, and so far he hadn't spotted any other riders on a weekday morning. Good, he wanted to be inconspicuous, it's why he'd donned his old clothes. He didn't see any cars from visitors in the driveway as he neared the house.

He heard the dogs barking inside and thought he recognized one deep voice.

He paused on the driveway, checking again to make sure he could still find the way. It was one of two he could sense, within range.

His grandfather stepped out to see who it was, tall and upright. Why, George thought in surprise, he looks just the same, white-haired and slender, but still vigorous. It seemed impossible, so much had changed in his own life in such a short time.

His grandfather's face lit up to see him. He opened the door again to let the dogs out and called back into the house, "Georgia, he's back."

The dogs rushed out, all of his grandfather's and both of his own. Llamrei danced in alarm, and he automatically calmed everyone, shushing the dogs. His grandfather looked surprised at the sudden quiet.

George dismounted, holding the reins, a bit shy now that he was here. His grandfather embraced him, then stepped back to look him over. He spotted the different clothes, except for the coat and vest. He saw the saber attached to the saddle and walked over to it, fingering the straps that held it. George had forgotten it was there, it was just part of his gear now.

Watching his grandfather, George fondled his dogs, deep-voiced coonhound Hugo with his paws planted on his chest, and Sergeant, sniffing him all over.

Gilbert walked around Llamrei and returned to his grandson.

"Fine mare," he said. "Where's Mosby?"

"Taking a rest. He had a hard hunt Saturday night."

"Night?"

"It's a long story," George said. His grandmother was standing in the open doorway at the top of the porch stairs, watching them.

"I daresay." Gilbert gave him a searching look. "Seems like you could use some rest, too. Come inside. We'll put your horse up in the stable, and you can tell us all about it."

George gave his grandmother a long hug at the top of the steps, and then they all went inside. She sat them at the kitchen table, and George looked around with fresh eyes, marveling.

He could clearly hear the buzz of the fluorescent lights and the hum of the refrigerator motor. Behind that was the sound of the house's furnace kicking on and off to maintain the temperature. Floating over it all, like a high thin note, was the smell of the cleaners she used, the partially filled garbage can under the sink, the contents of the fridge when she opened it. He heard a car go by on the road and could almost feel his ears swivel to track it.

The lights, suspended from the high ceiling, seemed very bright.

His grandmother said, "Why are you limping, dear?" He shrugged it off, then searched her face looking for traces of Gwyn. They were there, in the slender shape, the dark hair, and the mouth—enough to convince him. Her hair had never turned gray, but she was getting frail and was clearly approaching the end of a normal human lifespan.

His grandfather watched him. "Let's give the boy something to eat first, Georgia. It's good just to have him home."

They spoke of inconsequentials while they ate, easing back into normality. Gilbert filled him in on events at the hunt, and Georgia talked about the doings of their neighbors. George said little, but smiled in appreciation at their stories. He couldn't keep up this reserve much longer, though, and dreaded starting.

He pushed his plate aside and cleared his throat. "Grandmother, how much do you know about your father?"

She stilled at the question. Why, she knows quite a lot, George realized.

"I knew he was somehow unnatural, he never aged. I was almost a teenager before I realized, you know how children are. I knew he had a way with animals that was uncanny. I could never ride like he did, or train my dogs as well. I don't think he noticed. I did, though. No one handled horses and hounds like he did."

Gilbert patted her hand as she spoke.

"He was away a lot, but many fathers traveled. He was distant, but then a lot of fathers were. It wasn't until I was almost grown that I understood that his distance and his lack of change were part of him and had nothing to do with me."

"Did you ever ask him about it?" George said.

"Only once, when I was fifteen. I worked up the nerve on a day when he seemed especially relaxed. I'll never forget, he looked at me with the saddest expression, as if something were going to happen that he couldn't save me from. It scared me. 'Never mind what I'm like,' he said, 'just remember that I loved your mother, and you, too.' That didn't satisfy my curiosity, but I was afraid to ever ask again."

Gilbert said, "He had a reputation for fair dealings, but he was away a lot and he unnerved his neighbors at Bellemore when he was here. There were few visitors to the house, unrelated to hunt business. I met your grandmother hunting, and after that, you couldn't keep me away."

They smiled fondly at each other.

"I was a regular visitor, the only one, I think. After we married, it was a great surprise to us when he vanished so soon, his life seemed so unchanging."

Georgia said, "I never believed he just died. But there was nothing to look into, it was very neatly documented, and so we had to let it go and get on with our lives."

"And then you sent those strange notes," his grandfather said, "and we wondered again."

George began his tale of being lost in the Bellemore woods and meeting the buck, his voice becoming less tentative and more matter-of-fact as he went along.

His grandmother had cleared the plates long since. Now she was at the stove making a fresh batch of tea for them.

George sat in silence, fondling the ears of his dogs. They hadn't left his side since his return.

She said, slowly, "My father was never around for Halloween. I always spent the night with a friend. It was a neighborhood curiosity, especially when the next day was a hunting day. I guess now I know why."

"So, why did it have to be you, at the wild hunt?" Gilbert asked.

So far, they hadn't scoffed at his story. It fit well enough with their old memories of Gwyn, and they let him tell it without interruption. He'd taken them as far as the setting and the people, and something about the importance of the great hunt and the politics.

Now he would have to tell them more about what he was.

"Grandfather, how much do you know about my father?"

Very little, it turned out.

"Léonie, your mother, wanted to travel after college. It was the fashion and there was no reason not to indulge her. She was planning to work her way east across Europe, starting with Ireland." He rubbed his chin. "She never got past Wales."

"Did you know Gwyn met her a few times as a child, on her pony at Bellemore?"

"No, I never did. I guess she wasn't supposed to be there and so she never told us."

"She wouldn't have known who he was," George said. "Just some charming man on a horse who admired her determination with her pony."

"Imagine him looking in like that," Georgia said.

"It saddens them that their human children live such short lives, and that they can't stay to see it."

Gilbert coughed. "Anyway, when your mother got to Wales, she stopped calling. Instead, she started to write letters. Long, flowing letters, many pages each. We kept them, we kept all the papers, her writings, his things, everything."

"I know. I want to go through it all, but I can't do it right now, on this trip."

He realized what he'd said the instant it slipped out. They'd thought he was back for good, and the dismay was clear on their faces.

He tried to prepare them. "You don't understand. My father was like Gwyn, sort of, only more so."

He leaned forward, leaning his elbows on the table and propping his chin on his hands. "You know the 'Horned Man' inn signs, with the antlers?"

They nodded.

"That's a remnant of an old Celtic god, Cernunnos. I'm not sure how the connection works, but that's where your in-laws come from."

His grandfather leaned back in his chair. "I know this is real, I've seen the sword on your saddle. I knew Gwyn and I trust you, but this is… very difficult."

"That's almost exactly what I said." George laughed quietly.

He stood up and led his grandmother back to the table. "Stop fussing at the stove for a moment."

When they were both seated, he reached for the horned man, grateful that the kitchen was large but mindful of the lights in the ceiling.

His grandparents caught their breath, and Georgia reached for her husband's hand. She raised her free hand to her cheek as her eyes widened.

He was afraid of scaring them worse, and so stood motionless, letting them take a good long look. Then he turned slowly all the way around for them.

"There's more," he said, in his deep, alien voice.

His grandfather swallowed. "Continue."

He pulled up the form of Cernunnos. He was thankful that there was no sense of his personality to complicate things.

Gilbert stood up and walked over, reaching for the antlers, and George bent his knees to make that easier. His grandfather turned back and lifted his wife up, leading her over to George. "Come on, dear, it's alright."

She stroked his furry cheeks as he bowed his head to her, careful with the long antlers. "How handsome," she murmured, scratching him between the ears.

He inhaled deeply, imprinting their scents, the smell of family. Then he backed away and pulled back both forms.

He let them sit down first before he joined them, wary of their reaction.

Gilbert abruptly stood up again and brought over a bottle of bourbon and three glasses. Georgia shook her head, but he poured some out for his grandson and himself. "Here you come back and I start drinking in the middle of the afternoon."

The chuckle broke some of the tension, and George continued with his story.

~

"So you led the Wild Hunt Saturday night?" Gilbert asked.

"I know it sounds like a fairy tale when you say it that way, but it was deadly serious. People died, one of them innocent."

"Someone you knew," his grandmother said.

"She had a family and a betrothed, and she gave her life to save another girl."

A sad silence held them for a moment.

"You're planning to go back," Gilbert said. "For how long?"

"For real, to make a life there. I fit that world. I may live as long as they do, and there are other things, not as easy to show you." He looked at them apologetically. "And I have family there, too."

"Are you sure you want to do this?" his grandmother asked.

"Who can be sure? But at least I get to make a choice."

His grandfather deflected the awkward emotions by turning businesslike. "So, how will this work?"

"I'll be back for visits, and soon. I'll need to arrange to move a few items. May I take my parents' things for a while when I come back?"

Gilbert waved his hand. "Of course. What about your job, your home, your friends?"

"I'm going to need some help winding things down, but we can make a plan together. I'll come back in a few days and we can swap notes about the best way to do it. I want to ask Gwyn how he arranged his affairs at Bellemore, too. Maybe I should set up something like that."

"Alright," his grandfather said briskly. "I'll jot some ideas down. Can you arrange some regular communication so we have some way of reaching you?"

"I don't see why not, but I'll have to figure it out."

They spent a few more moments sketching things out.

George stood. "I'll take the dogs with me now—thanks for looking after them."

He glanced around the kitchen.

"What is it, dear?" his grandmother asked.

"I'd like to bring someone a gift."

"What sort of thing?"

"Oh, just a token, you know, like flowers."

She smiled. "Has she ever tasted oranges?"

George laughed. "I don't know—what a good idea. How did you know it was a woman?"

She brought him a net bag of oranges from the fridge. "You have the look of a courting man, I've seen it before." She clung suddenly to his free hand. "Bring her to meet us someday."

She stepped back, then, releasing him. "And tell my father that I miss him and wish him well. Invite him to come see an old lady sometime."

Angharad walked out the kitchen door when she heard Cabal barking, Ermengarde eagerly trying to keep him company with her yips. She was surprised to see George trot into the work yard in his old red coat, and then she noticed the dogs at his heels, a tall lanky blue-tick hound and a medium-sized yellow dog with upright ears and a pointed muzzle.

He's been home, she thought, dismayed. Has he come to say good-bye? She held her breath.

The dogs sniffed each other over carefully, wagging. George gave her a cheerful greeting as he dismounted. "I've brought some of the family to meet you."

Relieved, she said, "This must be Hugo, I suppose," looking at the handsome hound with his long ears.

"Yes, and the feist is Sergeant." The yellow dog looked up at his name.

He reached up and removed the bag of oranges which he'd wrapped in his grandmother's kitchen towel to keep clean. "These are from my grandparents. Do you know this fruit?"

He opened the bag for her, and she took one out, holding it in her hands and inhaling the fragrance. "I haven't had one of these in a very long time. They don't travel well."

She turned back to the kitchen door, saying over her shoulder. "Come in and we'll share them."

He put Llamrei away in the stable and walked up the back steps bringing all the dogs along with him. They flopped in a pile near the woodstove and lost little time in drowsing off.

Angharad looked at them in amusement. "That didn't take long."

"They know friends when they see them," George said. She glanced up at him and caught his eye.

She busied herself cutting up two of the oranges and they sat at the table, peeling them messily and devouring them with simple enjoyment.

⁓

They stood side by side together at the basin of the sink to wash the sticky juice off their faces and hands. George smiled at the pleasure of being clean again, his mouth tingling with the tart sweetness of the fruit.

Still smiling, he looked down at Angharad who was saying something he didn't hear. He turned and bent his head, drawing in the scent of her hair. She stopped talking. He exhaled and did it again, and then he kissed her, strong and lingering, wrapping her in his arms, and breathing in her scent all the while, intoxicated, focused.

He felt her arms slip around him under his coat, holding him tight as she returned the kiss. He loosened one arm, freeing his hand to hold her head as he tilted it back to pull her closer against him. Finally he drew a shuddering breath and stopped, just holding her, softly upright in his embrace.

Angharad leaned back in his arms, her eyes shining. They looked at each other for a few moments, speechless.

He released her and groped his way, weak-kneed, to the kitchen table. She laughed shakily and joined him there, at her customary seat on the opposite side. They didn't say anything, then Angharad reached out one hand across the table, and he grasped it loosely. They smiled at each other, content.

She let go of his hand and reached for the sketch book that was always somewhere within reach. "So, you're staying then?" She turned to a fresh page and began idly drawing something.

He looked at her fondly. "How else will I ever get a picture of my oak tree? I found it, now I want to remember it."

"I have other scenes in mind, too." She sketched for a moment without speaking. "So, how do you feel about children?"

His eyes widened and his smile, at first tentative, bloomed across his whole face.

She smiled back. "I'm not getting any younger, after all."

Gwyn walked into the stables late in the afternoon. Ever since this morning people had come to him to tell him about George riding out, wearing his old red coat. Idris asked Alun about it, but couldn't get any definite answer from him.

It didn't seem like him to just leave without a good-bye, Gwyn thought. He had to check for himself, and he found George's big gray horse still in his stall. Surely he wouldn't leave his horse behind, would he?

I shouldn't be this concerned, he thought, as he walked back out into the yard. I have many descendants, and a whole year to make a plan for the great hunt, if I must. But this felt right, he was the right man.

Movement caught his eye, and there was George riding in through the curtain gate, followed by two strange dogs. He had a broad smile on his face, and when he caught sight of Gwyn, he shouted, "Yes!" across the intervening space, with great good cheer.

His delight was infectious, and Gwyn returned the smile, hiding both his uncertainty and his relief. While George dismounted and introduced him to his dogs, he thought about what this would mean. Will he someday be my rival for Annwn, blending the blood of Cernunnos with my own?

As he dismounted George thought, Gwyn seems happy to see me stay. Though I suppose everyone would look happy to me, at the moment. He couldn't stop smiling.

He checked on Mosby and Afanc, and then dropped in on one of the grooms. "Can I change my icon? Is that possible?"

"No problem at all," was the reply.

Alright, then. No more staring into the past, to Talbot, and Gwyn, and Cernunnos. Time to look forward, to found his own family. Let it start with me, whatever brought me to this point.

"Make it a big bare winter oak, please," he said, "instead of the lion." He sketched out what he meant on a scrap of wood.

George sat in the huntsman's office alone in the evening.

The glow of all the good wishes at dinner and afterward at the hunt staff meeting was beginning to fade. I'm glad everyone seems so pleased at my decision. I hadn't realized how much it mattered to some of them.

It warmed him, but he couldn't tear his mind from the afternoon with Angharad in the kitchen. That shone so brightly it cast all the other smiling faces into shadow.

He looked down at his green sleeves. Alun couldn't move fast enough when he got back, peeling that red coat off of him. I must've given him a scare, he thought.

Well. Better read up on where we're hunting tomorrow in the old logs. He half rose out of his chair to walk to the shelves, then dropped back down again.

No, he thought, there's something else I need to do first. He pulled the current hunt log to him and opened it onto a fresh page. He wrote the year with a flourish as well as he could and started to write.

Saturday, 31 Hydref / Sunday, 1 Tachwedd - Nos Galan Gaeaf
On this day …

GUIDE TO NAMES & PRONUNCIATIONS

MODERN WELSH ALPHABET

A[1], B, C, CH[2], D, DD[2], E[1], F[2], FF[2], G, NG[2], H, I[1], J,
L, LL[2], M, N, O[1], P, PH[2], R, RH[2], S, T, TH[2], U[1], W[1 2], Y[1]

[1] These letters are vowels. The letter 'W' can be used either as a vowel (when it is said 'oo' like in the Welsh word 'cwm' (coom) meaning 'valley') or as a consonant (when it is said like it is in English, for example in the Welsh word 'gwyn' (gwin) meaning 'white'). This is the same with letter 'I' which can also be used as a consonant (when it is said like an English Y like in 'iogwrt' (yog-oort) meaning yoghurt.

[2] Letters that are not in the English alphabet, or have different sounds. CH sounds like the 'KH' in Ayatollah KHoumeini. DD is said like the TH in 'THere'. F is said like the English 'V'. FF is said like the English 'F'. NG sounds like it would in English but it is tricky because it comes at the beginnings of words (for example 'fy ngardd' - my garden). One trick is to blend it in with the word before it. LL sounds like a cat hissing. PH sounds like the English 'F' too, but it is only used in mutations. RH sounds like an 'R' said very quickly before a 'H'. TH sounds like the 'TH' in 'THin'. W has been explained in the sentences before about vowels.

It helps to remember how Welsh is pronounced in order to translate the unfamiliar orthography into familiar English sounds. The language has changed over time and so has the spelling. People with very long lives tend to be conservative in how they spell their names.

Some nicknames are descriptive, occupational, or locational, as they are in English (e.g., Tom Baker, Susan Brown, John Carpenter, Meg Underwood)

Bongam - Bandy-legged
Goch - The red(-haired) one
Owen the Leash
Scilti - The thin one

PRINCIPAL CHARACTERS & PLACE NAMES

HUMANS

Conrad (Corniad) Traherne
Father of George Talbot Traherne, husband of Léonie Annan Talbot.

George Talbot Traherne
Huntsman from Virginia. His parents are Conrad Traherne and Léonie Annan Talbot.

Gilbert Payne Talbot
Father of Léonie Annan Talbot, husband of Georgia Rice Annan.

Georgia Rice Annan
Father of Léonie Annan Talbot, wife of Gilbert Payne Talbot, daughter of Gwyn ap Nudd (Gwyn Annan).

Léonie Annan Talbot
Mother of George Talbot Traherne, wife of Conrad (Corniad) Traherne.

FAE & IMMORTALS

Alun (AL-an)
Servant to the huntsman of Gwyn ap Nudd.

Angharad (ang-KAR-ad)
Artist affiliated with Gwyn ap Nudd's court.

Arawn (air-AH-oon)
Prince of Annwn, predecessor of Gwyn ap Nudd.

Beli Mawr (BEH-lee MA-oor) - Beli the Great
Father of Lludd Llaw Eraint (Nudd) and Llefelys.

Brynach (BRIN-akh)
Great-nephew of Eurig ap Gruffyd.

Ceridwen (ke-RID-wen)
Scholar, healer, magician at Gwyn ap Nudd's court.

Cernunnos (ker-NOO-nus) - Master of Beasts

Deity takes the form of an antlered man.

Creiddylad ferch Nudd (krey-THIL-ad verkh NIDH)
Daughter of Lludd Llaw Eraint (Nudd), sister of Gwyn ap Nudd and Edern ap Nudd, one-time wife of Gwythyr ap Greidawl. Lady of Edgewood (Pencoed) to Gwyn ap Nudd.

Cyledr Wyllt (KIL-eh-der WILT) - Cyledr the Mad
Son of Nwython. Warrior of Gwythyr ap Greidawl.

Dilys (DIL-is)
Mother of Thomas Kethin, mistress of Thomas, Lord Fairfax.

Edern ap Nudd (EE-dern ap NIDH)
Son of Lludd Llaw Eraint (Nudd), brother of Gwyn ap Nudd and Creiddylad ferch Nudd, father of Rhys ab Edern, grandfather of Rhys Vachan ap Rhys and Rhian ferch Rhys.

Edneved ap Gwilt (ed-NEV-ed ap GWILT)
A scholar.

Eurig ap Gruffydd (EI-rig ap GRIFF-ith)
Husband of Tegwen, great-uncle of Brynach. Vassal of Gwyn ap Nudd.

Gwyn ap Nudd (GWIN ap NIDH) - Gwyn Annan
Son of Lludd Llaw Eraint (Nudd), brother of Edern ap Nudd and Creiddlyad ferch Nudd. Father of Georgia Rice Annan. Prince of Annwn.

Gwythyr ap Greidawl (GWI-thir ap GREI-dul)
Ex-husband of Creiddylad ferch Nudd.

Hadyn (HAY-din)
Weapons-master to Gwyn ap Nudd.

Hefina (heh-VIN-a)
Assistant to Ceridwen in the infirmary.

Helyan (hel-I-an)
Guard training with Hadyn.

Huw Bongam (HUE BON-gam) - Hugh Bandy-leg
Innkeeper of the Horned Man in Greenhollow.

Idris ap Hywel - Idris Powell (IH-dris ap HIH-wel)
Marshal to Gwyn ap Nudd. 2nd in command.

Ifor ap Griffri - Ifor Moel (IH-ver ap GRIFF-ree), (IH-ver MOYLE) - Ifor the Bald
Steward and administrator to Gwyn ap Nudd under Idris Powell.

Iolo ap Huw (YO-lo ap HUE)
Huntsman to Gwyn ap Nudd. Iolo is a diminutive of Iorwerth.

Iona (YO-na)
Breeder of ponies and small horses.
Iorwerth Goch (YOR-werth GOKH) - Iorwerth the Red(-haired)
A scholar.
Islwyn (I-sluin)
A whipper-in, great-great-grandson of Iolo ap Huw.
Ithel (IH-thel)
A lord, father of Merfyn.
Llefelys (lhe-VEE-lis)
Son of Beli Mawr. Brother of Lludd/Nudd. Uncle of Gwyn ap Nudd, Edern ap Nudd, and Creiddylad ferch Nudd. King of Gaul.
Lludd Llaw Eraint (LHIDH LHAU er-AYNT) - Nudd/Lludd of the Silver Hand
Son of Beli Mawr. Brother of Llefelys. Father of Gwyn ap Nudd, Edern ap Nudd, and Creiddylad ferch Nudd. King of Britain.
Madog ab Owen Gwynedd (MAA-dog ab OU-ain GWI-nedh)
Son of the Prince of Gwynedd. Discovered a way to the new world around 1100.
Mederei Badellfawr (meh-DER-ey BA-dell-VA-oor) - Mederei Great-Griddle
A female bodyguard to Creiddylad ferch Nudd. Warriors carried iron pans for cooking on their backs while traveling.
Merfyn ab Ithel (MER-vin ab IH-thel)
A whipper-in, son of Ithel.
Mostyn (MOS-tin)
A tailor in Greenhollow.
Nudd
See **Lludd Llaw Eraint**.
Nwython (NWIH-thon)
A warrior of Gwythyr ap Greidawl, killed by Gwyn ap Nudd. Father of Cyledr Wyllt.
Olwen (OL-wen)
Cloth-mistress to Gwyn ap Nudd.
Owen the Leash (O-wen)
Leader of three men guarding people from the Cŵn Annwn.
Pwyll Pen Annwn (PWILL pen ANN-un) - Pwyll head of Annwn
An ally of Gwythyr ap Greidawl and friend of Arawn. Lord of Dyfed.

Rhian ferch Rhys (HRII-an verkh RHEESE)
Foster-daughter of Gwyn ap Nudd, daughter of Rhys ab Edern, granddaughter of Edern ap Nudd, sister of Rhys Vachan ap Rhys. Junior huntsman to Gwyn ap Nudd.

Rhodri ap Morgant (HROD-hrii ap MOR-gant)
Distant nephew to Gwyn ap Nudd, cousin to Rhian ferch Rhys and Rhys Vachan ap Rhys. Diplomat to Gwyn ap Nudd. Musician.

Rhys ab Edern (HREESE ab EE-dern)
Son of Edern ap Nudd, father of Rhian ferch Rhys and Rhys Vachan ap Rhys.

Rhys Vachan ap Rhys (HREESE VAKH-an ap HREESE) - Rhys the younger, Rhys Junior
Foster-son of Gwyn ap Nudd, son of Rhys ab Edern, grandson of Edern ap Nudd, brother of Rhian ferch Rhys. Steward of Edgewood, to Gwyn ap Nudd.

Scilti (SHIL-tee) - The thin one.
From Irish Cailte, Caolite.

Tegwen (TEG-wen)
Wife of Eurig ap Gruffydd.

Thomas Kethin (KETH-in) - Thomas the Swarthy
Son of Thomas, Lord Fairfax, and Dilys

Trefor Mawr (TREH-vor MA-oor) - Trevor the Great
A famous way-finder.

LUTINS (loo-TANH)

Armelle (ar-MEL)
Betrothed to Tanguy.

Benitoe (BEN-ih-toe)
Whipper-in. Betrothed to Isolda.

Brittou (BRIH-too)
Stable manager to Iona.

Huon (HOO-on)
Kennel-man.

Isolda (i-SOL-da)
Daughter of Ives, betrothed to Benitoe.

Ives (EVE)
Kennel-master. Father of Isolda.

Maonirn (MA-oh-NIRN)

Groom at the Horned Man inn.

Orry (OR-ri)
Handler of bloodhounds (lymers).

Tanguy (TAN-ghee)
Kennel-man. Betrothed to Armelle.

HORSES

Afanc (AH-vank) - Water-horse, monster
Huntsman's horse inherited by George. Black gelding.

Eleri (eh-LEH-ri)
Pony for Benitoe. Bay mare.

Gwladus (GLA-dus) - Ruler
Pony for Benitoe. Gray mare.

Halwyn (HAL-wyn) - Salt
Pony for Benitoe. White gelding

Llamrei (LHAM-ry) - Legendary horse of Arthur.
Huntsman's horse inherited by George. Chestnut mare.

Llwyd (LHUID) - Gray
Huntsman's horse inherited by Rhian.

Mosby (MOZ-by)
George's horse. Dapple-gray Percheron/thoroughbred gelding.

HOUNDS - CŴN ANNWN

Cŵn Annwn (COON AN-nun)
The Hounds of Hell. See Annwn.

Aeronwy (f) (ei-ROO-nui)
Anwen (f) (AHN-wen) - Very fair
Briallen (f) (bri-AL-len) - Primrose
Cythraul (m) (KEH-thral) - Devil, Demon
Outsider.
Dando (m) (DAN-doe)
Elain (f) (eh-LAIN) - Fawn
Outsider.
Goronwy (m) (go-RON-wee)
Outsider.
Holda (f)
Rhyfelwr (m) (hreh-VEE-lur) - Warrior
Deceased

Rhymi (f) (HREM-ee)
Outsider.

DOGS (OTHER)

Arthur
A bloodhound (lymer).
Bran
A terrier owned by Angharad. Deceased.
Cabal (KA-ball)
A terrier owned by Angharad.
Ermengarde (ER-men-GARD)
A terrier (puppy) owned by Angharad.
Hugo
A blue-tick coonhound owned by George.
Myfanwy (mih-VAN-wee) - My lady
A terrier owned by Gwyn ap Nudd.
Roland
A bloodhound (lymer).
Sergeant
A yellow feist owned by George.
Taffy (TAF-fee) - diminutive of David
A terrier owned by Gwyn ap Nudd.

EVENTS

Nos Galan Gaeaf (noos GA-lan GAY-a) - The night of the calend of winter
The first day (night) of winter. October 31, the eve of November 1, the eve of All Saints' Day (All Hallows), Hallowe'en. (Celtic dates begin in the evening).
Nos Galan Mae (noos GA-lan MAY) - The night of the calend of May
The first day (night) of summer. April 30, the eve of May 1.

PLACES

Annwn (AN-nun)
Part of the Celtic otherworld, traditionally the underworld. See **Cŵn Annwn**.

Bellemore (BELL-more)
Gwyn ap Nudd's estate in Virginia, a fixture of the Rowanton Hunt.

Cor Tewdws (KOR TEW-dose) - College of Theodosius
Monastery and school in Glamorgan, Wales. It was a primary center of learning in Britain until the Norman Conquest.

Daear Llosg (DEI-ar LHOSK) - Burnt Ground
The meadow on the slope north of Greenway Court where funerals and cremations are held.

Dan-y-Deri (dan-ih-DEE-ri). Also **Danderi**. - Below the Oaks
The village visited by the great hunt.

Llys y Lon Las (LHIIS eh LOON laas) - Greenway Court (Court of the Green Lane)
The name of Gwyn ap Nudd's manor, later borrowed (before 1750) by a human visitor, Thomas, 6th Lord Fairfax, as a name for his wilderness estate and hunting lodge at White Post, in the Shenandoah Valley.

Pant-glas (PANT-glaas). Also **Pantglas**. - Greenhollow
The name of the village below Greenway Court.

Pen-y-Coed (PEN-ih-KOID). Also **Pencoed**. - Edgewood
The name of Creiddylad's estate, granted by Gwyn ap Nudd.

IF YOU LIKE THIS BOOK…

You can find illustrations of George's pocket-watch, hunt button, family arms, and the oliphant at: PerkunasPress.com/wp/books/the-hounds-of-annwn/to-carry-the-horn/

Please tell your friends about this book. You can link to it on my website and let people know on Facebook or Twitter.

The next book in the Hounds of Annwn series, **The Ways of Winter**, is scheduled to be released in Spring, 2013. Find out more: PerkunasPress.com/wp/books/the-hounds-of-annwn/the-ways-of-winter/

Sign up for my newsletter to stay informed of new and upcoming releases:
PerkunasPress.com/wp/about-us/

You can contact me at PerkunasPress.com. You can also follow me on Facebook: Facebook.com/PerkunasPress

If you let me know about any discussion groups or fan-fic on other sites and provide a link, I'll link to them on my website.

Please consider writing a review wherever you bought this book, or on sites like Goodreads, or on your own blog.

Please help me make this book better for everyone by reporting any errata to me. Since page numbers vary by format, let me know what Chapter contained the problem and some nearby sentence. The first five people who report more than 5 errors (typos, formatting) will receive a free trade paperback edition, suitably corrected. If you would like to be credited in a corrected edition, just let me know when you contact me.

EXCERPT FROM THE WAYS OF WINTER

I'm sorry I ran away, Mother. I want to come home now.

Seething Magma's great head raised, in the dark underground cavity, and she interrupted her meal of crushed rock. At last, she thought, relief flooding her limbs. It had been almost a thousand years since she'd heard from her youngest child.

Where have you been? she scolded, then emended, **Never mind, just come home.**

I can't! He won't let me go. Granite Cloud's wail roused her mother's alarm. Nothing could hold an elemental.

I'm coming to get you, Seething Magma projected decisively. She shook herself and prepared for travel, pinpointing her daughter's location from her thoughts.

No, you can't. He'll get you, too.

Seething Magma settled back down thoughtfully. **Maybe you better tell me all about it. I'm sure we can find a way.**

George kept Angharad company in her kitchen as she prepared the dough for an apple pie. Almost a month of marriage had not diminished her charms for him in the least, but he couldn't spend the whole afternoon just watching her. Too bad.

It was the inactivity, he thought. The second of the early winter storms had just ended this morning, after three days of snow. Hunting had been stopped since the first days of December. At least that allowed him to be more flexible in his domestic commuting schedule. His young junior huntsman Rhian had been handling hounds on Thursday mornings for hunting, and Sunday and Monday mornings for the hound walking, allowing him to come from Gwyn's court into Greenhollow and spend time with his wife (I can't believe it, my wife!) three nights per week. He was grateful Rhian was improving her confidence with handling the pack so rapidly.

Now, with hunting stopped from the snow and hound walking restricted to the front grounds of the manor house, his hunt staff had conspired to give him a full week off. He had just arrived yesterday, anticipating at least a week of delayed honeymoon. His own dogs, the coonhound Hugo and Sergeant, the yellow feist, looked like they didn't plan to stir from the vicinity of the kitchen stove, but he knew Angharad's terriers Cabal and Ermengarde would roust them if it looked like the people were going to play in the snow.

Angharad broke the silence. "Did I tell you? I liked your grandparents, very much. I'm glad I had the chance to meet them."

"What about your family? You've never told me much about them."

"You'll have to wait for a visit to Gwyn's father in Britain. They're all in the old world, around the court, even the children."

George had a hard time getting used to the notion of her having a dozen children, all of them older than him. At thirty-three, he was a well-grown human, but she was a fae, more than 1500 years old, and had lived many lives by his lights. He had blood ties to the fae himself, but no one yet knew if he had their gift of longevity, if he would be more than a brief interval in her life. It was an unstated worry that brought a note of urgency into their relationship.

He still found it a miracle that she wanted to be with him anyway, especially given her position as a renowned artist. He was far more intimidated by her artistic gifts than by the age difference.

"Have you found an apprentice yet? I know you asked your mentor Bleddyn about it," he said.

"These things take time, often many years. I just let it be known I was available if anyone was seeking."

She'd been painting up a storm since they met, revitalized, and was offering to share that with someone, as masters did.

She filled the pie dish with sliced apples and sealed the upper crust in place. Popping it into the oven, she washed her hands and walked over to join him at the kitchen table, patting him on the shoulder as she went by. He grabbed her with one arm around the hip and held her there, tight against his side, breathing in her scent. She melted against him and looked down at him suggestively.

The pounding on the door was very unwelcome, just then.

Angharad sighed and opened it, letting in Thomas Kethin, Gwyn's head ranger. He stamped the snow off his boots on the doorstep and unwrapped the wool muffler from his dark and weathered face.

"I'm sorry to interrupt you two, I am, but we have a situation and I need George's help."

She offered to take his coat, but he refused. "The latest batch of Rhys's invitees has just arrived at the Travelers' Way, and the inn is full up and can't accommodate them. We've got to get them up to the manor."

"I feel for you, in all this snow, but what can I do about it?" George said.

"They're not exactly a cooperative group," Thomas said, wryly. "We have fae masters of several crafts, each prouder than the next, and a few korrigans, as well as other riffraff mixed in. They are not getting along with each other, and they aren't inclined to recognize my authority. I don't fit their old world ideas of what's proper."

"But I'm just the huntsman," George said.

"You can use Gwyn's authority as part of the family and I think that would do the trick."

George was reluctant to leave his warm nest but he recognized that Thomas had a point. He pushed back his chair and stood up. "Sorry, sweetheart, but I think I must.

"Of course you need to," she said. "There will be other times." Ignoring Thomas standing there, trying to look somewhere else, she gave him a hug and a long kiss.

"There. Something to remember me by."

And if I can make my legs work again, I'll just walk on out of here, George thought, dazed.

In a few moments he assembled what he needed for a couple of miles of riding through the snow. He spoke to Thomas as he prepared, "Do they all have horses?"

"There are five wagons, carrying equipment and a few passengers. The rest are mounted, even the korrigans. I think we might as well sweep up all the other folk from the inn while we're at it, in case the snow gets deeper."

George whistled up his dogs and plunged out into the dark afternoon, deepening the path to the stable to saddle his horse.

George looked up at the dark sky with its threatening clouds. The snow may have stopped but more was clearly on the way.

He and Thomas had the street to themselves at the moment and were able to ride side-by-side down the shallower snow in the middle, where the villagers had organized a log drag, a pole pulled behind a pair of horses that swept the top layer of snow to the side. They'd been sending a team out for the village streets every few hours for the last several days, and already the difference between the dragged and packed path and the untouched snow was a foot. The full depth was approaching eighteen inches. Householders had cleared their own paths but were having a hard time keeping up with the persistent snowfall.

George had seen heavy snow occasionally in Virginia near the Blue Ridge, but even here in this otherworld version of the landscape, this much snow this early was considered unusual.

He stopped briefly at the Horned Man inn to speak with Huw Bongam, the innkeeper. He gave his reins to Thomas to hold and stamped the snow from his feet before going in.

The main room was packed and noisy. The more fastidious fae were off in a group along one side, but the bulk of the crowd were korrigans. George had never seen so many of the dwarf-like folk all in one place. He'd only met the smith and his family at Greenway Court and a few traders as they came through.

Some of the fae were as tall as George, at six foot four, but none were as broad. Huw Bongam had no difficulty spotting him as he came in, and made his way through the crowd. "Go back out on the porch, huntsman, or we'll never be able to hear ourselves." He pulled a cloak around himself and both stepped outside, where Thomas was waiting with the horses.

"I'm on my way to help Thomas with a new group at the Travelers' Way," George said. "Thought we might bundle up some of what you've got and bring them with us, the ones who're headed for Edgewood."

"Well, you'd be doing me a favor, and that's no lie. I've got more than I can handle. I'm used to housing folks who are snowbound for a few days, but this call of Rhys's for skilled craftsmen at Edgewood has brought out all the ambitious folks from Gwyn's domain, and a few from the old world, too. Do you know, I've even got a few lutins, looking to expand their opportunities?"

"Where are you putting them all?"

"It'll be the hayloft soon, if you don't take some of them with you."

"Alright, I'll go on and see what we've got at the Travelers' Way and get them ready to move out immediately, without stopping here. If you could sort out your 'keepers' versus the ones that want to move one step closer to Edgewood, tell them I'll be back in about an hour with Thomas to lead them to Greenway Court."

"I'll do that," Huw replied.

Thomas spoke up. "Not all of the newly arrived people are prepared for this much early winter. Can you spare the loan of any blankets for the trip to the manor house?"

George added, "What about horses or wagons for the folks here? They'll have trouble walking in the snow, even if we help break more trail."

"I'll sort out some transportation and wraps for the trip, as much as I can spare, if you can get it back to me as soon as you can," Huw said.

"Much appreciated," George said. "If you can provide your own drivers, we'll house them and they can bring back the empty wagons, weather permitting, plus any villagers who might be feeling trapped at court."

With a nod, Huw went back inside and George remounted.

He rode with Thomas past the crossroads with the stone bridge on the right and turned into the cul-de-sac on the far left that led to the Travelers' Way. All the peace and quiet of the snowy streets fled as they heard the raised voices and clangor of the newly-arrived expedition.

George hung back for a moment as Thomas rejoined the party. He saw five wagons with goods and people, now shivering in the cold. There were a few fae on foot, and a couple of korrigans, but most of the travelers had heeded the instructions to come mounted or with transport, and even the korrigans were mostly mounted on sturdy ponies, though they didn't all look like seasoned horsemen. To his dismay, he saw what must be wives and families for a few of the travelers, so there were several children to think of.

Thomas's reappearance drew the loudest speaker like a lodestone draws iron.

"A fine welcome this is, no one from the court and two feet of snow. How are we supposed to proceed?" This was from a tall fae, on the older side of middle-aged.

He put himself in front of the other fae as if he had taken charge of them, and they seemed to permit it, though George thought he detected some hidden smiles as he continued to make a fuss. "I demand some civilized shelter in this wilderness. This is not what we were led to expect."

Thomas said, with great self-control, "My lord Cadugan, allow me to present George Talbot Traherne, the great-grandson of Gwyn ap Nudd." He bowed from the saddle, and beckoned George forward.

"At last," Cadugan said, gratified. "Edern ap Nudd summoned me as steward for the Edgewood lands, on behalf of his grandson Rhys. I'm eager to see that all of us get there as quickly as possible."

"I am pleased to meet you, sir, and all of you here," George said in his best political voice. "I apologize for our unseasonable weather, but we have yet to find a way to keep the snow from falling." This mild quip broke some of the tension, and the fractious crowd started to relax now that someone had appeared to take charge of them, someone agreeable to their leader.

One of the korrigan elders, a bearded man in practical woolens over a blue silk waistcoat came up to join Cadugan. He bowed. "I am Tiernoc, elected leader for the journey for my folk." He offered his hand up to George.

George didn't dismount because he wanted the height to help direct the crowd, so he bowed low over his saddle to shake hands with the korrigan— very low, since Tiernoc was only about four feet tall.

"Are the two of you the leaders of everyone here, for now?" George asked.

"That's right," Tiernoc said, and Cadugan nodded.

"Alright, here's the situation. We can't put you up at the inn because it's full with other snowbound travelers, and you're too many to just try to house in Greenhollow's homes. We're going to take your group and a party from the inn which is also headed to Edgewood and bring all of you up to Gwyn at Greenway Court. From there you'll be able to get to Edgewood via the Guests' Way and a brief passage to the Edgewood Way."

"How far is Gwyn's court?" Cadugan said. "We're not prepared for this weather."

"It's two miles, and the snow is deep. We have more wagons and horses coming from the inn, and as many blankets as they can spare. We'll organize trail-breakers in front. Everyone who can't ride we'll put into wagons so that no one's on foot."

Cadugan looked unhappy at this. "Can't we stop and warm up first?"

"I'm sorry, but the snow could restart at any time—look at the sky. Better to do one last push and be under sure shelter no matter what the weather brings next," George said.

He walked over to Thomas, who had a group of four men to help. "You were right, like oil on troubled waters. You have two centuries of experience and they wanted a member of the family. Save me from the status-conscious." He shook his head.

"I'm headed over to the inn to get that batch organized. If you'll give me two of your men and keep two for yourself we can each get our groups into a trail-breaking order and then shuffle them together as they cross the bridge. What do you think?"

"That'll work," Thomas said. "Heavy horses in front, then light horses, wagons, and ponies at the rear. Don't forget blankets for this group, I don't like the looks of some of them in the wagons. And don't delay, that snow won't hold off forever."

Before entering the inn, George set Thomas's two men to sending on one of Huw Bongam's wagons to the other group, then coordinating the wagons of the inn's party. They'd line those up in the road at the head of the line and free up some space in the inn yard to maneuver the horses. George had a private word with one of the grooms to hold his horse tacked up but under shelter to spare him as much of the cold as possible.

He walked into the inn's main room, bringing his dogs with him, and beckoned Huw over. "Do you think we could send some hot tea down to the Travelers' Way? There are about forty people there and some of them are miserable."

"I've already taken that in hand. The wagon they're getting has fifteen blankets and three gallons of tea. Let me go see about the rest of the preparations in the stable yard."

"Good work."

Many of the crowd had turned to watch him standing in the entrance. George knocked loudly on the door frame for silence and addressed the crowd. "In one hour we will lead a party from here with a group from the Travelers' Way up to Greenway Court. If you're trying to go on to Edgewood, I strongly advise you to join us, since the snow could start again at any time. We can house you at the court until the weather allows you to continue your journey."

"Be warned," he continued, "the snow is deep and it's about two miles. We will break trail as we go and there should be room in the wagons for anyone who isn't mounted, but I urge you to ride if you can to leave room for others. Can I see a show of hands for anyone who plans to join us?"

A rising hubbub filled the room at the news, though George didn't doubt that Huw Bongam had already warned them this was coming. About a dozen fae raised their hands, and many more korrigans. Five lutins made their way through the crowd to the front, too, all dressed in red and not much taller than the korrigans.

George called again for silence. "If you don't have a mount and must have a place in the wagons, come up to me now for a moment. I'd also like to see a leader for each group, someone who can keep track of its members before and during the ride so that we don't leave anyone behind. Everyone else, start packing. And be quick about it."

Two fae and a korrigan joined the lutins in front as most of the rest of the crowd dispersed to pack their belongings.

The elder fae spoke first. "I'm Meilyr. All of us are from elsewhere in Gwyn's domains and came at his call. We have four in our party who are traveling to Edgewood as masters in their crafts. One of those is a teacher for Ceridwen. There are seven others who are seeking family long lost to them. I'm one of those."

"Will you hold yourself responsible for their names and making sure of their whereabouts for our journey to the court?" George asked.

"I will."

"Do any need wagons?"

"The craft masters brought equipment but we have our own wagons to haul it. All are mounted."

"Thank you. Please assemble your wagons on the party already out front and take your instructions from the rangers there."

The lutins came forward, led by one middle-aged lutine. She said, "I'm Rozenn. Some of us are looking for lost family, and others are seeking employment. I'll be responsible for our names and well-being, but we will all need places in the wagons, with our goods."

"Thanks, Mistress Rozenn. Please bring your people and your goods to me here. I'll hold all the wagon loads in one place until we know how many will be required."

As she left, Huw Bongam returned. "Do you know how many wagons you'll need from here yet, huntsman?"

"So far, it looks like there are five lutins and their gear who will need transport, but the rest are accounted for. So, just the one wagon. What's the news from Thomas?"

"He thinks he only needs the one wagon I sent him for his group, so it's not as bad as I feared. I'll send out two drivers who can bring them back when the weather permits." He paused. "It makes me think of Isolda, your party of lutins needing a driver. I can't get used to her being gone. She'd have loved the adventure."

George let his sadness show for a moment and gripped his shoulder. He turned back to the senior korrigan who was waiting patiently to speak.

"I'm Broch, and I'll take charge of the fifteen of us from Gwyn's domains. We, too, are craft masters and traders, hoping to re-open the route to Edgewood. We've brought our own wagons, and a few of us are riding as well. I've already sent our folks to assemble in the road with the others."

He looked at George with apparent curiosity. "Did I hear Huw Bongam call you huntsman? Are you Gwyn's new huntsman? We came through Danderi recently and heard all about it."

"I'm sorry, I didn't introduce myself properly. I'm George Talbot Traherne, Gwyn ap Nudd's great-grandson and, yes, his new huntsman."

"I heard that someone died at the start," Broch said, tentatively.

"That was Isolda of whom we were speaking. She had just started working as a driver, the first lutine to do so. She was just eighteen and newly-betrothed, and she gave her life to save Gwyn's foster-daughter from death at the hands of Cyledr Wyllt."

"Who became the quarry of the great hunt."

"Yes. He's gone now." There was satisfaction in George's voice.

"Excuse me, but someone said you were human."

"It's true, more or less. I was brought here when the old huntsman was murdered. It's a long story, for another time."

Broch persisted. "They also said you hunted as the horned man."

"As I said, a long story. We can speak at the manor house later."

Broch took the dismissal in good humor and went off to organize his companions.

One person was left, a young fae roughly George's age. Unlike almost all the fae George had met, he was red-haired and freckled.

"Not part of Meilyr's group?" George said.

"No," he said, smiling sardonically. "I'm just a lowly provincial musician—Cydifor. But I have hopes. No one said anything about Rhys Vachan having any musicians at Edgewood."

"I've been there and I don't remember any. But, you know, his cousin Rhodri is one, himself?"

Cydifor's face fell, and George laughed.

"Don't worry. Rhodri's not there to stay for the long-term, and in the meantime he's likely to prove a friend. I imagine he's tired of playing by himself for his own amusement. Do you need transport?"

"I have a mount, but I would appreciate space in a wagon for my gear, to ease the burden on her."

"No problem," George said. "Bring it here with the lutins' bundles and then go mount up."

George took a look around as Cydifor hurried off. He waved a hand at the locals who were still in the inn's main room and went off to check on the assembly in the road.

George and his men finished loading the borrowed wagon and helping the smaller lutins scramble in. Their driver hastened out to join them, still munching the end of his meal and fastening his coat.

As he mounted up to ride the length of the group in the road, George considered how long it would take to get the two groups together and then up two miles of snowy road before dark or the next storm. Probably about two hours, if nothing breaks down. He pulled out his pocket watch on its chain and confirmed that he had about two hours of daylight left. It was going to be close.

He spoke to Meilyr and Broch as he passed and got their assurance that everyone in their groups was accounted for, waved at Cydifor, and confirmed with Mistress Rozenn that all the lutins were set, with blankets piled around them and George's dogs at their feet.

"Alright," he called to Thomas's men. "Let's move 'em out."

The horses at front of the line, including his own heavy Mosby, started out first, packing the snow down more tightly for the wagons that followed them. The korrigans, on their smaller horses and ponies, followed at the back. The squeak of the dry snow combined with the rumble of the wagons and the creak of the horses to make it a noisy departure. Some of the drinkers at the inn waved from the doorway as they pulled out, the light behind them shining out onto the road under the darkened sky.

They didn't have far to go. George held them short of the bridge and saw Thomas leading his group out of the gloom from the other side. All the riders were as well-bundled as possible, and the people on the wagons made good use of Huw Bongam's blankets.

George walked Mosby over to confer with Thomas. "How do you want to do this?"

Thomas said, "Two of my men at the back, two along the sides moving up and down to keep them moving, and the two of us in front. I'll have one of them do a count as they go by, so we know how many wagons and riders. Let me start out ahead to make sure there's no special problem with the road. You come along on your horse at the head of the line to reassure them as we go." He gave some last instructions to one of his men, then turned and crossed the bridge.

George turned back to the foot of the bridge, a grin tugging at one side of his mouth. He was going to be the master of a wagon train, if only for a couple of hours. Too bad he didn't have a cattle herd to go with it and a good Stetson hat.

He faced the two lines of riders and wagons and raised his hand for attention. The groups quieted.

"Listen up. We have about two hours of daylight and it should be enough. We're going to cross this bridge and go up the road on the far side of the stream, to the right. It's a gentle slope, but uphill all the way. At the end is the lower gate of the manor house and one more brief climb up to where we will unload and get under shelter.

"Keep track of your neighbors. Don't leave the line under any circumstances. If anything happens, a child falls overboard, anything, call for help from one of Thomas Kethin's riders. Make sure your group leaders know where you are and, leaders, keep track of your people. You don't want to be outside overnight, wandering in the dark.

"We're going to go in groups. All riders on larger horses first, beginning with the group from the inn, then those from the way. Stick together with your group. Wagons next, starting with the lutins from the inn and then the rest of the inn party, the other wagons," gesturing at the group from the Travelers' Way, "then the riders on shorter animals, all together."

He paused. "Any questions?" No one replied.

Thomas trotted back over the bridge and joined him. "There are footprints, someone small, headed up the road since we came through earlier. Keep an eye out for him."

ABOUT THE AUTHOR & PERKUNAS PRESS

Karen Myers writes, photographs, and fiddles in the picturesque foxhunting country of the Virginia Piedmont. She can be reached at KarenMyers@PerkunasPress.com.

A graduate of Yale University from Kansas City, Karen has lived with her husband, David Zincavage, in Connecticut, New York, Chicago, California, and for the past several years in Virginia, where they both follow the activities of the Blue Ridge Hunt, the Old Dominion Hounds, the Ashland Bassets, and the Wolver Beagles.

Perkunas Press, founded in 1993, is pleased to enter into a new era of independent publishing in ebook and trade paperback formats

Made in the USA
Charleston, SC
17 December 2012